THE
EDGE

THE
EDGE

LUCY GOACHER

THOMAS & MERCER

Text copyright © 2022 by Lucy Goacher
All rights reserved.

No part of this book may be reproduced, or stored in a retrieval system, or transmitted in any form or by any means, electronic, mechanical, photocopying, recording, or otherwise, without express written permission of the publisher.

Published by Thomas & Mercer, Seattle

www.apub.com

Amazon, the Amazon logo, and Thomas & Mercer are trademarks of Amazon.com, Inc., or its affiliates.

ISBN-13: 9781662506277
ISBN-10: 1662506279

Cover design by Lisa Horton

Printed in the United States of America

For my family

PROLOGUE

POPPY

I've never seen so many stars. They're swirled across the sky, reflected on the tips of the waves. It's dark here, truly dark, far enough away from civilisation to let the starlight in. And that starlight stretches on ahead of me, above and below, as far as I can see.

It's like I'm stood at the edge of the universe, looking back.

'I knew you'd love it here,' he says, nuzzling my hair. He tightens his arms around me, holding me from behind as we both gaze out at the sea. 'It's like a painting, isn't it? *Starry Night Over the Rhône.* We'll have to paint our own. *Starry 3 a.m. Over the English Channel.*'

'Not quite as glamorous.'

'I don't know. Depends on who you ask.'

Our words crystallise in the freezing air, twinkling in the starlight as a mist. Usually the coast is blustery and loud, tangling my hair and making my eyes water, but tonight there isn't even a breeze. It's as though we're frozen in a perfect moment of stillness, with just the sound of waves lapping on the beach below to remind us that time is passing.

I shiver.

He pulls me tighter, dipping his head to press a kiss against my shoulder.

'Are you okay? We can go if you're too cold.'

'Don't you dare move,' I say, grabbing his arms with my gloved hands. He laughs softly in my ear.

This night is too beautiful to cut short. I've dreamt of nights like it my whole life, but that's all they were: dreams. Now it's reality. The touch of another person, the beauty of nature, the connectedness we feel to each other and it . . .

I lean into him, feeling him press back. Despite our thick coats and the winter air biting our noses, I feel his heat. I feel mine.

This moment is beautiful, but part of me hungers for the next.

We'll ride our bikes back along the coast to my room and kiss in the dark. Undress each other in the dark. We'll hold each other as our cold, bare skin becomes warm and the world around us falls away to nothing, leaving just us, there, together, wrapped up in each other like twin butterflies in a cocoon.

The stars glitter around us, and my cheeks glow.

I never knew my life could be like this, that the empty space I've always felt could be so perfectly filled by someone else. Someone I met by chance. We lie together night after night, skin to skin, opening our hearts to each other like trinket boxes filled with secrets. He knows the smell of baking reminds me of home, and how sunsets remind me of my sister. He doesn't judge me for my shyness, he takes my hand and leads the way. When I'm with him, I don't feel the need to hide from the world behind the easel in my bedroom. He puts me in the centre of his camera lens and pushes everyone else out of focus, like nobody matters except us and the moment we're in. And every time he presses Capture, he gifts me more confidence than I ever thought possible.

After almost two months, he's pulled me so far out of my shell that I've forgotten where I left it.

'Look, there!' he says, pointing past me to the sky. Light streaks through the stars, shooting down towards the horizon. 'Make a wish.'

'I wish—'

'Shh, don't tell me! It won't come true if you tell me.'

As the shooting star disappears, I speak the wish in my heart. *Let this moment last forever.*

I know exactly how I'll paint this tomorrow. I'll black out the canvas and pick out the details in white: the shimmering crests of the waves; tiny pin-prick stars; the streaking meteor; and us, wrapped together, two figures in love.

We haven't said that yet, but I feel it. It's in the comfortable silences when we're out walking, and the things he breathes into my hair when we're entwined in bed.

'*I adore you, Poppy. I've never felt like this before.*'

I haven't had a relationship before, but I know how these things go. It's love when the boy says it's love. He has to say it first.

But I feel it now – and I feel brave. He's changed me in these past few weeks. I used to feel frozen in public, like everyone was staring at me and judging me and laughing at me, and sometimes I couldn't even face leaving my room. But I try to speak up in classes now. I make eye contact with strangers. I go cycling on my own, exploring nature, getting lost. I've even started going to sales assistants' tills instead of heading straight for the self-checkouts. These are tiny things, really, baby steps, things everyone but me has been doing their whole lives – but for me, these steps are leaps.

Right now, under this diamond-speckled sky, I will leap again.

'Thank you for suggesting this,' I say, turning to look at him. He's a beautiful shadow, just stars shining in dark eyes. Like he's made of something celestial. 'I love it here, and . . . I love you.'

For a moment, everything is still – then his eyes seem to shine more.

'I've wanted to say that to you for ages, but I thought you'd think I was an idiot. I love you, too, Poppy.'

He pulls me to him again, and my arms wrap around him in the familiar way. But it feels different this time. Tighter. We're both

3

shaking, laughing, feeling a comfort in the embrace that I can't explain. I feel utterly safe in his arms. Utterly seen.

'Oh, I have something for you.' He unwinds his arms and pulls something from his pocket. It's a necklace. I see the glint of a chain and a pendant hanging from it.

'You didn't have to get me anything.'

'I know, but I wanted to. Anyway, you might hate it, so don't thank me too soon.'

I laugh, and he carefully fastens it around my neck. I feel for the pendant in the dark. It's a smooth strip of metal worked into two curves and a point. A heart.

'Thank you. I love it.'

'Really?'

'Really. I love it, and I love you.'

'I love you, too.' Although I can't see it in the dark, I hear him do what he always does: raise a finger to his chest and swipe an X-shape against the fabric of his coat. 'Cross my heart.'

I stand up on my tiptoes and he pulls me into a kiss – deep but gentle. Unrushed. The sea churns through me, splashing through every nerve, and I drown in happiness. I drown in him.

I want to feel these kisses every day for the rest of my life.

We turn back to the twinkling stars and their reflections in the sea below the cliff edge. The sky, this man, our love – it's magic.

I lean against him again, swaddled in his arms like a newborn, and smile.

'I bet the sunsets are amazing from here,' I say. 'Maybe we could bring Clemmie when she's next back. I can't wait for you to meet her. I think you'll like each other.'

'Oh, definitely. Your sister is going to *love* me. I guarantee it.'

His hands stroke up my arms, to my shoulders, and flatten against my back.

And he shoves me over the edge of the cliff.

CHAPTER 1

6 Months Later

I never cared much about sunsets, but Poppy did.

Years ago, when she was small and our parents used to put me in charge on Sunday afternoons, she'd beg me to take her all around London so she could find the best spot to watch them from. What started as simple outings became weekly expeditions: me marching her between Tube stations with my memorised sunset timetable and watch; her with a worn tourist map and felt-tipped pen to mark off the locations. I took her to every park, every bridge, every free-to-enter viewing platform. We spent one afternoon huddled together under an umbrella on Primrose Hill, her insisting we stay *'just a little bit longer, in case things cheer up,'* while the rain pelted and the wind howled, my glasses splattered in droplets and her map flapping in her hand. She told me years later in one of her letters that Primrose Hill was her favourite spot, her best sunset memory, but we saw nothing but grey that day. She must have gone back without me.

This is how I try to remember her: pink cheeks in the rain; windswept ginger curls; bare feet sticking out from under the curtain by her bed, whispering excitedly about settling snow or moonbeams or the glimmer of sunrise, pleading with me to come and see.

I can almost hear her saying it now, feel her tugging on my hand the way she used to.

'*It's so pretty, Clemmie! Turn around and look. Look!*'

But I don't turn around. I don't look. I follow the dull grey pavement east until it winds into a Tube station and artificial light replaces natural. I head underground.

My sister was the one who loved sunsets, not me.

The platform is busy. I walk down it, weaving through couples coming home after dinner and students who are just starting their nights out. A train screeches somewhere in the tunnel, blasting dirty air ahead of it. It's twenty seconds away, maybe less. A UK Listeners poster is tacked on to the wall at the far end of the platform, a phone number and green text: *However alone you feel, we'll always be here to talk.*

In other words: *Don't jump.*

I glance around at the crowd, scanning faces. I used to think – not that I ever thought about it much – that if someone was suicidal, you'd know. Surely they would look sad, and cry, and act strangely? They would openly hate life. They would have a big, obvious sign around their neck, emblazoned in neon lights: *Depressed and going to end it all!*

The reality is different.

Suicidal people smile. They go to work, do their shopping, wave to the neighbours. They hide their feelings from the people they care about.

Statistically, I've learnt that most of the 6,500 yearly suicides in the UK are men, mid- to late-forties, or teens and young adults – but on this platform, tonight, the person thinking of suicide could be anyone.

That man in the suit could be struggling at work, going through a divorce, losing kids in a custody battle, not talking. But the old woman sitting alone and knitting may have just lost her husband of fifty years. The cheery lady in a supermarket uniform could be on antidepressants. The girl laughing and joking with her friends may feel hollow inside from years of bullying.

One moment a person can be singing Christmas songs, dancing in the kitchen, sparkling with warmth and light and love and a million hopes for the future – and the next they can have taken their own life.

Like Poppy did.

The train thunders past, noise and air slapping my face and tearing long brown strands from my ponytail. I close my eyes against the blur of carriages, and I'm there: chalky earth beneath my feet, salt air gusting around me, waves roaring on the beach far, far below the cliff edge.

Not all suicidal people call helplines. Some reach out to friends, to loved ones. Sometimes people in distress just need someone to talk to, someone who knows them, someone who will take their hand and lead them away from the edge.

That's what Poppy needed that night. She needed to know everything would be all right. She needed to know she was loved. That's why, when she stood on that cliff edge in the dark, she called me.

But I didn't answer.

And she jumped.

I leave Aldgate Station and walk my usual route through Whitechapel. Tourists clog up the pavement at various points, tour groups circled around guides describing the grizzly details of Jack the Ripper's murders, pointing out Victorian crime scenes that have long since been demolished and turned into flats.

It's a morbid legacy for the five women who were murdered: their lives reduced to nightmarish photographs and stops on a tour.

They were human beings before they became victims. People forget that.

It's dark when I get to the helpline. I head inside, up several flights of stairs, and sign the log-in book at reception. *Clementine Harris, 21.52.* Our branch is a simple office space with a lounge area, kitchen, some private rooms, and a phone room. Leafy plant pots are in every corner and every surface has a box of tissues. The white walls are covered in pinboards and posters with well-meaning messages in friendly fonts.

However alone you feel, we'll always be here to talk.

I wasn't there for Poppy when she needed me most, and there's nothing I can do to change that, but I can be there for the others.

And there are so many others.

'Clementine?' Brenda, one of the branch supervisors, waves at me from the kitchen opposite the phone room, beckoning me in as she makes several cups of tea. 'I didn't expect to see you here again. Didn't you do a night shift a few days ago?'

'Yes, Friday into Saturday. I'm trying to do two or three a week.'

Brenda purses her lips as she pours out the milk. 'Clementine, you mustn't overdo it. We're very happy to have you, but we only ask our volunteers to do one or two night shifts a *month*. Please don't feel you have to give more than three or four hours a week, day or night.'

'It's no trouble,' I say, handing her the milk bottle top she's hunting for. 'I have the time.'

'It isn't an issue of time. Listening can be a very draining process, and you're still new to this. You might not realise when too much is too much. I wouldn't want you to feel overwhelmed.'

'I'm not overwhelmed.' I pass Brenda a spoon for the sugar and take the milk to put it away – anything to speed the conversation to a close. 'I like to be helpful.'

'Yes, I've noticed.' She smiles. 'Well, as long as you're comfortable, nobody here is going to limit your hours. But come to me if you need to, all right?'

I take a few mugs of tea and carry them into the phone room with Brenda. Some volunteers are on calls already, hunched forward at their desks with headsets on, while others read or chat in whispers to pass the time. I vaguely know a few names, a few faces, but even the strangers greet me with kind smiles and friendly waves. It's always like that here.

'. . . Buckingham Palace to Frieda by the door, I'll take the London Eye, and our resident Picasso over there can have the Tate Modern.'

I put the last tourist mug in front of a man with dark curly hair. He's leant back in his seat with his boots on the desk, drawing in a sketchbook with his headset on.

'*Thanks*,' he mouths silently, smiling. Then he returns to his call. 'Would you like to talk about it?'

A phone rings behind us and a listener answers it, but quickly goes back to their book.

'Another snap call,' Brenda mutters. 'There have been lots of those lately. Alan counted twenty-six the other day! It must be the time of year.'

'Why would the time of year make more people call and hang up?'

'It's younger people, usually. The summer holidays give kids more time to call for a joke, and then there are all the exam results that come in during August. It's a stressful time for them, poor dears. It's one thing to pluck up the courage to call, but quite another to manage to speak.' Brenda touches my arm. 'Oh, did you want a tea? I forgot to ask.'

'No, I'm fine. Thank you.' I pull off my backpack and claim a free station in the corner, away from the others. 'I just want to get started.'

'All right, but remember what I said. No overdoing it.'

I smile back at her. 'I won't.'

I unpack my bag. I set up my station as I always do: heavy folder on the left; notebook on the right; ball-point pen clicked and ready.

At a glance, this could be my desk in the library at Harvard. Tucked away in a corner of the Molecular Biology section, colour-coded folder of notes open, Jenna whispering to herself as she scans through a thick textbook beside me. It could be a night of cramming and caffeine, of knowledge and progress.

But it isn't.

I sit down and open my folder. It's a listening guide I put together from the materials and training I received, with sections for all possible eventualities during calls. There are resources and phone numbers I can refer people to, solid facts to help them, but also suggested responses. The other listeners echo them around me during their calls.

'How are you feeling?'

'I'm sorry, that must be hard.'

'Would you like to talk about it?'

Their words are full of easy, effortless compassion, as though comforting others is second nature to them.

It is not second nature to me.

I need a handbook.

Phones ring sporadically around the room, and I wait for my turn. I flick through my folder, rereading words I've already memorised, and scroll down the usual Reddit forums on my phone: r/BereavedBySuicide; r/SuicideWatch. I reply to a few posts, tapping out responses to titles like *Wish I was dead* and *I'm not good enough* and *Someone tell me not to do it.*

I need my handbook for those, too.

When my phone rings after midnight, I'm ready for it. I take a deep breath, centring myself, and block out the rest of the phone room. I press the answer button.

'Hello, UK Listeners?'

There's a noise from my headset, some slight static or breathing, that lets me know someone is on the other end of the line. But they don't speak. I consult the checklist in my folder, the one I follow for every new call. *Let the caller know you're there and that you want to listen. Be available. Be kind. Give them a reason to trust you.*

'Is there something you'd like to talk about?' I ask, making sure my voice is soft and welcoming, but firm enough to sound in control. 'I'm here to listen, whenever you're ready.'

Still nothing. There's another noise, maybe from the phone brushing against something. This could be one of the snap callers Brenda mentioned: the people who phone us, don't talk, and almost immediately hang up. It could be a nuisance call from a pervert or a time waster.

Or it could be genuine. It could be the most important call of someone's life.

No matter how alone this person might feel, as long as I stay on the line, they won't be.

'I know you're there,' I say. I pause between sentences, giving the caller space. I think about what Brenda said earlier. 'I know it can be daunting to talk to a stranger, but that's what I'm here for. Anything you say to me now is just between us, and I won't judge you for it. I'm here for you. Whenever you're ready to talk, let me know.'

There's a slight sniffle, and then a voice. 'Okay.'

I straighten up in my seat, pen at the ready. Good.

'Hello. How are you feeling tonight?'

I wait, but the answer doesn't come. There's some kind of noise, but I don't know what.

11

Not all callers are quiet. Some people barely wait for me to respond before they spill their life stories, getting everything off their chest in what feels like a single breath. Those calls are a lot easier.

I check my folder again. *Be kind. Be empathetic. BE PATIENT.*

I swallow the blunt, probing question I was about to ask. These calls are not lectures I can interrupt with a raised hand, or textbooks whose chapters I can skip until I get to the section I need. We go at the caller's pace, and their words must be coaxed out, not forced.

What would Poppy say?

'I'm sorry you felt the need to call this number tonight. I know whatever you're going through or feeling right now must be very difficult, but I promise you I'm ready to listen. Whatever it is you have to say, you can say it to me.'

The words are right, but they feel wrong in my mouth. I aim for soothing, for gentle, but they come out empty and disingenuous. It's as though I've picked up a script for a role I was never supposed to play.

But I must be doing an okay job, because the caller responds.

'I . . . I don't want to feel like this any more.' The voice sounds male. It's small and defeated.

I glance at my guide. *Always find the purpose of the call. There is often a central issue the caller is facing, and highlighting this to the caller can help increase the possibility of future healing.*

'What is it that you're feeling tonight?' I ask.

'Nothing.'

'You feel empty?'

'No, I feel like there's nothing left for me. Like . . . like everything that was good is gone. I just . . . I miss her so much.'

As he stifles a cry, I pick through the coloured section dividers in my folder and flip to one: *Breakdown of Romantic Relationships.* I've had this call a few times now. I'm prepared.

'Missing someone is a horrible feeling,' I say, reading the typed words on the page and pretending they don't apply to me. Next is a recommendation for an open-ended question to prompt him into a monologue. 'What happened?'

'She's gone, but . . . but she wasn't that kind of person. It doesn't make any sense. It's never made sense.' He sniffs heavily. 'She wouldn't do that. Not my sister.'

'Your sister?' This must be the wrong section. 'What happened with your sister?'

'She died. She . . .' He struggles for breath. 'They say she killed herself.'

My own breath catches in my throat. I see Poppy smiling at me in my head, two paintbrushes holding her curly ginger hair in a bun. Everything about her is warm, like she's lit by a sunrise.

I turn away from her.

'I'm sorry to hear that,' I say, flipping back to the pages on bereavement in my guide. 'I'm sorry for your loss.'

'It doesn't make any sense. She was fine. She was *happy*.' His voice spikes in anger. 'Happy people don't kill themselves!'

I know the response to that even though I don't have it written down. 'Depression affects more people than any of us realise. People often hide their true feelings. Even the most cheerful person could be—'

'I can't believe that. Maybe for other people, but not for her. It was so sudden. It – it didn't make any sense. I don't understand it. I can't. Everyone says she did it but nobody can say why. There was no reason. It came from nowhere.'

My pen shakes in my hand like my phone did six months ago. I hear Dad's voice again in the call I *did* answer.

'Clem, it's . . . it's Poppy. The police came this morning and they said they'd . . . they'd found her in the sea, and . . . and . . . she's gone,

love. She didn't make it. They . . . oh God, they think she did it on purpose.'

I steady my hand.

'It can be hard for us to understand other people's reasons, but often—'

'I'm not talking about other people, I'm talking about Rachel! My sister! And she told me everything!' He sniffs desperately, and I hear swallowing. There's a bottle there, liquid sloshing against glass. His words, I realise, have been slightly slurred since the beginning.

'We talked all the time,' he mumbles. 'Told each other everything. We were close. I was always there for her, always. I always made time for her. If she was suicidal, why didn't she tell me?' He takes another messy gulp of his drink. 'Why didn't she even say goodbye?'

There's nothing in my handbook about this. There's no section titled *How to Cope with Your Sister's Sudden Suicide.*

I wish there was.

'I know it feels impossible to process something you can't understand, but with time, the pain will lessen. Time heals.'

'*Time heals,*' he repeats mockingly. 'I've had time. Two years of it. But it never gets better.'

'Two years?'

'Yeah. And it still hurts like it was yesterday.' He takes another drink, laughing hollowly. 'It's not gonna hurt any more after tonight, though.'

Four out of five calls to the helpline are from people who need someone to talk to. The other call is from someone who is feeling suicidal – but rarely does that person actually intend to take their own life.

Assess seriousness, the Attempting Suicide section in my handbook says. *Ask about means. Get caller to move to another room while you talk.*

'What do you mean, it's not going to hurt any more?' I ask.

The caller doesn't respond. I hear movement, like he might be getting up. The alcohol bottle – empty – clatters to the ground.

'What's going on?' I ask. 'Are you feeling suicidal?'

The question is too blunt. He laughs at me down the line, but without any joy. His breathing is hard and messy. Small, painful whimpers sneak out.

'Have you taken any steps this evening to end your life?'

'Yeah, loads.'

'What do you mean?'

'Ten flights.'

I dig my pen into my notepad, scrawling out the calculation even though I already know what it means. Ten flights is a block of flats, a high-rise building. One hundred feet, at least.

'Where are you?'

'Why, so you can call the police to come and stop me? Have them section me again?'

'No, we don't do that. Your call is anonymous. That means the only details I have about you are the ones you give to me, and I can only pass them on to emergency services with your permission. If you give me your name and address, I can—'

'No! No address, no permission.'

'All right, we don't have to go into specifics. But I just want to know if you're in any immediate danger. Where are you?'

'A roof.'

A weird, staticky noise in the background sharpens: wind. He's so high up, I can hear the air whipping around him.

He's going to jump, just like Poppy did.

I can't let him.

'Are you by the edge?' I ask it calmly, like I'm asking when his birthday is. That's on the first page in my handbook: *Callers' lives*

15

often feel chaotic and disordered. Be a calm, steadying voice for them to cling to.

'Yeah, I'm by the edge.'

'Would you consider moving away or going back to the staircase? Just while we talk?'

'We already talked.'

'There's more to say.'

'No! We're done.' His words are angry again, and more slurred. He's become bolder. Braver. 'I don't want to talk any more. I'm sick of talking and nobody listening. I just . . . I just want this to be over.'

There's a noise, almost like a grunt. A sound of exertion.

He's climbing. He's getting ready to jump.

'Tell me about Rachel,' I say, trying to distract him.

'She got hit by a train.'

I wince. 'No, tell me what she was like. As a person. As a sister?'

'She was happy. She had plans. She . . .' The tears are back. Maybe they never left. 'She wouldn't have done this. I keep telling them that, but they don't listen. They don't care. There wasn't even a note, but they don't care. She didn't do this!'

'There are people you can talk to,' I say, consulting my handbook. 'Counsellors, bereavement support groups. They can help you process the loss.'

'No,' he cries. 'I don't want that. I've tried! I've had the pills and the doctors and months on the psych ward. *Accept it*, people say, *you have to accept it*, but I can't accept it. It doesn't make sense. They say I'm mad, but she wouldn't do this. She'd never do this. But I can. I'm going to.'

The wind gets stronger. I imagine him, this formless caller, on the edge of a block of flats, dangling a foot over the edge. Crying. Hating himself. Longing for a life he can never have again. About to end the one he does.

And Poppy stands right next to him, ready to do the same.

My guide says to listen, to respect the choices our callers make – even if they choose to die. But I can't.

I throw my arms around him and pull him back from the edge.

'Wait! Please, don't do this.'

I listen to the staticky wind. There's breathing there, too.

'You're not supposed to say that,' he says quietly.

'I know. I respect your choice, I do, but . . .'

My handbook doesn't have a page for this. It says to listen, not talk – but listening won't help this person. I push the folder away, and take off my glasses so I can cover my eyes. I have to find the words from somewhere else.

'My sister took her own life six months ago, and she didn't leave a note either. I know how confusing it is when you don't have a reason for why a loved one is dead, and how it feels as though it can't be right, that someone must have made a mistake, because there's no way *your* sister would ever, ever . . .' I rub my forehead, sighing. 'I couldn't make sense of what happened to my sister either, but suicide is something that rarely makes sense at all. For a deeply unhappy person, being unhappy is the reason. Feeling suicidal is the reason. And as much as my sister's death feels out of character, it wasn't, because she did it. She made that choice. And, well, looking back . . . There are signs. Something wasn't right, and I can see that now. Perhaps there were signs for your sister, too? Perhaps acknowledging those signs will help you accept the choice she made, even if you don't understand why she made it?'

The caller doesn't respond.

'Are you still there? Hello?'

'You're the reason,' he says.

'What?'

'The signs were there and you didn't see them. You didn't care. She was crying out for help and you ignored her. You're the reason she's dead.'

For the first time tonight, he keeps speaking without me prompting him.

'People think I'm like you, that I was too selfish to even know she was upset, that I let her die, but I wasn't. I was *always* there for Rachel. If she was upset, I'd have known, but there was nothing. Nothing! I've been over it a hundred thousand times. No note, no signs, no reasons. Even the inquest couldn't find anything.'

I find my voice again. 'I know it can be hard to accept, but your sister had *her* reasons. For the bereaved, no reason could ever be—'

'But she didn't have a reason! Why aren't you listening to me? You're just like them, aren't you?'

'Who?'

'The others. All of them. Mum, police, the bloody coroner. They all say the inquest is final. Suicide. Case closed. But the case was never even open!' His words get faster, more desperate. 'They saw someone hit by a train and they *assumed* it was suicide, then they picked her life apart trying to prove it instead of finding out what really happened. They didn't care about her, about who she was or if it was out of character. They say she threw herself under that train, but she didn't. I *know* she didn't. I have proof. But they won't listen. Nobody ever listens. They put me in the psych ward, they put me on drugs, but they never listen. They never believe me.'

I shove my glasses back on and grab my handbook, rifling through it for something, anything. I shouldn't have deviated from it. This was a mistake. I'm supposed to listen, not *talk*.

'Let me give you that support group referral. There are excellent ones all over the country. Where are you? Which county?'

'No! No more support groups. I'm done. I'm sick of being the only person who knows what he's talking about while everyone else calls me crazy. I'm sick of not being believed. I'm . . . I'm sick of missing her.'

My fingers shake as I flip through my folder. There has to be a way to help him. There's always an answer.

'It gets better,' I say, seizing on a printed phrase. 'Everything gets better eventually.'

'Not this. Not while they're still out there.'

'What do you mean? Who's out there?'

'Them. *Them.* The person who pushed Rachel in front of that train.'

I press my pen into the page of my notebook, the ink bleeding out from the nib.

'You don't believe me either, do you?'

'I . . .'

'I knew you wouldn't. Nobody does. They say I'm in denial, but they're the ones who won't face the truth. I tried to think like them, to accept it, but I couldn't. She didn't do that. I can't prove it, I can't prove any of it, but I know what happened. I *know*. And I can't live with knowing any more.'

He chokes out a pained cry, sobbing.

'Please,' I say, wishing I knew his name, 'step back from the edge and let's talk. I know it feels difficult right now, but let me help. There must be something I can do to help?'

He sighs, then inhales. 'There is.'

The wind around him has died down a little. It's calm. He's calm. Maybe now I'll be able to get through to him, convince him to –

'Nobody believed me, but you can. You can keep the truth alive. For Rachel.'

'No, please, wait—'

'Whatever anyone says, my sister didn't kill herself. She was murdered.'

And before I can say anything else, there's a gasp, a clattering noise, a distorted rush of wind, and, eventually, a thud.

The call disconnects.

CHAPTER 2

My headset is silent. No staticky wind, no words. Just the heavy, dead air of nothing.

Somewhere in the UK, a man has just fallen to his death – and I'm the only person who knows it.

'Are you okay?'

There's someone beside me. An office chair is pulled over and a man is leant forward, his hand resting on the back of my seat. I stare straight ahead.

'He jumped,' I find myself saying. 'He jumped off a roof.'

My brain repeats the sounds to me: the gasp, the wind, the thud. Other sounds seep in.

The sea thrashing against rocks.

A woman's scream.

Poppy's.

'I'm so sorry you had to hear that,' the man says. 'I can't imagine.'

I take off my headset and rest it on the desk. My folder is still open on the resources pages: a list of dozens of websites and phone numbers that the caller didn't want to have.

He didn't want to be talked out of it. He wanted to die.

But why did he gasp?

I hear it again, over and over. He gasped when he fell. It scared him. Terrified him.

He regretted it.

Did Poppy feel the same? Did she die regretting it? Did she fall from that cliff edge clawing the air and screaming for help? Screaming all the way down? Screaming even though there was no one there to hear her?

I should have answered. I should have been there to stop her. I should have –

'Hey,' the man says gently, touching my shoulder with his fingertips. 'It's all right. You're okay.'

I look up from my desk, from the unused resources and useless notes, and focus on the man beside me. He has kind eyes. They're brown, like his beard and the curly hair pulled into a messy knot on his head, and they're fixed on me. He's tall and broad, but his voice is gentle, quiet enough to shield our conversation from the other volunteers in the room. I forgot there were others. They continue on with their shifts, whispering softly, turning pages of their books. Oblivious that a man has just died.

'Do you want to talk about it?' he asks kindly.

My hands shake on the table.

'I tried to get him to stop, but he did it anyway. I couldn't save him.'

The man shakes his head and moves his other hand to my wrist, giving it a firm squeeze.

'He knew what he wanted to do, and he did it. You couldn't have changed that outcome, okay?' He rubs my shoulder slightly. 'I heard you. You asked for his details so you could get him help, but he wouldn't give them. You did everything you could for him. He didn't want this to end any other way.'

The man gives me a half smile, reassuring me, squeezing my wrist again.

'It's not your fault, Clementine.'

I gave this man a cup of tea earlier. He smiled then, sketching as he spoke to a caller. '*Do you want to talk about it?*' he asked them, in the same kind, gentle way he's talking to me.

Like I'm one of *them*.

I clear my throat, pulling my hands on to my lap and straightening up. He stays leant over, but retracts his hands to his knees.

'I know it's not my fault,' I say. I brush some stray hairs behind my ears – the ones the train pulled free earlier on the Tube platform. 'It's just the first time I've had that happen on the line.'

The man nods. 'It's tough. Most of the time people call us to talk, or to be talked down, but when you get a serious one . . . Sometimes they just want someone to stay with them while it happens. I've had that before, listening as someone fades away. Awful, but somehow peaceful, too.'

My call wasn't peaceful. It wasn't someone slipping away to the gentle lullaby of soothing words. It was an abrupt, violent end.

There was fear, regret, and, for a fraction of a second, indescribable pain.

Or more than a fraction of a second. Perhaps the fall didn't kill him. Perhaps he's still clinging on to life somewhere, dying slowly, feeling that pain, drowning in it.

Hoping that, somehow, the person he spoke to on the phone will save him.

Did Poppy think the same as she was falling?

'Shall we go and talk to Brenda?' the man asks. 'It'd be good to talk this over, get some clarity.' He touches my wrist again, shrugging. 'It really is normal to feel bad after a call like that.'

'I'm fine.' I push my thoughts away and smile at him. 'It was just a shock, that's all. I'm fine.'

He raises his eyebrows. 'Are you sure?'

'Of course. Really.'

I busy myself with tidying the desk for my next call. I flip the folder back to the checklist at the front, line up my pen, turn over to a fresh page in my notebook. Some of the words I scrawled stand out through the paper: *10 flights. Rachel. Believes suicide was murder.*

'I might nip to the toilet, though. Excuse me.'

I smile again and exit the phone room before he can say anything else. Brenda waves at me from her office as I head down the hall, and I wave back, still smiling. I don't go to the toilets. I leave the helpline office and head to the stairwell, but instead of going down, I go up. I go to the roof.

It's rained again. It's been raining on and off all day, dense clouds bringing heavy showers between bursts of sunshine, scrubbing the air clean.

I once told Poppy that heavy showers before sundown can contribute to an impressive sunset, and she never forgot it. She went out in all weathers, all seasons. She never wrote off a day until it was over.

I breathe in the clean, cold air.

When Dad called to tell me about Poppy's suicide, I didn't believe him. Why would I? Two months earlier she'd been her usual self: bouncing around Mum and Dad's house singing Christmas songs, drawing things, dancing, laughing, smiling, chirping on and on about her Fine Art degree, how pretty Brighton is, which painting projects she had planned for her second term.

That's the Poppy I've known my whole life. Six years younger, always interrupting my studies to chatter about foxes, or to drag me out the front door to watch a sunset. The sister who left me daily doodles on the bathroom mirror, and saved up letters to give me when I came back from university for the holidays.

She was a creative, vibrant, bursting-with-joy person.

But she was shy. The child psychologist Mum took her to said it was social anxiety: extreme nervousness around others. She found it hard to make friends at school. She didn't like to leave the house, especially by herself. She wouldn't talk to strangers. If we went out for dinner, she'd hide behind her menu and Mum would order her food for her. She refused to go to the art club Dad signed her up for one summer, crying all the way there and not letting go of my hand when we tried to drop her off. For the past three years, I've come home from university to a stack of letters on my bed because she simply couldn't face going to the post office and asking for them to be airmailed.

Those were the signs.

After Christmas, when she'd sung her songs and gushed about her first term until I was thoroughly sick of hearing about it, I flew back to Boston and got back into my PhD research. We talked every so often: I'd like an article she shared with me, she'd send me a photo of her latest Brighton sunset. I never checked in with her because I didn't realise I needed to. I remembered the Christmas smiles, not the childhood fears. I'd been living away from home for so long that I assumed she'd grown out of it.

I never considered that she was isolated and alone, hiding in a different bedroom from the same old fears. I never thought to ask her if she was actually okay. Maybe if I had, I'd have known that she wasn't. And if I'd known, I could have done something about it. I could have stopped her.

I *should* have stopped her.

But I didn't answer. I ignored her call. I didn't check the voice-mail until the next morning, after I already knew she was dead.

The sound of it taunts me again: wind on a phone receiver; the churning of waves. Silence.

Whatever she wanted to say to me, she never got the chance. Her last words died with her.

The caller's words come back to me, spiked in anger.

'*They say she threw herself under that train, but she didn't. I* know *she didn't . . . She was murdered.*'

He believed that. Even after an inquest and medical intervention and counselling and two years of healing time, he truly believed his sister would never have taken her own life. He was certain it had been taken from her.

I think of Dad's call again.

'*They found her in the sea, and . . . and . . . oh God, they think she did it on purpose.*'

I couldn't believe those words at first, either. It felt wrong, out of character, as though he was talking about someone else's sister. Not mine. Not shy little Poppy with her smiles, her skips, her bright eyes, her tugging hands. The police had got it wrong. She wouldn't do that. She'd *never* do that. Someone must have made a mistake. There must be more to it. She wouldn't. She couldn't. There was no reason for her to . . .

I cross my arms, digging my nails into my palms.

The psychological studies on suicide bereavement are very clear on this: to heal from it, you have to accept it. To move on, you have to let the questions go.

The caller couldn't do that. He got stuck in denial. He decided he'd rather die blaming the vague shadow of a murderer than face a future with the truth: that his sister was dead because she wanted to be.

The air is chilly, and rain starts to fall in a light drizzle. The concrete roof is slick, puddles reflecting the taller buildings around me. I walk to the edge.

Six months ago, in the early hours of 23 February, my eighteen-year-old sister rode her bicycle to the top of a cliff outside Brighton and threw herself off. That was *her* choice. *Her* decision.

She didn't leave a note. She didn't call anyone else to say goodbye. She died silently and alone.

And that was what she wanted, however much I wish it wasn't. I can't make excuses for her, or explain away her actions as the caller explained away his sister's. I can't cling to a hope that isn't there.

Yes, I should have answered Poppy's call that night, I should have helped her see she was loved and precious and had a future worth living, however bad the present was – but, ultimately, she was on that cliff because she wanted to be. Nobody forced her there. Nobody talked her into it. Nobody pushed her.

She made the decision to die all on her own, and pretending otherwise is a selfish delusion.

There's a barrier at the edge of this roof to prevent falling, but it's not impossible to climb over. Anyone could do it. Even someone drunk and crying.

Poppy stood on the cliff edge alone – but I was there for the caller on that roof tonight. I tried to save him, and I stayed with him until the end.

At least I gave him something Poppy never had.

I head back to the phone room. The man I spoke to earlier is talking on his headset, the same soft and gentle tones in his voice. He's leaning back in his chair, one foot on his desk and the other crossed over it, head to one side, sketchbook on his knee, doodling away during the call. Casual and easy-going. Calm despite whatever he's hearing on the other end of the line.

Poppy would never have been able to volunteer here and talk to strangers on the phone because of her social anxiety, but if somehow she had, she'd have been like him. Instinctively kind, empathy and compassion pouring out of her like sunshine, so easily she could draw and save lives at the same time.

I'm not built for this, with my handbook of stock phrases and emotional cues.

She should be the one here, not me.

I sit down at my desk. There are two mugs there – one of Trafalgar Square, the other of the Science Museum – plus a stack of sugar cubes, a small cup of milk, and three custard creams. There's a drawing on a square napkin, a little cartoon version of the volunteer I spoke to earlier: laced boots, denim shirt, dark beard and curly hair. Waving.

> *Wasn't sure if you were a coffee or a tea drinker, so I got you both. And some biscuits!*
>
> *PS – I'm Jude, by the way.*
>
> *PS 2 – You're doing a great job. :)*

I glance at him – Jude – but he's looking away, his attention on his caller. I take the Science Museum mug and pour a splash of milk into the coffee. The smell of early morning labs and library all-nighters centres me.

I switch my phone back on, ready for another chance to do the right thing.

In a way, I envy tonight's caller. He couldn't accept that his sister would take her own life, that she was unhappy, and blaming someone else for her death preserved her for him. When I think of Poppy, everything is tinged in sadness: her smile becomes stretched and forced; her laughter hollow. But the caller's sister is forever joyful. Her smiles are like butterfly specimens beneath glass.

The only person I have to blame for my sister's death is myself.

CHAPTER 3

I stare up at the ceiling as sunlight streaks through a gap in the curtains and rush-hour traffic rumbles in the street outside.

I dreamt of her again.

It was a picnic, maybe, or a holiday somewhere. Us on a beach, her hand pulling mine away from my book, begging me to take her swimming. She laughs and shrieks when we hit the water, jumping in the waves, but then I can't find her. Her hand is no longer in mine. She's not laughing any more. She's face down in the water, ginger curls tangled with seaweed and her limbs broken. A piece of paper floats by, pulled away by the current: her suicide note. The reasons why. Lost at sea, for ever.

I never saw Poppy's body. A dog walker found her bicycle and bag on the coastal path near Seaford the morning after she jumped, and the police recovered her body from the beach below a few hours later. Even though her bag had her ID in it and her phone was found on the cliff edge, my parents had to go to Brighton to identify her. Dad did it. He didn't want Mum to see. But he told us she looked like she was sleeping.

In my dreams, she's never sleeping. She's twisted, bruised, bloated. Even though she was only in the water for a matter of hours, my unconscious mind focuses on the worst-case scenario, however scientifically unlikely. In one dream, her waterlogged skin hung off her bones like rags on a scarecrow. In another, her flesh had been gnawed away by fish.

I'm grateful for the nights she's face down.

Did last night's caller dream of his sister, too? Did he revisit the tracks where she died night after night, watching her fall, again and again, into the path of the train that killed her? Is that what he saw? Her suicide?

Or her murder?

I sit up and rub my tired, aching eyes. I know what woke me. Liam is in the kitchen, his favourite playlist turned up and his singing twice as loud. Other noises are familiar: the bangs of the fridge as he puts the butter away before remembering the jam; the almost violent discarding of a used knife into the sink. His breakfasts are always a messy rush before he has to run out to work.

I grab my glasses – the round tortoiseshell ones Poppy picked out for me. I can never get back to sleep in the mornings. Sometimes I join Liam, drinking strong coffee, making the polite conversation of two strangers in a tiny flat. But today I keep my door closed, and reach for my phone.

I enter search terms into Google: *news suicide death building roof fall fell jump body man male discovered UK*. I scroll through the pages of results, but it's old news articles, other people. Nothing current that could be the caller I spoke to last night. No name or image to go with the voice.

It's probably too early for it to be reported. It's been less than twelve hours, and the authorities would have to contact next of kin before releasing information to the press. There's paperwork to do, procedures to follow.

Unless, of course, nobody's found him yet.

What if there was no dog walker, no passer-by? He could still be out there somewhere, lying in some remote building site or beside a derelict building. Flies on him. Birds picking at his eyes.

29

Like Poppy, I prefer to think of him face down, too.

My phone vibrates in my hand with a new message. It's from Jenna. They're always from Jenna.

> *Hey Clem! I just left the lab (at 3 a.m.! I know, your bad influence finally rubbed off on me) and thought I'd text you since it's actually a reasonable human hour in London. How're you doing? Things are good here. No undergrad papers to mark, so it's experiment city over here right now. Missing my fave lab partner, though. Could use a few of those midnight pajama brainstorming sessions we used to have. Pretty soon Prof's gonna realise you were the brains of this operation all along and revoke my funding.*
>
> *I really really hope you're doing okay, Clem. You can talk to me any time, you know. Seriously, ANY time. I'm here for you. x*

Jenna Kim. Her icon smiles at me, red lips pulled wide and head tilted, the blurred background of a bar behind her. It's new. Usually she's wearing a lab coat and mock-squinting at an empty test tube – a parody of the picture of me that made it into last year's Harvard prospectus. Her hair is different, too. It was blunt against her shoulders – a solid, glossy black – but it's longer now, the ends lightened.

My thumb hovers over the reply button, shaking.

This used to be my life. Harvard. Red-brick buildings, green courtyards, leafy orange trees. The feel of a lab coat. The smell of books. Jenna grabbing my hand, the way Poppy did in my dream, and pulling me out of the library and into the falling February snow.

'*Come on, Clem! Time to celebrate!*'

Her warm American accent fades to silence, and I close the app without replying. Like always.

So much has changed since that last night in Boston.

Too much.

I put my phone back on the table and get up, stretching until my shoulders click. I need coffee.

My bedroom is as bare and undecorated as the day I moved in, but the main room of the flat is an explosion of Liam: hand-painted plant pots brighten dark corners, colour-clashing framed artwork covers the patchy walls, and a rainbow of ten different cushions are crammed on to a drab three-seater sofa. The salt and pepper shakers on the tiny dining table are flamingos. The fridge is covered in second-hand magnets from other people's holidays.

The kitchen is silent and Liam is gone, but his tracks remain: toast crumbs, splodges of jam, a wet towel dropped outside the bathroom at the far end of the flat. I pick up after him as I wait for the kettle to boil, even though the chalkboard on the counter says: *Don't you dare clean this up, C! It's my mess! Drinks later??*

Poppy was like Liam when we were growing up: used cups stacked up by her bed; yesterday's socks on the floor. She was always too busy creating to be clean. When Dad and I went to Brighton to clear out her room in the halls, it was just the same. Half-drunk drinks. Socks she'd never wear again.

I scrub at the kitchen counters like I did yesterday and the day before.

I don't mind Liam's messes. I don't mind Liam, either. I thought I would initially, because the flat is small and his personality is anything but, but he gives me my fair share of space. When we cross paths, he launches us into easy conversation, saying enough for the both of us as long as I smile and nod in the right places. He always invites me to spend time with him – dinner, movie nights, offers of baked treats – but I make my excuses.

31

I was supposed to go back to Harvard after Poppy's funeral, but I didn't. I couldn't. Mum wasn't well. She said I should go, she insisted, but how could I when she was a shell of herself? When she barely slept? When most days she couldn't even make it downstairs to help in her own café and Dad had to stay up half the night doing the baking for her? She needed me around, they both did, so I stayed.

But not in the house. Not in my childhood bedroom with the emptiness of Poppy's room on the other side of the wall, and her messy life packed up into neat little boxes. Liam – a pink-haired stranger with dark stubble and a Geordie accent – ordered a smoothie from me at the coffee shop one day, complaining about the weirdos who'd responded to the online ad for his spare room. It was nearby, cheap, and still available, so I took it. I paused my PhD and my funding. I paused everything, indefinitely.

Until this Thursday, anyway. Nine a.m. at Eastbourne Town Hall.

Poppy's inquest.

Every sudden or unexplained death requires an inquest: an official investigation into the causes. In three days it will be Poppy's turn. For the last six months, the Eastbourne coroner's office has been gathering information about Poppy's life and death, and using it to piece together exactly what happened to her. On Thursday, that information will be presented to us, and a conclusion given.

We know some of it already – the when, the where, the how. But we don't have the why.

The inquest could give us that.

There isn't always a reason for suicide, and often there isn't a motive, I *know* that, but . . . what if there is? What if we're one of the lucky families? The coroner could have found something to explain all this – or if not explain, at least hint. Mean texts could suggest she was bullied. Missed deadlines could show stress.

It might not be a definitive answer, but it would be something. It would be enough.

And after that, we can draw a line under it. There will be nothing left to wait for; no hanging threads or secrets left to come out. My parents will know I didn't answer Poppy's call, but at least we'll be able to say she died by suicide – due to bullying, due to stress, due to missing home. Due to *something*. And we can move on with our lives.

But what is there to move on to?

Poppy will still be gone. With or without a motive, I still let her down by ignoring her call. I could have saved her, but I didn't even try. Will my parents ever forgive me for that? Will I ever forgive myself? Do I even deserve forgiveness?

I pull off my glasses and press my hands against my face, forcing the emotions back inside. Deep inside. I put my glasses back on.

I can't imagine a day when things are normal again.

But maybe, after the inquest, I can try.

When every corner of the flat is spotless, I shower and get dressed, selecting a plain T-shirt, a cardigan, navy trousers, and lace-ups from my wardrobe. I scoop my dark hair into its usual ponytail. Poppy loved colour and patterns, but I always wear the same combination of sensible clothing. I don't have much of a choice; I only brought one bag with me from Boston. I didn't realise at the time I wouldn't be back for six months.

I trail around the flat. What now? I've read all my library books. The new posts on r/SuicideWatch on Reddit take only minutes to reply to.

The time between today and Thursday stretches ahead of me like an infinite expanse of space: cold and lonely. But it isn't a void. In the darkness, black holes suck my conscious mind towards them, trapping me in the gravity of thoughts I don't want to have but can't avoid.

Why would she do it?
It wasn't like her.
This doesn't feel right.
You should have stopped it.
She's dead because of you.

I wrench my mind away before it reaches the event horizon, and grab my bag, phone, and keys. I need to keep busy.

I stop in the kitchen on the way out.

Drinks later?? Liam's handwriting on the chalkboard says, as though I'm a normal twenty-four-year-old Londoner who's earnt a much-needed evening out with a housemate. As though Liam and I are actually friends.

I take a cloth and wipe the invitation away.

Liam doesn't know me, and if he did, he wouldn't be asking.

CHAPTER 4

I follow Regent's Canal east, dodging dog walkers and mid-morning joggers on the towpath. The canal is the same as ever: stained green with algae, lined with narrowboats, and overlooked by alternating stretches of buildings and bushes.

There are memories waymarked along the path. Poppy's favourite boat, the one with a planter of sunflowers on the roof. The bench the four of us always sat at when we came out for Sunday picnics.

It seems wrong that these things exist when she doesn't.

The bridge comes into view around the corner, and Mum and Dad's place with it. It's a tall, narrow building, set back a little so it overlooks the canal from the other side of the bridge. It used to be a creaky bric-a-brac shop when Mum inherited it from her great-aunt Tabitha, and she and Dad moved us here from Cornwall to fix the place up to sell. Seventeen years later, we're still here. Mum fell in love with the twisting staircases and oddly shaped rooms, so Dad converted the ground floor into a café – Tabitha's – and made the rest of the floors residential for us, one room at a time. He made it a home.

Poppy and I used to share a top-floor bedroom, one long enough to have windows on both sides of the house. When she was little, Poppy would flit from one side to the other, feet poking out from under the curtains, nose pressed to the glass to watch the sunrise over the bridge or the sunset across the canal. Even after Dad divided the room into two, I'd still hear the squeaking of her bedsprings as she knelt up to look at the moon or check for snow.

Her window is empty now, but a glimmer of sunlight picks something out. An old nose print on the glass. A smudge of her left behind.

I push on up the ramp through the trees and turn right on to the busy bridge.

Tabitha's is almost full. It's pretty inside, with round wooden tables, green walls and plants, and the occasional oddity discovered during the clear out of the old shop. Mum's home-made cakes and pastries are under bell jars on the counter, and the menu is hand-painted on boards above it.

Hand-painted by Poppy.

Her art is on the walls, too. A London landmark on every canvas, but fused with nature. Buckingham Palace covered in ivy. The London Eye's viewing pods as red roses. Big Ben with daisies trailing down its sides.

I try not to look at them.

Dad, with his dark beard and shaved head, spots me as soon as I walk in.

'Clem, love, what are you doing here?' He throws a cloth on to a half-cleaned table and pulls me into a hug. 'You don't have to come in after night shifts.'

'I know, but I thought I'd help out anyway.'

He keeps me wrapped up in one of his bear hugs, his arms holding me tighter than they used to.

'How's Mum doing?' I ask.

'It's a good day today, sweetheart. It's a good day.'

'Oh, is that my Clementine? You know you don't have to come in after night shifts, love.' Mum, ginger like Poppy and with even curlier hair, delivers two coffees to a couple by the door and comes to give me a hug of her own. I've been taller than her since I was eleven, but she doesn't seem to have noticed. She pulls me into the same soft, head-stroking embrace of my childhood, and finishes it with a kiss.

'Come and see what I made last night! You'll love this.'

Mum takes my hand and leads me behind the counter to a line-up of colourful discs.

'Macarons!' she says, pointing. 'All different flavours. What do you think?'

The thought of sugar turns my stomach, but Mum is looking at me hopefully. I've never had a sweet tooth, but Poppy did. She was always there with Mum, licking spoons and testing offcuts, both of them singing along to Disney songs.

I used to shut my bedroom door so I wouldn't have to hear them while studying.

'They're lovely. They must have taken you ages to make.'

'Well, I couldn't sleep.' Mum clears her throat slightly, then tightens her short ponytail.

Mum's eyes are puffy and tired. She hasn't been sleeping either. Like me, she prefers to keep busy.

The silence stretches until Dad changes the subject, his big hands tucked in the pockets of his apron. 'Clem, how was last night? Good shift?'

'Did you help people?' Mum asks, clutching my arm.

I swallow an uncomfortable breath, trying to ignore the trio of sounds in my ears: the gasp, the rush of staticky wind, the thud.

I nod and smile the wide, stretched smile that hurts my cheeks, and my parents smile back. I practise in the mirror sometimes, dabbing Liam's concealer on the dark circles under my eyes. Pretending to be normal.

I grab a cloth and a tray without waiting for a response and head away from them, focusing on dirty plates and crumpled napkins. Don't look at the paintings on the walls. Don't look at Poppy's handwriting. Don't look at Mum and Dad, and the sadness that never properly leaves their faces, no matter how much they try to hide it.

There are seven tables inside the café, and the ones overlooking the canal always fill up first. It's picturesque out there today, as it often is: ducks gliding along the water, sunshine sparkling in the ripples. Poppy used to do her homework here sometimes, always sitting at the corner table, daydreaming instead of writing. Someone is sat there now, his own ginger hair turned fiery in the sun, books and notes stacked up around him, sipping coffee as he stares out of the window, lost in thought with his pen still twisted in his fingers.

I reach for the empty plate behind his books, and startle him. He jolts, coffee splattering over his hands and the table, the mug falling, his pen clattering away across the floor. He looks at me wildly, his corkscrew-like hair shaking, flecks of liquid on the lenses of his horn-rimmed glasses, cheeks burning red.

'I'm so sorry,' I say, ditching the tray of empties. The customer's books – heavy, expensive academic textbooks – are covered in splashes of coffee. I press my cloth on to them, trying to save the pages of text and diagrams. 'That was my fault.'

'No, no, it wasn't.' He coughs, choking down the sip of coffee that lodged in his throat. 'My fault, definitely. Should've been paying more attention. I'm an idiot. Sorry.'

He grabs a wad of paper napkins and mops at the table – but all he does is push the liquid on to the floor, and my shoes.

'Oh, Christ! Sorry!'

'Maybe you should leave the cleaning to me?'

He cringes, covering his face and shrinking down in his seat so his shirt collar is level with the table. Poppy used to do the same when she was embarrassed. She hated the thought of people watching her.

I keep wiping, absorbing coffee from book spines and the keys of his laptop.

'It doesn't look too bad, actually. I think you got away with it. Why don't I get you a complimentary coffee? Americano, was it?'

'Yes. I mean, no. No, thank you. I'm fine. I don't deserve one. Really. I'm just an idiot. Butterfingers. Please, don't worry about me. Sorry. And, um . . . how much do I owe you for the mug?'

He holds up the cup – and its detached handle.

'Nothing. Let's call that complimentary, too.'

I smile and pick up my tray again, adding the broken china and wet paper towels. I reach for a bundle he's holding, but he sheepishly pulls them away.

'I, um . . . I still need these ones.'

I'm about to question why when I notice a large wet patch on his trousers. I nod and leave him to it.

I take the empties to the kitchen, then fill a bucket and head back out with the mop. The ginger man with glasses is by the counter, trying to awkwardly sneak past with a cumbersome backpack and a stack of books in his arms. He jumps again when he sees me, and a heavy textbook slides off the stack and slams on to the floor. I dart around the counter and replace it for him, then hold open the café door for him.

'Oh, thanks. Again.' His glasses have slipped down his freckled nose. He bends over and uses the returned book to push them back up. 'Well, um, sorry again for the mess. Running away now. Bye.'

He smiles at the floor and shuffles off as fast as he can, juggling his books over his damp clothes as he bumbles out on to the busy pavement.

39

I used to juggle books. I'd check too many out of the library and end up with a precarious stack of them on my desk – my old desk, the one three thousand miles away, wedged in a postgraduate apartment with Jenna and Paolo and Raj. I can still remember the weight of them in my arms; the smell of the pages. The psychology and self-help books from the local library just aren't the same.

I set off to the corner table with my mop and bucket.

'Don't do that, love.'

Mum appears beside me, and she takes the mop.

'Your mum's right,' Dad says, stooping to grab the bucket. 'Go out, have fun, see friends. Relax a bit.'

Friends? I haven't had friends in London since school, and I lost touch with them years ago.

'Or you could catch up with your American friends,' Mum says. 'Call them, see how they are. Who's that nice one, the one who sent us flowers? Jenny? The Korean girl?'

'Jenna,' I correct automatically, even though saying her name out loud hurts my throat. 'And she's Korean-American, Mum.'

'Oh, that's right, sorry. *Jenna*. Give her a call.'

I think of the message she sent me this morning, and the hundred or so others I haven't responded to either.

Why does she keep sending them?

'We love having you here, but your mum's right. We can cope without you for one day, love. We'll be fine.'

They smile and usher me to the door, like they're doing me a kindness. They did the same thing after Poppy's funeral, with the same twitchy smiles. '*It's been such a comfort having you home, love, it really has, but you need to go back to school. Get your PhD. You don't have to stay here and put your life on hold for us. We'll be okay. Really. We just want you to be happy.*'

But how can I go back to that life when everything has changed?

'Now get out of here,' Dad says.

Mum and Dad wave me off, then watch me through the café windows. Their troubled expressions turn to smiles when they spot me looking, and they wave again.

I wave back, the cheery, carefree wave I always gave them when they were tearfully seeing me off at Cambridge or the airport. I pretend I'm still that person, as though I'm skipping off to see a film or hang out with friends, something normal and wholesome.

But instead I head home, grab my handbook, and take the Tube back over to Whitechapel. To the helpline.

If Mum and Dad don't need me today, someone else will.

YEWANDE

3 Months Before Poppy

Resting my library book on my knee on the night bus home, I circle a chunk of text and scribble a note in the margin.

Foreshadowing. You in danger, girl!!

My words stand out for a moment on the page, glossy and fresh, before drying down to become another voice in the crowd.

Theme of madness. V. important.

Mr Rochester is a total DICK!

This is ruining Jane Eyre *for me, but okay.*

I love these worn, torn, coffee-ringed university books. Every great novel comes with a running commentary from dozens, maybe hundreds, of other students who've read it over the decades. When? Who knows. These voices could belong to graduates, or dropouts, or retirees, or the dead. There's no way to tell. They live in the moment for me, waiting on every new page like comments on a years-old tweet I've only just stumbled across.

A community of ghosts, and I long to join them.

Thud.

I look up. The bus has emptied of partying students, and it's idling at a stop. A white guy heads down to the front, headphones on and bag slung over his shoulder, his long navy coat billowing behind him like he's a Regency hero in a windy field. A book lies by me on the floor. There's no one else around. It must have slipped out of his bag.

'Excuse me, I think you dropped your—'

But he's already nodding at the driver and stepping off. He didn't hear me. He doesn't know he's forgotten it.

I bundle together my book and his, and run for the front of the bus, but he still doesn't see me, so I jump out and call again. Then the doors click behind me and the driver pulls away.

The street is dark – and wet. Rain smacks down on me, dragging through my braids and splattering against my shoulders. Great. The man is striding down the street, water cascading from all sides of an umbrella. I shove the books under my coat and run after him. I call, but he can't hear me through his headphones. I have to lurch into his path to stop him.

'I have your book.'

He jumps and his eyes pop, his glasses speckled with rain. He pulls his headphones down. 'Excuse me?'

'I think you left your book on the bus.'

He frowns. 'No, I didn't, it's in my . . .' His Scottish voice trails off as he checks his satchel. 'Oh!'

'I think it must have fallen out. It was on the floor when you got off the bus and, um, I'd pass it to you now but I don't really have enough hands . . .'

'Oh gosh, of course. Let me help.' He steps closer to me and holds his umbrella over us both. It's big, the old-fashioned kind with a hooked wooden handle. Rain pounds heavily on top. 'Thank you for returning it to me. I nearly missed my stop because I was reading it, so I'm not sure how I managed to forget it!'

'I've done that a few times before, as well. Got halfway to Glasgow last time by mistake.'

He smiles at me, his floppy fair hair standing out against the dark background of the umbrella. I smile back.

'Well, um, here you go!' I've got too many books in my arms to hand his over, so I hold the stack out to him so he can take what's his.

He jams the umbrella handle under an arm and, with similar difficulty, takes two books. 'Um, which one is mine?'

I look at them, shifting a bit to catch the light of a nearby lamppost. He's holding two hardback books, both with navy fabric covers and stickers from Edinburgh University Library. The gold lettering glints. *Wide Sargasso Sea*. Times two.

I gape. 'We're reading the same book?'

'That's so strange! Are you studying it?'

'No, I'm a Med student. Are *you* studying it?'

'I'm a History student. I just wanted to read it for fun.'

We laugh incredulously. The rain continues to thrash down, bouncing off the puddles around us. I shiver – the kind that goes right down my spine.

'Sorry, you must be freezing. Okay, hmm, let's see . . .'

He checks both books and finds one with a red pen clipped in it – and red writing on the page. He tucks it into his bag and readjusts his umbrella.

'Okay, book returned. Your good deed of the day – night – is done, and you can get home and go to bed. Thanks. Really.'

We smile again and it turns awkward, neither of us moving, until I wave and step back into the rain. I pull my coat over my head and make my way back to the bus stop, checking my watch. Night buses are usually every half an hour. I look around. There's no bus shelter here, and the rain is as hard as ever. There's nowhere to hide from it.

Then the rain . . . stops.

'Hi. Me again.'

He's behind me, his umbrella stretched over my head. I lower my coat.

'You didn't get off the bus just to give me my book back, did you?'

'I couldn't let you leave without it.'

He sags a bit, looking guilty. 'Thank you, but you didn't have to do that. And you probably shouldn't have, actually. It's the middle of the night. There could be weirdos about. Other than me, I mean. When's the next bus?'

'About thirty minutes, I think.'

He winces. 'You'll be half frozen by then.'

'It's fine. I've got my coat.'

I shuffle back into the rain again, giving him permission to leave. But he doesn't. He frowns, mulling something over, then steps to cover me with the umbrella again.

'You don't have to stay,' I say, almost annoyed at his martyrdom. 'I'll be fine.'

'Oh, I don't care about you.' He pulls his book back out and opens it, leaning against the bus post. 'I just thought I'd have a little outdoor read before I head home. Mm, refreshing! This is my favourite spot, you know.'

'It absolutely isn't,' I say, laughing.

'It is!' He pulls his book to his chest so he can connect his index fingers together in an X. 'Cross my heart. I come here all the time. I usually stay about . . . ooh, thirty minutes? Give or take. It's just a wee coincidence you happen to be waiting for a bus right now, too.'

I cross my arms. 'There's no fighting you on this, is there?'

'I'm afraid not. You saved my book, and now I'm saving you from hypothermia. Sound like a fair trade?'

I sigh exaggeratedly and pull out my own book. We stand side by side under the large umbrella, reading.

'Which bit are you up to?' he asks after a while, craning his neck to see. 'Ooh, Thornfield Hall. I'm not there yet. Still in Jamaica.'

'I wish I was,' I say, shivering. 'The weather there is about as opposite to Scotland as you can get.'

'Are you from there?'

I scoff. 'I'm from Leeds!'

He almost drops his book. 'Oh, um, sorry, I didn't mean it like that. Typical stupid white male, right?'

'It's okay,' I say, laughing. 'My dad's Jamaican, so we go there to visit family every couple of years. Nigeria too, on my mum's side. I was just teasing you.'

We go back to our books.

'So, why Jean Rhys?' I ask. 'As literature goes, a postcolonial retelling of *Jane Eyre* can't be everyone's cup of tea, right?'

'Maybe not, but it is my cup of tea. I love books, always have, but the literary canon is *very* narrow, *very* white. So I'm trying to expand my reading. As a white man, it's not always comfortable reading, but it is enlightening.' He coughs a little awkwardly. 'I always pick books with the most annotations in them, so I can read what other people thought about them. It's like being in a book club.'

'Really? I do that too.'

He grins at me, laughing, and I grin back. My cheeks feel hot, even though my feet are wet and ice-cold tendrils creep up my legs and spine. I shiver without meaning to.

'Here, take this. I insist.'

Dumping his book on top of mine, he pulls off his tartan scarf and loops it around my neck, pulling it tight. It's soft and warm, like being swaddled.

My cheeks glow even hotter.

'It suits you,' he says. 'I'm Alistair, by the way. Alistair Forgetter-of-Books.'

'I'm Yewande Retriever-of-Books. And thank you for this.'

The bus comes early. He flags it down and rushes me to the door, his own hair becoming wet as he keeps the umbrella over me.

'Enjoy the book!' he calls as he ushers me onboard. 'Let me know what you think!'

'How?'

The bus conductor closes the doors before he can answer, tutting, eager to move on. I rush to the window, rubbing a hole in the condensation.

Alistair waves at me through it, the umbrella under his arm, miming the opening and closing of a book, the squiggle of a pen. He points at me. I look down.

I'm still holding his book as well as mine. I open it on the page where his pen is, and find eleven digits scrawled in the margin in red pen. A phone number.

The bus pulls away and he's lost around a corner, like a figment of my imagination. I settle into the nearest seat, hugging the books to my chest, feeling the warmth of his scarf around my throat.

Wide Sargasso Sea doesn't have a happy ending, but maybe I can write my own.

CHAPTER 5

'My daughter Yewande loved books,' Blessing, one of the helpline's frequent callers, says. 'She'd read them and write all over the pages, making notes and underlining the passages she liked best. I used to tell her off for it, I said it was a bad habit, but now those notes are all I have left of her. I read her books and it's like she is talking to me. But I can never talk to her in return. I can never say what I need to say to her.'

I know the feeling.

'What do you need to say to her, Blessing?' I ask.

'That I . . . I wish I had known how alone she was up in Scotland. That I am sorry for making her feel like she could not talk to me. And that I forgive her.'

'Forgive her for what?'

'For . . . for committing suicide.'

Blessing sobs – but muffles it almost immediately. She's pressed her hand over the phone so I can't hear her cry.

Scolding myself, I take my pen and scribble an addition on to her caller summary in my folder.

Blessing Arnold-Smith: fifties, bereaved, often calls out of loneliness. (Daughter Yewande – SUICIDE.)

Blessing calls a lot. This is my first time listening to her, but she's on the helpline's list of regular callers that Brenda keeps in her office. Sometimes callers have such a positive experience with the random branch the national number puts them through to that they request the direct number for further calls. For whatever reason, Blessing picked us.

She must be regretting it now. Was I too blunt with those questions? Did I make her say too much?

The notes I've made during Blessing's call – *Yewande, wears daughter's heart pendant every day, can't face donating daughter's books* – are on a fresh page in my notebook, but traces of the things I jotted down last night are dug into the paper: *Rachel, train, believes suicide was murder.*

There are so many of us with no answers. Blessing still longs for a conversation she'll never get, while last night's caller died believing suicide couldn't possibly be true. He was convinced his sister's death was murder.

I didn't believe him. I still don't. It's denial, wishful thinking. But . . . maybe there was more that he didn't tell me. He seemed so sure. Maybe he had proof? Maybe he couldn't find an answer in two years because there never was one?

believes suicide was murder

What did Poppy want to say to me that night? Was it sadness, or something else? Was she in trouble somehow? Was she scared? Did she –?

No. I shut my notebook and focus on the printed words in my handbook: facts, not speculation. Facts, not hope.

Poppy died because I was too selfish to save her. And that's it.

'Blessing,' I say gently, 'we don't use that term any more. People commit crimes, but suicide isn't a crime. Depression and suicidality are illnesses. Yewande was ill, and she took her own life.' I pause. 'I understand the frustrations of losing someone this way, but I'm sure the last thing she wanted was for you to experience the same pain she did. Be kind to yourself.'

Blessing sniffles. 'Thank you for being here with me. You're a good person. I wish my Yewande had had someone like you, at the end. I think it would have saved her.'

I want to believe Blessing's words – but all I can think of is last night's caller falling, like Poppy did.

◆　◆　◆

After my shift, I wander.

I head to the Thames and follow the river westwards, passing the Shard, the Tate Modern, the London Eye. Poppy's old sunset spots.

Eventually my aching feet take me up the steps of the domed, column-lined National Gallery.

We used to come here all the time. Poppy never liked crowds, so we made sure to come late in the day, when most of the visitors had trickled out and the place was eerily empty.

As I walk through the big, high-ceilinged rooms, I remember the way her smaller hand used to tug at mine, dragging me through the eras and movements.

'See here? They were just figuring out how to use perspective.'

'Isn't that lovely? He said Margate had the best lighting.'

'There's actually another painting hidden under this one, but you need an X-ray to see it!'

I only ever half listened, the way I only half looked when I took her out to hunt for sunsets. I'd sneak chapters of my latest library

50

book or go over exam revision in my head. Whatever she had to say, I was always doing something more important.

Even during those last moments of her life, I was doing something more important.

I sink on to the bench opposite a Turner painting. We'd always end up sitting here together, her pointing out this use of light or that blending of colour, me not really listening. The last time we came was just after Christmas. She sat beside me, hair escaping its bun, chunky Doc Martens swinging, one shoulder of her loose knitted cardigan falling down over her flowery dress as she talked.

I should have listened.

I take the Tube home at closing time – and someone grabs my arm as I leave the station.

'C! I thought that was you.'

Liam grins at me as he pulls level, his pastel pink hair drooping down from its usual slicked-back style and on to his dark, sculpted eyebrows.

'How you doing, hun?' he asks in his slight Geordie accent. 'Everything all right?'

'Yes, of course.' I clear my throat and try to assemble a smile. 'Everything's great. Just heading back to the flat.'

'Oh no, you're not.' He links his arm through mine. 'We're going for drinks.'

'Drinks?'

'Yes, drinks! You promised me, like, the day you moved in that you'd come out with me, but every time I try to organise it, you're busy. Well, you're not busy right this second, so we're doing it.'

'I can't tonight, I—'

'Have a headache? Need to read a library book before the loan runs out? Just don't want to be around me?'

Liam stops on the street outside the Tube station, arms crossed and face defiant. It's the same expression Jenna used when she'd drag me away from the lab to paintball, or comedy nights, or that little café by the river with the speciality hot chocolates. Defiant for my own good.

'I've heard all your excuses, C. Let me buy you a drink – just one drink – and then I'll never ever ask you again, okay? We'll consider it time served. But just this once, come and hang out with me? *Please?*'

I check my watch. It's almost 6.30 p.m., and I'm exhausted. I should go home and get some rest. Make a dinner I won't eat. Check Reddit until my eyes hurt. Lie awake through the darkest hours of the night, staring at my ceiling, desperate for sleep but dreading seeing Poppy in the water again, face up, accusing eyes fixed on me as the rest of her decays, my ears filled with the faint sound of the sea.

'You don't have to if you don't want to, but . . .' Liam shrugs at me, fiddling with the collar of his leather jacket. 'To be honest, I could really use the company. Been feeling kind of homesick lately.'

He shoves his hands in his pockets. Usually when I see him around the flat, he's tall and confident, joking about everything, but right now he seems a little shrunken.

Poppy moved away from home. Was she homesick? Did she need someone to talk to? Would that have changed everything?

'All right,' I say. 'Let's go for a drink.'

Liam gapes at me. 'What? *Really?*'

'Yes. Just one, though,' I add, as he bounces on his heels, grinning manically.

'Awesome! This is gonna be great.' Liam links his arm through mine again and steers me in the opposite direction from home, a skip in his step – the vulnerability of a few seconds ago forgotten. He launches into one of his stories as we walk to his favourite bar around the corner, and his chatter becomes soothing background noise – the kind of conversation you don't have to take part in.

I relax my arm against his, just a little.

One quick drink, for Liam's sake, and then I'll go home.

CHAPTER 6

'Wait, wait, wait,' Liam shouts over the bar's thumping music, pointing at me across the table. 'You're a scientist? Like, an actual scientist?'

'Yes. I'm a molecular biologist. I'd like to stay in academia and split my time between research and teaching.'

'Oh my God. You're such a nerd!'

Liam laughs into his cocktail, liquid sloshing precariously, and I take a careful sip through my straw. This cocktail is even more sickly than the last two. Or was it three? Four?

'I knew you were a nerd already, but not, like, a *total* nerd. Just a bit of one. You've got the whole sexy librarian thing going on, so it's a given, really.'

'Don't be ridiculous. Firstly, I'm not a librarian, and secondly, sexy is the last word *anyone* would use to describe me. Ever.' Now it's my turn to laugh into my cocktail. Snort, really.

Liam purses his lips, staring at me like he's accusing me of something.

'Come on, you're a babe! Really! You could do that thing where you pull your glasses off and shake your hair loose and everyone in here would love it. Honest.'

I raise my hands to my head – to tighten my ponytail.

'Tease.' He winks, reaching for his drink again and encouraging me to do the same. 'So, what's Harvard like?'

'It's great. The labs are incredible, so sophisticated, and the library is—'

'Yeah, yeah, but what about the parties? You and your friends go to frat parties and drink from those red plastic cups and stuff, right?' He clasps his hands beneath his dark-stubbled chin. 'Are you living the *college* dream?'

'Well, I'm a biology postgrad, and my friends are also postgrads, so . . . We are living our dream. It's just not that one.'

'Damn, I thought I was going to hear some wild stories. You don't stay in the library the whole time, do you?'

'No. Jenna doesn't let me.'

'Who's Jenna?'

'My partner.'

Liam's eyebrows sky-rocket.

'*Lab* partner, I mean. We work on the same research, and our theses are in similar areas. She's really intelligent, but also . . . cool? Like you!'

Liam flutters his fingers over his chest in false modesty. '*Moi?*'

'She's a nerd, too, I suppose, but you wouldn't know it. She's really outgoing and she's always trying to get me to go out, even when I want to stay in and read, and she knows before I do when I *need* to take a break. She's intuitive like that. And she's a lot of fun. She's the kind of person people immediately like, because she's interesting and clever and kind and always knows what to say . . .' I tighten my ponytail again, shrugging. 'We're very different.'

'You don't sound very different to me.'

He says it like he means it.

'Anyway, we live together in Boston with a couple of guys from Astrophysics. Paolo and Raj.'

'Whoa. Bet you guys are good at pub quizzes.'

'We are, actually!'

'What's your team name?'

'Pipped to the Postgrad.'

'That's terrible. Congratulations. Do you miss them? It must be hard being thousands of miles away from your mates. It's bad enough all mine being up in Newcastle, let alone on the other side of an ocean. Do you Skype them and stuff?'

'Yes, of course,' I say quickly. 'Every day.'

'So, what about romance? You got some nerdy Mr Right waiting for you back in Boston? Or *Ms* Right?'

I huff out a laugh. 'Absolutely not.'

'What? We've already established you're a certified sexy librarian babe, so don't act like that question is stupid. I bet those college boys are queuing up to date you. And not just the nerds, either.'

He's humouring me. Jenna used to do this, too. Men would approach her when we were out and she'd shove me towards them, saying: '*Oh, sorry guys, I play for the other team, but my friend Clem here is single . . .*' I hated those moments. Being thrust into the firing line, seeing the grinning faces fall as they looked between us – Jenna with her red lips, her short pleated skirts, her easy confidence, and me with my collars and cardigans and glasses, tall enough to be lanky, completely unremarkable in every way. But Jenna pretended not to notice their waning attention, their half-hearted compliments. She spoke for me, gushing like a museum curator in front of a priceless artefact, but the men and I always knew the truth.

She was the artefact. I was barely a gift-shop postcard.

'When was your last relationship?' Liam asks.

I rub my forehead. He's just being friendly, but I feel tired suddenly. 'When was yours? Do you have a boyfriend in Newcastle?'

Liam gasps, exaggerated like a cartoon character.

'Oh, right, so just because I have pink hair and great skin and work as a hairstylist, I'm *gay*?'

'You mean you're not?'

'No! Well, you know, maybe *sometimes*, but only on very special occasions.' He winks at me, running his hand through his hair. 'Nah, I'm pan. I'm all about the person, whatever gender they happen to be. What about you?'

'You didn't answer my question.'

'Which one? Oh, am I in a relationship? No. There was someone back in Newcastle, but . . . she's dead to me and I'm, like, totally fine about it! Not heartbroken or traumatised at all! Definitely don't have huge trust issues when meeting new people!' He sighs. 'Okay, your turn. Tell me about your love life!'

I gulp my too-sweet drink. 'There's nothing to tell. I don't really do relationships.'

'That's okay. Nothing wrong with being casual and non-monogamous – as long as you share the salacious secrets.'

'What? No! I mean I've never really been with anyone. Not properly.'

Liam's eyes go wide. 'Seriously?'

'There were a couple of guys back in Cambridge who liked me, and we went on a few dates, but . . . No, nothing serious.'

'What the hell? There's been nobody? There's been *nothing*?' He leans over conspiratorially. 'You mean you've never even got laid?'

I don't know where to look. I dig my nails into my hands, wishing this conversation would go away – and the memories. They swirl around me, the way the room does every time I blink for too long.

Fingers linking through mine.

Hot breath on my neck, my chest, my stomach.

The way my legs shook as time stretched and the universe collapsed around us.

The warm memories become cold and dark, drowned out by the sound of winter air and breaking waves.

'There was someone, all right? Once. But it was a mistake. It didn't mean anything. And it's definitely over.'

I gulp down the last of my drink. It's numbing in my mouth, washing away a taste I didn't know I still remembered.

I try so hard not to ever think of that night.

'I'll get another round,' I say, getting up. 'My choice, this time.'

'Fine. Oh, can I use your phone to text my mum? Mine's out of battery.'

I punch in the passcode – 3141, pi – and toss it to him, then head to the bar. I take deep breaths as I go, trying to plant my feet on what feels like a moving fairground floor. I try to focus on the present.

When I return to the table, Liam looks up from my phone screen and wrinkles his nose at the beer bottle I pass him.

'My choice,' I remind him.

'Speaking of choices, I'm curious. What's your type?'

'Of beer?'

'No, of person! Who do you go for?' He holds up my phone, flicking through full-screen images of male selfies. 'Hairy Chewbacca boy? Glasses geek? This guy with the shoulders? Ooh, that's a super-like for sure, right? Don't play coy, C. You're the one with Tinder installed. Cute profile pic, by the way. I think Josh, twenty-five, will like it. He seems like a nice, respectable gentleman. Look, he's got an emoji covering his—'

'Liam!'

The room feels ten degrees hotter all of a sudden. I grab my phone back and shove it in my pocket.

'Don't act so coy. You already had the app!'

'I only have this stupid app because Jenna stole my phone and installed it for me. I never used it. It was all her.'

She did exactly the same thing: holding the phone out of reach, swiping right on men I wasn't interested in. Men who certainly wouldn't have been interested in me.

'Quite a wing-woman, this Jenna. I like her.' He grins. 'Okay, fine, I'm sorry. I promise not to tease you about boys any more. I have one condition, though. You have to join me for a dance.'

'No way. I don't dance.'

'Those are the rules, and I'm afraid they're non-negotiable. Dating chat or dancing. Pick your poison.'

I know how I'd rather die.

Liam laughs as I grab him and drag him into the crowd towards the music and flashing lights, my backpack over my shoulder. At least this way he can't ask me any more questions.

We find a gap and he spins me so we're face to face. I don't know the song and wouldn't know how to dance to it even if I did, but Liam gets the beat immediately, moving his shoulders, flicking his hair. He grins and takes my hands, trying to get me to do more than awkwardly tap my foot.

I shut my eyes, feeling the extra sway of the alcohol in my system. I'm not a dancer. Jenna tried to make me one, once. The indistinct music of this bar melds into the noise of that one, the one from so many months ago. It's Jenna across from me in the crowd, dark bob swishing, smiling lips red, arms criss-crossing over her face as her hips sway, slowly and purposefully, to the beat I can't quite get. There are men around us, the men from the bar. A hand grabs my waist, a groin pressing against my back. Jenna pulls me free and claims me for herself, her arms looped lazily around my neck, her hips teaching mine what to do. In my pocket, my phone starts to vibrate. Jenna pulls it out for me, shows me the screen. It's –

No. Don't think of this. I can't think of this.

But alcohol lets the banned memory take hold.

It's Poppy calling. I don't factor in the time difference to notice it's 3 a.m. in the UK. I don't wonder what she's calling about. I don't care. I ignore the call and put my phone away. I put my hands back where they were. In that moment, there is only Jenna.

The memory comes in waves: the heat from our skin; the alcohol on our breath; my phone face down and forgotten on her bedside table.

When it rang the next morning with Dad's call, Jenna was still asleep next to me, her red lipstick smudged between us on the pillow.

And Poppy was dead.

'I've got to go,' I say to Liam, grabbing my backpack and burrowing through the crowd to the exit. I chase fresh air, and breathe it in deeply when I get out on to the street. I wish it was colder. I wish it was the kind of air that hurts to breathe, that pierces your lungs, that makes every breath a punishment.

It's my fault she's dead, and I don't deserve to ever forget that.

'Hun, are you all right?'

Liam catches up to me, pulling on his leather jacket.

'Just tired,' I say, hiding my face. I walk home in silence – or try to. Liam won't stop talking. His questions follow me all the way into our building and up the stairs.

'Hey, C. C! Talk to me, will you? What happened back there? I'm sorry if I upset you, if my stupid teasing went too far. Are you okay? Is it . . . your sister? Do you want to talk about her?'

I've never told him about Poppy. Not properly. Just that I'd come back for the funeral. Perhaps he knows the rest anyway. I busy myself with unlocking the door to our flat, glad to have my back to him.

'No. I'm fine.'

'Are you sure?' he asks as he shuts the door behind us. 'I'm here for you if you want to talk about it. Any of it. Any time. Really, I'm here.'

'I don't need to talk about it. I'm good. Like I said, I'm just tired.'

I meet his eye for the first time since we left the bar, and try to smile.

59

He sees through me, I can tell – but he's kind enough to play along.

'Well, you'd better go get some sleep, then! Thanks for humouring me tonight. I really appreciate it.' Before I can avoid it, he swoops forward and pulls me into a hug. He smells sweet, like one of the cocktails. One of the nicer ones. 'But you know, if you ever want to talk about being tired, I'm here.'

We part, and I don't know what to do next. I give him a thumbs-up. 'Uh, thanks.'

Liam grins and flashes me his thumb in return.

'Any time. Goodnight, sexy librarian! Sleep well.'

In my bedroom, I lean my back against the door. Tiredness aches in every cell of my body, and the cocktails make the darkness swirl in front of me. I see things in it: Jenna dancing; a man falling from a building; Poppy with crying eyes and wet hair – wet with blood.

I could have stopped that from happening. I *should* have. But I wasn't there for her.

Whatever her reasons, she died because I wasn't there for her.

I sink on to the edge of my bed. I can't go to the helpline, not like this, but I have to do something. I have to make a difference.

I open Reddit on my phone and reply to every r/SuicideWatch post I can find, telling these people they're not alone, they're loved, they have something to live for. I tell them everything I should have told Poppy that night.

But deep down, I know that no matter how many people I help, I'll never hate myself any less.

CHAPTER 7

Eastbourne is a tourist town, the seafront lined with pretty Victorian hotels, shops with postcards and buckets and spades, a pier, pebbles, stacks of striped deckchairs. But my parents and I are not going to the beach. We leave the train station and make our way to the town hall, a large red-bricked building with columns and a tower, to meet with the coroner. Confetti collects in the corners of the front steps, and a couple with a small baby tread delicately down them.

I wish we were here for something else.

We're directed to a court room. It's set up that way – two sides of seating, two front benches, space for a judge and jury. But there is no jury, and this isn't a trial.

There are people here already. Just a few. Some look official, perhaps police and pathologist witnesses due to give evidence, while someone with scruffy hair sits at the back and scrawls in a notepad. A journalist, probably for some tiny local paper. He eyes us as we trail past to take our seats at the front, already brainstorming the best adjectives for us: *morose, tired, devastated.* My skin feels itchy and hot beneath my shirt. Why does a journalist have to be here? Why does my sister's death have to be news? *Remember that body found under the cliffs back in February?* he'll write. *Well, here are all the gory details!*

The coroner, a man of about sixty with a neat grey beard and round glasses, enters from the side door. He sits at the front, presiding over us. The room goes quiet, and my stomach lurches.

After six months, it's happening. The answers are coming. I'll know exactly what happened that night, every last detail of it – and so will my parents. We'll have our closure.

The coroner stands.

'On the morning of Saturday the twenty-third February 2019 the body of Poppy Harris, eighteen years of age, was discovered below the cliffs at Hope Gap, East Sussex. This inquest has been called to determine several factors – who the deceased was, and when, where, and how they died. I will be calling witnesses to give statements and answer questions, and after I have heard their testimony, I will pronounce a conclusion to the inquest, stating whether to rule the death as accidental, unlawful, open, narrative, or suicide.

'To begin, I believe the deceased's father, Fred Harris, would like to read a statement about his daughter. Mr Harris, if you'd like to take the stand.'

Dad walks up to the front, to the witness box. He's breathing heavily. He's in an old grey suit, wearing Poppy's favourite tie: a strip of Van Gogh's *Starry Night*. The suit used to strain against his shoulders when I was younger, but it hangs limply now. I hadn't noticed it before, but he's changed. He's compressed. There are more lines around his eyes; his dark beard is laced with grey. He fishes his glasses and a sheet of paper from his pocket. I've seen him give speeches at family weddings in that very suit, timing the jokes just right and making the guests roar with laughter.

But today, he's shaking.

'My daughter Poppy was a lot of things,' he says softly. 'She was a talented artist who found beauty in everything she saw. She was a friend to anybody who needed one. And she was kind. Ever since she learned to talk, she only said nice things. She had a way of looking at the world where she'd always find the bright side, and she'd always share it. She was a ray of sunshine – even if we did butt heads about the state of her bedroom.'

Dad smiles a little, and I do too. He was like this at her funeral all those months ago: making sure we remembered her as she lived, not as she died. But today isn't a memorial.

'She was a cheerful little girl, always smiling, but she was very shy. She never had many friends, but she had us – me, her mum Heather, and her big sister Clementine. We were very close. This last Christmas, we made a gingerbread castle and played charades and laughed until we cried. We were happy. We had no idea that . . .'

Dad silently chews the next words, then turns over the page.

'Poppy had social anxiety, and social situations made her nervous. With us, with her family, she was a normal, talkative girl, but outside our house or around crowds, she could be scared and timid. When she told us she was applying to university in Brighton, we thought she was getting over her shyness. She moved away for the first time, and . . . she said she was happy. She was doing what she loved. We visited her as often as we could, and her mother sent cakes every week, and we checked in almost every day, but she always said she was happy. We didn't know . . . we didn't know she was struggling. She kept it to herself.'

He exhales heavily, centring himself.

'The Poppy we knew was bright and creative, but nervous. A little scared of everything. I brought the bike down for her because she wanted to explore the countryside, but in London she never went out on it alone. She was too nervous to cycle on roads or even take her hand off the bars to indicate. Some days she wouldn't leave the house at all because she was so shy. So . . . so to hear that she rode her bike so far, so late at night, on proper streets . . .' His voice cracks. 'She was brave. Whatever happened that night, my little girl left her shyness behind, and she was brave. Thank you.'

Dad looks at the coroner, who nods and indicates he can return to his seat. When he sits back down beside us, Mum slips her hand silently into his.

I keep mine pressed between my knees, trying to stop them shaking.

The coroner clears his throat. 'I now call Police Constable David Burnham.'

A dark-skinned man in a tailored suit takes the stand, straight-backed. He offers us a polite nod before giving his statement; he was part of the team that recovered Poppy's body from the beach that morning, after her abandoned bike was spotted by a dog walker at the top of the cliff near Hope Gap just before 7 a.m. The scene, Burnham states, was indicative of a suicide, especially with its proximity to Beachy Head, a known suicide spot. Nothing he says is new to me.

PC Burnham steps down, and the coroner replaces him with pathologist Dr Jennifer Morgan.

Dr Morgan smooths a blonde flyaway hair back into her bun. Those same delicate fingers prodded at Poppy through gloves, digging a scalpel through her flesh in a Y-shape to check her organs, removing them, weighing them, replacing them, sewing her back up. Those fingers photographed injuries and picked debris from her hair. They tracked over every inch of her body.

Poppy hated being watched. Why would she choose to die this way? Summoning the police, the coastguard, pathologists, investigators, journalists . . . Is that really what she wanted? To leave her body in the spotlight? To have her life scrutinised by strangers? *Why?*

I shake my head. I have to focus on the pathologist's answers, not my questions. The 'why's that I need will come later. They have to. For now, it is the 'how's.

'Were you able to ascertain time of death?'

'Yes,' Dr Morgan says. 'By assessing the condition of the body and factoring in water damage and rigor mortis, I was able to estimate time of death to be between the hours of four a.m. and five a.m. on the morning of the twenty-third of February.'

'And were you able to ascertain cause of death?'

Dr Morgan lists the injuries: three limbs broken in compound fractures; left shoulder dislocation; shattered pelvis; traumatic spinal damage; a skull fracture and accompanying laceration.

Mum is leant forward, her head down and her ears covered. Dad's fingers dig into her knee, and his other hand finds mine. It's clammy and desperate.

But I take small, calm breaths. This is just scientific analysis. Cold, hard facts.

I imagine the scene as a crash test dummy, little markers attached to the injured body parts. It is not my sister, who smiled and danced and painted.

I cannot let it be my sister.

Two hundred feet and a head injury. It was quick. At least it was quick.

It was not a straight fall, Dr Morgan states. Chalk in the head wound indicated a collision with the rocks on the way down, then another impact on the beach itself.

The dummy bounces, landing on its back on the rocks.

The physical injuries were particularly severe due to the sea's position, with water not yet covering the beach. The tide is estimated to have reached the impact site approximately one hour after the initial impact. Post-mortem analysis showed water in the lungs and an absence of oxygen in the blood.

Wait. No . . .

'This indicates,' Dr Morgan says, 'that the deceased was still breathing when the tide came in. The eventual cause of death was drowning.'

I can't see it as a dummy this time. Poppy, *my* Poppy, lies at the bottom of the cliff, face bleeding, both arms broken, unable to move, as the tide slowly, slowly creeps towards her.

She was alive. She was alive for an *hour*.

And her arms were fractured because she tried to break her fall.

The helpline call from a few days ago rings in my ears again: the gasp the caller made as he jumped.

He regretted it, and so did Poppy.

She tried to save herself.

She didn't want to die.

Why would she jump if she didn't want to die?

The person on the stand changes to the coroner's officer. Mum is crying and Dad is trying not to. I drag myself away from my doubts and focus on what the man is saying.

This is it. These are the answers I've been waiting for.

I'm about to find out why she did it.

'I was tasked with obtaining information about the deceased's life and the days leading up to their death,' the coroner's officer says. I've seen him before, picking through Poppy's things. Asking questions. 'During the discovery, I interviewed university staff and the deceased's housemates, and will summarise their statements. Full transcripts can be found in the disclosure documents.

'The deceased was described by staff as amiable and hard-working, but quiet. She did not enquire about mental health services at the university, nor partake in any clubs, therapy, or other student organisations. Her housemates described her as a loner, and despite their invitations, she declined to join them in any social activities. She kept to herself. One housemate described hearing her crying in her bedroom during the autumn term, but this was never brought up between them.'

The autumn term. Poppy wrote me letters during that time and gave them to me at Christmas. There was nothing in them about crying. Nothing about sadness.

And after Christmas, she didn't write any letters at all.

Why? Why did she suddenly stop wanting to share her life with me?

The coroner's assistant is still talking. He's small and indistinct.

'. . . records of the deceased's Netflix account showed she had watched various films and TV shows relating to suicide in the weeks before her death, including repeat viewings of an episode with a graphic suicide scene. The deceased's Google search history showed frequent research into the East Sussex coastline, including Beachy Head, a local suicide spot, and information on bus and cycle routes to the area. Three terms were searched shortly before the estimated time of death – *What fall height is fatal?*, *Hope Gap height in feet*, and *Does it hurt to die?*'

No. She wouldn't type that. How could she type that?

The coroner clears his throat again. 'During the investigation, did you find any form of suicide note or message?'

'No.'

We would have heard if they had, they would have shown us, but my heart sinks regardless. I hoped they'd found something tucked away in an unsent email or between the pages of a book. But they must have found something else in their search. Something to prove it. To explain it.

'Did you find any explanation for why she had cycled to the cliff edge? Did she tell anyone her intentions?'

'No,' the officer says. 'Her internet history shows she checked the route on Google Maps before she left the house, but no explanation was given. Her housemates were out together at a local club and did not see her leave.'

'Can you summarise the deceased's last hours?'

I wish I could run from what's about to be said, or that everyone else would disappear. I don't want them to hear it. Not the note-taking journalist. Not my parents.

Mum grips Dad's hand and Dad grips mine, holding on to me like a wave might break us apart at any second.

But they don't know what's coming like I do.

'CCTV from the morning of the twenty-third of February shows the deceased leaving her halls of residence with her bike at 1.24 a.m. and riding by herself through Brighton and along the coast. She is last spotted on a camera in Seaford at 2.39 a.m. before heading along the coastal path, and she is not seen again.'

'Before she left her halls of residence, did the deceased do anything to indicate she was in a fragile state of mind?'

'Yes,' the officer states, and he takes another breath.

Don't say it, I beg, digging my nails into my palm. *Please, don't say it.*

'The deceased tried to get in contact with her sister, Clementine Harris. At 7.19 p.m. on Friday the twenty-second of February, the deceased sent the message, *Hey, are you free to talk?* to her sister on WhatsApp. The deceased sent a second message at 12.48 a.m. saying *Text me.* Both messages were seen by Clementine Harris at 12.49 a.m. At 3.07 a.m. the deceased attempted to phone her sister, but the call went to voicemail. Although a recording was left, the only audible sounds on the message were ambient, with no words spoken. Call triangulation places the deceased near to the scene of her death when the call was made. It is believed she fell from that area shortly afterwards, and died within the next hour.'

Dad's fingers falter on mine, loosening.

'You . . . you never told us that,' he whispers. 'You never said she called you.'

I can't face looking at him, or Mum. Like a coward, I keep my eyes fixed on the coroner's officer as he walks back to his seat.

Dad's voice cracks. 'Why didn't you answer her?'

The room feels painfully quiet. I can hear the journalist's pen scratching on his notepad, feel the eyes of the sparse crowd on the back of my head.

'I didn't know why she was calling,' I say, clutching at that last straw of an excuse. 'She never told me she wasn't well. None of us knew. I thought she was happy. I didn't realise—'

'You could have *stopped* her, Clem.'

'Fred! Stop it,' Mum hisses. She leans over, grasping the hand Dad abandoned. Pulling on it. 'Look at me, Clementine. Please.'

I force myself to do it. Mum's shaking, her tired eyes shining, but she manages an empty, devastated smile. She pats my hand.

'You were busy with your studies, love. You were learning. We don't blame you. Isn't that right, Fred?'

Dad hesitates, his fists clenched on his lap. Then he exhales, and wraps his arm around me. 'We'll never blame you.'

But I can hear the disappointment in their voices.

The coroner stands again, but he doesn't call any more witnesses. His folder is closed; his hands clasped.

'I will now give my conclusion to the inquest.'

No, that can't be right. We haven't heard everything yet. There must be more. There *has* to be more.

'Given the evidence I have heard here today, I believe the deceased, Poppy Harris, was a vulnerable and lonely person who made a conscious decision to travel to a dangerous location. Her online research of the spot and its dangers, plus her fascination with suicide, is evidence of enduring suicidal ideation. She attempted to reach out to a family member shortly before her death, but was unsuccessful. While she left no physical note, only forty per cent of those who take their own lives do. It is my understanding that on the morning of the twenty-third of February 2019, Miss Poppy Harris took her own life and died by drowning, and I conclude her death to be suicide.'

◆　◆　◆

On the train back to London, Mum cries the whole time. Chest heaving, sobbing, her hands all over her face. Dad keeps his eyes on the flashing scenery, his knuckles white against the table, avoiding my reflection in the window.

It wasn't supposed to be like this.

The inquest was meant to give us answers. I knew it wouldn't be definitive, but I thought there would be enough to suggest a reason – something more than suicide proving suicidality. Even if there was never going to be an answer, it should have felt different from this. It should at least have given us closure. It should have been an ending.

But this won't ever end, will it?

I'll never know why she did this. I'll never be able to understand it.

And I'll never be able to forgive myself for letting it happen.

CHAPTER 8

I walk my parents to their front door, but I don't go inside. I can't. Not when Poppy's face smiles out from so many photo frames, and an old pair of her boots still rests on the shoe rack. Not when I know my parents don't want me there.

'Where are you going, love?' Dad calls as I head over the bridge. 'Clem!'

Liam rushes at me when I get back to the flat, his arms thrown wide.

'C, babe, I read about the verdict online. I'm so sorry.'

He wraps himself around me, pressing my head to his shoulder and enveloping me in the softness of his fluffy jumper. He smells of sugar. I cling to that smell, burrowing into it, following it to its root: Poppy in the kitchen with Mum, eating offcuts of cake, laughing, licking spoons, icing sugar across her cheek.

Blood on her cracked forehead.

'I made jam tarts,' Liam says, rocking me. 'Let's watch one of your nerdy TV shows and eat all of them. Or I could make us something else. We could go out, stay in, whatever. If you want to chat, we can, or we can sit in silence.' He squeezes me more. 'Whatever you need, I'm here.'

Like I should have been that night.

I pull myself free of Liam.

'I . . . I have to go.'

'Go? You only just got here.'

'I know, but I have to go.'

'Come on, sit down. Have a jam tart, or some water, at least.' He steps forward, reaching for me. 'You don't look well, Clementine.'

'See you later.'

He runs after me as I leave the flat and head down the stairs, his shouted words lost in the thumping music that always comes from the flat across the hall. I lose him on the street. I keep walking, head up, focusing on the horizon, on a kind of autopilot where the destination is anywhere but here. Shops are shutting, bars filling, workers heading home. It's a mundane Thursday and life is going on as normal.

What's a normal Thursday for me? A shift at the café in the morning, a shift at the helpline in the afternoon, and a meeting in the evening. The gaps of my day plugged until there's no space left for feeling.

I check my watch and turn, heading back the way I came towards the community centre.

The suicide bereavement support group runs weekly, in a classroom-like hall with the chairs rearranged into a circle. I first attended months ago, with Mum and Dad, but they stopped going after two sessions. '*I can't be around people who are still sad after ten years,*' I overheard Mum say to Dad as she cried in his arms, back when I was still staying in my old room. '*It's never going to get better, is it?*' But I kept going to the group. It was something to do; another place like Reddit or the helpline where I could tell people that it gets better, that things will change. I talk, but not about Poppy. Not about that night.

I say my stock phrases to others while trying to believe them myself.

I push open the door. People are here, but the meeting hasn't properly started. Olly, the group leader, is still doing his introduction, and I sit down as quietly as I can. There are some new faces. There are new faces every week, popping in and out. Some people come here, spill their hearts, and never return. Others come every week and never talk. Some pop by when they need to: birthdays, important dates, bad days. And some, like me, attend every session in the hope of finding an answer that never comes.

'This is a safe space,' Olly says, looking kindly at the newcomers. There's a fidgeting old woman, a tissue clenched in her fist; a skinny, bearded guy with vacant eyes; and a man in a suit. 'You're welcome to talk or listen, and nothing you say here will be shared outside these walls. Would anyone like to start?'

My skin feels clammy as I wait for someone to speak. Images of Poppy swirl around me, jabbing at me like needles: standing on a cliff, crying, waiting for me to pick up the phone; lying broken on the rocks below, legs paralysed, arms snapped, still alive as the tide comes in.

But they never gave a reason. She took her own life, but for no reason.

It doesn't make sense. Does watching a few sad films *prove* suicidality? Does a housemate hearing her cry *prove* depression? There was nothing concrete, was there? Nothing first-hand. Just those Google searches on the cliff edge: *What fall height is fatal?*, *Hope Gap height in feet*, *Does it hurt to die?* Questions asked for the first time moments before she fell. Frantic. Impulsive.

But she wasn't impulsive, she was stubborn. She never tore up a sketch or painted over a canvas. She waited in the rain for sunsets that would never come, no matter how many times I told her the clouds wouldn't clear.

The Poppy I knew wouldn't have typed those things.

The Poppy I knew wouldn't have done this.

But maybe if I hadn't abandoned her when I went to Boston, I'd have known her better.

The fidgeting old woman is speaking, her voice wrecked with grief, and I cling to it. It's her son. He went through a divorce, lost the kids. He couldn't cope.

A grim ripple goes around the circle. We listen to her cry, this bereaved mother who never expected to live to see her child die.

Mum's crying pierces my eardrums. I heard it down the phone when Dad told me the news, a deep, harsh wail, and I heard it again today: a softer, more pathetic weeping. She might still be crying now, Dad holding her on the sofa, the family portrait of us all smiling in a sunflower field above them on the wall.

Poppy's ashes in an urn on the table.

The old woman – Gail, her nametag says in neat handwriting – shakes her head when Olly asks if she'd like to continue. Olly adjusts his glasses and leans forward, addressing the newcomer a few seats along from me.

'What about you, um . . . Daniel, is it?' The young man's nametag is a scrawl, like a rage-filled scratch on the paper. 'Would you like to share, Daniel?'

He takes a breath, leaning forward a little – then slumps back, shaking his head. He thrusts his fingers into his messy hair, tugging on the mousy strands, staring at the floor. Still shaking his head.

Nobody's talking. I need horror and devastation, second-hand grief. Anything to push my own thoughts from my head. The grief. The guilt. The doubt.

A voice starts up on the other side of the circle. The man in the suit. He's talking about someone who died, a brother, and how he wishes that brother had reached out to him instead of suffering alone. Others chime in, telling him not to blame himself. He couldn't have known.

But I should have known. Poppy called me. *Me*.

74

If I'd answered, I wouldn't have these questions now. This man, the caller who fell, Blessing – all they wanted, and needed, was their loved ones to reach out to them. I had that, and I squandered it.

That was my one chance for this to make sense.

'Clementine, are you all right?' Olly asks, leant forward with his hands together. I realise I'm hunched over, curled in on myself.

The whole circle is turned to me – sad, lost, looking-for-solace eyes fixed on me – eyebrows and mouths twisted in encouragement. *Go on*, their faces say, giving as much of a smile as they can muster. *You can tell us. We're here for you.*

I take a raggedy breath.

'It was my sister's inquest today. Suicide. Officially.'

The woman next to me, Ruth, pats my shoulder, and knowing whispers hiss around the circle. *Those are awful. Like reliving it all over again. At least it's an ending.*

'I knew that's what it would be, but to hear how she died . . . It wasn't quick. She fell, but it didn't kill her. The tide did. It came in and she drowned. Her arms were broken from where she – where she tried to break her fall. As though she changed her mind, or . . .'

I dig my nails into my palms until it hurts.

'I know how she died, they were very clear about that, but . . . nobody could say *why*. And that's what I needed. I needed to know why she did this, because I don't understand it. It doesn't make sense. She didn't have a reason to take her own life. It wasn't like her.'

Olly inhales, but I continue before he can interrupt me.

'I know what you're going to say – suicide doesn't have a specific cause, there's never just one issue. But she had nothing. She was shy. That was it. The coroner concluded it was suicide because of some last-minute search history about death and falling, and the location and the type of movies she watched, but nobody could give a reason why she might have done it. They gave the effect, but not the cause. I *needed* the cause. I really thought they'd give it. I

75

thought they'd find something that would *make it make sense*. But they didn't. They looked, but they couldn't find anything. And that means there *was* no motive.'

Olly nods. 'Yes, this is often the case. I know it's painful and confusing, but it's a good sign that you can accept it. Sometimes a person feeling suicidal is as much of a reason as—'

'No, no, you don't understand. I'm saying there was no motive. Her actions don't make sense. I know I'm supposed to accept it and move on, but how can I? I'm a scientist, everything I do is facts and figures. Every outcome is predictable. But this wasn't. I wanted to excel at this. I wanted to speed through the five stages of grief and get the certificate to prove I was over it, but I can't. I can't because it *doesn't make sense*.'

I press my knuckles to my closed mouth. The room is small, but it feels like a lecture hall, like my voice is booming and everyone is tiered around me, looking down.

'And . . . and I don't know what to think. I can't believe she did this, she wasn't capable of it, she *wouldn't* – but maybe that's just what I want to think. Maybe I'm tricking myself, and hoping for some other explanation to wipe suicide off the table so I don't have to live with the guilt any more.'

'Why do you feel guilt?' Olly asks.

'Because she called me just before she jumped, and I didn't answer.'

The circle goes quiet: no reassurance, no support.

I can't tell them the rest. How much would these people hate me if they knew that while Poppy lay dying, I was with Jenna? I ignored two texts and a phone call. I had three chances to save her that night, and I missed them all. No, I didn't *miss* them – I avoided them. I *chose* not to help her. I only cared about myself.

'Clementine, it isn't your fault,' Olly says in his honey-balm voice, the one that's meant for the truly blameless. 'You couldn't have known what she was planning, or how that call would have gone. You can't blame yourself for her actions.'

'I can, and I do.'

'But you *shouldn't*.'

'Why not? There was no reason for her to do this. I *needed* a reason. If she was worn down from bullying, or stressed because of uni, or in debt, or *anything*, then . . . then it meant something drove her to it. There was an outside factor. But she didn't have that. All she had was that missed call. She was lonely. She needed me. And that means that if I'd answered, I could have saved her. I could have talked her out of it. She only died because I didn't answer.'

'Clementine—'

'No reason means *I'm* the reason.'

Fat, heavy tears leak down my cheeks. I cover my face, clawing at it with the pads of my fingers, like I can tear away the shame.

'A few days ago, when I was volunteering at the suicide helpline, a caller took his own life on the line – but before he did it, he said I should have known something was wrong with my sister, he said I was selfish, and it's my fault for not caring. He was right. It's my fault. She's dead because of me. And I'll never be able to forgive myself for it.'

Everyone stares. Even the newcomer with the scribbled nametag looks at me sideways, one hand still stuck in his hair.

The helpline phone call hits me again, the caller's sharp jabs finding their mark. I think of Mum and Dad's faces at the inquest; the betrayal in them.

I ball up, burrowing in on myself. I'm not used to tears. They appear in lumps, choked out of me like someone's wringing my neck. When Poppy was little, she'd cry like this. Desperate sobs and a strangled voice. Did she cry like this that night, too? When she reached out to me and got nothing back?

77

I feel hands on my shoulder, my arm. Gentle pats from the others in the circle.

You need to forgive yourself.

It'll get better.

One day, you'll be able to move on.

But there is no moving on. Not for me.

What am I supposed to do now? Go back to Harvard and pretend this never happened? My life there was everything I'd hoped for. Academia, research, friends. Jenna. For a moment, I had all of that – but I can't go back to it. How could I? The guilt will come with me. The shame will follow me wherever I go and whatever I do – but especially there. I don't deserve to live the life I always wanted when I cost Poppy the chance at her own. I don't deserve to even try to be happy.

I can't go back there. Not ever. Not when every time I look into Jenna's eyes, I'd see the stain of my sister's death.

My future died that night on the beach with Poppy.

I wish it had taken me with it.

I stand up and push through the circle, wiping at my face, at the sweat and tears and shame plastered all over it, and stumble out of the room.

My head spins like a roulette wheel, the ball of despair bouncing around, wondering where to land. Underground tracks? The Thames? The wheels of a speeding bus? It spins faster, and I spin with it, London blurring around me like one of Poppy's abstract paintings, red lights and blood and broken arms, and I beg it to cut to black.

'Clementine?'

A hand grabs my wrist and I'm jerked back to the present – out on the street, out of breath, on the edge of a road I don't recognise. The hand tugs me back from the kerb and I turn, expecting Olly, or maybe Liam, somehow, there to comfort me again – but it's neither.

The newcomer from the session stands there, breathless, mousy hair matted and wild, grey eyes searching my face.

'It's you, isn't it?' he says. 'I wasn't sure, I thought it couldn't be, but then you said about your sister, and volunteering, and hearing someone die, and . . .'

He's too close, too intense. We're alone on the street.

'What do you want?' I try to pull away, but he doesn't let go. 'Who are you?'

A bus thunders past us, whipping our hair.

'It's me,' he says, gripping my arm even tighter. 'I'm him. I'm the caller.'

CHAPTER 9

I stare at the stranger. He stares back, eyes bloodshot and ringed with dark shadows; cheeks hollow like a skull. His hand is tight on my wrist.

'No. You can't be him. The caller died. He *died*. I heard it.'

The gasp, the rush of air, the thud.

He died.

'I didn't die, because I didn't jump,' the man says. 'I meant to, I really did, I was supposed to, but I dropped my phone and it fell, it fell so far, and I . . . I couldn't face it. I chickened out. My phone fell, but I went home. I didn't go through with it.'

The voice is different. There's no buzz of phone-line static; no drunken slur.

It's not him. He's just a stranger from the support group clinging on to the narrative I shared in the circle; regurgitating the information I gave him about the call. He might be unwell. He might be unsafe.

'I didn't die, okay? I'm not lying. It was me. *Me*. I called, you answered, and I was pretty drunk, and . . . and I think I didn't talk for ages, right? But then I did, and I told you about my sister, about how she . . . went under a train. Do you remember that? The train? My sister?'

His face looks sunken and ill, but his eyes are alive. Desperate. Pleading.

'Rachel. My sister's name was Rachel.'

He says her name the exact same way the caller did: raspy and pained, like it hurts him to voice it. The same way I say Poppy's.

It *is* him.

I couldn't picture him before. He was a person-shaped ball of despair in my head, formless, anonymous, but even without the phone-line static and the slurring, I know this is him: early twenties, spindly, clothes hanging off him, mousy hair hanging in dirty clumps, beard uneven, skin ashen, face haunted.

Back from the dead.

'I thought you died. I thought . . .'

The strangeness of it hits me, that I would meet this person at this moment; that an anonymous caller to a national phone line would happen to be at my local community centre, at the weekly meeting I always attend. That he'd follow me when I ran out of it.

'Why are you here?' I ask. I glance around us, checking for other pedestrians, for witnesses. 'How did you find me?'

'Find you?' He pulls a face. 'I didn't *find you*. I mean, not on purpose. When I was on the roof, you told me to get help, and I thought maybe you were right, maybe I should try one last time, so I tried. Support groups, that's what you said. Well, I looked for one, and this was the only one running anywhere near me that wasn't some churchy crap, so I came here. But then you came in and I realised who you were, and remembered what I'd said to you, about your sister, and I wanted to apologise, but then you said—'

'You don't have to apologise for that.' The shock of him being here is wearing off, and the shame I was fleeing from returns, digging its cold fingers into my heart. Squeezing it. 'You were right. It *was* my fault. I should have been there for her. I . . . I should have answered her.'

81

Another bus rushes past us, and my stinging eyes follow it. How fast would it have to be moving to cause a fatal impact with a pedestrian? Where on the road would it reach top speed? Could I get there before the next bus passes?

'Wait, please.'

He tugs my arm again. I hadn't realised I'd moved.

'Look, what I said that night was wrong. I didn't mean it. Well, I did, at the time, but I was drunk and angry and I didn't know who I was talking to, I didn't care, and it's easy to forget there's an actual person answering those calls, and . . . and I wanted to hurt you, okay? I did, that's why I said that stuff, but I didn't mean to hurt *you*, because you didn't deserve any of that. It wasn't your fault. It wasn't, and I know that because—'

'It *was* my fault. It doesn't matter how much I regret it, I still let her down. I can admit that. I . . . I have to live with it.'

Can I live with it? I shrug his arm off.

'You didn't have to follow me out here. I don't need an apology. I don't deserve one. You should go back to the meeting. They can help you.'

I start walking away, but he chases after me.

'You're not listening, are you? I don't want to go back there. You're the one I need to talk to. You're the one who—'

'I can't help you! I can't help anyone!'

'I'm not asking you to! We're the same, don't you see? I didn't realise when we first spoke, I was only thinking about myself, but it was there then, too. You doubted your sister's suicide back then, didn't you? Just like I did. You knew something wasn't right. It didn't feel right, did it? It never has. And today confirmed it.'

'Yes, but . . .' I claw at my forehead. 'It's not real. It's just denial. Poppy killed herself, but I didn't want to admit it. I'm a coward. I have to accept that—'

'Your doubts are right. I had the same ones, and for good reason. You know it. You feel it! Your sister *didn't* kill herself.'

'She did!' I shout. 'She did, and I failed to save her.'

'No!' He lunges and stops me, his hands pressing on my shoulders. 'My sister's inquest put her death down as suicide, but it wasn't. I *know* it wasn't. They got it wrong. Is it so out there to believe they got it wrong for your sister, too?'

His eyes are wild again. He smells of stale alcohol and sweat, there are stains on his hoody, he looks ill. I see in him the person who called the helpline: the vulnerable, unwell young man who could no longer take comfort in the outrageous claim that helped him cope with his sister's death. Desperate. Delusional.

I cannot let that myself become that.

'You didn't believe me before,' he says, 'I get that, but please, let me explain. What you feel, that doubt? And the certainty that it didn't happen like they said? I feel it, too. I've lived it for two years. It doesn't go away. You can't run from it. It's gonna follow you, always. Every time you think you've left it behind, that you can finally be normal and accept what happened like everyone else, it comes back, even surer than before. And I know you know it, in your heart. You know she didn't kill herself. You *know* it. Right? Right?'

'I . . .' Hope flutters in my chest. Do I deserve hope? 'I can't imagine her doing it. I can't make sense of it. There's no reason for it. But what other explanation is there? She was there, at night, and—'

'Forget all that, okay? Suspend disbelief for a second. You have doubts, I have doubts. For one night, stop trying to feel what you *think* you should feel and actually listen to what your instincts are telling you. My sister got screwed over by her own inquest, and I'm pretty sure yours did, too. Give me five minutes of your time, and I'll prove it to you.'

Another bus speeds past us, reflecting us in its windows. My shirt is wrinkled from the train, and my face looks clammy with tears and grime. My hair is a mess, loose clumps of dark brown hanging from what was a ponytail. I can't remember the last time I ate, drank, or slept for more than three hours.

And next to me, the caller looks just the same.

'I can't. I'm sorry. I have to accept the inquest's ruling, and move on.'

I back away and he lets me, his hands finding their way into the pockets of his hoody. He shrugs.

'Okay, have it your way. Accept something you *know* isn't true. But you said you're a scientist, right? I thought you would have wanted to see my proof.'

I pause, my back to him.

'You have proof that your sister's death wasn't a suicide? Real, tangible proof?'

'Yep. And I'll share it with you.'

I bite my lip, glancing at a run-down burger bar across the street.

'All right. Five minutes.'

We sit in the window of the burger bar, me with a coffee, him with a milkshake, neither of us drinking them. Kids stream in and out, laughing in oversized T-shirts and pristine white trainers, enjoying the warm summer evening.

Outside the window, the horizon at the end of the street glows orange.

'So, what's your proof? Show me.'

The caller – Daniel – sighs.

'Can I explain things first? It might make more sense if I explain it.' He picks at the scrawled nametag stuck to his hoody, ripping it off and tearing it into strips. 'It never felt right. I know everyone says that, but I mean it. Rachel was happy. Really. She was a musician, a guitarist in this little indie band, and they used to do tours around Europe that cost them more than they earnt. She loved that. She went to Asia, too. Australia. She loved travelling. Our dad died years ago in a work accident – faulty firefighting equipment – and we both got a lump of the compensation payout. I think she would've burnt through all hers before she was twenty-five, if she'd lived that long. She'd booked her next trip before she died. Thailand. Apparently she was going to work in a beachside bar and do the open mics and get discovered by some record label exec who'd just happen to be on holiday there. That was the dream, anyway. No way would she give up on it.'

Poppy laughs in the kitchen, icing sugar on her cheek. She dances in her bedroom to Christmas songs, singing along. She beams as I unwrap her present to me – three pebbles from Brighton beach hand-painted with portraits of Einstein, Curie, Tesla – and beams even more when she opens mine to her: two tickets for a ride on the i360 viewing tower on Brighton beach.

'*Oh, thanks! I've always wanted to go on this! You have to come with me, Clemmie. We can go at sunset. When are you next back? Easter? Let's do it at Easter!*'

I fiddle with my cup, feeling the heat through the cardboard.

'I'd have known if something wasn't right with her,' he says. 'We talked a lot. We didn't keep secrets. Like, I knew she had tickets to Christine and the Queens before she died, and that she'd ordered new jeans for the gig. They arrived after the funeral. Who does that? Who orders jeans for a gig they're never going to go to? She ordered them the night she died.'

'They didn't pick up on that at the inquest?'

'They barely mentioned it. Had some psychology person pass it off as her being briefly undecided about suicide. Didn't see it as a massive sign of her not wanting to be dead. They focused on these tiny, insignificant things that apparently built up a picture of depression and being suicidal, but ignored the huge pile of stuff that showed she wasn't.'

I think of Poppy's inquest, and the way the coroner's officer mentioned her watchlist of sad films and TV shows. Was that all she watched? Or were those titles cherry-picked from a list of dozens of 'safe' ones?

'That's what it felt like today,' I say. For the first time, I don't dismiss my doubts; I let myself speak them. 'Confirmation bias. It was as though they were only considering the data that supported the conclusion they wanted, and discarding everything else.'

'And like they weren't actually interested in finding out what *really* happened.' Daniel grabs his milkshake. His fingernails are short and bitten. 'Yeah, exactly. Exactly! Like, they didn't actually care about Rachel, or showing who she was or what happened. She was just a name on a file to them, a suicide victim, and the inquest was just a formality to get the paperwork done.'

'It felt like they were talking about someone else today. A stranger. Not Poppy.'

'Yep. I know.' He pokes at his milkshake with his straw. 'How did your sister die? I mean, I know you said about the fall and the sea, but . . . what was the story?'

I take a sip of bitter, scalding coffee.

'She was away at university in Brighton. She left her halls at about one-thirty in the morning, back in February, and cycled along the seafront to a section of cliffs. And then the next morning she was found at the bottom of it.' I twist the cup in my hands. 'I can't deny how it looks, and why they assumed what they did, but . . .'

'Let me guess – she was happy, no note? Nothing in her own words to actually prove she did it? Yeah, same with Rachel. That happened at night, too. We were both staying at my mum's back then, almost two years ago. I got in around . . . eleven? And her door was shut. The next morning it was open, and her bed hadn't been slept in. She was caught on CCTV driving to this church by the trainline, which was weird because it wasn't far and she could have walked, easy, but she drove there, and there was this hole in the fence that we'd found years ago, a secret shortcut for when we were feeling brave, and that's where they found her. But like your sister, no note. Just tickets for upcoming gigs stuck on her pinboard, and new jeans in the post. But they didn't care about that. They saw a death on the tracks and did everything they could to prove she did it to herself. They didn't even consider anything else.'

Poppy went for a bike ride at night and fell from a cliff. Who's to say that wasn't an accident? Did they investigate that angle? That she, a nature lover, went there to view the stars, but tripped in the darkness? It wouldn't have been her first late-night excursion. I used to catch her with a coat over her pyjamas and doggy slippers, standing on tiptoes to reach the deadbolt on the front door so she could go searching for foxes at midnight, Mum's leftover sausage rolls stuffed in her pockets. Usually I'd get her back up to bed, but not always. Sometimes I'd unlock the door for her and we'd sneak out together, me holding the torch, Poppy whisper-calling to the foxes, her hand never leaving mine.

She wasn't scared of the night, because she was more scared of the people she'd see during the day.

'I don't know if the coroner considered misadventure,' I say. 'I suppose not. Poppy fell near Beachy Head, which is—'

'A suicide spot, I know.'

'Right. But . . . it just didn't seem like her? She was a shy, private person. She'd have done it in her bedroom, or somewhere quiet and out of the way. Not there. And not so . . . violently.'

'I know.' Daniel digs his fingers into the sides of his cup, bending it. 'Death by train is about as violent and destructive as it gets. Rachel was squeamish. She couldn't even hack a papercut. She wouldn't have done that to herself.' His eyes shine. 'No way. And I can prove it.'

He gets his phone out and slides it across the table to me, showing me a video looping on the screen. It takes me a second to realise what it is, and I shut my eyes at the right moment. It's the onboard footage from the train that struck his sister.

'I don't want to see that.'

'It's censored, so you won't see anything bad. Look at it. Please.'

I do. It's edited and slowed down, looping again and again, frame by frame. The view speeds along the tracks and a person in a striped top appears from a gap in the fence behind a bush. They don't leap in front like I expect them to; they fall. The arms swing, the feet stumble, and they disappear into a pixelated, censored blur at the bottom of the screen. And then the track is clear again, and the train speeds back towards the bush.

'Did you see it?' Daniel asks.

'Yes. I saw her fall.'

'No, not the fall. Just before it. Look at the bush. Carefully. Right there, by her back.'

The video loops a dozen more times, Daniel's bitten fingernail pointing to the right section, pausing it, restarting, trying to get me to see something.

'I'm sorry, I don't know what you're showing me,' I say. 'It's too fast. Is it something to do with the leaves? The shadow?'

'No.' He pauses the video and zooms in past Rachel's shoulder, picking out something pale. 'There, behind her. It's only for a split second, but it's there. See it? It's a hand.'

'A hand?'

'Yeah. The hand of whoever pushed her through that fence and in front of the train.'

I grab the phone and hold it up close, squinting, trying to make it out. It's blurry, yes, but a thin, white shape – like a capital L – sticks out from the bushes. I zoom out and hit play. The shape appears and disappears, visible just for a moment as Rachel starts to fall. Leaves shake and fly as the train approaches, and this looks like one of them – almost. It doesn't flutter like the rest. The rigid L-shape that was at Rachel's back flattens as she falls, smoothing out before withdrawing – like a wrist joint would after shoving with an open palm. The more I watch, the more I see what Daniel sees. Couldn't those darker pixels be the shadow of a thumb? The band of a watch or bracelet?

I watch the video over and over, my stomach churning in disgust – not just because of what I've seen, but because of my own eagerness to see it.

If that white blur *is* a hand – and it does look like it – then Daniel was right. His sister didn't jump that night. She was pushed.

'You have to show this to the police,' I say.

Daniel laughs joylessly, taking the phone and pocketing it.

'They've already seen it. They didn't care.'

'What? But it's proof that someone pushed her! I know it's not definitive, but surely if you explain—'

'I did explain.' He laughs again, rubbing his forehead. 'Dozens, hundreds of times. They showed this video at the inquest, but no one saw anything wrong with it. They missed it. I got a copy and I was at the police station every day for months, trying to get them to watch it again. I printed stills of it, and circled the hand so they'd see, so they wouldn't even have to watch the video, but they fobbed me off. They said it was just leaves, nothing else, and . . . I get it, it's hard to see, but it's *not* a leaf. It's not. I tried official complaints, and going to the coroner's office, and his house, and refusing to leave the police station, and I started petitions, and I talked to everyone who knew her and I gave the police the transcripts, but . . . they wouldn't listen. They didn't believe me. They, um, they sectioned me. Three times. They pumped me full of drugs and said I was delusional. Everyone did. Even Mum. They wouldn't even let me off the psych ward unless I pretended to believe it. Nobody wanted to see the truth, even though it was right there. But I knew. I knew someone killed her, and they'd got away with it. They got away with it because nobody believed me.'

He pulls his knees up and hugs them.

'So, I . . . I know exactly how you feel. You blame yourself for not answering that call, but it's my fault the police never investigated Rachel's death. They took one look at me and assumed she was just as mad as I am. I failed her.'

He rubs at his bloodshot eyes, then claws at his chest under his shirt. Something glints in the unnatural light of the restaurant: the silver chain of a necklace. He clamps his hand around its pendant and hunches over, looking away, and I see the back of his neck. The chain has rubbed his skin red-raw.

This is the caller I know: the one who stood on the edge of a building because he didn't want to live another day in a world that wouldn't listen to him.

But I'm listening.

'We can get her justice,' I say. Daniel looks up, stopping his rocking. 'I'll help. We can take this to the police and we'll make sure they look into it.'

'It's no use. They've blacklisted me as this nutcase and they'll never take me seriously. I got in the room with them a few times.

They'd looked at her file, and they kept bringing up stuff like the fact she checked train times before she died, and they said she planned it. They wouldn't believe someone else could've done that, could've planted it on her phone. It didn't prove anything.'

The report from Poppy's inquest echoes in my ears.

'Three terms were searched shortly before the estimated time of death – What fall height is fatal?, Hope Gap height in feet, and Does it hurt to die?'

My mouth goes dry.

'That's how they proved it? That was the main link to suicide?'

'Yeah, looking up train times and then dying on the tracks. They said it showed her intentions. But they found her phone nearby, and they never checked it for DNA or anything. Someone else could have typed it. It had a passcode, but she always used the fingerprint sensor. They could have overpowered her and unlocked it with her thumb. They could have set her up before they pushed her.'

Poppy's passcode was 1234. Her phone wasn't on her. It was on the cliff edge. They found it like that the next morning. She called me, dropped the phone when I didn't answer, and jumped. That's what the inquest suggested.

But Poppy never made phone calls. She hated talking on the phone. She'd answer if I called her, but she never initiated them herself. Even the most urgent questions were asked through text, not call.

But she called that night.

Nobody would have checked the phone for fingerprints. Why would they, when the police officer who attended the scene already assumed it was a suicide?

There's a rot inside me, a rot I've tried to ignore for six months. But now it spreads freely, finding its way up through my brain stem and digging into every lobe, every nucleus. Numbed for six months, my neurons begin to fire again.

'That's how they proved Poppy's death was suicide,' I say. 'She searched falling deaths before she fell, and they found her phone on the cliff edge. But . . . I don't believe she'd kill herself. It wasn't suicide. It can't be. Her death must have been an accident or misadventure, a mistake, but . . .'

I don't know if I can voice it. I see the evidence and what it must mean, but I don't know if I can believe it.

'But if it was an accident, why is that Google search on her phone?'

Daniel sits up.

'It got on there somehow,' he says. 'So either your sister typed it and then jumped, or—'

'Someone else typed it, and pushed her.'

I sink back in my chair, pressing my knuckles to my mouth.

Is that why her suicide has always felt so wrong to me? Not because of the guilt I tortured myself with, but because it was never suicide? Because I knew, on some level, that there was more to it? That she wasn't depressed? That she wasn't the type to go near the edge of a cliff by mistake? That someone else must have been involved?

But the pathologist didn't mention any defensive wounds. The police officer said there were no signs of a struggle. Just her bike by the fence, and her phone left on the edge. A clear suicide, just like Daniel's sister. But he has proof that it wasn't. He has a recording. What do I have?

'The voicemail,' I say, my voice cracking. 'Poppy called me before she fell, right after the Google searches, and she left a voicemail message when I didn't pick up. I listened to it later that day, after . . . after I found out she was dead. She didn't say anything, but I could hear the sea and the wind. I thought . . . I thought I was too late, that because I hadn't answered she'd already jumped and left the call running, but . . .'

I get my phone and navigate to the saved voicemail. I've only listened to it once before, but I know the sounds by heart. It's what I hear in the empty spaces of time between helpline shifts and Reddit sessions. It stalks my waking moments and my dreams.

I close my eyes, the phone to my ear. I'm there on the cliff edge, and muffled, buzzing audio becomes crisp, clear reality: cold, salty air, waves dragging against shale, darkness, a breeze.

No, not a breeze.

'What is it?' Daniel asks.

I don't answer him. I hit speakerphone and press the phone harder against my ear, covering the other one, sliding the volume all the way up, drowning myself in the waves and the static, over and over, until I can tune out the white noise and hear the sound hidden behind it.

Breathing.

Not the tearful, choked breathing of a suicidal girl, or the deep, scared breaths of someone trying to be brave. These breaths start as little sips of air, muffled, quiet, but become trembling and open-mouthed, lingering on the exhale, shaking with . . . excitement.

I remember how Poppy's breaths would sound as we panted after running for a train, or huddled together in the cold under an umbrella.

These breaths are not hers.

I silence the voicemail and slam my phone on the table, face down.

'What?' Daniel repeats. 'What did you hear?'

'Someone killed her,' I say, numbed by the horror of it. 'They . . . they pushed her, and then they called me. I could hear them breathing. That's *them*. I never missed Poppy's call, I missed theirs. Calling me was just a way to . . . to help stage it. To make it

93

look like a suicidal person reaching out. But – but that's the killer. Someone killed her.'

I press my face into my hands like I did at the support group, digging my nails through my hair – feeling a rage I have no outlet for. 'Someone killed her!'

'I . . . I didn't think it would be that,' Daniel mutters. 'I thought for sure your coroner had messed up, but I thought it was an accident, or misadventure, or whatever they call it, but this? *Another* murder? Just like Rachel? I . . . I didn't want it to be that.'

His hand, shaky and uncertain, touches my back – but I sit up abruptly, knocking it away.

'Who do you think killed Rachel?'

'What?'

'You've known she was murdered for two years. Who are your suspects? Who would hurt her like that? Who did you tell the police to look into?'

He opens his mouth, then shrugs, reaching for his necklace again.

'Nobody. Everyone loved Rachel. I don't know why anyone would have done that to her. It was probably a drunk or some random person. I . . . I think that's why the police didn't take me seriously. Because I couldn't give them a suspect. All I had was the image of that hand.'

I sink back in my chair again.

I can't prove what happened. Poppy was captured on CCTV cycling to Hope Gap alone, and she was found alone. There are suicidal searches on her phone, and an answerphone message with weak, muffled breathing that to anyone else could sound like hers.

I have nothing concrete to disprove the inquest verdict. Just the circumstantial nature of the things used to prove Poppy's intent, two minutes of disembodied breathing, and a feeling.

But feelings don't prove hypotheses.

'You're like me now, Clementine,' Daniel says. 'You know a truth that nobody else is ever going to believe.'

I stare out the window, trying not to cry.

This is what I wanted, wasn't it? I longed for something, anything, to explain why Poppy fell that night – all to escape my own guilt. But guilt still gnaws away at my insides; the same beast, but with different teeth.

I should have voiced my doubts six months ago, even if it made me seem irrational. I should have trusted my gut. Instead, my inaction helped whoever killed my sister get away with it.

The last of the day's light glows through the narrow gap between streets, soft orange being pressed down by inky black from above.

'Poppy loved sunsets,' I say eventually. 'She used to chase them all over London to find the best view.'

'She would've loved where I'm from. People say we've got the best light in the UK.'

Something stirs in my memory: Poppy and me in the National Gallery.

'You live in Margate?'

'Yeah. Well, I'm from there. I'm outstaying my welcome with a friend in Croydon right now. How'd you know that?'

'Poppy loved the Turner paintings in the National Gallery. Especially the seascape ones. She used to tell me all about them.'

'Oh. Rachel had this thing about dogs. She loved seeing them in their waterproof coats and little knitted jumpers. I used to take photos of them for her. I still do, sometimes. Even though . . .'

Daniel's voice trails off.

I glance at him. His eyes are big and teary, fixed firmly on the sky even though there's nothing left to see. He chews on his knuckles, his lips shaking. His sleeve has slipped down a little, showing a cross-section of barely healed cuts on his wrist.

'It was bad enough to lose her,' he says, his voice breaking. 'But to know that the person who killed her is still out there, laughing about it? Living their life after taking hers? That's . . . that's why I went to the roof the other night. That's why I called you. Because how am I supposed to live with knowing someone got away with killing my sister, and there's nothing I can do to find them?'

He pulls his necklace tight against his skin, clinging to it.

Is this my future? In two years, will I be blacklisted by the police, sectioned, branded as mentally ill and delusional for trying to make others see the truth? When Daniel told me this at the helpline, I didn't believe him. Me, with a sister who was a victim of the same crime. I assumed he was clutching at straws in his grief; that my doubts about Poppy's death were the wishful thinking of a guilty conscience. If I didn't believe him, why would anyone else believe me?

'*Prof's never gonna go for this,*' Jenna says in the library, yawning, our latest proposal draft coffee-ringed and scribbled. '*Not enough precedent.*'

'*Not in English, at least.*' I grab a stack of dictionaries from the languages section and return to our desk, checking the database of scientific articles on my laptop. '*You take that French thesis, I'll take the Spanish. The perfect reference is out there somewhere, trust me. We just need to find it.*'

'If there isn't enough evidence for the police,' I say to Daniel, 'we should go out and find more.'

He chews on his cheeks, his eyes shining as they meet mine. 'What do you mean?'

'We investigate for ourselves.' I sit up, my shoulders straightening into a familiar stance. 'All we need to do is collect enough evidence to convince the authorities to open up a new investigation. We can do that!'

'You can, maybe. But Rachel died two years ago. What's left to find? You think there'll be DNA on those tracks after all this time?'

'No, but that's not what I'm talking about. We're not detectives, but we can talk to friends, search through our sisters' things, find something that proves our theory, or at least disproves their suicide one. We can see if there's more CCTV of your sister, maybe from a different angle, maybe showing someone approaching her, and maybe someone else was spotted near Hope Gap the night Poppy died, and spotted again leaving it.'

I think of the way the kind, brown-eyed volunteer touched my wrist after Daniel's call at the helpline, offering me comfort without even a moment of hesitation. After more than a moment, I force my own hand across the table to grab Daniel's. He flinches.

'There are things we can do. Our sisters don't have to be helpless any more. We can help them. We can find who did this. We'll get justice for Rachel.'

For a second, I think he's going to rip his hand out from under mine – but he doesn't. He adds his free hand to the pile, gripping me back. His eyes go wide, a kind of childlike hope in them.

'And for Poppy,' he says. 'We're gonna get justice for Poppy, too.'

Today, more than any other day, I've heard Poppy's name from the lips of people who didn't know her. But from Daniel, it doesn't sound like it's from a stranger. It's like we're some weird family and our sisters are sisters, too. Rachel and Poppy. Names that go together. Two bright young women dead before they had a chance to thrive.

Daniel and I exchange contact details, and I give him my address. As I walk him to the Tube station to start his search in Kent, I feel my brain clicking into research mode. Plans form. My fingers itch to get started.

Six months ago, someone murdered my sister and staged her death as a suicide – but I know the truth, and I won't stop investigating until I can prove it.

CHAPTER 10

At Harvard, late nights were invariably followed by early mornings. No matter how sleep-deprived my body was, I always woke up alert, the previous night's work still set up in my head like a paused experiment waiting to be resumed. I'd brush my teeth, grab a coffee, and head back to the library or the lab, ready for action once more.

Friday morning feels like that.

I dress quickly and take the folder I assembled last night from my desk. It's brand new, grey with colour-coded dividers clipped in, already labelled.

Hypothesis

Inquest Errors

Facts Against Suicide

Poppy Background Information

Evidence of Murder

Suspects

The last two sections are empty, but I spent last night collating the others. I flick to the first page, as I would at the start of any new project: refamiliarising myself with the hypothesis I'm setting out to prove.

On 23 February 2019, Poppy Harris fell from the cliffs at Hope Gap and died. Further investigation without the assumption of suicide will reveal this death to have been murder.

Anger and disgust scorch the back of my throat, but I swallow those feelings down.

No. Emotional responses cloud one's judgement and are of no use in an investigation. I need to be clear-headed and calm. I have to treat this hypothesis as I would any other: rationally searching for the evidence to support my theory and presenting that evidence to the relevant authorities.

Because whatever I feel in my gut, hypotheses need to be proved.

Liam is bobbing around the kitchen in his gym clothes when I leave my room, music blasting from his headphones as he selects a piece of chalk for his daily message. I try to sneak past him, but he catches sight of me and jumps, the chalk snapping against the board: *You are amazi—*

'C!' He drags his headphones down around his neck. 'Sorry, did I wake you again? I was trying to be quiet during my workout, I swear.'

'Don't worry, I woke up on my own.'

'Okay, phew.' He scrapes his pink hair off his sweaty forehead, but it flops back down over one eye as he grabs a smoothie from the fridge.

I check the cat clock on the wall.

'Aren't you late for work?'

'Took some holiday. Three-day weekend, baby.' He grins and hauls himself up to sit on the counter, drinking his smoothie from the bottle. 'So, you're feeling better, right? After the meeting last night? You said it cleared your head.'

He asks it nonchalantly, even swinging his feet while speaking, but I know he's just as concerned as he was last night when he waited up for me to get home, and when his footsteps creaked on the floorboards outside my bedroom. He isn't a very good actor.

'I feel a lot better. The meeting helped.'

'You sure?'

Perhaps I'm not a very good actor either, but I don't want to tell him about Daniel, and Daniel's sister, and how I'm almost certain my own sister was murdered, too. I can't voice that yet, and not to him. I assumed Daniel was mentally ill when he first mentioned murder to me. Why would Liam think any different?

'Yes, I'm sure.'

'Cool!' Liam empties the smoothie bottle and wipes his mouth with the back of his hand, his stubble scraping his skin. 'So, you usually work Fridays, right? But your parents' café is shut today?'

'That's right.'

'Here's what I'm thinking. I've been in London for, like, almost five months now, but I've never done the whole tourist thing. I heard it's a heatwave, so let's get out there! You can show me around. We can go see some sights and then do a museum or something. The Science Museum? Or maybe the National Gallery? What do you fancy?'

'I can't.'

His bright, easy smile falters. 'Oh.'

'I have things to do today.'

'Is this another of your avoidance techniques? Are you fobbing me off?'

'No, I . . . I have a helpline shift.' I flash him my new folder. He won't remember the other one is black. 'I'm covering for someone. Sorry.'

'Oh.' He laughs guiltily, scraping his hair back again. It still doesn't stay. 'Look at me, making it all about myself again. Helping those people is *way* more important than art galleries or waxworks! Go be a good person.'

He jumps down from the counter.

'Seeing as you're busy, I'm gonna shower and head out solo and see where I end up. But you are *not* off the hook, young lady. I want a personalised walking tour of London at your earliest convenience, and you will not be wriggling out of it again. Okay?'

Despite everything, I smile. 'Okay.'

He flashes me a thumbs-up, like he did the night we went out for drinks.

'Good luck helping those people. I know you'll smash it.'

I give him a thumbs-up in return.

I will.

I head to Mum and Dad's house along the towpath. The morning is eerily hot already, uninterrupted sunshine glittering on the still water of the canal. My chinos and sensible lace-ups are not sensible today.

Poppy lived her life that way: too-thin dresses in winter, her big Doc Martens roasting her feet on hot summer days. I've always been too practical for that. SPF 50 every morning, an umbrella in my bag, insulated coats, cool cotton tops, frequent checks of the weather app. During summer, Jenna and I camp out near the air conditioning vent in the library, and go for our daily runs through campus in the evening when it gets cool.

That's how things used to be, anyway.

Is it hot in Boston today, too? Will Jenna go running in the evening like we always used to, or will she run in the sun without me?

I pull my phone from my pocket. The message she sent me overnight is still there on the notification bar. I pull down the preview again.

> *Hey Clem. I'm so, so sorry about the inquest. I'm sorry you have to go through any of this. We're all thinking of you, especially me. I know things are hard for you, I get it, but I wish you'd talk to me. We can just forget about that night. We don't ever have to talk about it. But please talk to me. I miss my best friend. x*

The air around me grows dense and stifling.

We never spoke about it. That morning, the morning after she kissed me on the dancefloor, threaded her fingers through mine, and led me home like she'd never done before, I woke up first. It didn't feel real, seeing her on the other side of the pillow, the sheets just barely covering her. I didn't know what to feel, what to do. Slip away before she woke up, or wake her up? Brush the hair off her face? Kiss her shoulder? Kiss her mouth? Was I allowed to do that? Would she return the kiss, or recoil from it? Was I another one-night stand who'd be awkwardly shown the door, the words she'd breathed in my ear the night before just the meaningless product of too much alcohol? Was that night nothing, or was it everything? Was it real? Did I want it to be?

I never worked it out. The phone rang with Dad's call and that part of my life ended. The feeling in my gut settled into shame. I didn't even look at her as I packed a bag and left for the airport.

I can't look at her now. Not yet.

I flick the notification away, unread, and hit the new name in my contacts list: Daniel Burton.

He doesn't pick up. The phone rings again and again as I walk past the bench and Poppy's favourite boat, going to voicemail three times. '*You've reached Daniel! Leave a message!*' a peppy voice says, one I don't even recognise. He must have recorded it years ago, before his life changed like mine did. It's a ghost of the person he used to be.

I call him for the fourth time, a flush of panic adding to the heat of the day. Why isn't he answering? We said we'd support each other in our searches, but I can't support him if he doesn't answer.

I see him, suddenly, as I did that first morning after I thought he fell from the roof: face up on the ground, broken, pecked at by birds – but this time, with a face I recognise.

I end his chirpy answerphone message and call again. This time, the dial tone ends.

There's a groan down the line.

'Daniel?' I stop on the towpath. 'Daniel, are you okay?'

'It's too early,' he mumbles. He yawns, muffling the second half of it. 'Why are you calling? Wait, what's wrong? Is something wrong?'

'Um, no, no.' I start walking again, exhaling. 'I just wanted to check in. Are you in Margate?'

'Margate?' His voice sinks as he remembers. 'Nah, I crashed at my friend's place in Croydon again. I . . . couldn't face going back there. Not yet.' It sounds like he turns over, rubbing his face. 'I'm not sure what the point is, anyway. What am I gonna find that's better evidence than that video from the train?'

'You just need to find one thing to corroborate that video, or to build up the possibility of doubt. The police might not have been convinced by the video, but can they ignore the video *and* another piece of evidence? I don't think so. You *will* find something.'

He sighs. 'You're one of those annoying, perky morning people, aren't you?'

There's a hint of the old him in those words, the one who left an upbeat, friendly message on his voicemail.

'Yes, I am. And the sooner you get to Margate, the sooner you can find something to make you perky, too.'

'Ugh, fine. I'm getting up. I'm going. I'll call you later.'

He hangs up, cutting off mid-yawn – but before I can put my phone away, he calls back.

'Wait, I forgot to ask. Did *you* find anything yet?'

'Not yet. But I will.'

A familiar restless energy pulses through me as I reach my childhood home, the kind I'd get the morning of an exam or experiment, as I spot the faint nose print on Poppy's window. For the first time in six months, I feel in control. Instead of ignoring my instincts, I'm doing something. I'm being proactive.

The truth is in that room, and it's within my power to go up and find it.

But when I lower my eyes to the café windows, something isn't right. We were supposed to be closed today after the inquest, but the lights are on and customers line the window seats and canalside outdoor tables. Olena and Harriet, the part-time staff, are both at the counter serving drinks, while Dad clears tables and collects empties, smiling at the customers. He approaches the window to speak to a ginger man with glasses, and I step behind the large willow tree on this side of the towpath so he won't see me.

It's a normal day – busier than normal, even – but Mum and Dad didn't call me in. They don't want my help.

They don't want me around.

When I got back to London six months ago and Mum and Dad pulled me into a hug – the first of its kind since Poppy was born: a triangle instead of a square – I knew everything had changed forever and nothing would bring it back. I knew one day they'd find out about the missed call and blame me as much as I blamed myself. And now they do.

But Poppy didn't jump. Poppy didn't call me. What I missed was a call from whoever murdered her, not a desperate cry for help from my sister. I could never have saved Poppy, even if I did answer.

Is that true? What if I had answered? I'd have heard the sounds of a cliff edge, and maybe even the killer themselves, and raised the alarm. Maybe I could have alerted someone about it. Maybe they could have found her on the beach in those minutes before she drowned. Maybe she'd be alive now, injured, but alive, smiling at me from her window, her nose pressed to the glass, still finding joy wherever she looked.

But nobody had a chance to save her that night because I didn't answer.

I have to make up for that.

I leave the towpath and head over the bridge, turning my face away as I pass the café to get to our front door. I hesitate outside it.

I've walked out of this door so many times before, Poppy's hand slipping into mine, needing me to be the confident big sister who'd help her navigate the world.

I will be confident for her again today. I will get her the justice she deserves.

I take a deep breath, turn the key in the lock, and step out of the sunlight and into the darkness of home.

CHAPTER 11

Home is just how I left it. It's like walking into a memory, one from a long time ago: the radio blaring out Christmas songs, Dad washing up in a Santa hat, Mum singing into a whisk like a microphone, Poppy covered in icing sugar and piping intricate designs on to biscuits, her hair secured in a bun with a wooden spoon.

The kitchen is empty now. No music, no laughter. Two mugs are on the draining board with two plates. Even though the sun glints on the canal outside, it feels cold in this room.

I head up the next flight of stairs. Framed photographs run up the wall, documenting twenty-six years of the Harris family: Mum with blue eyeshadow and Dad with a full head of dark hair, smiling in front of a Christmas tree – then two pictures later, I join them, and five pictures after that, Poppy does. As I climb, she grows. A bundle of blankets becomes a red-cheeked, grinning infant. Fair wisps of hair sprout into ginger curls. Pudgy arms grow long, knees become scuffed, teeth disappear and reappear and are pulled into place by two Christmases of braces. I walk with her through princess dresses and One Direction T-shirts until she becomes the Poppy I know: the arty girl in big boots and a floral dress and a baggy cardigan falling off her shoulder. Smiling like she means it.

I touch the frame. This was last December. Two months before she died.

No. Two months before she was murdered.

I get to the second floor, with its bathroom and Mum and Dad's bedroom, and cross to the staircase on the other side, the one that used to be a rickety spiral to an attic stock room back in the building's antique shop days. The third step creaks in the middle, like always.

There are two doorways on the third floor. On the left is the one to my room: a pale room with crisp white bedding, neat shelves of books and awards, posters of scientists, and a window overlooking the road. On the right is Poppy's: rich orange walls, her own art everywhere, clothes hanging out of an overstuffed wardrobe – and the last few months of her life packed up into unpacked boxes.

I haven't been inside since Christmas.

Mum is sitting on Poppy's bed, staring out at the canal. She turns quickly as the floorboard creaks beneath me, her teary eyes full of a hope that instantly fades.

She wanted me to be Poppy.

'Oh, love,' she says, rising from the bed and wiping at her cheeks. She puts on her usual cheery smile, but it has holes in it. 'I didn't hear you come in. What are you doing here?'

'I . . . came to check on you,' I lie. 'You weren't in the café, so—'

'Oh, the café! I completely forgot! I came for a lie down, but then . . . I should get back. I've done far too much dilly-dallying today as it is.'

She checks her face in Poppy's wardrobe mirror, rubbing her eyes. She catches me looking and smiles.

I don't like Mum's cheeriness. It feels macabre in this room, like confetti at a funeral. The room looks lived-in, but it isn't. The book on the bedside table will never be read. The sketches on the desk will never be finished. The uncapped hairspray bottle on the shelf will remain there until someone throws it away.

The room of a dead girl shouldn't look so full of life.

'I come up here sometimes,' Mum says quietly. 'It still smells of her. I hadn't got around to washing the bedding when she . . . Sometimes I pretend she's still away at university. I pretend she has her whole life ahead of her, and she's living it, just out of reach. Somewhere I can't see her. I tell myself she's happy.'

Mum's voice catches.

'I really thought they were going to say it was an accident.'

Fresh tears slip down Mum's cheeks, and I hug my folder to my chest.

She feels it too, doesn't she? The rot of doubt. Suicide doesn't make sense to her either.

She deserves to know the truth about the night Poppy died. She deserves to know that it wasn't suicide, that Poppy *was* happy, that she did nothing wrong as a mother and that someone else is to blame. Daniel's mother didn't believe him when he told her, but why wouldn't mine? She's the person who read me science books and helped me do homemade chemistry experiments in the kitchen and used to run her thumb over my cheek every night at bedtime, tucking in my old Doctor Who bedsheets, saying, '*Sleep well, my tiny genius.*'

She'll believe me.

I touch her shoulder. 'Mum, a suicide verdict doesn't mean it *was* suicide.'

'What do you mean, love?' Mum wipes her face, looking at me intently. Hopefully.

'The coroner doesn't know what happened that night, he simply made an assumption based on the limited evidence available to him. But it doesn't mean he was right. The evidence presented for suicide was circumstantial, at best. There was no motive, and nothing to suggest she was actually suicidal. That means it may not have been suicide at all. It may have been an accident, Mum, or even—'

108

'But she called you!' Mum rushes the words out, then wraps her arms around herself. 'She called you that night, Clementine. She needed you. We can't pretend that she didn't.'

I bite my tongue, hard. What use is claiming Poppy didn't make that call when Mum already thinks this is a way for me to weasel out of my guilt?

She blames me – and if that helps, maybe I should let her.

'I really should get back down to your dad. He must be run off his feet in this weather! I'm sure we'll be open late, too. You know what he says. That alcohol license pays for itself every heatwave!'

She smiles, managing to make it stick this time. Does she practise in the mirror, too?

'I . . . have some things to check up here,' I say, 'but I'll come down and help later on.'

'Oh, no, there's no need for that. You have a rest, darling. Enjoy the sunshine.'

She walks past me to the door – then backtracks, and places a gentle kiss on my forehead. She brushes her thumb across my cheek, just as she used to.

'Don't stay up here too long. It's not what she would have wanted.'

Mum leaves, and very gently closes the door behind her.

There are coats hanging on the back of it. Coats from years ago. Poppy's old green checked winter coat, the one with the too-long sleeves that she never grew into; the pink-and-purple polka dot rain mac she wore that time on Primrose Hill when she was convinced there would be a sunset.

I'm not the sentimental type, I never have been, but items jump out at me from all around the room, stabbing a visceral pain through my gut with the memories they trigger.

Felix the fox getting lost in the Natural History Museum, and me carrying a crying Poppy around on my back until we found his fluffy tail sticking out of the dinosaur exhibit.

Mum and Dad presenting Poppy with her own trophy after I left my high school leavers' night with an armful: *Best Little Sister*.

Dad smacking his hands on the side of the raft as we approached the top of the water ride at Thorpe Park: '*Hands up for the picture, everyone. Hands up. You too, Pops. And dooooown we go!*' And Poppy screaming beside me, one hand in the air, the other grabbing mine as we hurtled into the water.

No.

I tighten my ponytail and open my folder. I didn't come here to dwell on the bits of Poppy's life that I already know about. This is research and discovery. I'm in the library, scanning through archives and data analysis and theoretical textbooks, looking for new information. I will treat anything I find with objectivity.

And what I find cannot hurt me.

I repeat the phrase to myself as I kneel in front of the boxes of Poppy's university things, still in the corner where we left them. Dad and I went to Brighton together to collect them. I remember him folding her clothes so neatly into her suitcase, as though she was going on holiday. I ignore the pangs in my chest as I unpack art theory books she'll never read again, gloves that won't be worn, brushes that can no longer turn paint and canvas into a masterpiece.

I search through every compartment, every bag, every box of kitchenware. I smooth out discarded receipts slotted inside books and pockets and make a timeline out of them, working out her habits and noting them down in my folder: ready meals for one; a new pot of hot chocolate powder every week from the corner shop; treats for the cats she might see on her walks around Brighton. She never remembered to wear sun cream when she was little, but the SPF50 I bought her is half empty in her toiletry bag. My sensibleness must have rubbed off on her, because she has a first aid kit, too, and a box of condoms – both in case of emergency. Used Post-it notes are stuck together in a clump.

Buy milk!

Kandinsky for next assignment?

Text Clemmie about planning Mum's birthday.

Seminar 8.30 a.m.!!!

The mundanity of it hurts. There is nothing remarkable here, nothing extraordinary; she was a normal person with a normal life. Why would anyone have wanted to kill her?

Poppy's backpack was found at the scene and held as evidence until after yesterday's inquest. It's tagged, as are some of the contents. There are more receipts inside – groceries, overdue library loans – and, among other things, her sketchbook.

I flick through it hungrily, even though I don't know what I'm looking for. There are scraps of writing, little thoughts in her looping hand, but mainly it's stuffed with messy sketches and practice paintings, things done in miniature before she painted them out full size. I compare them to the stack of canvases: a fruit bowl still life, chalky in her book but glossy on the canvas; a view over the Sussex Downs, the trees in the foreground hazy blobs and then made up of individual leaves. I turn to the next canvas and my breath catches in my throat.

A cliff.

I slam it down, trying to fight off the thought of her lying at the bottom of it. Shakily, I pick through the sketchbook. There are a few pages dedicated to this painting, and it's easier to look at it in draft form. There's a red-and-white lighthouse at sea level with a streak of coast behind it, tested with blue skies and stormy ones, landscape and portrait. I pick up the canvas again. It isn't a painting of a cliff. The lighthouse is the focal point.

I love living by the sea!! she wrote underneath in her sketchbook.

The coroner presented her Google searches of Beachy Head as a fixation of suicide and its methods, and used it to prove she was planning to take her own life. No. She was just planning a painting. It was research. She probably didn't even *know* about the connotations.

I flip through the rest of the book, trying to dull my anger. There are projects and time-wasting doodles, and paintings that never made it to canvas. The colours grow darker as I turn the pages, and neighbourhood cats with scribbled, guessed names give way to lifelike charcoal sketches of eyes and torsos, of bodies, of slashes of pink and red paint that I can't squint into meaning. There are faces of people. Friends, classmates, teachers. A frowning girl with rollers in her hair. Someone sleeping in a lecture hall. A man holding up a camera, just a flop of hair and one warm, sparkling eye showing above it. The kind of eye that follows you around the room.

Poppy's phone is in an evidence bag. I unlock it – passcode 1234 – and check the portraits against people in her contacts and social media friends lists. I identify a few of them – her housemate with the hair rollers, some classmates – but others are strangers, possibly people spotted in public and sketched out later. I write down the names of the ones I can find, making a list of their contact details for later. Then I check through her phone for notes, for photos, for messages from anyone talking about Hope Gap or midnight cycling trips. I don't find anything. I grab her laptop and flip between the two, checking photos, recently opened files, search history.

She's still logged in to all her apps. Her Instagram page is a feed of beautiful squares: sunsets, paintings, street cats. '*I'm trying to post something new every day,*' she told me a year or two ago, when she lumped me with all the shopping bags so she could photograph the graffiti in an alleyway. I scroll all the way down to that graffiti: July 2017. Just before I left for Harvard. There are drawings of Boston peppered through the years since, along with London and Brighton. *Did this from a photo,* one caption says. *My sister Clemmie is studying there right now. :(Can't wait to go and visit her one day!*

But we never got round to organising a trip.

Her Reddit account is similar. I didn't realise she had one, but she posted fairly often in r/Painting to share her work. *The lighting here is amazing,* a comment on one of her Brighton paintings says. There are others.

> *This is so so so beautiful!*

> *Totally ethereal.*

> *Stunning.*

> *You're so talented!*

I check her other apps, too, digging out her charger when the phone battery starts to fade. She didn't post on Twitter much, but her likes are full of art, and TV show quotes, and discussions about feminism and trans rights and support for all. The last tweet she liked was posted the day before she died.

> *who else can't wait for summer?? bbqs, beach days, sundresses, toe rings, sunflowers, bees, butterflies, warm nights with the people you love <3*

Rage flares in me again. The coroner's officer must have seen this, surely? How could he see that and think she was suicidal? How could he ignore this?

Her message threads are peppered with smiling emojis. She smiled a lot in real life, too. There aren't many messages: a few to her housemates about their shared kitchen; a few to the other artists on her course about the syllabus. People have sent her messages since she died, though. They flood the top of her WhatsApp list.

Hope you're in a better place, Poppy.

Miss you!

RIP xxx

I note down their names and numbers, too. I have to contact as many people as I can. One of them must know something about that night – or at least something important about the weeks leading up to it. That's all I need: one piece of evidence to throw the suicide verdict into doubt. One thing to make the police take the voicemail seriously.

I scroll down far enough to find my own name in the list, with her last messages to me forever the final words between us: *Hey, are you free to talk? Text me.*

'*Come on,*' Jenna says, stuffing my books into my bag. '*I'm getting you out of the library. This calls for a celebration! Drinks are on me.*' She holds out her hand to me, grinning, flecks of snow still clinging to her beret.

At that moment, still just a friend.

'*All right, then,*' I say, exiting WhatsApp and sliding my phone back in my pocket.

'*Yes!*' She grabs my hand and we run down the steps of the library together, snow falling, laughing as we try not to slip over in the courtyard, her leading me into a bar that's already packed and warm.

'*To us and our amazing brains,*' she says later when she hands me a shot, chinking it against hers. Her other hand finds mine again. '*Come on, you. Let's go dance. And I won't take no for an answer.*' I scroll down Poppy's search history over the weeks before she died. Before the last-minute terms the coroner mentioned, there are searches for film reviews, artist research for uni, pictures of cats, new underwear. I follow that last link. It's something red and lacy. I check her suitcase: something red and lacy amid the floral patterns and multicoloured prints.

I wrap it up in one of her dresses. She wouldn't want me to see that.

I sink back on my heels. I've sorted through everything from the university boxes, but I still haven't found what I'm looking for. I double-check Poppy's things, laying the clothes out, checking for anything hidden away. I go back to her books, checking every page, making sure nothing is slipped between the leaves. I open bags, look inside compartments, tins, her jewellery box of beaded bracelets, every single container or possible hiding place – but they aren't there.

There are no letters.

She always gave me a bundle of letters at the end of every term, a big stack of drawings and notes tied up in ribbon and left on my bed. She was too nervous to go to the post office to send them individually, so she saved them. They were like a time capsule of the last few months: all her thoughts, feelings, hopes, dreams.

If anything was going to have a clue in it, it would be those letters.

But there aren't any. For the first time in years, there are no letters waiting for me. There's no trace of them. They weren't in the disclosure documents from the coroner – I grab it from Dad's desk downstairs and spread the pages across Poppy's floor to check – and they're not in the things we brought back from her university bedroom. We stripped that room bare.

No letters. Not a single one.

I claw myself to my feet and head into my bedroom – so visually stark after the explosion of Poppy's – and open the bottom drawer.

I kept all her letters. It was more out of awkwardness than love. What do you do with a stack of letters that you're not quite sure how to respond to? Shove them in a drawer. So here they are: almost three years of thoughts, wrapped up in ribbon. But missing the six weeks I truly need.

I pull out the ones she gave me at Christmas and undo the ribbon.

It starts with a long letter about her nervousness – and excitement – at starting university, then there's a postcard of Brighton Pier: *Wish you were here!* She tells me about attending Freshers Week events – *You'd be so proud of me, Clemmie!* – and what her classes and teachers are like. *The weather is always windy*, she writes on the back of a drawing of a bedraggled seagull, *but it means the air is so fresh! You wouldn't believe it. Come visit?? Can't wait to see you at Christmas! Finished your present today. Not sure if you'll love it or hate it, but I'm hoping for the first one!*

I hold the letters to my chest, wishing they were flesh and blood; that the words were as real as they sound in my head.

I never wrote back. We'd text occasionally, she'd send me news articles and I'd thumbs-up them, but I never amassed a term's worth of affection for her. It was one-sided, this outpouring. I always *meant* to write back. I meant to do a lot of things: arrange a trip for her to Boston; reply to her texts that night to find out what she wanted.

But now it's too late.

I take the other stacks of letters out and spread them across the floor, rereading my sister's life as I search for her latest batch. She nursed an injured bird back to health in a shoebox last year. She couldn't be sure, but she thought it came back every morning to sing to her from the tree outside. She wanted to visit Florence one day and see the paintings. She was going to miss me so, so much while I was away in Boston.

I have her letters from Cambridge, too. They're tucked away in a folder with the rest of my undergraduate materials. I used to throw them in the recycling at first, but Mum came to visit one day and pulled a hand-drawn postcard out, saying it would hurt Poppy's feelings if she knew I didn't keep her art. So I kept it. I never gave it a second look, but I kept it.

I give it a second look now.

She was barely twelve when I moved away, drawing cartoon figures and colourful stars. But the assorted scraps become detailed, shaded, lifelike by the end. A ginger cat, Henry, would hang around on the towpath sometimes, and she'd feed him treats. She drew him a lot: cutesy at first, but a professional illustration by the end, simple pen lines washed with watercolour.

You're so talented! that Reddit user said to her. But I never said that. I took it for granted that she could draw, as though it wasn't extraordinary and a gift. I never appreciated the things she could do with a pen and a scrap of paper. I never told her she was talented. I never told her . . .

I trail back to Poppy's room and sink on to the floor, my sister's former life scattered around me.

There's nothing here, is there? There's no sign of her arranging to meet someone else that night, no message history to show an ongoing argument with a friend. She wasn't being stalked, she didn't have enemies, she hadn't ruffled any feathers. She lived a solitary life of sketching Brighton landmarks, photographing sunsets, befriending local cats, drinking hot chocolate mix alone in her room, and researching painting projects.

Her murder was even more random than I believed her suicide to be.

But *was* it random?

The killer used her phone. If it was a stranger, maybe they knocked it out of her hand on the cliff, or forced her to unlock it for them – but the police said there was no sign of a struggle. She had no defensive injuries. But what if they already knew her passcode? What if they knew her well enough to know who I was to

117

her, and how she always wrote letters to me? Maybe they were mentioned in them. Maybe they knew they had to cover their tracks.

Maybe they took the letters.

I grab the sheet of names and contact details I've collated, running my finger down it. Is one of these friends her killer? Did the person who pushed her to her death text her *RIP x* the next day?

I drop the folder and claw at my scalp, hunching over.

If I'd taken an interest in her life instead of being so focused on my own, I'd already have the answers I need. She texted me that night, twice. *Hey, are you free to talk? Text me.* Why? What did she want to talk to me about? Was she scared for her life? Did something feel off to her? Did she know what was coming?

If I was a better sister, I'd already know.

I reach out for the one untouched thing on the floor: a small plastic bag of the items Poppy had on her body when she died. My fingers are numb, as though they're frostbitten, as I press on the silver chain through the plastic.

Jewellery.

Small silver studs in the shape of cats. Thin silver rings. A necklace with a fox on it. A second necklace is caught up in the chain: a pendant made of two thin strips of metal, silver and rose gold, twisted into two halves of a looping heart.

My sister knew me well enough to send me magazine clippings and give me personalised Christmas gifts, and yet I don't even recognise the jewellery she died in. This heart necklace could be anyone's.

I wish it was.

I toss the bag of jewellery back on to the floor, and play the voicemail on my phone again.

No letters, no suspects, and no motives. No clues of any kind.

CHAPTER 12

It's evening when I finally head back on to the towpath, slipping past the café – now a candle-lit canal-side bar – with Poppy's phone, laptop, and notebooks crammed in a backpack with my folder. I haven't given up. This is the same as checking books out of the university library to continue my research at home. I know that sometimes it takes time to find what you're looking for.

The towpath is dark, and empty. I walk along it alone, hearing music and laughter from the residences over the wall, and seeing snatches of crowded bars on the commercial side. The streetlamps cast down wide circles of light that glisten on the still water, and leave a gulf of darkness between them. I pass from one spotlight and into the gloom.

I was sure there would be something conclusive in Poppy's room. I have nothing I can take to the police. The defeat weighs on me, heavy like a stack of failed exam papers. I'm not used to failure. When I seek answers, I find them. If I have to work every day for a month, scrounge for extra supplies, translate an entire thesis with a Spanish-to-English dictionary at 3 a.m. to find a single specific reference, I do it. In academia, you get out as much as you put in. Hard work gets results.

I suppose I have to accept that the real world works differently.

Poppy's favourite boat shines in the next block of light, the paintwork glossy and the sunflowers pointing east, back towards the café. Waiting for the sun to rise.

My phone vibrates in my pocket and I check the screen: Daniel.

'Are you in Margate?' I ask as soon as I answer.

'Hello to you, too. And yeah, I'm here. Well, kind of. The train was delayed and then I got off a few stops earlier so I didn't have to . . . you know. Go past the place where she . . .'

Died.

I didn't think about that. Every time Daniel wants to go home, he passes the exact spot on the train tracks where his sister Rachel died. He has to relive it over and over.

I see Hope Gap in my dreams every night, but I've never had to go there.

'I'm still walking,' he says. 'Might've taken a few detours. I kind of don't want to go in there, you know? Last time I left, Mum and I didn't leave things on good terms. She wanted me to go on meds again. I didn't want to take them. I shouted a lot. I don't know if she even wants me there.' He sighs. 'So, what did *you* find?'

'Nothing.' I swap the phone to my other ear, wishing I had a better answer. 'Well, not nothing, because in this case, absence is itself a possible clue. But nothing tangible.'

'What are you on about?'

'Poppy used to write me letters while I was away and leave them on my bed for me during the holidays. She did it for years, telling me what she was up to and how she felt and doing little drawings for me. It was almost like a diary. But I didn't find any letters in her things.'

'You looked everywhere?'

'Yes. They're not in the inquest documents or in her boxes from uni. I even checked her room here, even though she hadn't been here for weeks when she died. There was nothing.' I swap ears again. 'If she knew her killer, if she felt like she was in danger somehow, she'd have written about it. What if the killer knew that? What if they did something to the letters? What if they destroyed them to cover their tracks?'

Daniel breathes shakily down the line. 'Oh my God, Clementine. You think it was premeditated? Planned?'

'I don't know for sure, but I think so. I don't think it was random.'

We walk along together in silence: me in London, Daniel in Margate.

'I'm sorry you didn't find anything,' he says after a while. He breathes in sharply and exhales. 'I keep worrying that—'

'Are you smoking?'

'Yeah. So?'

'You know I'm a scientist, right? I've dissected lungs. Don't smoke.'

He inhales again, slowly, taking his time to completely fill up his lungs, before exhaling even slower. 'Sorry, what was that? I couldn't hear you over the blissful calm of nicotine. Besides, you know I'm suicidal. Reminding me of the risks makes it even more enjoyable.'

I slow on the towpath.

'You're still suicidal? As in, right now? Is this one of *those* phone calls?'

'Um . . . No. I guess it isn't. I guess I'm not.' He sounds confused by that. He fumbles with his lighter for a moment. 'Dad repaved our driveway once. This was back before he died, obviously, so I was about . . . eight? Nine? And Rach was a couple of years older. Anyway, turned out we were one slab short, so Dad left a gap by our front door, kind of like a welcome mat, and we pressed our hands into the cement, all of us, me and Rach and my parents. And for so long after Dad died it was a reminder of him, and it was nice, but then Rach died and suddenly it was about her, too. And I can't look at it. I can't stand it. And . . . and just a few days

121

ago, I thought Mum was going to be the last of us left. The last one to look at those handprints. That's what I wanted. But then I met you, and . . . I don't think I want that any more. Like, don't get me wrong, the feelings haven't gone away or anything, but I'm the last voice Rachel has. I have to speak up for her, and get her justice. I have a purpose now. Something to live for.' He sighs, and I hear him scraping his nails through his hair. 'So, thanks.'

I know exactly what he means. I was at my lowest when he followed me out of the support group yesterday. What would I have done if he hadn't persuaded me to look at his video? Would I be here now? Would the truth about Poppy's murder be hidden forever? I owe Daniel so much already.

But I've never been good at talking about feelings.

'Same,' I say, shoving my free hand in my pocket. 'It's good to have a purpose. I just wish ours was something more pleasant.'

'Right? Next time, let's team up to investigate tax fraud at a biscuit factory.'

'I don't really like biscuits.'

'What? That's it, we can't be friends. We're strictly a one-off investigative team and then we go our separate ways. Who doesn't like biscuits? Honestly . . .'

His laugh fades to silence, and the sound I've become so used to hearing forces its way into my ears in its place: waves. The cliff. The voicemail.

'Where are you?' I ask, unable to keep the panic away.

'I'm on the beach. Just chilling by the . . . Oh,' Daniel says, cupping his phone. 'The waves. I didn't think. I didn't know you could hear it . . .' He trails off, fumbling with a lighter. 'Sorry. I can move?'

'No, no, it's okay. It sounds different.'

I focus on the real sounds, not the remembered ones. I listen to his deep, smoky breaths, the gentle waves lapping against sand, not rock. It isn't the same.

There's a scuff somewhere behind me on the towpath. Another pedestrian.

'I might stay on the beach tonight,' Daniel says. 'It's warm. I could lie here and look at the stars, then try again in the morning. I'm too tired for any of that stuff tonight. I know once I get there I'll keep looking and looking and looking until I find something, but what if there's nothing to find? What then?'

'Then you call me, and we talk about it.'

'But you didn't find anything, either.'

I look up at the stars. London is too big, too bright to see much of the universe, but a few constellations punch through the glare, like beacons. I shift my backpack, feeling the weight of the resources I'm taking home with me.

'I didn't find anything today, but I will tomorrow. And so will you.'

'Oh God, you're just as insufferably perky in the evenings as you are in the mornings, aren't you? If you figure out a way to bottle optimism, send some my way, yeah? I'm gonna need it for tomorrow. Night, Clementine.'

'Night, Daniel. Stay safe.'

'Yeah, you too.'

I put my phone away. I hope there's something for him to find tomorrow. I hope he doesn't end his day as defeated as I feel.

There's a scuff behind me on the pavement. The person behind is getting closer, their pace increasing. They sound like they're in a rush. I move to the side, slowing down a little to let them eventually overtake, but they don't. I glance back at them. They're in a pocket of darkness between lampposts, nothing but a vague black mass – and their footsteps have slowed, too. They've matched mine. I pick up speed again, walking fast; the person's feet do just the same.

There are no other footpaths here, no exits on to roads or into carparks. The walls on the right are high; the industrial warehouses on the left deserted. The light under the bridge ahead is out.

I glance back again when I'm under it, catching the person just as they dip into the darkness with me. It's a man. Broad.

Jenna never liked me walking alone across campus at night. '*You've gotta be careful*,' she said. '*You never know what kind of weirdos are out there in the dark.*'

Sweat flushes across my chest, my face. I gulp down my breaths. It's just the heat, and the person behind me is just out for a walk, like me. He walks as fast as he can, like me. He leaves the path, turns left over the bridge, and winds his way through a shortcut to the flat – like me.

I rush up the steps to my block of flats, fishing around for my keys – and drop them. I scrape them back up, fumbling for the right key, trying to find it.

There are footsteps behind me; a vague reflection in the glass door. An arm raises.

Is this what happened to Poppy that night? Did she sense someone behind her? Did someone follow her in the dark?

Did she even see her murderer's face?

I wedge my keys between my knuckles and turn.

'Get away from me!'

'Oh, gosh, all right. Sorry!'

The figure stumbles back a few steps. Glasses and corkscrews of ginger hair glint in the orange streetlamp. It isn't a broad man at all: it's a slight one, one with an armful of books and violently flushed cheeks. The hefty backpack strapped to his shoulders just makes him look big.

I keep my fist clenched around my keys.

'Who are you?' I ask.

'Alexander!' he squeaks, before clearing his throat. 'My name is Alexander Edwards.'

'What are you doing here?'

'I . . . live here?' He jangles the jumble of keys in his hand. 'Flat 4B. You know, the one with the music? Across the hall? We're neighbours, I think.'

'I've never seen you here before.'

'Oh. Really? I've been here for, um, two months now. And I, uh . . . I wave. Sometimes.'

He shifts his books, using the corner of one to push his glasses back up his nose.

'So, you weren't following me?'

'What? No! Gosh, no! Let me prove it, look.' He approaches, slowly, and unlocks the main door, staying an arm's length away to give me space. 'See? I live here.'

'Oh.' I go in through the door and he follows me in, scurrying up to his post box, burying his nose in it. 'Sorry about that. It was dark, and . . . sorry.'

'It's all right,' he says from inside his box. 'I'm sorry for startling you. I lost track of time because your parents didn't kick me out of the café like they usually do at closing, so it was dark when I left, and you were ahead of me, but I didn't want to get too close and scare you, so I hung back a bit, but then you kept looking back, and I wasn't sure what to do, and then you couldn't open the door, so I thought I would help, but that made you jump, and . . .'

He closes his post box, magazines and an envelope resting on top of his stack of books, and shrugs.

'The café,' I say. 'You're the one who sat near the window the other day. The one who spilt his coffee!'

He cringes. 'Yes, thanks for reminding me. And thanks for helping me clean it up. No harm done to the books. Although I managed to get orange juice on them today, which may be another matter entirely.'

He pats them, and his post slips off the top. I pick it up for him, checking the handwritten address on the envelope. Flat 4B, across the hall from me.

'Thanks. I only recently started going to that café. I love the view. I, uh . . . I didn't know you worked there when I picked it.' He cheeks are still pink. 'Honest.'

'It's strange that I've never noticed you before,' I say, as we head up the stairs. 'I've heard your music enough times.'

'Oh, that's not mine. It's my flatmate's.' He glares up in the direction of our floor. We can already hear the thumping through the stairwell. 'I've asked him to turn it down, but he won't. Says it helps him focus. Sorry about that. It must annoy you and your boyfriend.'

'Boyfriend?'

'The one you live with? With the pink hair and the . . . the muscles?'

I laugh, shaking my head. 'That's just Liam, my housemate. We're not *together*.'

'Oh. Oh! Um, well, sorry if the music annoys you. I'll have another go at getting it turned down. That's why I camp out at the café, actually. It's much easier to focus there.'

'Are you a student?' I ask.

'Yes, at Imperial.'

I glance at his books. 'Sciences?'

'Astrophysics.'

'Oh, two of my housemates at Harvard study Astrophysics.'

'Harvard?' he asks, his eyes bright.

'Yes, I'm studying for a PhD in Molecular Biology there. Or I was, until a few months ago. I'm taking a break.'

'That's incredible. What's your thesis?'

'Novel mechanisms of hypoxic metabolic reprogramming in metastatic cancers.'

'Oh, under Professor Jeffords?'

'Yes. How do you know that?'

'Who *doesn't* know that? He's top of the field.' He pauses to puff a few curls off his face. 'He gave a talk at Imperial last year. I, um . . . I always sneak into all the other science departments' special guest lectures. His was great.'

Jenna and I took over Professor Jeffords' classes that week, taking it in turns to host seminars and give lectures to undergrads. It was thrilling, seeing students note down *my* words, ask questions they trusted *me* to answer. It solidified what I wanted to do with my life: research, then teach my research to the next generation of great minds.

Yet here I am in London, three thousand miles away from the classroom, working on a hypothesis I may never be able to prove.

We reach our floor, and he comes to a stop with his back to his flat.

'Well, um, I'll let you get back to your housemate. Sorry for scaring you, and thanks for picking up my post.'

He smiles at me, awkwardly, as though he doesn't quite know what to do with his face.

He keeps staring.

'Oh!' I still have his letter and magazines. I shake my head and slip them on to his stack of books. 'Here you are. That article about cybernetics looks good.'

'You can have it, if you like. Go ahead. Take it.'

'Oh, no, I couldn't. It's yours.'

'Okay, what about this? I read it, and if it's any good, I'll pass it on to you. It'll be no trouble. I know where you live, after all.'

He smiles at me – not awkwardly like before. His glasses have slipped down his nose, and his arms are too full to push them back up. I feel a strange urge to do it myself.

'Well, um, it was nice to properly meet you . . .' He scrunches his face up. 'I'm such an idiot. I never asked you your name, did I?'

'It's Clementine.'

'Clementine,' he repeats, nodding, muttering it a few times to make it stick. 'I'm Alexander. I already told you that, didn't I?'

'Yes.'

'Great. Well, sorry for introducing myself twice, not asking your name, and blathering on about nonsense after scaring you half to death on the towpath. Hopefully our future meetings will be a little less mortifying. Goodnight!'

We head to our front doors and unlock them – but as soon as he does, there's the unmistakable sound of many books thudding on to the floor. I turn to find him with one foot over the threshold, frozen with his arms out. He glances back at me as though hoping I wouldn't still be here.

'Do you need a hand?'

'No, I'm fine. Just enjoying another mortifying moment that will haunt me every time I try to fall asleep.' He kicks the books out of the way of the door and slips in after them, pulling the door to. 'Goodnight.'

He waves at me with his now-free hand – and I return it.

'Were you talking to someone out there?' Liam calls from the sofa when I walk into the flat. He's draped across it in a T-shirt and boxer shorts, a desk fan pointed right at him. He moves a cushion to his lap. 'What? It's bloody boiling in here.'

'I was talking to the man in the flat opposite. Alexander.'

'He the one with all the hair?'

'Yes.'

'Aw, he's cute! Did you get his number?'

'What? No. He just . . . he comes to the café, and we bumped into each other on the way home. He seems nice.'

'Nice, huh? Is he as nerdy as he looks?'

'He's an astrophysicist.'

'Oh my God. Mega nerd. You should have invited him in for some tea, Earl Grey, hot.' He emphasises the last word, winking. Then his eyes narrow, and he sits up. 'How was today? Good shift?'

It takes me a moment to remember my cover story of going to the helpline.

'Um, yes. Lots of positive outcomes.'

'That's great! You're really – hey, where are you going?'

I pause outside my bedroom. 'I've got some work to do.'

'Work?'

'Reading. New library books. Research for the helpline.'

'C, I mean this in the nicest possible way, but – you look exhausted. The last thing you need right now is to *read*. Come and sit.'

Liam pats a space on the sofa, then clears his throat and gestures to the plates on the coffee table. 'This evening your resident pastry chef has prepared chocolate-and-caramel brownies, cheese breadsticks, and, as a special treat, some kind of experimental fudge that didn't work and may possibly rot and/or break your teeth. What do you say? Snacks and some bad TV? Some old school sci-fi? You need to relax, hun.'

I grip the straps of my backpack. I want to go through Poppy's messages again, and check her files, and start emailing her friends – but the bag is a bigger weight on my shoulders than I realised. Liam's expression is like Jenna's again.

'*No, seriously, forget the books! No more books!*' She wrestles the latest edition of *Lewin's CELLS* off me and throws it in the laundry basket, planting herself in front of it with her fists raised like an old-timey boxer. '*You are coming with me to the movies or so help me, I will fight you and drag you there unconscious. Either way, you're having a break.*'

'That sounds great, it does, but . . . I can't right now. Night, Liam,' I say, and shut my bedroom door behind me.

Some things are too important to take a break from.

SASHA

8 Months Before Poppy

I crouch on the roof of a half-collapsed building, raising the scope of my sniper rifle. Jax sneaks down the dusty road below, legs bent, pistol up.

'You're being tailed,' I say into my mic.

Jax twitches. 'Where? How many?'

'Two in the buildings on your left, one following behind.'

'Damn. Should I cut across the field and make a run for it? It's a straight shot to the generator.'

'No, you need the cover. They'll pick you off easy otherwise.'

'Well, I can't see them.' Jax checks a doorway beside him, pistol pointing to every corner of the room. 'Looks like you'll have to pick them off first.'

'My favourite. Okay, go into the next doorway on your left. The ones in the buildings have to jump down to get across to the next roof, so we can take them out there.'

'Where am I going?'

'Up the stairs to the first floor – that's second floor to you, yank. They're gonna jump from that ledge above, see it? Get under it. It's a blind spot. If I miss, you take them out.'

'You're not gonna miss.'

'Hey, there's a first time for everything.'

Jax gets into position. The enemies in the buildings get stuck at a locked door before the jump, but I can't get a clean shot through the window. I move my scope back to the road.

'Jax, watch for the third. I've lost him.'

Jax's gun moves down from the sky to the road. He crouches.

'I can't see him. Damn, they're coming.'

I focus back on the roofs. Two soldiers step out from a ruined hallway, eyeing a jump they can't make. I fix my crosshairs on the first one, flexing my fingers, ready to flick to the second man after the first shot.

'Ready?' Jax asks.

'Yup. One, two – no!'

A gunshot blasts and red splatters on to my screen: *YOU DIED*. My avatar – Mira, a woman protecting her homeland from US invaders – switches into third-person view, crumpling from a perfect headshot that blasts her off the edge of the roof. Behind her, the third US soldier stands at the top of a staircase, spinning in gleeful, crouch-spamming circles.

'What hap— Oh crap, grenade!'

Text appears in the corner of the screen: *JAXXON102 DIED*.

Then text takes over the whole screen: *MISSION FAILED*.

'We were so close!' I want to hurl my controller at the TV, but instead I punch a sofa cushion. 'We were right there!'

'Grenades! Who the hell throws grenades *there*?'

'Bloody Americans, man,' I mutter. 'No offence.'

'None taken, it's totally true. We're the worst. Crap. I'm thinking maybe doing a four-person campaign with just two of us was kinda a bad idea?'

'You wouldn't be saying that if we'd won.'

'I guess not.' Something rustles on Jax's mic, and I hear his familiar open-mouthed popcorn chewing. 'We going again? I think if I'd yeeted one off a building earlier, we could have done it.'

'Don't talk about yeeting people off buildings. Too soon!' I take a slug of Coke, stifling a yawn. 'Sure, let's go again.'

'You sure? What time is it there? Don't you have class tomorrow?'

'It's only one fifteen a.m. Chill.'

'I don't wanna be responsible for you failing algebra, or whatever.'

'Algebra? It's Animation, you arse.'

'You're the ass, Miss *Go Inside the Building, That'll Work*.'

'You wanna take point next time, be my guest. But you literally would've had three straight headshots if you'd gone for the field.'

'Yeah, but at least I'd have died the way I lived – running away at full speed from American jerks who wanna end me.'

I stretch out on the sofa, Minecraft leggings tucked into mismatched socks. 'Were you the kind of kid who used to get wedgies every day at school?'

'Used to? I've got one right now. Need pliers to get them out these days.'

I laugh, setting up our next campaign. Jax shoves another handful of noise in his mouth.

'You gotta mute your mic when you do that.'

'Never.' He crunches even louder. 'You love it. Mom keeps me stocked down here in the basement.'

'You're such a cliché. Do you have one of those little bum-fluff moustaches you're too proud of to shave?'

'Hey, leave my bum-fluff out of this. Bet you're the gamer girl cliché, right? Playing this with a full face of make-up and a low-cut tank top?'

I catch sight of myself slouched in the TV's reflection: hair scraped up into a messy bun, a definite double chin going on.

'How do you even know I'm a gamer girl? I'm actually a fat, bald, middle-aged dude called Frank who's using a voice manipulator.' I pull the mic right to my mouth, breathing into it as deeply and creepily as I can.

'What? But I'm also a fat, bald, middle-aged dude called Frank. Oh my God, we're soul mates.'

I flick through campaigns. 'What are you feeling, something new? Or should we try a redo? I think we were getting a lot closer.'

'Screw it, let's give it another go. All aboard the train to certain death!'

'Hey, have some faith. It's not *certain*, just incredibly likely.'

We materialise back in the ruined town, a table of supplies in front of us. Jax – a shirtless bodybuilder, basically – strides forward and grabs a sword and a pistol. I take my favourite sniper rifle.

'Hey,' Jax says, his avatar facing mine. 'So, like, my mom and I are visiting family in Scotland in, like, a month, and I was thinking I might come down to England for a bit. See Big Ben, you know? And so, like, if maybe you wanna see Big Ben too, we could meet? It's okay if not. Actually, it was a stupid idea. I'm sure you don't wanna meet a weird guy from the internet. Forget it.'

His avatar strides off to get into position. I raise my rifle and shoot him in the knee, crippling him.

'What the hell?'

I stand in front of his hobbled character.

'You're on, Jax. Let's do a London campaign.'

I press the button to heal him, my avatar crouching beside his. Jax crunches his popcorn again. Then we're both upright, guns out and ready for action.

'Okay, find the gas and get to the generator. Let's go.'

'Hell yeah,' he says. 'As one Frank to another, we got this.'

CHAPTER 13

It's quiet tonight on the night shift. It's like that sometimes: a few volunteers talking for hours with their callers, while snap calls and brief chats interrupt the silence for the rest of us.

I sit with my headset around my neck, staring at my phone screen.

It's been two days since I reached out to Poppy's friends and tutors and housemates, and most of them still haven't responded. The ones who did couldn't tell me anything useful.

I already told the inquest people everything I knew, Emily – the housemate pictured in hair rollers in Poppy's sketchbook – wrote back on Facebook, seven hours after first reading my message. *She was shy and didn't ever want to hang out. I didn't really know her. Sorry.*

Other replies were similar.

I hadn't spoken to her in months, sorry.

I knew her from class but we never talked much.

We only swapped numbers so she could send me her lecture notes from when I was ill. She seemed great, though. Sorry for your loss.

Her fine art tutor responded this morning.

Your sister Poppy was a bright, talented student who is dearly missed by the rest of her class. I wish I could be more help, but unfortunately she never approached any Brighton University faculty member or the Student Union about her mental health, so we were unable to provide her with any support for her mental health needs. I wish I was able to say something that would bring you comfort, but unfortunately we had no prior knowledge of her state of mind. I am deeply sorry for your loss.

I refresh my email again, hoping something more useful will land in my inbox.

Should I have been more direct? I messaged these people asking for information about Poppy's final weeks – who she talked to, who her friends were, if she was upset about anything. Perhaps I should have led with: *I think my sister was murdered and I need your help to find the killer.*

But Mum's quick shutdown of the conversation when I tried to tell her about it is still fresh, as are Daniel's warnings about his own experience. If people think I'm blaming Poppy's suicide on a murderer because I'm mentally unwell, they won't tell me anything – and if I do find evidence, they may not believe it. I have to be careful. And there's always the chilling thought at the back of my mind: what if one of the contacts on her phone is the murderer? It probably isn't wise to let them know I'm looking for them. Not yet.

I sigh. No new emails, and no helpline calls. I came here for my shift tonight so I didn't let anyone down, but there's nobody here to help. I need to help *someone*.

I open my Reddit app and check the subs I follow. r/ SuicideWatch is an echo chamber of depressive statements, constantly updating with cries for help from around the world. I switch to r/BereavedBySuicide, and find the same desperate tone.

He's been gone a year. Does it get easier?

I miss her so much.

Why did this have to happen?

I used to tell these people the things I told myself: that it isn't healthy to question a suicide; that we must accept there will never be clear-cut answers. I don't have anything comforting to say to them now. I'd visit this forum not just to help, but to *be* helped. After Poppy's death, I assumed suicide was an exact science, an effect with a specific cause, and the reason I couldn't understand Poppy's was because I hadn't studied the concept enough to know what it was yet. I thought surrounding myself with like-minded people would eventually lead me to the answer.

But we've never been like-minded, have we? I have no place here.

I navigate to another sub – r/AskReddit – and publish a new post.

> *If a loved one's death was ruled as a suicide but you felt it was suspicious, how would you go about getting the police to investigate it?*

I'm out of ideas. It can't hurt to outsource the question.

'Got you a coffee,' someone says a few minutes later, sliding a Science Museum mug on to my desk. 'Tiny bit of milk, no sugar, right?'

The dark-haired volunteer I spoke to the night I thought Daniel died sinks into the seat next to me with his own mug: the National

Gallery. His curly hair is loose tonight, brushing his shoulders, and his brown eyes twinkle as kindly as I remember.

'Yes. Thank you . . .'

'Jude,' he says, tapping his chest.

'Thank you, *Jude*.'

'You're welcome. So, pretty quiet tonight, huh?' He leans back in his creaking chair with his feet on the desk.

'Yes. Very.'

'I prefer to be busy, but if fewer people *need* to call us, that's a good thing.'

He smiles, and I sip my coffee. It's cold in the phone room, the office AC cranked up high to contrast with the stuffy London heat we can no longer feel. Jude is dressed for it – paint-flecked boots, turned-up jeans, a checked shirt, and a cardigan – but I'm not. I wrap my fingers around the mug, absorbing its warmth.

'Are you cold? You look cold.'

I shake my head. 'It's fine.'

'No, seriously, it's freezing in here.' He pulls off his cardigan and offers it to me. 'Take it.'

I try to refuse, but he leans over and slugs it around my shoulders. He puts his feet back up on the desk.

'Cosy, right? Oh, and it's fresh out of the laundry. I promise.'

The woollen fabric is warm on my shoulders, some of Jude's heat woven through it.

'Are you sure?' I ask. 'Don't you want it?'

'Nah, I'm good. You go ahead.'

I slide my arms into the chunky cardigan, feeling it drape loosely over me. When I reach for my mug again, one shoulder falls down like Poppy's used to.

I pull it back up.

'My first ever solo night shift was like this,' Jude says. 'I got one phone call all night, and it was someone asking how to install

137

new drivers on their PC. And I know technically we're supposed to shut things like that down, but I talked that guy through it for about twenty minutes. So I did manage to help someone that night. What was your first night like?'

I try to remember. There were training sessions, practice calls, monitored calls, and then after a few months I could take calls by myself. I had my handbook and my notebook, and I approached the shift like I would an experiment in the lab: focused, calm, and running through a list.

'It was busy. Well, busier than this.' I gesture to the quiet room, the other listeners either on the phone or passing time in their silent alcoves. 'But I don't remember who I talked to.'

'That's good,' Jude says. 'Some calls stick with you, but you've got to let the rest go. Otherwise you end up worrying about a lot of people you can't ever check up on. That's not healthy.'

I take another sip of coffee, shifting in my seat. Sometimes I go through my old comments on Reddit, clicking on the usernames of the people I've replied to, seeing how they're doing now. Sometimes they're fine, posting about *Game of Thrones* or indie rock, but other times they're back in r/SuicideWatch – or worse, they haven't posted at all.

I don't think I ever told Daniel how much of a relief it was to know he was still alive.

'What do you do to pass the time?' Jude asks. 'Are you reading something on your phone?'

I turn my screen off, hiding Reddit.

'Just a book.'

'Ah. I draw.' He taps the sketchbook resting on his lap. It's so like Poppy's. I have hers tucked away in the investigation folder in my bag. I take them everywhere with me now.

'I've always been one of those people who doodles while they're on the phone, so I can do it between calls as well as during.'

He scratches the pencil against the paper, smudging a shadow with his finger. Poppy used to do that: cross-legged, head tilted, tongue poking out. She could create something beautiful in less than ten minutes.

'Do you draw?'

'No. I can do scientific diagrams, but not art. My sister's the arty one.'

'Really? What's her style?'

He gives me a brief smile before looking back down at his sketchbook.

'She . . . I don't know. What's yours?'

'Oh, I do all sorts. I'm a graphic designer – freelance, hence the night shifts – but I like illustration best. I do jokey cartoons, some life drawing, portraits. Portraits are my favourite. See?'

He holds up his sketchbook. There's a lifelike image there, a middle-aged man clawing at his thinning hair. His face is caught in the moment between emotions: crying in despair; flaring with anger. There are lines and wrinkles, light and shade. Sad, glistening eyes.

'Who is he?' I ask.

'A caller I spoke to earlier. He said his marriage is over and he's about to lose everything he's worked all his life for. He hung up before we could really get into it. I hope he got something out of it.'

The attention to detail is incredible. The skin is shaded except for a strip on his finger: the tan line left behind by a missing wedding ring.

'That's wonderful,' I say. The comments left on Poppy's artwork come back to me. 'You're very talented.'

'Thanks.' Jude slaps the sketchbook back on his knee, pencilling in some finer details.

'How do you know what he looks like?'

'I don't. You know how when you talk to a caller, your mind sort of fleshes out an imagined face to fit the voice?'

I shake my head.

'Oh.' He laughs. 'Well, when *I* talk to a caller, I imagine them to be a certain type of way. I'll get this distinct impression of them. As we talk, I sketch them. When people call us, they show us parts of themselves that nobody else gets to see. That's what I try to capture.'

'But it's so lifelike. How do you do that without a reference?'

'The reference is in here.' Jude taps his head, then tucks a stray curl behind his ear. 'I can see them clearly. I just have to put it on paper.'

My brain doesn't work like that. I see bits and pieces and join them up into a person – Poppy's baggy cardigan, her ginger hair twisted up with a paintbrush – but I can't see specifics. Blue eyes like mine, I remember that, but what shape were they? What was her nose like? I see her without seeing her. She's there, but translucent somehow. Like a ghost.

'I'll show you some of my others.'

Jude pulls his feet down and squeaks his chair closer to mine. He flicks through his sketchbook, showing me the faces that match the stories.

'This guy failed his second year at uni. His voice was completely flat. No emotion. Said his parents would disown him. And this guy, he'd just lost his wife to cancer. Sixty years they'd been married. And this woman, she's one of our regulars. Her daughter took her own life a year or two ago and she struggles a lot. And then here—'

'Wait, wait, go back.' Jude flips back to a middle-aged black woman with her braided hair tied up in a silk scarf, smiling kindly while tears leak down her cheeks from her crumpled eyes, her fingers twisted around a necklace with a heart pendant. 'That's Blessing.'

'Yeah, that's right.' Jude cocks his head at me. 'You've spoken to her, too?'

'Yes, and that's . . . Well, I never properly pictured what she'd look like, but that's her. I . . . recognise her.'

'Now you're getting it.'

Jude resumes his rustling through the pages, and my eyes glaze over a little. The sketchbook is thick, full of dozens, maybe hundreds of faces. So much despair. So many stories.

'Did you ever draw a young man who couldn't accept his sister's suicide?'

Jude stops, and looks at me. 'Why?'

'I was just wondering.'

Jude purses his lips and flicks through the pages in chunks. He finds a page and hands it to me.

It's not the Daniel I know. Not only physically, but emotionally: there's a twisted scowl to his face; a meanness in the lips. Dark shadows and irises make his eyes seem hollow.

He looks frightening.

'I spoke to him once. He got very angry, very quickly. He said . . . Well, he had demons.' Jude takes the book back from me and closes it. 'He's the one you spoke to the other night, isn't he? The one who jumped?'

The phone call seems like so long ago. So much has changed since then.

'Yes, that's him. But it turns out he didn't jump. I've spoken to him since, and . . . he's alive still.'

'He is? Wow. You should be proud of yourself, Clementine. You *did* get through to him. I hope he can take the steps needed to get better. He needs help, but not the kind we can give him.'

Not within the confines of our training. But there are different kinds of help.

Jude creaks away slightly, leaning back in his chair again. A few voices murmur softly on the other side of the room, and a phone rings. But it isn't either of ours. I think about unlocking my phone, checking my Reddit notifications, checking on Daniel in case he's up at 2.38 a.m. on a Monday.

'How did you get into volunteering?' Jude asks, scratching away at his sketchbook again.

'A flyer came through my door asking for volunteers. I contacted the branch and signed up.'

'Just like that? Out of the blue?'

'Well, no. There was . . . another reason. My sister. She died near Beachy Head six months ago.'

'Oh. I am so, so sorry.'

Jude reaches across the narrow space between us and touches my arm through his cardigan.

'Do you want to talk about it?'

I think for a moment. I could tell him everything, spilling my secrets to this soft, gentle person, feeling the warmth from his borrowed cardigan and his kind brown eyes.

But he's following my script. Right now, I'm just another wounded person, and he's trying to fill his time with me.

And he wouldn't believe me anyway.

'How did you get into volunteering?' I ask, sitting up straight. He smiles and returns to his drawing.

'Well, a few years ago, I tried to end my life.'

He says it without pain or embarrassment. He isn't shouting it to the phone room, but he isn't hiding it from anyone, either. He pulls back his checked sleeve, showing a tattooed wrist. He traces the thick, vertical scar the art covers.

'I wasn't well. A relationship had ended, I was at the end of my rope, I felt lost . . . I wanted to die. That was it. But before I could finish, my mum rang me. She must've had this weird sixth sense or something, because it was like she intuitively knew I needed her. I didn't know it, but she did. And when I talked to her, I knew I couldn't end it. Not like that. So I didn't.'

He doesn't pull his sleeves back down. He rolls them up, letting the old scars breathe.

'I got help, physically *and* mentally, and decided to come here, to train to be a listener. To try to do for others what my mum did for me. Because that's the most important thing, I think. Just being there for someone. Giving them that time. Brenda's always telling me off for doing too many night shifts, but I hate it when I'm away for too long. I'm always worrying that I missed picking up the most important call of someone's life.'

A few days ago, those words would have sent me into a spiral of guilt about Poppy. But now I know better.

Jude's phone rings.

'Ah, there we go. I'll leave you to your book, Clementine.' He smiles and answers his caller, turning over a fresh page in his sketchbook.

I retreat back into my own cubicle, leaning over my phone. Nobody's replied to my r/AskReddit question yet. Perhaps nobody will. I open WhatsApp instead. There's a green dot next to Daniel's name. I press the call button.

'You're up late,' he says when he answers. 'Or early, I guess?'

'I'm on a night shift at the helpline,' I whisper. 'It's quiet. I saw you were online.'

'Yeah. Can't sleep.'

'You can get tablets to help with that.'

'I know, but they knock me out so bad I can't wake up from the nightmares. I'd rather be awake.'

I know what he means. My box of prescription sleeping pills are almost untouched in a drawer at the flat, along with the anti-depressants the doctor insisted on giving me. I never opened them.

'How are things going down there?' I ask.

'Not good. I still can't find anything. I was thinking that maybe something had got lost, or maybe she had a secret diary or some-thing, so I pulled up the carpet and was trying to get the floor-boards up too before Mum stopped me. She looked worried, but hey, I haven't been committed yet. *Yet*. I convinced her I'm back to look for a suicide note, so at least she thinks my mad search is for something rational, I guess.' Daniel rubs at his face. I hear the scratch of his beard. 'Did you hear back about those emails you sent?'

'A few, but I didn't get any new information. It was mostly just people saying they didn't know her, and that they were sorry for my loss.'

'I got that a lot. I kept asking and asking, thinking it might trigger something, but most of her friends ended up blocking me.'

'They blocked you? Why? All you wanted was to know what happened to your sister.'

'Yeah, but all *they* wanted was to move on. I can't blame them, I guess.' He sighs. 'What if there's nothing out there? What if there's literally nothing I can do to prove it?'

It's my own fear. I left Poppy's room empty-handed and defeated, and every useless email response I get just adds to that defeat. The answers are always there in science: things get proved or disproved. An experiment succeeds or fails. There's a scale to it, yes, but there's no flying blind.

I cannot guarantee that Daniel will find anything to prove his sister's murder, just like I can't guarantee I'll be able to prove Poppy's.

'Get some sleep,' I say, 'proper sleep, and have another look tomorrow with fresh eyes. Tomorrow will be different.'

'It's after midnight. It's already tomorrow.'

'No, it isn't. It's not tomorrow until the sun rises.'

Jude is still on his call beside me, his pencil scratching, his comforting words flowing effortlessly. His cardigan is soft on my shoulders, the sleeves long enough to pull down over my hands. I pretend I have his softness, his calm.

'Don't give up,' I say to Daniel. 'There are answers out there, and we're both going to find them.'

◆ ◆ ◆

Jude and I walk out together at 6 a.m. after our shift, the street now glowing with a low streak of sunshine.

'Thank you for the cardigan,' I say, handing it back to him.

'Thanks. Much nicer out here, isn't it?' He suns his arms, turning them over. From a distance, you can't see the scars at all. Then he grabs something from his bag. 'I've got something for you, too.'

He hands me a piece of paper with one of his sketched portraits on it.

It's me: sharp eyes, dark hair, the slight bump in my nose. But I'm not *me*. There's kindness there that doesn't belong, and an ethereal lightness to me. Softness.

I realise, suddenly, that it's eerily similar to the portraits in Poppy's sketchbook.

'I think we learn a lot about each other, volunteering here,' he says. 'And I've learnt that you're someone your sister would be very proud of. Don't forget that.'

He touches my arm – not hard, not a grip, but a quick, gentle squeeze.

'She would want you to be happy, and move on.'

He smiles kindly, head slightly bowed, and we part – him probably on his way to some studio apartment filled with light and canvases; me back to the flat, back to emails with no answers and social media accounts I've already picked clean.

My phone chimes with a notification, and I check it. It's a comment on my r/AskReddit post.

> *I'd play detective for sure. Retrace their steps, hunt for clues, talk to everyone. I wouldn't take no for an answer. Then I'd find who did it and kill them myself.*

I stuff Jude's drawing into my helpline folder and head for Aldgate Station – but I don't take the Circle Line north like I usually do. I take the District Line west, to Victoria. I buy a return ticket to Brighton and board the first train I can.

Tomorrow is now today, and today is the day I find something I can use.

CHAPTER 14

We used to come to Brighton when Poppy was little. We'd cram on to a train with the other day trippers and be there in about an hour, stepping off into fresh coastal air and sea breezes. The individual trips blur together now, leaving behind a fuzzy, sun-tinted impression, like a highlight reel made of old-fashioned film. It's all sensory: wafts of vinegar, sun cream, and hot sugared doughnuts; the itchy feeling of sand clinging to sticky legs, and pebbles jabbing into backs. I can taste the candyfloss dissolving on my tongue, hear the wooden boards of the pier beneath my feet, feel the plastic of the horse under me while the carousel spins, Poppy beside me, both of us rising and falling as the music plays, smiling, laughing. Alive.

Brighton is greyer than I remember, as I push through the oncoming crowd of commuters and exit the station. Despite the heatwave, there's no summertime magic in the city today. This isn't a day out at the seaside, it's a fact-finding mission.

If there are no clues about Poppy's murder in her bedroom for me to find, the city where she died is the next best place to look.

I follow a sign for the North Laine area which Poppy mentioned in her letters, and make my way through narrow streets of rainbow bunting, vegan cafés, piercing parlours, art shops, and vintage boutiques. I try to imagine her walking this same route last winter, wrapped up in her red coat and bobble hat, cheeks and nose flushed pink, stopping at every shop window but too shy to ever go inside.

Poppy's Instagram feed is full of illustrations of her favourite haunts – the Brighton landmarks she visited again and again, in all weathers. Consulting Google Maps, I navigate my way around the city to each of them.

Brighton Pavilion is as majestic as in her paintings, even with its lawn scorched by summer. There's a green dolphin fountain hidden away in a courtyard in The Lanes, the water run dry. Queen Victoria stands on a plinth on the edge of Hove, and a row of multi-coloured beach huts lines the promenade across the road. The West Pier is burnt-out and skeletal in the lapping waves of the English Channel, its half-crumbled legs as spindly in real life as they look in Poppy's jagged sketch. And on Brighton Pier I find the light-up red sign, the green fortune teller's caravan, the roller-coaster, and her favourite place to watch a sunset, looking west.

If I cross the pier and look east, I can make out the white cliffs towards where she died.

At every location, I head into nearby cafés and businesses and show them Poppy's photo – the one of us together on the bench – and ask the same questions: '*Do you remember seeing this girl outside in February? Was she ever with somebody else?*' But nobody recognises her. There's no trace of her any more. It's as though she was never here at all.

It's a macabre treasure hunt. If Poppy were alive and I were merely killing time before meeting her after a class, perhaps it would be fun, like orienteering with a compass and a map in the forest. But without her, it feels like one of the Jack the Ripper tours I always pass on my way to the helpline.

'*And here's where the dead woman walked, and here's where she always came to watch the sunset, and here's the very spot where she died a truly horrific death. Any questions? All right, let's move on . . .*'

There's a photo of Poppy on her Instagram feed. She didn't post many selfies, she preferred to hide, even online, but one of her last few posts is of herself. The sea is behind her and the sky is a spectrum of colour, the escaped curls under her hat burning even more orange in the light, her face pulled into a smile.

But it isn't just 'a smile'. Her eyes are crinkled in the corners, her cheeks are flushed, her mouth is pulled wide. It's the smile she gave me when I walked into the kitchen at Christmas, when she jumped up and hugged me and wouldn't let go.

It's the smile that shows her joy at being with someone she loves.

My phone dings and a notification pops up at the top of the screen, the bar overlapping the top of the sunset. *Tinder: You've been super-liked!*

I hit the notification and let it take me away from the photo of Poppy, burying her behind a new app window. It hurts too much to see that smile.

Tinder loads. There's another smiling image: a man this time, with floppy blond hair, glasses, muddy wellington boots, and a red knitted jumper, leaning against a wooden fence in the countryside. The photo is ringed with blue.

I'm sick of other people's happy, normal lives. I stab at the home button to get away from all my apps, but I miss and hit something else. A blue star pops up, then another screen.

It's a match! Tinder says, a photo of my face appearing in a heart-shaped bubble next to the stranger's. I'm smiling in my photo, too. Smiling at Jenna as she took a photo of me in the snow.

I get rid of it as quickly as I can, and pull up my home screen. It's almost eleven. I head back down the pier, weaving through the summer tourist crowds, and cross over from the promenade to get back into town. I stop at a small café on the way and buy myself a coffee, and use their bathroom to freshen up. Grime clings to me from the night shift and the journey, but washing my face in the sink doesn't help. My eyes seem redder than before, any traces of Liam's concealer lost from under them. I finger-comb my hair into a neater ponytail and chew on a handful of mints. It'll have to do.

Poppy's former housemate Emily – the sketchbook drawing with the rollers – is working full-time in Primark over the summer, and she works Mondays. She never told me this, but I dug into her social media accounts and found enough references to piece it together.

#working9to5

Staff discount yaaaassss #primarni

#ihatemondays

I work my way across a busy street, crowds and buses clogging up my path, and into the shop. It's equally busy and chaotic, clothes littering the floor, hangers clattering. It takes me a while to find Emily, but eventually I spot her outside the changing rooms, in a crop top and jeans with a high ponytail, ushering a queue of women into cubicles one at a time. I grab a T-shirt off a rail and join them.

'One item? Take this and go to number three.' She looks only at the T-shirt, not me, and tries to hand me a board with a one on it.

'Emily?'

She looks up now.

'I'm Clementine Harris, Poppy's sister. I'm sorry for coming here like this, but can we talk?'

Her face goes slack, like she doesn't know how to react.

'I'm working,' she eventually says. 'Just take the number.'

I don't. 'I have a few questions. It would really help me if you try to answer them. Please?'

She rubs her lips together, her powdery mauve lipstick somehow still pristine. Then she sighs. 'Fine. Rick? Rick! Come take over here for a sec, yeah? I've gotta, um . . . help this lady pick some jeans.'

Her colleague takes over and I follow Emily to a corner of the shop. She keeps glancing around furtively, even when we stop behind a large shelf of bags.

'What is it?' she asks, crossing her arms. Her tone is combative. 'What do you want?'

'I wanted to ask you about Poppy.'

'I already told you everything. She was shy, we didn't see her. I don't know what else you want me to say.'

'I know, I read your statement. The thing is . . .' I think about Daniel being blocked by his sister's friends, and his own mother sectioning him. 'I'm trying to piece together her last few weeks, just to get a better impression of what happened. I want to understand why she did it. And I thought maybe you could help.'

'Why me?' Somehow, she crosses her arms even further, jutting her jaw out. 'I barely ever saw her.'

'Maybe not, but you lived with her. In your interview, you said you heard her crying sometimes in her room. You're the only person who ever noticed anything like that.'

Emily blinks at me. 'So?'

'*So*, can you remember when you heard her crying? Was there a reason for it? Did she ever mention anything to you?'

'I don't remember.'

'Can you try? Please? I know you weren't friends as such, but you must have spoken sometimes. You must have noticed something.'

Emily looks away, dragging her nails up and down her arms.

'I really didn't know her. We'd see each other in the kitchen and stuff, she'd say hi, but that was it. I – She –' Emily sighs. 'Look, I'm not proud of it, but I thought she was weird, okay? I didn't *want* to be friends, even though she kind of tried to be. Our flat would go out a lot and I'd just, like, forget to invite her. So she was there alone a lot.'

Emily looks at me, then looks away again. She fiddles with her hair, her nails, the hem of her top.

'She was lonely, I guess.'

I know my sister better than any inattentive housemate. Maybe she missed our parents, but Poppy was used to being alone. She *liked* being alone.

'Are you sure she was lonely?'

'Yep,' Emily says quickly. 'Must've been.'

'But you can't say for sure that's why she was crying?'

'What else would it be? She didn't have any friends.'

'Well, there could be lots of other reasons. Did someone upset her, or argue with her? Did she feel unsafe? Was there anything to suggest she was scared? Please, Emily. Think. I *need* to know why she was crying.'

'I don't know why.'

'Well, can you remember when she cried? Maybe we can narrow it down, somehow. Which term was it? Autumn, or spring? Before or after Christmas? Right before her death, or—'

'I don't know!' Emily snaps.

'Why not?'

'Because I never heard her crying!'

She peeks up at me, her mouth scrunched and her eyes glistening like her eyeshadow.

'I lied, okay? I feel so bad about it now, but I thought she was weird and I pushed her away, and then suddenly she was dead and the police came and this officer guy wanted to talk about her, but, like . . . I didn't know anything about her, and I was ashamed that I didn't know, and I thought they'd judge me for not knowing, so

I . . . I lied. Just a little lie. Because she must've cried a lot, being alone in her room so much. And if I'd been a nicer person, I'd have known that.'

Emily pats at her face, trying to blot her tears away without ruining her make-up.

'You never heard her crying?' I repeat, trying to process it. '*Never?*'

She shakes her head, biting her lip. 'I'm sorry. I had no idea she was suicidal. I would've been nicer to her if I had.'

Emily turns away and starts straightening things on a shelf, sniffing.

She lied. There were no tears, and no history of Brighton sadness. The coroner concluded that Poppy was 'clearly' unhappy in the months leading up to her death – *because* of Emily's statement. Emily's statement was the only piece of evidence that pre-dated the clifftop Google searches. If Emily hadn't lied, maybe the coroner would have explored other options. Maybe the police would have been involved. Maybe Poppy's killer would have been caught.

'Excuse me, could you help me with maternity clothes? I'm not sure about sizing.'

A customer smiles politely at Emily from behind us, cradling her baby bump.

'Yeah, sure.' Emily shakes off our conversation, flicking her ponytail over her shoulder. She points. 'Maternity's over there. I'll take you.'

Emily starts off with her customer.

'Emily, wait.' I try not to sound angry, but it leaks out regardless.

'I'll be with you in a sec,' she tells her customer, before trudging back. 'What? I have to get back to work.'

'Are you *sure* you never saw her with anyone? Or noticed anything unusual or . . . suspicious? Did anyone ever—?'

'I don't know *anything*. Seriously. I wish I did! I wish I could say the right thing and not have to hate myself every day for excluding her. I wish I could help you, but I can't. Now can I get back to work so I can stop thinking about this, please?'

I grip my backpack straps. 'Yes, of course. Sorry.'

She sets off towards her customer – slowly.

'If I remember anything, I'll message you,' she says. 'But I've been thinking about this every day for, what, five, six months? And I haven't been able to find a reason for it yet. Honestly? She seemed okay. She seemed happy.'

◆ ◆ ◆

I trail back down to the beach and cross the pebbles to get to the sea.

It glimmers and sparkles, lapping gently against the stones, inspiring a hundred different drawings in Poppy's sketchbooks – but I hate it. This water killed her. Not the fall, not the physical injuries, but the water. It covered her and flooded her lungs as she tried to fight it, broken limbs useless, legs paralysed, unable to scream. This water pulled her to its depths, even though her body never left the shallows.

I want to hurl stones and scream, but I sink to the ground instead.

There are no avenues left to explore. Poppy confided in no one. No one in Brighton noticed her. She didn't have friends. She didn't tell anyone anything about what might have brought her to the cliff that night, or who might have followed her there.

Brighton is as much of a dead end as her bedroom was.

Coldness sweeps across me, chilling my skin. The horizon of the sea is gone: there is only fog. A sea mist rolls across the beach, drenching the promenade and surrounding streets in murky dullness. The sun is blocked, and the mist swirls in the air like smoke.

I stay on the beach, the stones digging into my legs, until my whole body is shivering. I imagine the chill travelling through every cell, punishing each one in turn.

Poppy was happy here. Shy and solitary, yes, but happy. Her art was thriving, she loved the city, she had wholesome hobbies to fill her time with. But because of Emily's statement – Emily's *lie* – her happiness was erased. That one remark about her crying alone in her room obscured everything: every positive tweet; every cheery Instagram post. It was too easy for the coroner to take that one piece of evidence to create an entire narrative around it.

That wouldn't have happened if I'd acted sooner. I could have searched Poppy's things months ago, I could have made this journey when the sight of Poppy in her red winter coat was still fresh in people's minds, and I'd have been able to offer the coroner another perspective. I could have alerted the police. But now it's too late. The inquest has concluded. The trail has gone cold. Nobody remembers my sister – or if they do, they remember her wrong. They remember the lie the killer wanted them to.

Whoever pushed her didn't only rob her of the future she should have had – they also rewrote her past. And I'm not sure there's any way left for me to restore it.

I leave the beach and head east, passing Brighton Pier, the marina, and miles of imposing chalk as I follow a path along the undercliff. My feet ache, my throat is dry, and my bare arms shiver, but I keep walking, only ever seeing a few dozen yards in front of me, my destination lost to the mist.

On this macabre walking tour of my sister's life, there's only one place left to see.

The undercliff walkway runs out and I climb to the top of the cliffs, following the coastal path as it skirts a town called Peacehaven and slowly starts to descend downwards to an estuary.

The sea mist has cleared a little in the breeze, thinning out enough to give a patchy view across the water – to the curving town of Seaford and the abrupt high point of Seaford Head. On the other side of it is Hope Gap, where Poppy died.

I head down the slope.

My phone beeps in my pocket – once, twice, more. I haven't told anyone where I am. It could be Mum and Dad asking after me, or Liam checking up on me, or Daniel with news of his own search.

I unlock my phone and open the notification.

Tinder: New message from Harry!

It isn't any of my friends. It's the stranger from before – the smiling, outdoorsy man with blond floppy hair and glasses and a comfy jumper, posed in front of a strip of idyllic countryside. A string of messages are below his name.

> *Hi*
>
> *Sorry if this is weird*
>
> *I just have to ask*
>
> *Are you Poppy's sister?*

The hairs on my cold arms stand up even further. I read the question a few times, trying to get it to sink in. Am I delirious? This can't be real. How does this stranger know Poppy?

Yes, I write back. *Who are you?*

> *A friend*
>
> *I know her*

Knew her

Before she died

Poppy didn't have any friends. Everyone said it. She was a loner. Alone.

What do you want? I type.

Can we talk?

What about? I ask.

About her

About what happened

Why she did it.

The mist swirls thickly again, blocking out everything around me. I can't see Seaford Head any more, or the edge of the cliffs beside me. I feel disorientated. Nauseous.

I get it if you don't want to talk

And I'm sorry for springing this on you

But your profile came up this morning and I looked at your pictures and saw the one of Poppy

And I realised you must be her sister from all the science stuff

So yeah

If you want to talk I'm free tonight

I navigate to my Tinder profile and check the photos Jenna uploaded for me. The last one is me with Poppy, her hair ginger like Mum's and mine dark like Dad's, as we sit together on the family bench on the towpath.

I touch the screen. Her smile is so bright, so wide. Her arm is around my waist, her smaller body leaning into mine, squeezing me, getting as close as possible. I have my arm around her shoulder, the automatic protective stance of the older sibling.

I go back to Harry's message.

Tonight? I send back.

Yeah

I'm busy right now but I can meet you later

The Grey Hare? 7?

I scroll back up to his previous messages: *Can we talk? About her. About what happened. About why she did it.*

I've walked for three hours and many miles, draining myself, pummelling the soles of my feet and deepening the ache in my shoulders, to get to Hope Gap. To see where my sister's life ended. But I turn my back on it and begin the slow, painful walk back to Brighton.

I'll be there, I send.

Whoever this Harry is, he has information. And I'm going to get it.

ELIZA

11 Months Before Poppy

I turn up the new Spiritbox album, scoop Ratilda out of her cage, and stretch out on the bed, Ratilda crawling over my legs. I open Tinder.

Things start as they always do: a man with a pouting mirror selfie and a firm, hard swipe left from me to get rid of it.

Snapchat dog filter – I prefer humans, actually. Left.

New to Cardiff, looking for a tour guide! – Not sure that implying dating you is like volunteering for a dull, unpaid job is the best strategy to stand out from the crowd. Left.

New here, show me around? – For God's sake . . .

Man smiling with kid: *The kid in the photos isn't mine.* – Then why the hell are you sharing pictures of them online? Left.

Looking for a partner in crime to go on adventures with. – Wow, coincidence, I'm looking for a generic phrase person to do generic phrase things with. Left.

I love food and TV and holidays. – Plus breathing and circulating blood around your body, I expect. Left.

Why do none of you bitches on here reply lol. – Really? You don't know why? Left.

Looking for someone beautiful, intelligent, respectful, compassionate, hilarious, and sexy. Bonus points if you have brown hair and eyes. – I know I am, but what are you? A jerk, that's what. Left.

Cheeky chappy from England. Here for uni. Looking for the Stacey to my Gavin lol. – How original! Oh my God! I have literally never seen this exact joke on any kind of dating app ever before! Left.

Looking for a girl for my friend and me to play with. – I think I just threw up in my mouth a little bit. Left.

That same stupid picture of Machu Picchu everyone has. – Left.

Three pictures of his boy-racer car. – Turn left at Rejection Avenue and keep on going.

Bio entirely in emojis. – ←

In your town for one night only. – And dragging a collection of STIs with you, too, I bet. Left.

Why the hell should I message you first?? – Wow, I love being made to feel like communicating with me is a chore. Literally my kink. Left.

Photo of a bare torso and pulled-down jeans: *Daddy looking for a bad girl to punish.* – Ah, definitely one to introduce to the parents. Left.

Looking for a reason to delete Tinder. – And I'm looking for a personality. Left.

My 3 kids are my world and no girl is EVER going to replace them so don't even try. – Don't worry, I won't. Left.

Eight blurry selfies taken in the seat of a car. – What is this, the man/car version of a centaur? Left.

Looking for a girl who doesn't take herself too seriously. – AKA won't mind you refusing to commit because you want to shag other people. Left.

Only here to get laid, don't get attached. – At least he's honest about it. Left.

Looking for my next ex girlfriend. – WHY? Left.
Looking for the Stacy to my Gavin! Not this again – Left.
Looking for the Pam to my Jim. – Urgh. Left.
Searching for the Morticia to my Gomez.

I pull my finger away from the screen.

Frederick, 21. Long black hair, black clothes, black fingernails. His eyeliner-ringed eyes are dark and intense, staring straight at me as the snake wrapped around his arm does the same.

Right.

It's a match!

Our pictures – him with the snake, me with Ratilda perched on my shoulder – join together in a heart. I chew on my lip ring. I need to say something. What should I say?

I start typing something out, but his message pops up first.

Nice rat.

Nice snake, I reply. *This is Ratilda, destroyer of my house-mate's cushions. Who's that?*

This is Edgar, eater of cockroaches and my enemies.

Do you have a lot of enemies?

Not any more.

I smirk, tapping out a message with my own black-nailed fingers.

What do you do, Frederick? Aside from reptile-based revenge?

161

I'm a student of pain and torture. I seek to bring fear to children and adults alike across the globe, the mere mention of my occupation filling them with an inescapable, visceral terror. I will be the monster they fear, the fate they dread.

He pauses.

Dentist.

Wow. I have never matched with such pure evil before. What made you want to go into such a sadistic line of work?

Who among us doesn't wish to be feared like a vengeful god? To look down upon our cowering victims and inflict deep, traumatic pain that will stay with them for the rest of their lives?

He pauses, again.

Also, the pay is good.

How will you spend your blood-soaked riches?

I shall purchase Spiritbox tickets, and have many familiars, and wear only the highest quality fingerless gloves.

May I also suggest Kat Von D eyeliner? It's the best on the market. Pricey, but lasts all day. Perfect for striking fear into the hearts of small children.

Thanks for the recommendation! I'll add it to my shopping list. So, Eliza, what do you do?

I am a student of the dark arts. I seek to learn the secrets of the human mind, to take the spongy grey matter and bend it to my will. All shall fall once I have mastered my craft.

I wait for a beat, like he did.

Psychology.

I feel your power already.

Ratilda nuzzles my neck, her little paws clinging to my skin. I stroke her from nose to tail, smiling.

What do you want to do with a psychology degree? Frederick asks. *Aside from manipulating the masses, of course.*

I'm interested in criminal or forensic psychology.

Catching murderers?

Yes. I'd love that.

Really? What are the signs someone could be a murderer?

It depends on the person. Some are outwardly unhinged — the kind who chop off heads in the street — while others are cool and calm, hiding beneath layers of lies. But there are certain signs. Psychopaths don't yawn when others do, because their brains can't form bonds like other humans' can.

An average person can't resist yawning when they see someone else do it. It's a natural impulse.

What other signs are there?

People look to the left when they lie. Murderers often return to the scene of the crime, or join the search for missing persons. They like to feel involved. Special.

I'm typing out more when there's knocking on my door. Hard, angry knocking. I huff and open it.

'What?' I ask Hayley. She's wearing a pink bedsheet, her blonde hair a mess. There's a love bite on her neck.

'Turn your music down! Oh my God, I can't even hear myself think. And *yuck*, put that rat away! Ew!'

I take Ratilda off my shoulder and hold her out towards Hayley. 'Who, her? This little thing?'

Hayley backs off, her face screwed up.

'Music off. It's, like, so rude.'

I raise my eyebrows. 'Rude? It's not even half eight yet.'

'That's not the point.'

'No, the point is that I don't want to have to listen to you and whichever guy you've got over shagging for hours. So if you're going to be screaming guys' names and have your headboard banging against *my* wall, I'm going to block it out with whatever music I want to. Okay? Or should I get in touch with the long-distance boyfriend of yours and see what he thinks about it?'

Hayley glares, her cheeks flushing.

'All right, freak, keep your music. You're just jealous because nobody wants to sleep with a fat weirdo like you. I bet you've never even kissed anyone but that rat.'

She slams her bedroom door as hard as she can, rattling the walls. I hear her screech over the music: '*That goth loser is such a bitch!*'

I settle back on my bed and pick up my phone. There's a message waiting for me.

> *I'd love to pick your brain about all this. I could learn a lot. Would you like to meet up sometime?*

I chew on my lip ring again, my music barely drowning out Hayley's insults on the other side of the wall. Screw it.

> *Are you free now?* I ask.

There's a pause, then Frederick's reply pops up.

> *Absolutely. Have you ever been to the old pub by the cemetery? I hear it's haunted. Nine o'clock?*

> *I'll be there.*

I get up, put Ratilda back into her cage, and freshen up before leaving: extra eyeshadow, my darkest lipstick. I grab my bag as another message arrives.

How do you know I'm not a murderer trying to lure you to your death? Frederick asks.

I don't, I reply. *But if you are, I'm sure I'll figure it out.*

I pull on my leather jacket and flick off the light, leaving my music blasting.

Hayley won't even know I'm gone.

CHAPTER 15

I get to the pub just after seven. It's tucked away in the North Laine and looks warm and inviting, stacks of dripping candles and fairy lights glimmering against dark wood, with leafy plants wedged against walls and indie music on the stereo. It's modestly busy, people in T-shirts avoiding the chill of the lingering sea mist out-doors. It seems to have followed me inside, the coldness cloaking my flesh even as I glance around the pub, to find a blond-haired man waving at me from the corner.

Harry looks the same as his photo: floppy hair, glasses, a knit-ted jumper.

I take a seat opposite him, my backpack on my lap.

'Hi, Clemmie. I'm Harry.'

'It's Clementine,' I say, more sternly than I mean to. Poppy was the only person who ever called me Clemmie. She was the only person I allowed to.

'Oh, right, sorry. *Clementine*. Well, thanks for coming. I got us some lager. I don't know if it's your cup of tea, but it's local and—'

I gulp down a few mouthfuls, grateful for any kind of liquid. He does the same, then sits there, fiddling with his glass, staring.

'This is a bit awkward, isn't it?' he says. 'I don't quite know where to—'

'How did you know my sister?'

'Straight in then? Okay.' He takes another quick sip of lager. 'We were friends.'

My gut squirms. Poppy didn't have friends in Brighton. She barely had any in London, shy as she was.

Jenna used to use Tinder a lot. Once, she came back to the flat fuming because the woman she'd set out to meet – Scarlett, a dancer – had turned out to be a hairy barista called Todd who thought he could change her sexuality. People lie all the time on the internet, don't they? Perhaps Harry is lying now.

'Were you at uni with her?' I ask. 'Are you an artist?'

'God, no, I can barely draw a stick person. No, we both love animals, so we'd talk about them a lot, and the countryside, and nature in general, really. She'd send me pictures sometimes, drawings. I can't draw to save my life, but I'd send her photos back. Sunsets, animals, that sort of thing. I volunteer at a wildlife rescue centre – I'm training to be a vet – so I'd always send her pics of the foxes who came in, and she'd send me back pics of the foxes she saw in the street.' He stretches his leg out, pointing at his fox-print socks. 'I love foxes.'

He wraps his hands around his glass.

'We used to talk a lot. Every day. I . . . I really cared about her.'

I dig my nails into the backpack on my lap.

'If you cared about her, why weren't you at her funeral?'

He wasn't there. Her housemates weren't there. Nobody from Brighton came at all. If this man cared about Poppy, if they really were friends, he'd have been there.

'I didn't know she was dead.' He stares at his half-empty lager, swilling it around in the glass. 'We talked every day for a month or two, we were really close, but then she just stopped replying. When I didn't hear from her, I thought maybe she just didn't want to be friends any more. Maybe she felt things were awkward. But then a few days ago I saw my dad's copy of the local newspaper and it was open with a little picture of her on it, talking about a suicide verdict, and . . .' He shakes his head, abandoning the glass. 'I had no idea.'

Something about this isn't right. It feels off. *He* feels off. How could he not know?

'But you said you were friends. Didn't you notice she wasn't around?'

'I was up in Surrey. That's where my vet course is. I just come back for the holidays to help on my parents' farm.'

'But surely someone would have told you about it? A mutual friend?'

'We didn't have mutual friends. I only knew *her*. And . . . we never actually met. We only ever texted.'

'What?' I think back to her social media accounts, her Reddit posts. 'You met online?'

'Kind of.' He rubs his neck. 'Look, I won't lie, it's a little embarrassing, but . . . we matched on Tinder. We hit it off right away, we got on so well, but I had to go back to Surrey for uni, and she was studying down here, and, well . . . to be honest, I wanted to date her and she didn't want to date me. So we were just friends who texted.'

The words don't quite go in.

'Tinder? My sister was on Tinder? Are you sure?'

'Yes, I'm sure. We matched months ago.' He rubs his forehead. 'Sorry, *obviously* it was months ago. We matched in early January, in the few days between her arriving and me leaving. It was definitely shortly after New Year's. I remember her saying her resolution was to explore more of the countryside on her bike.'

'*What's your New Year's resolution, Clemmie?*' Poppy asked, silver confetti in her hair from Mum's party poppers, the music and explosions of the fireworks on the TV. '*Mine's to get up to Devil's Dyke on my bike. Dad's bringing it back to Brighton for me!*'

He's telling the truth. He knew her. But it doesn't make sense.

Poppy was too shy to buy items from sales assistants or talk to her housemates. How could she talk to strangers?

Jenna used to show me her app sometimes: profile after profile of smiling faces, messages popping up, dates being arranged.

I can't picture that for Poppy.

'I searched Poppy's phone and I didn't find anything related to Tinder,' I say. 'There weren't any dating apps. And I don't remember seeing your name come up, either. I went through her messages and contacts. All of them. You weren't there.'

'Really?' His face falls. 'Oh. Maybe she deleted it? She . . . died in February, right?'

'Yes. The twenty-third.'

He gets his phone out and scrolls on it. I watch from across the table, seeing it upside down: a WhatsApp conversation with Poppy's name and photo there, but the screen filled with unanswered messages from Harry.

Hey! Did you see the sunrise this morning??

Still sleeping?

Hi, you okay?

Ground control to major Pop

You been eaten by foxes or something?

Are you okay?

It looks like my thread with Jenna.

'That explains why there was only ever one check mark, I suppose. My messages were sent, but not delivered to her phone. Um, the last time she replied was the day before that.' He scrolls back up to a photo: a fox in the middle of a dark street.

Look who I found on the way home from the post office!

'Why would she delete your information?' I ask.

'I don't know.' He scrolls further up, photos of sunsets and foxes and cats and art flashing by. I see the photo of Poppy from her Instagram, the one of her with the sunset behind her. She definitely sent them. He turns off the screen and looks up at me. 'I was her friend. Even if she didn't feel the same way back, we were friendly. I swear.'

I drink some more of my lager. I'm dehydrated and my thoughts feel thick and slow. The lager only slows them down further.

Poppy on Tinder. It doesn't make sense. It doesn't feel right. Why couldn't I find the app on her phone? Why have I never heard of Harry?

He leans forward, burying his hands in his sleeves.

'Ever since I read about her death, I can't stop thinking about her. If she'd just talked to me that night . . .'

He rubs his face as my guilty conscience twists inside me.

'I have to know, Clementine. Why did she do it?'

He stares at me, eyes begging for an answer. He knew her. He cared about her. They were friends. Friends who met on Tinder.

'Did she match with anyone else?' I ask, saying the words as soon as they come to me. 'On Tinder?'

'Well, yeah!' Harry laughs, leaning back in his chair with his pint. 'Of course she did.'

I blink at him.

'How else did you think she met her boyfriend?'

Even though I saw Poppy's picture on Harry's phone and he knows details about her he couldn't possibly know otherwise, he's got the wrong person. He's mistaken.

'She and him matched around the same time we did, after it, I think, and . . . well, I think maybe that's why she didn't want to date me. Because she liked him more. And that's okay! I mean, it happens a lot.' He clears his throat. 'But I was happy to be her friend. Honestly. I didn't make it weird for them. I was happy *she* was happy with someone, even if it wasn't me.'

'My sister didn't have a boyfriend.'

Harry looks at me as though I'm mad. 'Yes, she did.'

Pain stings in my temples, threading inwards. This can't be true. Not Poppy. Not shy, nervous little Poppy.

But then I remember the breaths on the voicemail. The unlocked phone. The Google searches she didn't write.

'Who? Who was he?'

Harry frowns. 'You haven't spoken to him?'

'This is the first I've ever heard of a boyfriend.'

'Because . . . because Poppy didn't put a label on it, you mean? Maybe they never made it official? Did you think he was just a friend when you saw him at the funeral?'

'He wasn't at the funeral.' I try to think back to that day: the sunflowers on her coffin; the slideshow of photos I couldn't bear to look at. 'There was no one from Brighton there. It was family, mostly. A couple of old teachers, old school friends. People I knew. That was it. No boyfriend. I've never heard of a boyfriend. Neither had the coroner, or her housemates. There was no mention of him at the inquest. There was nothing on her phone about him.'

The killer used Poppy's phone after they pushed her. They'd have to know her passcode to unlock it.

A boyfriend would know her well enough to know her passcode.

'That's . . . that's weird,' Harry stammers. 'I'm not making this up, I swear. She *told me* she was seeing someone. She was smitten with him. We always talked about this kind of stuff. Our Tinder

171

matches, our dates. Well, my matches, and my lack of dates. I think she wanted me to find someone, too, so she encouraged me to keep using the app, and to tell her about it. We talked in a sort of code. I'd tell her who I matched or met up with, and we'd give them anonymous nicknames. The Lithuanian, Chihuahua Chick, i360 Selfie Girl, that sort of thing. Mine were always different, because, you know, I couldn't find anyone else I liked, but she just had him.'

'And what nickname did he have?'

'The Photographer.'

I pull my folder out of my bag and flip to the red section: *Suspects.* I uncap my pen, ready to add information to the empty page I have clipped in.

'What's that you've got there?'

'Who is he?' I ask, ignoring Harry's question. 'The Photographer?'

'Oh, I don't know.'

'You don't know his name?'

'I told you, we always spoke in code. I never even asked.'

'Did you see a picture of him?'

'No.'

'A description? Hair colour, eye colour? Anything?'

'No, she never said.'

'What *do* you know about him, then?'

'Not much, really. Just that he's into photography and . . . and they'd go do arty things, and he made her happy, and he'd take her to loads of different places to watch the sunset together.'

I grip the pen so tightly it almost snaps, thinking of the Sunday sunsets Poppy and I watched from all over London.

That was *our* thing.

'What about astronomy?' I ask. 'Did he ever take her to see the stars?'

'I don't know. She mostly talked about the sunsets.'

'Did she have plans to see him the night she died?'

'She didn't mention anything. It was just that fox picture she sent to me. It was a Friday, wasn't it? I don't think they normally saw each other on Fridays. He worked evening events, I think? You know, photographing gigs and things.'

'Did he have a temper? Did they fall out? Were there any arguments?'

Harry huffs embarrassedly, hiding behind his drink. 'You're really overestimating how much we talked about him. I didn't ask questions, okay? I . . . I liked her, still. Not in a creepy, pining over her from afar kind of way, but the feeling didn't just go away. So, aside from being polite, and listening to her when she wanted to talk about it, I really didn't want to know.'

I stare at the two useless words on the page: *The Photographer.*

My sister texted Harry – a stranger – about her new boyfriend, but she never texted me about either of them. Why not? Why didn't she tell me about this part of her life? Why would she keep it a secret?

'She was really happy,' Harry says, smiling sadly into his empty glass. 'I know I didn't know her like you did, but I could tell. She was in love. So for her to end her life that way, and end the relationship . . . Well, there must not have been a relationship to end any more.'

'What do you mean?'

He sighs heavily. 'He broke up with her, didn't he? That's why you don't know him. He broke her heart, and it broke her. She didn't want to live without him. And, I don't know, maybe she deleted all trace of him before she did it? And deleted me, too. Depressed people get like that, don't they? They push people away. I wish I'd known. For months, I assumed she'd ghosted me because things got awkward. I had no idea she was gone. I . . . I kept hoping she'd change her mind and pop up again one day, like she used to, but without the boyfriend this time, so I could finally meet her in person, and tell her how I felt, and take her with me to feed the foxes.'

Harry stands up. 'Do you want another drink?'

'No. No, thank you.'

'Well, I definitely need one. Be right back.'

He hurries to the bar, clawing at his hair with both hands, trying to dispel a pain I know too well.

Poppy had a boyfriend. They used to view nature together. She purposefully left her room in the middle of the night to head to a cliff edge.

Did they go together? Did he ask her to meet him there? Did she go alone and he followed her?

Did he push her and cover it up?

I glance around the pub. It's got busier, friends laughing over pints, and couples twisting their fingers together by candlelight. Men are everywhere: behind the bar, in the seats, walking along the street outside.

Any of those men could be him. The Photographer. Harry has no idea what he looked like. There were no photos. How am I supposed to know who I'm looking for?

But then he comes to me, sharpening into focus as Jude said the callers at the helpline do in his head: the pencil drawing in Poppy's sketchbook. The man half hidden behind a camera, his one eye burning with an intense emotion I can't place.

The Photographer.

I dig her sketchbook out of my bag and rifle through it, my fingers shaking, until I get to the end of her used pages. There he is.

It's more sinister than I remember. The one visible eye is dark and intense, and the eyebrow is harshly curved. Maybe Poppy saw it as a smile, but it wasn't. It's a smirk. A challenge.

Catch me if you can.

I run my fingers across the stubs of torn-out pages that separate The Photographer from the rest of the clean, untouched sketchbook. His eye smirks its sinister smirk at those empty pages – at the evidence that's now missing.

The sketchbook was in Poppy's bag that night. He pushed her, then tore out the pages that showed his face. He unlocked her phone with the passcode he'd seen her use and deleted himself from it. He blocked Harry; deleted Tinder. He planted the Google searches. He called me. He taunted me in the voicemail, his breath barely perceptible, eye smirking, the hands that killed my sister touching all her things, tainting them, destroying any trace of evidence that might lead back to him.

Apart from this one drawing – the drawing that tells me nothing.

He wanted to gloat.

I glance around the pub again, focusing on eyes, searching for professional cameras. The Photographer could be anyone in this city. He could be in this pub. He could be right in front of me.

'Got you another one anyway, Clemmie. Sorry, *Clementine*.'

Harry hands me a pint, but I don't drink it. I can't remember how to drink. My body feels disconnected and strange, my brain lurching between terrible thoughts.

Did The Photographer follow the news about Poppy's death, waiting to see if anyone figured it out? Did he go to the inquest? Did he celebrate the verdict?

Did he go down the wooden steps to the beach that night after he'd pushed her and stand above her, smirking, as he waited for the tide to come in and finish the job? Did she call out to him to help her? Did she love him, even then?

The ladies' toilets are at the back of the pub, and I make it into a cubicle just in time. Tears streak down my face as I grip the edge of the bowl, trying not to think about it, trying not to picture it.

But how do you get rid of an image like that?

How can I forget?

I wash my face at the sink afterwards, the red pinprick dots of burst capillaries around my eyes the only colour left in my skin. I dig out a handful of mints from my bag and chew on them as I shove the folder and sketchbook back inside, out of the way. I don't have information to put into the sections any more. I only have more questions.

A boyfriend. Why didn't she tell me? Why didn't she write me her usual letters? They'd have been all about him. Did the killer destroy them that night? Or did she never . . . ?

I swallow a jagged lump of mints.

The last thing Poppy sent to Harry was a photo of a fox, with a caption.

Look who I found on the way home from the post office!

The post office. For years, she could never face sending my letters to me via airmail because it meant talking to a cashier. She left them in bundles for me on my bed, wrapped up in ribbon.

But there were no letters in her things.

Did the killer somehow destroy them that night – or did she manage to send them before he could?

Jenna's name is still at the top of my most-used contacts when I unlock my phone, even after six months, but I scroll past her name. I hit Raj's, and wait.

'Clementine?' he whispers, his voice comfortingly familiar – and dismissive. 'I'm in the library. Can I call you back later?'

'That's Clem?' I hear Paolo say, followed by a struggle. 'Clementine! I am here. Are you okay? You haven't returned our texts! We're worried. Jenna says—'

'Did any post come for me? At the apartment?'

'Um, uh, yes? I think I remember some things. Junk, I thought. I put it on your desk.'

'Was there anything from the UK? Airmail? With a handwritten address?'

'I don't remember exactly. Raj? Did Clementine get airmail? With a written address?'

'It would have been a while ago. March, maybe. Did I get something in March?'

'Um, okay, he says yes. There was a parcel, he thinks? With drawings on it. A star, an orange dog—'

'A fox.'

She sent them to me. For the first time ever, she plucked up the courage to send a bundle of letters to Boston – but I wasn't there to receive them.

Paolo inhales sharply. '*Oh*, is this . . . from your sister?' He swears in Italian. 'I did not know it was here. I am so sorry. If I knew there was something sitting here this whole time, I would have . . .'

'I need to know what they say,' I say to Paolo. 'It's important.'

'Of course, I can go home right now and—'

'I need you to open them and, I don't know, take photos, scan them in, whatever. But I need to see every letter. I need copies, as soon as you can get them to me.' The tears come, even though I try to fight them. 'I need to know who hurt her.'

I wipe at my nose, sniffing – hearing nothing but my own repressed sobs.

'Paolo? Are you there?'

I check my phone. The battery's dead.

The letters are in Boston. They're *safe*. And as soon as I charge my phone, I can read them and find out just who The Photographer is.

I pull the sketchbook back out of my bag and flick to his face, to his sinister *catch me if you can* expression.

I can catch him. And I will.

CHAPTER 16

There's nothing more to be done in Brighton. At least not tonight.

I make my excuses to Harry and head back to London by train, my investigation folder open on the table. I jot down everything I can think of about The Photographer in the *Suspects* section: the sunset outings, his job photographing gigs, him meeting Poppy on a dating app. These things could be important later on. Once I charge my phone and sort through the scanned letters Paolo will have sent me, I'll know more about The Photographer. I'll know enough to be able to find him.

And I will find him.

Liam is on the sofa watching TV when I get back to the flat. I try to slip past him to my bedroom, but he hears me. He turns and leans his elbows on the back of the sofa, the TV flickering behind him, his head at a cutesy angle.

'Hey, stranger. Where have you been?'

I wonder if he can smell the sea air on me, whether he remembers I'm in the same clothes as yesterday.

'I had to go back in for another helpline shift. A few people were off sick.'

'That's a long day. You need a break! Come join me. I made brownies.'

'Thanks, but I need sleep. I'm exhausted.'

He checks my face, his eyes lingering on mine. 'Forget exhausted, you look half dead! Are you okay?'

'I'm fine, I just need to sleep.'

I say goodnight and head to my room. What I *need* right now is a charged battery.

I plug my phone in next to my bed and wait for it to have enough energy to turn on. Once it does, it chimes and vibrates with missed calls and texts from Paolo, and one from Jenna.

> *Clem, I'm so sorry. I had no idea she'd sent something to you. I'm gonna get it to you straight away. x*

I check my email, but there are no scans or photos of any letters yet. I raise my plugged-in phone and call Paolo.

'Clem!' he scolds. 'Where did you go? We've been trying to reach you for hours.'

'Sorry, my battery died. Did you open the parcel yet? It was letters, right? A bundle of letters tied up in string? What did they say? Have you scanned them yet? I need to know about her boyfriend. I don't have a name yet, but I think he was involved. Did they mention a boyfriend?'

'I . . . I don't know.'

'Can you check? Please?'

'I can't.'

I check my watch. 'Why not? Are you still in class?'

'Clem, we don't have the parcel any more.'

'What?'

'I . . . I thought you wanted it sent to you. Jenna FedEx'd it as soon as we got off the phone. She insisted. And she didn't open it. She said it was private. None of us saw what was in there. It's already in the mail.'

179

I feel sick again. I had the answers, they were *right there*, but now they've slipped through my fingers. How long does it take to receive something from the US? Days? Weeks? And what if it gets lost in the post? It made the journey across the Atlantic once, but what if it isn't as lucky next time? What if I lose my one chance of identifying Poppy's killer?

'Is the parcel tracked? Was the packaging secure? When is it supposed to get here?'

I hear Paolo's muffled voice repeat the questions, and another muffled voice feed him the answers.

'Very secure. The parcel has a tracking link, Jenna will send it to you, and delivery should take three to five days.'

Three to five *days*. Today is Monday. I might not get the letters until Saturday.

'We're sorry, Clem. We thought this was what you wanted. We were trying to help.'

'Okay,' I say – tersely. I can't keep it out of my voice. 'Thanks. Bye.'

I end the call.

It's not their fault, I *know* that, but I can't trust my own anger. I sit on the edge of the bed with my phone, smacking the ignore button every time it pops up with a name: Paolo, Paolo, Raj, Paolo, Jenna – Daniel.

I answer.

'Clem! There you are.'

'I'm here. Is everything okay? Are you okay?'

'I am now, but I was worried. I've been trying to reach you for hours. Did you turn your phone off after your shift last night?'

I remember the stack of missed calls that popped up when I turned my phone on.

'Sorry, my battery died while I was in Brighton. I only just got back.'

'Brighton? You went to Brighton?'

'Yes. The emails weren't working, so I thought I might find something if I approached people directly.'

'And did you find something?'

'Yes.' I lean back on the bed, craving its comfort – but my body is too tense to feel it. 'Poppy had a boyfriend. I had no idea, I couldn't believe it, but one of her friends told me she was seeing someone, and they had proof. There were messages where she talked about him. And . . . I think it was him, Daniel. I think he's the one who murdered her.'

There's a pause before Daniel responds. He's probably out smoking again, pacing the streets like he always does when he can't sleep. I try to picture it, him pacing in Kent, rather than the cliff. Rather than Poppy.

'Who is he?' he asks, breathlessly. 'Who's the boyfriend?'

I rub my forehead, feeling the day's grime on my skin. 'I don't know. I didn't get a name or description, and it looks like he deleted himself from her phone afterwards. But I know he's a photographer. There's a drawing of him in her sketchbook.'

'There is? I bet the police can identify him from it!'

'They can't. His face is hidden behind a camera. It's not enough.'

'Really? Damn.'

'But there might be something better in Poppy's letters.'

'Letters? I thought you said there weren't any letters?'

'I found them. Well, sort of. She posted them hours before she died, but to Boston. They've been sitting in my bedroom all this time.' I swallow down the guilt of it, tucking it away for later. 'My friends have forwarded them to me. So, by Saturday, I should know all about him. She'll have written about him, I'm sure of it. There could be pictures or photos. A name. He deleted himself from her phone and ripped out pages of himself from her sketchbook, but he couldn't destroy what she'd already sent. This is how I'll find him.'

'Whoa. That's amazing.' But his voice is dull, down. 'You're gonna know everything.'

He goes quiet again, inhaling and exhaling. It reminds me, suddenly, of the silence before he spoke during our helpline call.

'Is everything okay, Daniel?'

'Yeah, I just . . .' He swears, and it sounds like he kicks something. 'Sorry. I'm happy for you, I *am*, but I'm just . . . I'm jealous, okay? I've been trying to prove Rachel's murder for two years, and all I've found are dead ends. Then you get a breakthrough like this after two *days*.'

'I'm sorry.'

'No, don't be sorry! I'm glad you've found this. You deserve it. I wouldn't want you to waste years, like I did. But . . . but I feel like I'm never going to find anything now. There are no magic letters for Rachel that are gonna give me the answers.'

'Keep looking.'

'I have been looking! Her friends won't talk to me! There's nothing in her stuff!'

'I found Rachel's friend by chance. I wasn't looking for him, but he found me on Tinder and messaged me and—'

'Wait, you're on Tinder?'

'The point is, Poppy had a friend I didn't know about. And if we hadn't crossed paths like this, I wouldn't know about the letters *or* The Photographer.'

'The Photographer?'

'Her boyfriend. That's what she used to call him. So Rachel may have had a friend like that, too. The person who has that information for you might be someone you simply don't know about yet. Maybe a driver saw someone approach her that night, or a neighbour saw something, or she had an online penpal she

182

mentioned things to. You've got to keep trying, Daniel. Don't give up.'

It's easy to say these things to him now, but a few hours ago, I felt just as hopeless as he did.

'Okay. I won't give up. I *will* find something.' He almost sounds like he believes it. 'When will you get the letters?'

'In three to five days. That's when I'll know who he is, and when I can go to the police.'

'They're gonna take you seriously, Clem. I know it.'

'I hope so.'

The glare from the ceiling light is painful. I squeeze my eyes shut, but it isn't enough. I cover them, too.

'Daniel, I . . . I should have known she'd leave letters for me. I should have gone back to Boston. If I'd gone back, I'd have found them. I'd already know all this. If I'd known six months ago, who-ever killed her could have already been arrested. I'd know why he did this to her. But I didn't go back, and he nearly got away with it. He's been free for six months. She was classed as suicidal, and he's been free. It isn't fair, that he's living his life while hers was—'

The floor outside my bedroom creaks, but Liam doesn't knock. He's outside again, worrying about me, trying to understand what's wrong with me. I roll and pull the duvet over me, cocooning myself, muffling out the world so it's just Daniel and me – the only two people who could ever understand.

'I'm going to find him, Daniel. In three to five days, I'll know enough to find him.'

But right now, three to five days feels like an eternity.

183

CHAPTER 17

Over the next four days, I prepare my investigation folder to give to the police once the letters arrive.

I do a thorough rundown of Poppy's personality, likes and dislikes, her anxiety, her hobbies, her outlook, her character – and how her actions were *out* of character. Using the disclosure documents from the inquest, I highlight the errors made by the coroner: Emily's false testimony about hearing Poppy cry; the cherry-picked films and series mentioned when the pages of her Netflix history show she watched dozens of cheerful ones too; how Poppy's research of Beachy Head was for an art project; the convenient clifftop Google searches; the breathing on the voicemail that doesn't sound like Poppy's.

I check her phone and find one blocked number: Harry's. Their WhatsApp messages have been completely wiped, including any photos shared between them. I even reinstall Tinder, hoping there will be a record of her match with The Photographer, but her account no longer exists. There's a saved password for it, but it doesn't connect to anything. I've researched Tinder enough to know how unlikely it would be to find any clues there, even if he hadn't deleted her account: when one person unmatches, the entire conversation is erased by default. Torching her account was just for fun.

I pad out the folder with the things I *do* know, and have sleepless nights about the things I don't.

Who is The Photographer? And why did he kill my sister? Until I get the letters, I have no way of knowing.

◆ ◆ ◆

'Well, if it isn't my favourite flatmate,' Liam says, waving at me from the kitchen as I head for the front door on Friday morning. He's sat up on the counter, legs crossed in fashionably ripped jeans, his pop music blasting from the speaker. 'Morning, C!'

'Morning. Any deliveries?'

'No, nothing yet. What is it you're waiting for? A Klingon rhyming dictionary?' He turns down his music a bit, winking.

'Something like that.'

I check the tracking link Jenna forwarded to my email: the parcel is in the UK, but the expected delivery is tomorrow. I put my phone away again, sighing.

'You're stressed,' he says. 'I don't know what you've been getting up to in that bedroom of yours, but you need a break from it. No more library trips or days spent hunched over a laptop, okay?'

He jumps down from the counter, the chalkboard still scribbled with yesterday's message: *Don't worry! Be happy!*

'I'm on a later shift today, so I've got the morning free for you. How about I make us some smoothies and we veg out in front of the TV? Or I could teach you some yoga moves? I mean, it's *hot* today, but you can have the fan on you. Or, ooh! I could pamper you. Manicure, pedicure, face mask, haircut . . .'

He's a whirlwind of ideas, fluttering around me, touching my shoulders, my hands, my hair. His cheeriness, however well intended, is exhausting. Before I can duck away, he pulls my hair loose from its usual ponytail and runs his fingers through it, inspecting it.

'I could take off an inch or two, easy. Make things a bit neater. When did you last get it cut?'

'I don't know. Back in Boston, I think.'

'So, like, six months? Hun, it's time for a trim, for sure. What do you think? This much off?'

He holds up a section of hair, his fingers clamped two inches from the ends.

It takes a long time for hair to grow. Years. How old is this bottom chunk? Three years? Four? Five? Was it there with me in Cambridge when I was taking my final exams? Did it come on that family holiday to Dorset where Poppy tried to hop across a river and ended up soaked to her skin, squealing with laughter like the rest of us, a frog stowed away in her wellington boot?

One day, someone will cut off the last piece of hair that lived at the same time she did.

I sweep my hair out of Liam's fingers and back into a ponytail.

'Maybe another time. I'm helping out at the café today.'

'Oh, okay. I'm glad you're going back there. It's good to have a routine.'

I already have a routine, but spending every waking hour checking unhelpful emails and scouring Poppy's already picked-clean social media sites is feeling less productive by the day. I've run out of things I can do. I *need* those letters. I *need* to know who The Photographer is.

'Let me know if you need anything, though,' Liam says. 'Whatever it is, I'm always here to help. If you ever need to—'

'How do you find a stranger online?' I ask, cutting off whatever Liam was saying.

'What do you mean?'

'I mean, is there a way to locate someone on the internet even if you don't know much about them? So, maybe if you didn't know their name or what they looked like, but you had the location where they lived, and a hobby.'

'What hobby?'

'Photography.'

'Err, well, people who do photography are usually on Instagram, and it usually tags your location when you post, so you could maybe filter through people using local hashtags, and see who comes up? But, um, why? Did you see a pretty guy with a camera on your way to the library and forget to ask for his number?' He pulls a face. 'Are you trying to stalk a *boy*?'

A familiar sickness rears up in me as I think of the drawing of The Photographer in Poppy's sketchbook. An eye, a ruffle of hair, a hand gripping the camera and pressing the shutter. Those fingers must have trailed through Poppy's hair, linked through her fingers – pushed her from the cliff.

'No, I . . . I was just curious.'

'Sure, sure.' He winks at me again. 'But if you want to stay here with me and stalk boys on the internet, I'm happy to be your accomplice. In fact, I would love it.'

I fiddle with my pockets. Why does he want me to stay?

Liam is the sort of person other people naturally gravitate to. After months in London, he should have a collection of bold, gregarious friends to drink cocktails, dance, and visit art galleries with. He should be busy every night and every free day. But instead he stays in this tiny flat with just me for company, and he acts like that's enough.

Jenna was the same. She could have had any best friend she wanted, but she settled for me: a friend she had to drag away from her books for a bit of attention; a friend who doesn't answer her messages.

She asked me months ago if I wanted her to forward my post, but I swept her message away like the rest of them. I couldn't face talking to her then, and I still can't. I went to Raj and Paolo for Poppy's letters instead. Even now, there's a new message on my phone from her with the latest tracking details, and asking how I am. Reaching out to me.

But I can't reply. Not when every thought of being with her takes me back to Poppy alone on that beach. Will there ever be a day when it doesn't?

'I have to go.' I head to the front door, but Liam stops me before I open it.

'Wait, C. Come here.'

He pulls me into a firm hug, arms wrapped low around my shoulders, and sways me. It's so abrupt, I don't know how to respond.

'C, we're friends. I care about you, even if you feel mostly indifferent to me and wish I'd stop hugging you.' He sways me more, chuckling. 'I just want you to be happy, okay? Because you deserve it.'

He pulls back and gives me a firm kiss on my forehead.

'I *know* you're not okay right now. After what happened with your sister, you have every right to not feel okay. But don't shut everyone out. I'm here for you, whether you need a shoulder to cry on or a big fat distraction. Anything goes. And the offer of a haircut still stands, by the way.'

He smiles at me, beaming, his arms still around me.

His hair has flopped down over one eye, and the other sharpens like a pencil drawing.

'Thanks, but I still have to go.'

I disengage from the hug as quickly as I can and get out into the hallway, shutting the door behind me.

'Oh!'

Alexander jumps back, eyes bulging wide behind his glasses, a magazine clutched in his hands.

'Hello?'

'Sorry, you startled me. I was just about to slide this under your door. Particle physics today. Interesting stuff. Thought you'd like it.'

His glasses droop down his freckled nose and he pushes them back up, attempting a smile. It comes out a nervous, goofy grin. His eyes dart to the door behind me, as though checking Liam isn't eavesdropping. Then he passes the magazine to me.

'Page thirty-four. I marked it with a Post-it, in case you couldn't find it. Not that I think you don't know how magazine numbering works . . .'

'Um, thank you.'

I think about going back into the flat and throwing it on the pile with the rest of the unread clippings he's slipped under the door, but think better of it. I unzip my bag and slide it in between Poppy's sketchbook and my folder.

'Colour-coded dividers! Must be a big project you're working on. Is it for your thesis?'

'It's . . . Yes. But I'm a little stumped right now. I'm waiting on some new data, and I can't really do much until I get it.'

'I hate that! It's awful when you're raring to go but don't have the tools to do it. One time when I was working on red dwarfs, my lecturer—'

Music blasts through the walls of Alexander's flat, the bass reverberating so much that we can feel it through our shoes. Alexander cringes, fiddling with the straps of his own hefty backpack.

'Sorry, my flatmate is a complete git. I have to sleep with earplugs, and even that doesn't help. Does it keep you up, too?'

'No, I can't really hear it from my room.'

'Well, that's something, at least.' He covers his ear, and points to the stairs. 'Where are you off to?'

'I'm helping at the café today.'

'Are you? I was just heading there myself. Shall we walk together by the canal?'

My instinct is to say no and find another route – but if I do that, I'll be stuck with thoughts of Poppy and The Photographer, checking every face I pass, looking for a charcoal eye, a sketch of hair.

Perhaps Liam is right, and a distraction is what I need.

We walk together along the towpath. Alexander talks with his hands: big, sweeping movements, so absorbed in his thoughts that he doesn't notice he almost knocks a cyclist into the canal when talking about *The Martian*.

After what feels like only a couple of minutes of back-and-forth conversation and energetic nodding, we're at the café.

'. . . and that's why *Star Trek: Discovery* is the best thing to happen to the franchise in years,' Alexander says.

'I agree completely, but it feels as though we're in the minority.'

'Well, everyone else is wrong, and one day they'll come around. Resistance is futile, after all.'

We head into the café, smiling, and part. He joins the queue, and I head for behind the counter – but Dad steps into my path and stops me.

'Clementine, what are you doing here?' His automatic smile is broken. Today he has to manually pull it into place, and it doesn't stay long. 'I thought you were having some time off? Mum said you weren't feeling great the other week. You don't need to be here.'

'But I want to be here. And you need the help.'

I reach for an apron, but Dad stops my hand.

'No, love. We don't need your help.'

There's frost in his words, despite the lingering heatwave. The café is busy, and I've been welcomed here on dozens of days when it wasn't.

It isn't that he doesn't need my help; he just doesn't *want* it.

'Have you been having some proper rests? You look very pale. How about a spot of sunbathing? Or reading by the canal? That sounds nice, doesn't it? Much better than working!'

He laughs, a firm hand pushing me out the door. I look back for Mum, but she's busy at the counter. She hasn't seen me.

She doesn't know what happened to Poppy yet. Neither of them do. They should.

'Dad, I need to tell you something. It's about Poppy's death. She didn't—'

'Not now, love. Please, not now.' He sighs, pressing hard on my shoulders. 'Mum told me what you said the other day, about not believing the inquest verdict.'

'Yes, because—'

'Clementine, I don't want to hear it. We need to heal, all of us, and talking like that won't help. Your mum was very upset the other day after what you said, and I can't have that happening again. It's a good day for her today. Let's keep it that way.'

The conversation is over. He ushers me off the premises – not unkindly, but firmly. He hugs me before he heads back inside, but not with his usual strength. It's as though his heart isn't really in it.

I don't want to sit by the canal, and I don't want to go back to the flat. I want to do something. I want to make progress. I want to help somebody. Anybody.

I shift my backpack and head towards the nearest Tube station. I can be at the helpline in less than an hour.

CHAPTER 18

I take my usual desk in the back corner of the phone room. It's only as I'm unpacking my folder that I remember it's the wrong one, filled with investigation notes instead of my helpline handbook. I think about packing up again and leaving, but someone appears beside me, the smell of coffee wafting between us.

'Hello, Clementine.' Jude smiles, passing me a mug and keeping another for himself. 'I just got here myself. How are you?'

Before I can answer, his phone starts to ring. He apologises and hurries to his seat, grabbing his sketchbook and sliding on his headset. 'Hello. I'm here to listen.'

I sit down, too.

So what if I don't have my handbook? I wrote it. I know everything that's in it. I can cope without it for once.

It's a quiet shift. Jude chats with his caller, but my line doesn't ring. It's another hot, sunny day, and sunshine makes people feel differently, sometimes. More hopeful. Maybe it's the weather and the building pressure in the air, but I feel more hopeful, too.

The letters are in the UK, and I should have them by this time tomorrow. My folder is prepped and ready. The inevitable police investigation I trigger will find CCTV I couldn't, and trace phone records I don't have access to. The police will find Poppy's killer, and justice will be done.

I truly believe that.

The calls pick up as the afternoon wears on. Instead of short bursts of anger or sadness, the calls are long and lingering, made by people who are calling to talk rather than to be talked down. It's like that in the daytime: prisoners not coping with incarceration; housewives dreading picking the kids up from nursery. Lonely people seeking social interaction of any kind. I try to copy Jude as I talk to them, saying far less than I usually do, asking open-ended questions to help them face their problems, letting them know that I'm listening.

I didn't need my handbook after all.

I pack up my things at the end of the shift and check my silent phone, hoping for a notification to do with the delivery of the letters, but there is a text from Jenna.

Hey Clem. The parcel should get to you tomorrow. I'm so sorry for not noticing it sooner. I'm sorry for everything. After you went back to England, I—

I flick the notification away, unread as always. There's a stack of missed calls, too. I turn my screen off and toss the phone in my bag, then head for the exit.

'Hey, Clementine! Hang on.' Jude rushes up behind me, slinging his satchel over his shoulder, a pencil wedged behind his ear. Poppy used to do that. He points to a group of other volunteers in the hall. 'We're going to the pub for some drinks, maybe some food. Fancy joining us?'

An automatic 'no' is already in my mouth, but the volunteers wave and smile and beckon me over. I don't recognise them, but they seem to know me. I've never paid much attention to the people I share this room with. I suppose I must have shared shifts with Jude long before I noticed him.

Poppy was always, *always* shy – but she didn't want to be. She used to say it was a cruel genetic mistake that I got all the confidence while she got all the social skills, and she was right. I thought nothing of joining the hockey team, or debate club, or moving abroad, or giving lectures, or talking to strangers, but Poppy couldn't do any of those things. She longed to, though. She'd whisper the right words to me at family events, but could never voice them herself. She hid behind me. She needed someone to take her hand and do these things *with* her.

I never did that enough while she was alive.

I feel the ghost of her hand tugging on my wrist now, whispering lines into my ear.

This is what Poppy would have wanted me to do.

'All right,' I say to Jude, nodding. 'I'll come.'

The pub has a traditional feel, with stained-glass windows, padded bar stools, and thick wooden tables. It's crowded. We squeeze around a table, and Jude comes back from the bar with a tray of chilled drinks. The other helpline volunteers all know each other and settle into an easy, familiar chat about partners and children, traffic and hobbies.

'Clementine here is a *scientist*,' Jude says, as a middle-aged woman bemoans her son's GCSE results. 'So if he needs a tutor for the retakes, you're covered!'

The woman playfully whacks Jude's arm, but turns to me regardless. 'Are you really a scientist? That's amazing! What field?'

I tell her about my work in Boston, which inevitably triggers the questions about Harvard.

'*What's it like?*'

'*What's your IQ?*'

'*What do you do for fun?*'

I haven't thought about Boston properly for a long time. I try not to. I keep the memory of it unfocused, like a reflection in disturbed water. I never let myself wait for the ripples to settle.

But as I talk, the old routine settles back into my mental calendar, pushing aside café shifts and stints at the helpline and the last sleepless week of investigation. My life wasn't always this. I had friends, hobbies. We'd sit around tables like this one, talking about science, talking about the future; Jenna's warm, easy smile always seeking me out, the way Jude's does now.

'Are you going back in the autumn?'

The question knocks the wind out of me.

For so long now, I haven't been able to imagine any sort of future for myself. Not beyond one plagued by guilt and grief and unanswered questions. But I have those answers now, don't I? I'm on the brink of knowing *everything*; of setting the record straight about what happened to Poppy.

Once I've done that, what comes after?

I picture boarding a plane, climbing the steps to our apartment, fighting with the lock that always, always sticks the first time, unpacking my things, straightening the books on my desk, sitting on the sofa with Jenna as we grade papers, laughing, chatting about *Star Trek* theories, her lounging with her feet hanging over the armrest, casual, friendly, just like we were before.

Can we ever go back to how it was before?

'I'm not sure,' I say to Jude. 'Maybe. Does anyone want another drink?'

I'm grateful for the queue at the bar because the long wait gives me time for the conversation to move on, far away from Boston and the things I no longer want to talk about.

After the next round, the volunteers begin to peel off home. I go to the toilets and return to find our table empty, my backpack gone.

'Clementine! Over here!'

Jude waves at me from a side table, one with only two seats. My bag is there, and another drink. I join him, putting the bag between my ankles so I can feel it.

'Sorry, the others ditched us and I didn't feel right hogging that huge table. Is this okay?'

'Yes, it's fine.'

A barman collecting glasses leans over to light a candle between us. The orange glow flickers in Jude's eyes.

'They're fun, aren't they? The other listeners. We come here a fair bit. Shifts can be so isolating sometimes, it helps to sit together and reset back into normal life. It's easy to take the negativity of the phone room home with us.' He sips his drink. 'I'm really glad you came out tonight, Clementine.'

'Me too.'

Aside from that one night with Liam, this is the first time I've had a 'normal' evening with friends in six months. But noting that fact ruins it, reminding me in a rush of *why*.

'I don't want to pry,' Jude says gently, 'but I know you're struggling right now. If you want to talk about it, I'm here. Honestly, no judgement, whatever it is. But you don't have to feel it alone.'

He smiles his usual kind smile – the one I usually turn away from. Do I need to talk about it? I have Daniel to confide in, but his uncertainty brings no comfort to mine. Perhaps an outside perspective is what I need.

I tuck some loose hair behind my ears.

'I found out something about my sister recently. Before she died, she had a boyfriend.'

He tilts his head a little – the polite version of a shrug. 'And was that unusual?'

'Very. She was incredibly shy, I doubt she'd ever even kissed anyone before, let alone talked to a boy. Apparently she was in love with him, and then she died.' I twist my drink in my hands, feeling the coolness of the condensation. Getting up the courage to share the theory. 'I think he had something to do with it.'

Jude sips his beer, nodding.

'I can guess what happened.'

'You can?'

'Of course. It's what happened with me.' He taps his wrist. 'When my heart was broken, I thought there was nothing to live for, too. It wasn't the only reason, but it was the catalyst for me. I'm so sorry your sister felt the same way.'

'No, that's not what I meant. She didn't take her life because of heartbreak.'

'Heartbreak is a kind of grief, Clementine. I know from the outside it may seem . . . insulting, almost, to say that, because death is a complete loss, but heartbreak shakes you to your core. It *hurts*, physically. It's like there's a piece of you that the other person has taken, and you can never get it back. They're gone, but not through illness or death – they just don't want you in their lives any more.' He shakes his head. 'I wouldn't wish that feeling on anyone.'

Jude's words make more sense than I expect them to – but they're not relevant. Not to Poppy.

'I'm going to find out who he is,' I say. 'The boyfriend.'

Jude pauses mid-sip. He swallows carefully and places his glass back down on the table.

'Is that wise?'

'Why wouldn't it be? He's responsible for her death.'

'No.' Jude smiles sadly, touching my wrist. 'You mustn't think like that. Poppy made her decision, and while it may have been triggered by what happened between her and her ex, it wasn't his fault. You can't blame him. He probably already blames himself.'

'But—'

'Don't go looking for him. Please. It isn't healthy. With a death like this, we want someone to blame, but there isn't anyone. There's no closure to be had. We have to find it within ourselves. Finding this man won't bring you any comfort, I promise you.'

He's being obtuse. I have a folder of evidence in my bag to prove to him why I'm right, why this is far more than a case of a broken heart triggering suicide – but I keep my backpack at my ankles, zipped shut.

He's used to talking to people with mental health needs. I don't want him to accuse me of having them.

'My sister posted letters to my address in Boston before she died. I only just found out. That's why I didn't know about the boyfriend. But they're being delivered tomorrow, and I'll know all about him. I'll read everything she wrote. I'll know exactly what happened between them.'

'Wow, that's . . . going to be difficult to read. Her final words to you. I can't even imagine.'

I fiddle with my glass.

I hadn't thought of that. I thought about finding out about the killer, getting his name and picture to the police, catching him – but these are the last letters Poppy will ever send me. The last time I see new words in her handwriting; the last time there's something left to discover about her. They'll go into the drawer in my room with the others, shut away from the sunlight, left to gather dust. And she will be truly silent.

'What was she like?' Jude asks, knowing just what to say, as always. 'Tell me about her. Tell me all the fantastic things there are to know about Poppy.'

In the candlelight, Jude smiles at me, open and inviting.

And I smile back.

CHAPTER 19

Jude and I leave the pub sometime later and walk towards the Underground together. The air is hot and dense with humidity, pressing in on us, buzzing with friction. Raindrops start to fall. They're rare at first, just the occasional ding against the roof of a parked car, but the noise increases. The occasional spot becomes a sheet of rain, streaking lines through the lamplit street in front of us, hitting us like bullets.

'Wild weather!' Jude cries. 'Come on!'

We try to run for the Tube station, but we're soaked in moments. We make it across a road before Jude grabs me, laughing hysterically, and points to a door with a tiny alcove above it. He pulls me against it, his arms locking me into the small patch of street that isn't pulsating with thrashing rain. I grab him back. He holds me there, our skin dripping, as the rain cascades deafeningly around us.

It's as though we're on the other side of a waterfall.

Jude is still laughing, good-natured even in a downpour. I find myself laughing, too.

'We may have timed our exit a little badly there,' Jude says, reaching past me to wipe his face with the back of his hand. 'Pretty much the worst moment we could have left. Let's see how long it's supposed to last.'

Jude contorts, trying to fish out his phone without exposing either of us to the rain. 'Oh my God, that's biblical.' He shows me his weather app, a satellite projection of a huge, dense raincloud directly over London, neon crosses marking lightning strikes. One lights up the street around us, followed by a deep rumble.

'Screw this, let's get an Uber. Where do you live?'

He orders one to my address and gets his phone back into his pocket. His puts his arm where it was: looped around my shoulder, pulling me towards him and shielding me from the rain. We're cramped together, chest to chest, wet clothes sticking to each other. Rainwater trickles through our hair, tracing cool, meandering paths against our skin.

'. . . and it was down a street like this,' a woman in Victorian attire with a huge umbrella shouts, dragging a wet tour group with her past our alcove, 'where Jack the Ripper would hunt for his victims. Dressed as a respectable gentleman, he could lure vulnerable women to quiet, secluded spots and—'

Thunder roars around us. Somewhere nearby the rain sets off a car alarm. The tour group rushes away and the back street becomes empty once more.

'This definitely isn't how I expected tonight to end,' Jude says, still laughing. He shifts a little, looking at me directly. His dark curls hang over his face, dripping. He shakes, clawing them away. Then he reaches over and gently tucks a bit of wet hair behind my own ear, brushing a raindrop from my cheek. He doesn't pull his hand away.

Our thin, wet tops are like second skins, a permeable membrane that connects us. I can feel the warmth of his body through them. My hands feel awkward suddenly, too aware of themselves and where they rest, and I don't know where to look. But Jude keeps looking at me. The moment reminds me of Boston, suddenly.

That night in the snow, Jenna taking my hand, stopping in shop doorways to brush the snowflakes from my cheek, her eyes on my lips, her lips finding mine, or maybe mine finding hers, and—

A car screeches to a halt on the road, beeping, and we both jump. Jude steadies me.

'That's our ride. Ready?' He grabs my hand. 'Run!'

He drags me through the waterfall and bundles me into the back of the Uber, then climbs in after me. He says something and the driver sets off, tutting, as the windows steam up.

I heave my backpack on to my lap and tear it open, checking on my folder, the sketchbook. They're dry. I lean back, sighing – thankful for sensible, waterproof purchases.

'What's that?' Jude asks before I shut the bag again, trying not to let any drops sneak in. 'Oh, your handbook? Is it okay?'

'It's fine.'

'Good.' He flips open his leather satchel and checks on his own sketchbook. 'Phew, mine too. Good thing my knitwear isn't dry-clean only, though.'

He grabs a fistful of his cardigan and squeezes, the wrung-out water leaking on to his already wet jeans. Looking down, my white T-shirt has gone see-through. I cross my arms over my chest.

The city is a blur of lightning and artificial light as we're driven north-west. I can't place where we are. Jude, still laughing, talks about getting caught in the rain in the countryside once and hiding in an old barn with a bull he didn't realise was there until too late. I tell him about Poppy demanding we wait on a wet Primrose Hill for the sunset.

The car stops abruptly and the driver says my address.

'How much do I owe you?' I ask Jude, digging out my purse.

'Nothing. It's fine. It's my fault you got caught in the rain anyway.'

'Don't be silly.' I press a note into his hand. He takes it, warm fingers touching my skin.

'Thank you for coming out with us tonight. The others loved you. They told me before they left.'

'Oh.' I don't know what to say to that. 'Um, thank you for inviting me.'

'Any time. Seriously, you're always welcome to join us. We go every Friday, but you and I could always go somewhere another day, if you wanted to.'

'I mostly do night shifts.'

'Well, I know a few local places that do early morning coffee. The good kind. We could always make it breakfast instead.'

I picture it: a table for two, small cups of artisan coffee with steam rising from the swirling froth, warm eggs and toast, Jude's face, smiling as always, the glow of sunrise all around him.

I know what Poppy would want me to say – but this time, I won't say it.

'Um, I should go.'

'Of course. Goodnight, Clementine. I really enjoyed—'

I climb out into the rain, staring up into it like a cool shower.

Forget Boston. Forget Jenna. Forget that night, with its magic and beauty and charm, because that's when Poppy died. That night was cursed. Forget it. *Forget it.*

I rub my face, and head for the flat.

A figure sits on the steps to the flat, head bowed, a bottle beside them. Their hands are fumbling in front of them, a tiny glimmer of orange appearing and reappearing. A lighter. They're trying to light a cigarette. They can't do it. The lighter glints again as the person throws it at the ground, the damp cigarette joining it. The person looks up, showing me their face. Their messy, mousy brown hair. They pull their hood down over their eyes, hunching forward.

I run the distance to the steps, the rain blinding me as I splash through puddles. I cover my eyes, squinting.

'Daniel?'

Daniel looks up, his eyes large and blinking unevenly. He's soaked, his clothes hanging baggily from his thin frame, water dripping from his ratty hair.

'Where've you been?' he asks. His words are slurred, and his lip trembles. 'I called you. I called you so many times, but you didn't answer. You told me you'd always answer.'

His face is wet, but it isn't just the rain. Even in the unnatural glow of the streetlamps, I can see the painful redness in his eyes, the puffiness, the deep, dark shadows. He's crying. Why is he crying?

'I needed to talk to you, but you weren't there. I needed you, Clem. But you weren't there.'

Guilt surges through me. There were missed calls on my phone when I saw Jenna's text. I assumed they were from her, I chucked my phone in my bag, and . . . kept it on silent.

'Daniel, I'm sorry, I—' My voice catches. This is like that night. I was out, having fun, and someone I care about needed me. But I didn't care. I didn't check. I ignored my phone, and someone died.

I can't let that happen again.

'I'm so sorry,' I say again, sitting next to him on the steps. I touch his shoulder. 'What is it? What's wrong? Did you find something in Kent?'

'No!' He rubs his face, sniffling. 'I didn't find anything. There's *nothing*. I can't prove who killed her. I don't know who would. I . . . I've failed her.'

'You haven't. You're doing everything you can. It isn't your fault if there's nothing to find.'

'But you said there *would* be something!' He flinches away from me, shaking my hand off him. 'You got my hopes up, like . . .

like I could be normal and not a nutcase, but I still am. Nobody believes me. This is just how things were before!'

He hunches over again, grabbing at his hair, rocking. I reach for him, but he smacks me away.

'Stop it! Stop trying to comfort me! Whoever killed Rachel is gonna get away with it for ever, and it's my fault. I didn't do enough. I'm stupid! I'm crazy! I—'

'Is everything okay here?'

Daniel's shouts die in his throat, his face frozen in a snarl.

Jude stands in front of us, wearing his usual concerned expression from the phone room. He must have been watching from the car.

I wish he hadn't been.

'It's fine,' I say hurriedly. 'Daniel's a bit upset tonight, but it's fine. We're good. You can go.'

'It's no trouble,' Jude says, stepping a little closer. He looks at me pointedly. 'I can stay.'

'Stay?' Daniel says. 'Nobody's asking you to stay, mate. Mind your own business. This doesn't concern you. Jog on.'

Jude doesn't move.

'What are you staring at? Piss off!'

Jude glances at me. 'Clementine, what—?'

'*Clementine?*' Daniel repeats. He rounds on me. 'You know this weirdo?'

'Yes. His name is Jude. He's from the helpline. We had a shift earlier, and then we went for a drink, and—'

'Oh, a drink? That's where you were while I was waiting for you? Getting drinks?' He staggers to his feet, pointing wildly. 'Snogging in the back of an Uber?'

'Hey,' Jude says quickly. 'Let's just sit down for a bit, yeah? Take some deep breaths?'

'Don't tell me what to do. You don't know me. Do you even know her? Do you know what happened to her sister? To both our sisters?'

'Daniel,' I say, leaping up after him. 'Calm down.'

Recognition passes over Jude's face. 'Daniel, is it? I do know you. We've spoken before, at the helpline. We talked about your sister.'

'You don't know anything about my sister!'

Daniel lunges at Jude, but I pull him back.

'I remember him. He's just like the rest of them. Everyone thinks like him, Clem. Nobody will ever believe me.'

'They will,' I soothe. 'You'll find something. I can go to Kent with you. We'll prove it. We can—'

'Get you help,' Jude says loudly. 'I know some great counsellors, and the best support groups. I can refer you. We can get you the help you need. It won't always hurt like this. You can get better, Daniel.'

'I'm not mad!' he shouts. He backs away from us, grabbing for the bottle on the steps. 'I know what happened. It happened. It happened to her sister, too. If I'm mad, so's she.' He tries to take a swig of vodka, but there's nothing left. He bashes it against the wall in his fist, broken glass fragmenting like rain. Then he points at me. 'She's a psycho, too.'

'Daniel, you're . . . you're bleeding.'

'Huh?' He checks his hand: blood drips from his palm, diluting to a misty pink in the rain. He shakes it off. 'It doesn't matter. None of this matters. What's the point of anything any more? I . . . I . . .'

He slumps back down on to the step, burying his face in his hands. Even with the thrashing rain, I can hear him sobbing.

Jude steps towards him, but I stop him.

'Daniel,' I say, winding my arm around him. He doesn't push me off this time. He grabs my other arm, leaning into me, crying against my chest. 'It's okay. Let's get you upstairs, okay? Jude will help.'

'Okay. Let's go upstairs.'

Jude and I scoop him up, taking an arm each over our shoulders. Daniel sags, but we manage to get him into the building and up the stairs to the flat. Jude digs a knitted hat out of his bag and presses it to Daniel's palm.

'Sorry,' he mumbles, not looking up. 'I'm sorry.'

'You're back late,' Liam calls from the sofa as we come in. 'I hope you're hungry, because I gave in and ordered pizza and I've also made the mother of all Victoria sponge ca—'

He gapes at us, then gets to his feet and approaches, wrapping his arms around himself. 'What's going on? Who are they?'

'Uh, friends,' I say. 'Do you have a first aid kit anywhere? Daniel's hurt his hand.'

Daniel sniffles beside me, head still down, tears and rain dripping from his cheeks.

Liam, pink and perfect as usual, hesitates – then nods. 'Yeah, sure. Hang on.'

He disappears into the bathroom and digs it out of the cabinet. Jude and I get Daniel on to the sofa. Liam returns, hovering as Jude chucks his open satchel on the floor and drags the coffee table over, then grabs the first aid kit. Liam looks between us all: Daniel, a mess; Jude, calm and reliable as he always seems to be; and me, somehow in the middle of them. He pulls me aside.

'Okay, seriously, what's going on? You've never brought a guy back before, and now you rock up with *two*? And you're covered in blood?'

I check myself: blood is smeared across my already wet T-shirt, diluting out to pink. 'It was an accident, and they're from the helpline. Jude is a listener, like me. He was dropping me off, but Daniel was already here.'

'Daniel?' Liam frowns. 'Who's Daniel?'

I forgot I never told Liam about him. I decide on a half-truth.

'He's from the support group. We met a couple of weeks ago, and I've been trying to help him.'

'Well, that looks like it's going well.' Liam bites his lip. 'Is he okay? Why is he bleeding? Why is he here?'

'He . . . he's not well. But I can help him.'

'Hey, buddy,' Jude says to Daniel in his soothing phone-room voice. 'How are you doing? Do you want to talk about it?'

Daniel shakes his head violently, hunched over.

'Okay, that's fine. We don't have to talk. But I do need to look at that cut. Is it okay if I—?'

'No!' Daniel snaps his arm away from Jude and clamps it to his chest. 'I . . . I'll do it. I just . . . Don't touch me. Please. Just leave me alone.'

He hunches over again, rocking on the sofa, knees pulled up to his chest, twitching like a spider trapped under a glass. Jude nods and we back away towards the bedrooms. The flat is so small that it's barely any distance.

'I'll talk to him,' I whisper. 'He'll be all right.'

'You don't know that,' Jude says. His tone is different from usual. Colder.

'Yes, I do.'

Jude opens his mouth to say something, but glances at Liam. 'Hey, do you have some spare towels anywhere? He could use one. He must be freezing.'

'Yeah, of course,' Liam says. 'I'll dig some out.'

'Thanks, mate.'

Liam glances between us, then heads to the bathroom again. When he's out of sight, Jude rounds on me.

'You're in contact with someone from the helpline?' he whispers incredulously. 'That's against our policy. We never give our personal details, we *never* get involved in their lives. You don't know him. He could be dangerous.'

'We met by chance, and he *isn't* dangerous.'

'Then what was that outside? He tried to punch me. He pushed *you*.' Jude takes a furious breath and sighs it out. 'You shouldn't have done this. What were you *thinking*?'

His tone cuts me to the core. It's the same as when my physics professor gave me a dressing down about a failed exam in front of the class – but it was a computer error. I'd got full marks but been assigned the wrong grade. I hadn't done anything wrong.

I knew it then, and I know it now. I cross my arms.

'I think you should go.'

Jude blinks at me like he can't believe it. Then his face hardens.

'If that's what you want, fine.'

Jude heads back to the sofa and grabs his satchel from the floor, tugging the buckles closed. He leaves his bloody hat on the table. 'Hope you feel better soon,' he says to Daniel. Then he strides down the hallway and opens the front door.

A magazine falls across the threshold, like it was leant against the door. He picks it up and comes back in to hand it to me.

When we're close, he whispers again.

'You think you can help him, but what if you can't? He's delusional, you know that. He's chasing a murderer who doesn't exist. It's not healthy, and . . .'

'What?'

'I heard you the first time you spoke to him, Clementine. I heard what you said about your sister, about how you thought her suicide didn't make sense. I don't want him infecting you with this delusion, or giving you false hope. You need to heal, not chase phantoms. The helpline rules are there for a reason, for callers *and* for listeners. They're there to protect you.'

'From what? From *him*?'

Daniel is scrunched up on the sofa, shaking, staring at nothing. He looks like a child.

'You don't know him.'

Jude's face, usually so friendly, seems harsh and bitter. There's no warmth in it now; no crinkle of kindness around his eyes. It's as though he left his empathy in the phone room.

I don't recognise him.

'I don't know you, either,' I say. 'Daniel needs help and you resent me giving it? You want me to turn him away? No wonder you always look so relaxed at the helpline. You don't even care about the people on the other end of the line.'

I snatch the magazine out of Jude's hand and point at the door.

'You can go now.'

Jude walks a few steps before turning back, shaking his head. 'I hope you know what you're doing.'

And for the first time since I've known him, Jude leaves without a smile.

The door bangs shut and Liam shuffles up beside me.

'Everything okay, hun? What was that about? Why did he leave? I couldn't – I mean, I *didn't* hear.'

I sigh and take the stack of towels from him. 'Thanks, but I can take it from here.'

'What? I'm not leaving you alone with a guy who's both bleeding *and* crying. Let me help. I'm good at first aid. I did a course. Well, one class. More of a pamphlet, actually. But I can help.'

I smile at him, at his fun hair and colourful T-shirt and cheery manner, and turn back to Daniel. 'Thank you, but I'm the only one he'll talk to.'

'Okay, if you're sure. Give me a shout if you need me, okay? Seriously.'

He gives me a reassuring shoulder squeeze and heads inside his bedroom, closing the door with deliberate slowness. I raise my eyebrows at him, and he closes it properly. I head over to Daniel, draping a towel around his shoulders and sitting beside him.

I sigh and hug my knees, too.

'Daniel, I should have checked my phone. It was loud in the pub and I didn't hear it, but that's no excuse. I promised you I'd always answer, but I didn't. You needed me and I wasn't there. I'm sorry. I mean it. I let you down.'

The words are painful. They come out covered in barbs, carrying hundreds of different unsaid apologies.

Daniel looks up. His wet eyes are big. His mouth trembles into something like a smile.

'You didn't let me down. Don't say that.' His unhurt hand finds mine, his cold fingers wrapping around mine. 'I'm just drunk and horrible tonight. I'm sorry, too. You didn't deserve that. I just . . . Damn it, I really thought I'd find something back there. But it feels like I stirred it all up again just to hurt myself.'

He leans into me again, and I wrap my arm around him.

'Don't fob me off this time,' he says. 'What happens if I can't find anything? What do we do then? If I can't prove it? If the video still isn't enough?'

I rub his shoulder, trying to give him any kind of comfort I can.

I wish I knew.

CHAPTER 20

I stare up at my bedroom ceiling, unable to sleep.

I bandaged Daniel's hand and set him up on the sofa with a blanket, but that isn't what he needed from me tonight. He came here for comfort and reassurance. He wanted me to tell him everything would be okay and we'd find his sister's killer, but I couldn't do that. I couldn't lie. If the police didn't believe video evidence of a hand pushing Rachel in front of that train, would anything else really change their mind?

It's entirely possible he'll never find out who did this, or why.

He must resent me, even if he doesn't say it. He's had two years of this, obsessing every day about a murder he can't prove, but I've made greater strides than him in a week. I know who I need to find.

The Photographer.

I reach for my phone in the dark. There are twenty-six missed calls from Daniel earlier tonight, and dozens of messages. I dismiss them, guilt twisting in my gut, and check the delivery app in case there's an updated estimate for tomorrow.

But the words on the screen say something else: *Package delivered.*

I sit up. Poppy's letters are here. They're *here*.

I get up and look for them. I check all around my bedroom, but Liam must have put them somewhere else. I creep out to check the rest of the flat.

I left the fairy lights on for Daniel, like a night light, and their glow illuminates him now. He looks different when he's asleep. The physical markers are still there – an uneven, overgrown beard, greasy hair, the thinness of his malnourished wrists – but there's a sense of calm on his face. The despair that manifests in his conscious self as nervous tics and deep frown lines has lifted, leaving behind a glimpse of the person he was before all this. He's shifted in his sleep since I tucked him in, and now he hugs one of Liam's fluffy cushions to his chest, lips slightly parted, a piece of hair dancing with every breath. I want to tuck it behind his ear and out of the way, but I leave it to flutter.

He needs to rest, and I need to read.

The kitchen countertops and other surfaces are empty. I check everywhere I can think of, using my phone torch for extra light, but there's no sign of a parcel or envelope. Liam must have put them somewhere strange.

I open his door and a faint beam of light from my phone hits him, face pressed into the pillow, hair uncharacteristically dishevelled, shirtless.

'Liam?' I whisper, trying not to wake Daniel on the sofa. 'Liam, where's my parcel? Where did you put it?'

'Tomorrow,' he groans, rolling on to his back and covering his face with an arm. 'It doesn't come till tomorrow.'

'But the tracker says it's been delivered. You must know—'

He snores lightly, his bare chest rising and falling as he sleeps.

I check the tracking information again. *Package Status: Delivered – left with neighbour 4B.*

Alexander's flat.

I pad out of Liam's room and close the door behind me. It's gone 2 a.m. I can't cross the hallway and knock on the door like I want to, not when Alexander is sleeping – but his housemate's music is still thumping, loud enough for me to hear with a hallway and two sets of walls between us.

I knock on Alexander's front door, hard, and don't stop until someone opens it.

'Yes?'

Alexander squints, his glasses wonky, in a NASA T-shirt and checked pyjama bottoms. Then he recognises me, and straightens his glasses.

'Clementine! Um, what are you doing here? Is it the music? It never bloody stops. I've asked him to turn it down, but he—'

'I'm here for my parcel.'

'Parcel?'

'Yes, a package. You signed for it earlier and I'd like to collect it. It's important.'

He scratches his head, his hair even messier than Liam's. 'I don't know anything about a parcel. I've been at the café all day. I didn't sign for anything.' He glances pointlessly around the dark flat. 'Jay must have done it. Come in, come in. It must be around here somewhere . . .'

He flicks on the light, wincing at its artificial brightness. The flat is a mirror image of mine: one main room leading to a small bathroom, with two bedrooms flanking the side. But it doesn't have Liam's decorative flair. There's something sterile about it, as though it's not quite lived in. Alexander's books are stacked on the coffee table, along with his laptop, but there are no dirty or drying plates by the sink, no pots of coffee haphazardly left out on the counter. Aside from the music blasting from the far room, you wouldn't know somebody lived here.

'Sorry,' Alexander says. 'He's a gamer and he does these competitions in different time zones, so I get *this* until about five a.m. usually.' He yawns, checking around the kitchen. 'Right. Parcel, parcel, parcel . . .'

It's a pointless search. There are no stacks of letters or paper anywhere, and no obvious place to rest post. Alexander checks a few drawers, just in case.

'Are you sure it's here? I never saw anything.'

I show him the tracking information. 'Yes, it's definitely here. I need it, Alexander. It's important.'

His cheeks go pink. 'Oh. Maybe Jay took it into his room by mistake? Wait here, I'll go and check.'

He bustles down to the far bedroom – the mirror of my own – and slips inside, shutting the door behind him. The music is too loud for me to hear anything. After a while, Alexander rushes back out, rubbing his ears, cheeks even redder – a brown Jiffy bag tucked under his arm.

'I thought he was going to punch me then! Said I scared him and he got taken out by a sniper. Anyway, is this it?'

He hands me the Jiffy bag. I hold it carefully, feeling the slight scrunch of the paper and inner bubble wrap around a familiar, solid shape: a bundle of letters. Drawings are scrawled across the packet – stars, a fox, Brighton landmarks – but the writing is neat and precise, my new address written on white paper and trimmed so it doesn't block out a single drawing. Jenna. Even though I asked Paolo, it was Jenna who sent this.

I turn the packet over. It's open.

'Sorry,' Alexander says again, quickly. 'I think Jay thought it was for him. He does it with my things all the time. But I checked, and he put everything back as soon as he realised it wasn't his.'

I fish inside the packet, wishing he wasn't watching me, and pull out the letters.

It's like every other bundle Poppy ever left for me: colourful ribbon; folded paper; postcards; magazine cuttings; her rushed, looping handwriting.

I shove them back inside.

'Letters from a friend?' Alexander asks, rocking on his heels.

'Yes. Well, thank you. Goodnight.'

I don't wait to be shown out. I head back to my flat, staring down at the familiar illustrations and Jenna's neat words, feeling the weight of them in my hands. There are answers here. I'm going to know. I'm –

'Clementine?'

Daniel peeks over the back of the sofa, his hair matted from the rain.

'Sorry,' I whisper on the way to my room. 'I didn't mean to wake you. Go back to sleep.'

He rubs his eyes. 'Where did you go? What's that?'

'Poppy's letters. They were delivered to the flat across the hall.'

He's properly awake now. He sits up, fingers clutching the sofa.

'Did you read them? Do you know who he is?'

'No,' I say. Daniel sighs. 'I haven't read them yet.'

'What are you waiting for? We've got to check them. Now.' He turns around on the sofa, throwing a blanket over his shoulders like a cape and gesturing for me to join him. 'Come on. I'll help.'

'Are you sure? You don't have to be here for this.' I hug the parcel, wondering how to phrase it. 'I don't want you to be upset because I have this, but you didn't find anything in Kent. You know, after how you were earlier . . .'

'Oh, piss off.' He turns on the lamp and crosses his legs on the sofa, pulling the coffee table closer. 'As if I'd let you do this alone. I want to know who this bastard is, too. Sit.'

He doesn't need to tell me twice. I kneel on the floor opposite him, tightening my ponytail, and open the package again. I've done this before. In the lab, couriers would drop off samples for us and I'd unpack them, pulling out delicate glass slides cushioned in bubble wrap or wedged in boxes, entirely aware of how important they were. I do the same with the letters, sliding them out as though they're made of glass, too.

But it isn't like being in the lab. This isn't a sample to tick off a list and put into storage. It's personal. Everything here has meaning.

This term's ribbon is blue. I pull it loose, crisp writing paper and handmade postcards keeping the stack together on the table. Poppy always arranged them in the same way: in chronological order, dated, the first letter on top and the last at the bottom, so I could read through like a diary.

'How shall we do this?' Daniel asks. 'Start at the beginning, or—?'

'Last first.' I turn the stack over and take the letter that was on the bottom. It's in an envelope, so I pull it out and unfold it. The thick paper is Poppy's favourite, the kind Mum bought her last year with a poppy embossed in the corner. The one for special occasions.

I read the first line.

Hey, Clemmie! Surprise – you've got mail!

Pain burns in my chest, and the words blur on the page.

These are the last words she ever wrote. This is the last thing she said to me.

And I should have read it six months ago.

'Do you want me to read it to you?' Daniel asks gently. 'I don't mind. Really.'

'No,' I say, composing myself. I sit up straight again and smooth out the letter, trying to be brave.

This is going to hurt – but I can't let it. I can't be sentimental right now. One day, I'll be able to sit down and read these letters and appreciate every little thing about them and feel the pain and cry and scream and curse – but not today. Today I have to focus.

Today I owe it to Poppy to view these letters as data, and do what I do best: make the connections to prove my hypothesis.

Emotion comes later.

Hey, Clemmie! Surprise — you've got mail! Wish I could be there to see your face when you get this. Bet you weren't expecting it, right? Thought I'd be brave and actually go to the post office for once, so if you're reading this, it worked! I spoke to a random human and paid for a service! I know, I know, you never got what the big deal is about post offices anyway, but trust me: they're scary.

ANYWAY, thought I'd send you this lot before you came home for Easter (you are coming home for Easter, right??), mostly because I cannot keep Ben a secret any more. I want to talk to you about him so badly! Honestly, Clemmie, I know you're all like 'who needs romance when I have science', but he is dreamy and smart and artistic and just so, so lovely.

I've never felt like this before. I never knew I could fall in love. I hoped I would, one day! But to actually experience it is so different. He gets me. We're already making all sorts of plans for him to come to London this summer and see the galleries, and we do things all the time around Brighton. He says he's got a surprise for me tonight, and I'm supposed to leave around midnight and cycle to Seaford to meet him on the coastal path after he finishes work, somewhere near Hope Gap. Romantic, right?? I just hope I can find it in the dark! He told me not to tell anyone about it yet, or us, but you won't get this for days, so I'm not technically breaking my promise!

Anyway, I'm rambling. You're going to love him though, Clemmie. You have to come home this summer when he's here to visit! He says he can't wait to meet you.

I'm sure I'll have lots more to tell you tomorrow, but that's for another letter. Maybe I'll start posting them weekly from now on! And you could write back. What do you think?

Lots of love, Poppy x

I stare at her name, anger and sadness and a hundred other emotions building inside me.

'What does it say?' Daniel asks. 'Was it from that night?'

'Yes.'

'And? Does it prove anything?'

'Yes. She . . . she went to Hope Gap because he invited her. He told her not to tell anyone. It was a secret.' I pass him the letter so he can read it, too. 'Ben. That's his name. Ben told her to meet him there. Ben planned it. Ben is the killer.'

'Oh my God,' Daniel says, the letter shaking in his hand. 'Ben who? Are there pictures? There must be pictures. Who the hell is he?'

I turn the stack back over and rifle through it, looking for glossy photographs or photobooth strips or lifelike portraits, but there aren't any. There are only drawings. Not lifelike like the one in Poppy's sketchbook, but cartoony, Disney-style: her with a messy ginger bun and her floral dresses and Doc Martens, him standing taller – much taller, brown haired, green eyed – passing her a heart-shaped puff of candyfloss on Brighton Pier, a starling murmuration peppering the sunset behind them, seagulls squawking love songs as they fly past. There are ones like this from all over Brighton, in the spots from her Instagram page that I visited alone. Them sitting on the edge of the dolphin fountain, smiling coyly; holding hands as they walk past the rainbow beach huts along the promenade. Each time he is a caricature of turned-up jeans and boots, a different scarf flapping in the coastal wind, smiling, taking pictures, pointing excitedly.

'Do you recognise him?' Daniel asks. 'Was he on her friends list or anything?'

I get my phone out and check her contacts and social media for Bens, but the only one who comes up is our Uncle Benjamin. In the collection of RIP messages she got after her death, there are no Bens.

'She must have mentioned his full name somewhere.' I arrange the letters back into their stack, and start at the beginning. 'There'll be enough clues in here to piece it together.'

The first few letters aren't helpful. Poppy talks about being back at uni, her housemates, the sea air, the frost – things I don't have time to appreciate right now. I skip through to the parts I need. The parts that make me sick.

Poppy and Ben match on Tinder on a Wednesday afternoon. He super-likes her. They talk about art and their favourite painters, then swap numbers to share their own work: her paintings, his photography. After a week of solid texting, they go for a date. She's nervous; he puts her at ease. They don't kiss until their second date. He buys her candyfloss and they watch the sunset from Brighton Pier. They see each other a lot: restaurant dinners, chilly picnics on the green, sleepovers. He asks her to meet his family when they come to visit in April. She invites him to come to London over the summer holidays.

She was happy. So was he. He makes her laugh, he holds her tight, he makes her promises and swears them by making an X with his fingers, crossing his heart. She thinks she's in love, and he might be, too. She wants to tell him. He invites her to Hope Gap in the early hours of 23 February.

She goes. She dies.

And he was there with her.

'This is proof,' I say. 'She wasn't suicidal, and she was lured to the cliff that night. I know she never says his last name or where he worked or even what he looked like, not properly, but this is enough, isn't it? The police will have to investigate. They'll have to take this seriously.'

Daniel nods. It's a while before he can find any words.

'She wrote so much. She . . . she really loved him. You can see her falling in love on the page. She trusted him.' Daniel clenches his fists. 'That makes it so much worse.'

I wipe my eyes, staring down at my sister's cheerful, jolly, ridiculously happy words. She was oblivious. She had no idea she was falling in love with a killer. She never doubted him, not even for a moment. She trusted him so much that she cycled to her own death in the middle of the night without questioning it.

She was easy prey. She was vulnerable.

She was alone.

'She texted me that night,' I say, even though the self-preservation part of my brain has tried so hard to forget. 'Twice. She had something to tell me, hours before the call. It was this, wasn't it? She would have said she was going out at night. I could have told her not to. I could have seen it was suspicious. I could have saved her. I could have stopped this.' I lean forward, covering my face. 'It's *still* my fault.'

'No, Clementine. It's all right, it's okay.'

Daniel pulls my clawing hands away from my head and holds me – more a straightjacket than an embrace. I lean against him, his clothes still damp from the storm, his bones jutting against mine, breathing in the stale smell of sweat and cigarettes and vodka. I let him flood my senses, drowning out the freshness of the sea; the salt water on my lips; the desperate, weak cries from Poppy's throat; the bite of the waves; the deep, aching void in my chest where hope used to lie.

'It's not your fault,' Daniel says into my hair. 'Don't blame yourself, ever. Ben did this, not you. He's responsible. He's the one who killed her.'

'I know.' I sit up, wiping my face. 'And I'm going to be the one who catches him.'

CHAPTER 21

I wait until a reasonable hour – 8 a.m. – before calling the police. There are no direct numbers listed online, but I dial 101 and manage to get put through to the Brighton and Hove area.

'This is Sussex Police, how may I help you?' a woman says.

'Hi, I have new information to report about a case from earlier this year. Is there someone I can speak to about it?'

'Not directly, but I can take your report and pass it on to the correct police department, who may contact you for further information.' I can hear the woman typing. 'What case is this regarding?'

I catch Daniel's eye across the coffee table, the folder, letters, and investigation materials we've been studying all night spread across it. He warned me again about his own experiences with the police in Kent, and how he was quickly branded mentally ill and disbelieved for his claims, even with proof.

'Poppy Harris. She was found dead at Hope Gap in February in an apparent suicide, but I have new information that . . . needs to be looked into.'

Daniel nods at me, mouthing a word: '*Perfect.*'

'And you are?'

'Clementine Harris, her sister.'

It takes a while to give the operator all the details. Daniel stays with me, sometimes scribbling notes on what I should say – and what I shouldn't.

'So, you believe Miss Harris wasn't alone the night she died?'

'I have evidence to prove that, yes.'

The operator types something extra on her computer. 'All right. Well, I'll send this through to the relevant department, and—'

Liam's door creaks open.

'Uh, thank you! I'll be available to discuss this and share all information any time. Goodbye.'

'Morning, you two,' Liam says cheerily as the call ends, ducking to grab a smoothie from the fridge. 'Who was that?'

'Uber,' Daniel says, reacting before I can even think of an excuse. 'Clementine left something in the car last night.'

'What did you lose?'

'Um, a library book.'

'Oh no. Hopefully someone'll get it back to you. Anyone want some breakfast, by the way? I'm thinking eggs on toast.'

We decline, and Liam clatters about the kitchen with the pans.

'Feeling better today, mate?' he asks Daniel. 'You looked a bit worse for wear last night, what with the rain and everything. How's the hand?'

Liam points with a spatula, smiling. Daniel gets smaller somehow, checking his palm as though he forgot about the bandage there. It's grubby now, no longer white and pristine. He clears his throat.

'It's fine, thanks. Don't think it was too deep.'

'Oh good! You can help me with the washing up later, then.' Liam winks and returns to the frying pan. 'Let me know if you need anything, by the way. I've got clean clothes you can have, and feel free to use any of my stuff in the bathroom. Body wash, deodorant, you name it. I think there's a spare toothbrush under the sink, too. As I said, feel free.'

Liam turns his music on, humming along, cheeriness oozing out of him. Daniel curls in on himself, twitching the neck of his dirty T-shirt to his nose. He grimaces, and grabs one of the towels he slept under last night.

'Er, thanks,' he says, and disappears into the bathroom with his head down.

'Okay, what happened last night?' Liam asks, the second the shower starts up. 'Is he okay? Are you? Forget eye *bags*, you've both got suitcases! Did you get *any* sleep?'

'No,' I admit.

'What's going on, C? Is he really okay? He looked rough last night, but he's even worse today. What happened?'

'He was upset, that's all. He'd had a bit too much to drink, and accidentally cut his hand on a bottle.'

'He seemed more than upset to me.'

I squirm. What Daniel needed last night was to talk to me, but I was unreachable. Is it any wonder he broke down the way he did when he was left alone with his despair for so long?

'It was the alcohol,' I say. 'He had too much and overreacted. That's it.'

'But he's better now, yeah? He's not, like, a danger to himself?'

'No, of course not. He's fine.'

There's a clatter in the bathroom, a cascade of products in the shower, followed by an angry, muffled swear word. Liam raises a dark eyebrow at me.

'Irritable, maybe, but he's fine. He's not like he was last night.'

'And what about you?'

I get up and busy myself with refilling my coffee mug. I've had several already. 'I'm fine.'

'Come on, C. I'm not an idiot. You're exhausted.' He crosses his arms. 'Look, if you need a break, you can go to bed. I'll watch Daniel.'

'Watch him?'

'Yeah. That's what you're doing, isn't it? Making sure he's okay? Helping him deal with . . . whatever it is he's dealing with. You don't want him to be alone. Well, he can be not alone with me. It doesn't have to be your job just because you're the person he came to.'

'It's not like that. I'm not babysitting him. If anything, he's babysitting me.'

'What?' Liam turns down the hob, abandoning his eggs, and rounds on me. 'What's going on, C? Tell me.'

I sigh, rubbing my forehead.

Liam's eyes are bright and hopeful, his cheeks and lips as rosy as his hair. He lives in a different world from me, and from Daniel. He isn't plagued by insomnia; he doesn't share our trauma. If I told him Poppy was murdered, would he believe it? Would those bright, hopeful eyes narrow and survey me like they did Daniel just now, judging me, picking me apart, and brand me a danger to myself based on something he simply doesn't understand? Would he insist on babysitting me, too? Would he call for professional help? Would he assume I'm mad and suddenly treat me like a liability, like all of Daniel's friends did to him?

I want to tell him, I do, but . . . not until I know the police have reopened the case.

Not until I'm sure he'll believe me.

'Does your offer to help me find someone online still stand?'

'Uh, yeah? Why?'

'Because it turns out my sister had a boyfriend none of us knew about, and I need to somehow find him even though I don't have a last name or a photograph.'

225

Liam blinks at me, but goes with it. 'Okay, what *do* you have?'

I explain about the letters and show him Poppy's drawings, listing everything I know about Ben so far – except for the fact that he's a murderer. As far as Liam knows, I'm still looking for information about Poppy's suicide. It's still within the realms of normal behaviour.

'It's not a huge amount to go on,' he says. 'Was there anything else in them?'

He reaches for the letters, but I collect them up and stuff them inside the folder, closing it. Poppy never properly named Ben or gave me the details I need to find him, but she was open about everything else. Too open. There are pages of her falling in love, joking about new underwear, experiencing things for the first time . . .

I remember the pack of condoms in her suitcase, and the lacy red underwear. Those were for him, weren't they?

Liam doesn't need to read those private moments. I didn't even show them to Daniel.

'I told you everything I know. If you can help me find him, I'd really appreciate it.'

Liam pulls me into a hug.

'Of course. I'm gonna get you your closure, C. I promise. I'll find you all the Brighton Bens, and then we can go through and do a process of elimination kind of thing, seeing if they've got brown hair or do event photography. If we can't find him for sure, at least we can rule some other Bens out. I can get you closer to finding him, and getting answers about your sister.'

Liam rocks me, his sweet-smelling embrace getting tighter.

'Thank you,' I say, hugging him back. 'It'll be great if we can give the police somewhere to start.'

Liam flinches. 'The police?'

The bathroom door squeaks open.

'Oh,' Daniel says, as I pull myself out of Liam's hug. 'Sorry, I didn't mean to interrupt . . . You said something about clothes?'

Daniel stares at the ground, the door pulled tight to his towel-covered body, most of him hidden.

'Of course!' Liam grins and disappears into his bedroom, keeping up a commentary as he gathers some items. 'What are we thinking, jeans and a jumper? You'd look good in blue, I reckon. Are boxers okay? How do you feel about faux-fur?'

Liam delivers a bundle to the bathroom and the door snaps shut again with a murmured 'thank you'. Then Liam comes back to me. His stare is intense – and doubtful.

Doubting my mental state.

'Did you say something about the police?'

'No,' I say quickly, tidying up the coffee table. I wish there was an easy way to make him drop it.

'Yes, you did. You said finding Ben would give the police somewhere to start.'

'I meant the coroner. I know the inquest is closed, but the coroner might want to know any new information. So if Ben knows why Poppy took her own life, and it's different from what the inquest concluded, then perhaps the verdict should be updated.'

I hate lying about her like this. Knowing what I know, having the proof of it just inches away in a folder, it feels like a betrayal to once again talk as though Poppy's death was a decision she made for herself. I believed it for so long, didn't I? I believed the lie the killer put in place to frame her.

I don't enjoy lying to Liam, either. Would it be easier to be honest? He's always been kind to me, and surely that wouldn't change if I explain it properly and show him the letters? I'm sure he'd –

'C,' Liam says, sharply enough to make me jump. 'Who were you on the phone to earlier?'

The bathroom door opens again and Daniel comes out, hair towel-dried and fluffy, the grime and blood of last night washed away. He's about my height, but he looks much smaller in Liam's clothes, the sleeves of a blue colour-block jumper hanging almost to his fingertips. He rolls the sleeves up, then remembers the harsh red scars on his wrists, and rolls them back down again.

'Um, hi,' he says, as Liam and I stare at him.

'Liam, didn't you have something in the frying pan?' I ask.

'Oh crap! My eggs. Thanks for the reminder.' Liam flashes me a thumbs-up – a half-hearted one – and returns to the kitchen area. Although he continues cooking, I can tell he's watching us through his flop of pink hair.

I grab our evidence from the coffee table, and gesture for Daniel to follow me into my room.

'Did the police call back yet?' he asks in an undertone, pulling the door closed.

'No.' I check my phone again, just in case. 'Not yet. But Liam said he'd help me find people called Ben on Instagram, so we might be able to give the police some extra details when they call.'

'You told your housemate about this?'

'Some of it. He knows Ben was Poppy's boyfriend, but nothing else. I thought about telling him, but . . .'

'You were worried he wouldn't believe you. I get that. I literally showed people the video of my sister getting murdered, and people still didn't believe me. They didn't *want* to believe me. But once they hear that the police are involved, it validates it. You're no longer, you know, the crazy person with a theory. That label is kind of hard to shake off.'

He stretches his sleeves all the way over his hands, balling the fabric up in his fists.

'It's happening for you. These letters are everything you need. The police will believe you, they'll catch this guy, and you'll be able to set the record straight about your sister. And it's not just because of the letters, it's everything. It's you. You never lost hope, or gave up. You kept looking, you went to Brighton, you found leads no one else had been able to. That's the scientist in you, isn't it? You finish what you start. Poppy is so lucky to have a sister like you. Someone who can do this for her, and do it well.'

He smiles sadly, fiddling with his sleeves again.

'Clem, I need to go.'

'What?' I check my phone again. 'But the police haven't even called yet. I don't know what to say to them. I might say the wrong thing.'

'You won't. You don't need me for a phone call. You don't need me for any of this. I can admit it.' He smiles again. 'You've done so much for your sister, and I need to do it for mine. I need to go back to Kent.'

'But you only just left there. I thought you couldn't find anything?'

'I'm not sure I was looking properly.' He slumps down on the bed, sighing. 'I was looking for a stranger, a weirdo who was hanging around that night – but what if the murderer wasn't? What if she knew the person who pushed her? What if they lured her there that night, like Ben did to Poppy? I need to go back. I know it's been two years already, but—'

'You don't have to say anything else. Go.'

I sit down next to him. 'You say I did all these things and found extra information because I'm clever, but the truth is, I was lucky. The friend with the lead about the boyfriend approached *me* by chance, just because my Tinder account happened to be within range of his in Brighton, and he recognised Poppy's photo. I was in the right place at the right time. So go be in the right place at the right time. Do it for Rachel.'

Daniel's eyes shine, and he fishes out the necklace tucked beneath Liam's jumper. He clutches it. 'I'm sorry to abandon you like this. I wish I could stay and support you.'

'It's fine. Really. I'll be okay.'

'Good.' Daniel rubs his nose, recomposing himself. 'As long as you introduce things slowly when they call you, and don't blurt everything out at once, it'll be okay. They'll believe you. And then all this will be over.'

The excitement fizzing in my bloodstream fades a little.

Over is a relative term. My investigation may be over, Ben's time as a free man may be over, but nothing else will change. Poppy will still be dead; life will still be worse.

Years in prison versus a lifetime of grief, loss, and regret.

I know which punishment is worse.

CHAPTER 22

After Daniel leaves for Margate, I wait for the police to phone back.

To keep busy, I type up my notes, reorder my folder, and take clear photos of all the evidence. I open Instagram, Twitter, and Facebook and search for Bens in the Brighton area, scrolling until my eyes hurt. I increase the distance on my Tinder app to include Sussex and flick through hundreds, thousands of men's faces, looking for photographers, for Bens, for anyone resembling the man in Poppy's drawings. I dig through the social media accounts of bands and nightclubs and music venues in Brighton, looking for photo credits. I sit at my desk, jittery from coffee, sick from tiredness, staring between a page of suggested phrases for the call and my phone screen, waiting for it to light up with a call from Sussex Police.

But it never does.

Sunday is the same: no returned calls, no sense of urgency from Sussex Police. I wait until midday and then call 101 again, repeating the process.

'I have new information about an old case,' I tell today's operator. 'It's urgent. It's about my sister's death. I think she was . . .' I bite my tongue, remembering Daniel's warnings about saying too much too soon. 'I gave my information yesterday, but no officers have got back to me yet. I need to speak to somebody. Immediately.'

'I'm sorry for the delay,' he says. 'They might be backed up at the moment. It's a busy station. But don't worry, your report *was* passed on, and someone will deal with it in due course. All right?'

It isn't all right, but I say yes anyway.

I try not to think about the time that's being wasted. Instead, I focus on the positives: it gives me more time to prepare my folder and gather extra evidence. And to find Ben.

Why did he have to have such a common name? Facebook comes up with a never-ending list of Bens, and so does Instagram. I send out another volley of texts and emails to Poppy's housemates, classmates, and university tutors, asking if they ever saw her with someone matching Ben's description, or if she mentioned spending time with a boyfriend. Emily sends back a brief message.

> *I used to hear talking in her room but I thought it was the TV or something. I never saw anyone. She was super-private. Sorry.*

How is it possible for her to have had a serious relationship without anyone noticing? I pick through her letters again, and use a yellow highlighter on the copies in my folder.

> *Things are going so well! Ben says he doesn't want to put any pressure on me, so thinks it's best not to tell anyone about us yet, just in case something goes wrong or I change my mind. As if I would!! He's perfect!*

> *We meet up at the seafront a lot for sunsets, but he works nights, so sometimes he doesn't come over until 2 or 3 in the morning. Sometimes I feel like Juliet waiting on the balcony for Romeo! Only with more seagulls, and a happier ending.*

I wish I could tell you about him, C! In real life, I mean. But he says it'll be such a good surprise when you finally find out. You won't expect it one bit! I haven't told him about these letters yet. That can be his surprise when he comes to visit us at home when you're back, and you already know everything about him.

He knew what he was doing, right from the start. He made sure not to be spotted, not to leave a trail. That way, when he deleted himself from Poppy's phone and tore out the pages of drawings of him in her sketchbook, nobody noticed their absence. He disappeared as though he'd never been there at all.

But Poppy never told him about the letters she was writing for me. He never knew there were pages and pages of evidence against him that would ruin the calculated plan he'd carried out.

Good.

I spend the rest of Sunday trawling social media for Ben, checking hashtags, searching for every male photographer who was in Brighton earlier this year. Liam helps, too, but we come up with nothing: Bens with bad photos; sunsets and scarves from people with a different ethnicity; gig photographers with solid alibis.

We can't find him anywhere.

I lie awake in bed that night, staring at the ceiling.

If Ben isn't on social media, how else am I supposed to find him? And *why* isn't he on social media? Poppy said he loved photography, so why wouldn't he share that online? Why would he have set his profile to private? He got away with Poppy's murder, didn't he? As far as he knows, everyone believes it was a suicide. Case closed. He's got away with it. He didn't know about the clues she'd left for me in the letters, or that I've finally received them. If he thinks he's got away with it, why is he hiding? What's there to hide from?

I grip the sheets in my fists.

Poppy was in love. She thought Ben was, too. Every time he kissed her, touched her, promised her something with his fingers making a cutesy X over his heart, she thought he was genuine, that everything he said to her was true – but it wasn't. He wanted her to keep him a secret from the start. He made her think it was a romantic game, or a surprise for me, but it was a way to cover his tracks. He planned this.

Doubt creeps through me in the dark, settling as nausea in my stomach.

If he was covering his tracks from the beginning, how do I even know that Ben is his real name?

My phone rings and I snatch it from the bedside table – but it isn't a call from Brighton.

'Daniel,' I say, settling back on the pillows. 'Hi. Found anything?'

'Maybe. I don't know.' He exhales, the familiar sound of his smoking drifting down the line. He must be out pacing the streets of Margate again. 'I've been trying the boyfriend angle, just in case Rachel was seeing someone, but the only people who'd talk to me didn't know anything. But I found something, I think. Maybe. I'm not sure.'

'What is it?'

'A flyer. Rachel was into music, she was a musician, and she loved vinyl. I found this flyer for a vinyl swap night at a pub, like the kind you'd find stacked up by the bar or on a table or something. It was mixed in with some magazines.'

'And you think she went?'

'I don't know if she went, but I think someone wanted her to. There's a number written on the back of the flyer – and I mean, like, *written*. Handwritten. Like someone wanted her to call it. And there was a name and a smiley face below it. Dylan. But . . .' A car passes Daniel, and he waits to finish his sentence. 'But there weren't any Dylans in her phone contacts or social media.'

I prop myself up on an elbow.

'Did you call the number?'

'Yep. It was disconnected. Which could mean he wrote it down wrong, or—'

'He changed numbers. You need to get in touch with Rachel's friends again, and mention the name. Dylan, was it? Maybe someone remembers something, so if you ask them—'

'Way ahead of you. I've already messaged everyone about six times today, just in case. I don't know if she ever called him back, so maybe it's pointless, but it's something, right? It's a lead, at least. A name to cross off the list.' He takes another drag on his cigarette. 'Crap, sorry, forgot to ask. How'd it go with the police?'

'They still haven't called me back.'

'Oh. I guess it's early days, isn't it? And Brighton isn't exactly a saintly town. They must have a lot of guys with black eyes to process over the weekend. You'll hear something tomorrow, for sure.'

'I know. I hate waiting, though. I hate feeling as though I'm wasting time.'

'You like being in control, I get you. This makes you powerless, right? Knowing the truth but not *quite* being able to prove it to others yet? Welcome to my world.'

I sigh. 'How have you coped with this feeling for so long?'

'Um, if you recall how we met, not very well!' He laughs. 'Spite makes it easier to cope. Spite and support. So, thanks.'

'Any time. I just hope neither of us have to cope with this much longer.'

◆ ◆ ◆

After a few hours of sleep, Monday dawns into another Sunday: emailing, researching, building up my folder as I wait for the phone to ring. I check Poppy's letters against maps and her Instagram account, trying to pinpoint the places she and Ben went together. She mentions an Italian meal on 25 January, so I email all the Italian restaurants in the area to ask about bookings and CCTV. I do the same with coffee shops on certain dates, and reach out to the candyfloss stalls on Brighton Pier, and email the local council itself, asking about access to security cameras on the pier, and whether a couple matching Poppy and Ben's description were spotted between January and February.

Of course, I don't get any positive responses.

I try Reddit, too.

How much evidence is needed for the police to reopen a closed investigation?

Are there any cases of a suicide verdict being later changed to murder?

What's the best way to trace a stranger when you only have their first name and a location?

I get some responses, but unfortunately the last post is flooded by men boasting about tracking down girls they've spotted on Tinder. *Take screenshots of her photos and then reverse image search. Girls usually post their pictures everywhere for likes so you'll get her social media from that, and then you can DM her without having to match first.*

But I don't have a photo of Ben, so that advice is no use. I use the Google Lens app on my phone to photograph Poppy's drawings and search the internet for them, but neither Poppy or Ben posted them online. The drawing from Poppy's sketchbook brings up shopping pages for expensive cameras, not the identity of the person behind it.

The phone still doesn't ring.

I'm sick of the same four walls by Tuesday. I head out to the library, taking buses so I don't risk losing signal in the Underground. I return the books on suicide and depression that I've had stacked up on my desk for months, and check out new ones: *The Psychology of Murder, Why Men Kill, Abusive Relationships, The Science of Murder, Famous Murder Investigations.* I bring them back home and start reading, noting down anything that could be useful.

I check in with Daniel, but Dylan is proving to be as elusive as Ben is for me.

'Nobody knows a Dylan,' he says on the phone that night, pacing the streets once again. '*But*, apparently she mentioned something about a drummer with tattoos to a friend.'

'A drummer with tattoos sounds like the sort of person who might go to a vinyl swap night.'

'Exactly. But why hasn't anyone else heard of this guy? They'd have been seen together, right? Someone would remember that? I guess I have to keep asking around. Maybe the person with the best information is someone who doesn't even realise they have it.'

Wednesday dawns, and by the afternoon my patience has worn thin.

'Hello, Sussex Police?' a man says when he answers my latest 101 call.

'Hi. I understand the police are very busy, but I called twice over the weekend about new information relating to a death from earlier this year, and it can't wait. I need to talk to someone as soon as possible.'

'Did you file a report with us?'

'Yes, I gave all the details I was asked for. I was told it would be passed on to Brighton and Hove station.'

'Ah, Brighton and Hove is a very busy station. If you wait a few days, I'm sure someone will eventually—'

I swear under my breath, covering the phone with my hand. I want to throw it at the wall.

The calm, orderly approach isn't working. No, I don't want the police to assume I'm unhinged or clutching at straws in my grief

237

like the police in Kent did to Daniel, but how am I supposed to get through to the right people when I can't say how serious the new evidence is? I haven't specifically told these operators answering my calls that I'm trying to report a murder, so why would anyone be in a rush to get back to me about it?

I tighten my ponytail. It's time for the truth. I won't blurt it out or get angry; I'll stay calm, presenting my information in a rational way. I'll make sure I'm believed.

'Madam? Are you still there?'

'Yes. Look, I didn't want to blurt this out over the phone, but the new evidence I have suggests that my sister was—'

Loud, repeated buzzing interrupts me. It's the entry phone by the front door.

I sigh. 'Sorry, I'll have to phone back.'

I stomp to the front door, covering my ears. 'Who—?'

'It's me,' Daniel says, not waiting for me to finish my question. 'Let me in. I found something.'

I pace the tiny kitchen area as I wait for him to make his way up the stairs. Liam has scrawled a new message on the chalkboard: *If we can't find that dickhead, karma certainly will!* I hope he's right.

I open the door as Daniel gets to the top of the steps. He's out of breath, but still rushing.

'I need – to use – your phone charger,' he says, pushing past me to get to my bedroom. I get a glass of water from the kitchen and follow him.

He's on the edge of my bed, phone plugged in, shaking it in his hands as he waits for it to charge enough to turn on. I pass him the water and he gulps it down, wiping his mouth with the back of his hand.

'What's happened? What did you find?'

He pummels the power button on his phone, and the screen lights up with a start-up sequence.

'I was asking around about Dylan, seeing if anyone had heard *anything* about Rach seeing someone, or if they had any information about that night, and it turned out that, like, a friend of a friend of hers is the sister of someone I went to school with, and those girls lived on the road by the church, by the gap in the fence, where she . . . where she died, so I contacted the girl I knew, Kelly, to see if she or her parents remembered anything from that night, and she didn't, she didn't know, but she said there was a woman down that road who loved wildlife, who has trail cams, motion-activated ones, and one of them points at the street. So I talked to the woman and it turned out she kept everything archived. She had a photo from that night. She sent it to me, and I . . .'

He presses something on his now-functional phone and passes it to me: it's a photo of a car driving behind a bird feeder. In the car, a woman in a black-and-white striped top and glasses is driving, while the man in the seat beside her points ahead, his other arm around her shoulder. Dark, shaggy hair blocks his face, but tattoos are visible on the man's arm. There's a dark leather bracelet on his wrist.

'It's him,' Daniel says, gulping breathlessly. 'Dylan. The guy who murdered my sister.'

CHAPTER 23

Daniel and I sit on the bed, staring at the photo of his sister's car on his phone.

'They died the same way,' he says. 'Men killed them. Boyfriends. People they trusted. Is this . . . a thing? Guys killing their girlfriends like that?'

'Yes.' I think of the books I checked out of the library, and the chapters on domestic violence. 'In around sixty-one per cent of cases, women who were murdered by men were murdered by a current or ex-partner. It's not uncommon. But . . .'

'What?'

'Well, those murders are often violent attacks, like stabbings or assaults. Crimes of passion. But Poppy's murder was carefully planned, and the killer went to great lengths to cover his tracks and stage it as a suicide. That's unusual.'

'Not that unusual, apparently,' Daniel says. 'Not if it happened to Rachel, too.'

I think, soberly, about the Reddit replies I received from men knowing how to trace girls from dating apps online. I clicked on a few of their names to see their other activity: misogyny, guides on how to trick women into bed. Is there a part of the internet that has guides on how to stage suicides? Is there a collective of men taught to do the same thing to innocent women?

'His face is covered,' Daniel says. 'How are we going to ID this guy? They trawled CCTV for the inquest, and they never spotted him before. This is all they got.' He digs around in his phone for the right files. 'There, see? There was this CCTV of her in the car at the crossroads, but—'

'The angle makes it look like she's alone.'

'Exactly, and that's why they never believed someone else was there. Same with this security footage from the church. That's her car there, but it's only one side of it. He must've been right next to her, there, out of shot.'

'Maybe they'll be able to identify him from the tattoos?'

'I can barely make them out.' Daniel flicks back to the video. 'What's that, a sleeve? Flowers, maybe? Animals? I couldn't tell you. And everyone has tattoos these days. They're not exactly rare.'

I think of Jude and the intricate art covering the scars on his wrists. I remember the designs being beautiful, but I wouldn't be able to identify them now. Perhaps nobody would recognise Dylan's, either.

I search the image for other clues. The man's hair is slightly long, and slightly wavy. He looks tall, sitting high in his seat, and his pointing arm is more thick than thin. Below his arm, as Rachel leans forward a little, something glints on her chest. A heart-shaped necklace. It's familiar, somehow. I've seen it before.

Daniel is looking at the image, too – but one hand is at his own chest, clutching the pendant that he always wears. The chain has carved red lines into the back of his neck, and he always grabs it when agitated and upset.

I hover my finger over the bright pixels.

'Is this the one you wear?'

He smiles again, but sadness pinches at its corners.

'Yeah. I know it's weird, because she had it on that night, but . . . I got it back after the inquest and I couldn't face putting it

241

away somewhere, or getting rid of it. It was hers, and it makes me feel better to wear it, or maybe not better, not really, but it reminds me of her, and what I need to do for her. So I keep it on me.'

He opens his hand, the pendant resting on his palm.

It's a heart, one side silver, the other rose gold. Up close and in the flesh, it's just how I expected it to be: the two thin strips of metal looped together at the top of the heart and overlapping at the bottom to form a stylishly uneven point.

The familiarity of it eats away at me.

I must have seen it on him before. Last weekend when he came out of the bathroom, maybe? Or one of the other times I've seen him grip it?

But . . . the chain is gold. Why do I remember it mixed in with silver? Why, when I look at it, do I feel these twists of . . . anger? And guilt? Why do I remember *holding* it?

Daniel tucks the necklace away under his top, patting it. I stare at the one on the screen.

A two-toned heart. Where have I seen one, or touched one? Mum doesn't wear jewellery often, and when she does, it's usually something chunky and colourful. Was it Jenna's? Did she wear it that night? No, I'd remember that. It's not hers. Poppy used to wear a necklace all the time, but it was always the same one, the silver fox with . . .

I feel it in my hand again: the small plastic bag containing the jewellery Poppy was wearing when she died. The fox necklace was there, with its long chain – and beneath it, wrapped in the silver strands, was another necklace. A heart necklace. Two types of metal twisted together into one.

But she only ever wore her fox necklace.

'We have to go,' I tell Daniel, grabbing my bag and raincoat and throwing him my umbrella.

242

'Why? What's going on?' Daniel asks, rushing out the front door after me. Alexander's housemate's music follows us down the stairs, thumping. 'Where are we going?'

'Poppy's room,' I say, not wanting to waste oxygen on words when my legs need it more. 'I have to check something. It might be nothing, but . . .'

'It might not be?'

'Yes. Come on.'

The air is cold today, the heatwave well and truly washed away in last weekend's storm, and the canal water is dull. We hurry along the towpath in silence, past the bench for family picnics, past Poppy's favourite boat. I don't point them out. I glance up at the café when we reach it, checking Mum and Dad are still inside. They are, and so is Alexander. He sits at his usual table in a cable-knit jumper, scribbling furiously enough for his curls to shake. He glances up, too, and waves with his pen. I raise my hand in return.

'Is this the place?' Daniel asks, squinting across the water.

I use my hand to adjust the hood of my raincoat, hiding my face. 'Yes. My parents live above it, but they're working right now. They won't see us.'

I rush Daniel over the bridge and past the café to the front door, keeping my head down.

I lead Daniel up the gloomy stairs to Poppy's room. He follows, but his footsteps slow when we get to the second flight, with its trail of framed family photos running up the stairwell.

'You know, I never pictured her as ginger,' he says, pausing at Poppy when she was around twelve, his nose close to the glass. 'Not at first. Before I saw the drawings in her letters, I thought she'd be more like you. Dark hair. Tall. You're really different.'

I'm at the last picture there will ever be of us: Mum and Dad beaming proudly, me in the Harvard jumper they insisted I wear, Poppy with her hair falling out of a bun. I look at her properly, reminding myself of the subtleties of her face. A wide smile. A single dimple on one side. Faint freckles on her nose and even fainter ones on her cheeks.

The silver fox necklace rests against her collarbone, as it always did. Didn't it? I head back down the stairs, peering closely at the photographs.

2018, 2017, 2016, 2015, 2014, 2013. Six years of the fox necklace my parents gave her for her thirteenth birthday. She wore it every day. She slept in it. I don't remember her ever wearing anything else.

So why was she wearing a heart necklace the night she died?

Poppy's room is almost exactly how I left it a week ago: her university things back in their ordered boxes; her existing mess left in its natural habitat. The bed is the only thing that's different. There's a fresh dent in it, as though Mum has been sitting there again.

I dig through the box on the floor until I find the small plastic bag of Poppy's personal effects. The fox necklace is there, like I remembered, and the rings and earrings. I press on the swirled chain, pushing it around like water, parting it – and a curve of rose gold peeks through. I open the bag and dump the contents on Poppy's bed, unravelling the gold chain from the silver, trying to get to the pendant.

Eventually, it pulls loose. I rest it in my palm, the way Daniel did with Rachel's necklace back at the flat. Two thin strips of metal, one silver, one rose gold, fused together and twisted into a heart, the tails of the point overlapping.

Just like the one Daniel is wearing.

He hasn't noticed. He's over at Poppy's wardrobe, picking through the stack of canvases resting against it, muttering about art.

I swallow the vomit rising in my throat.

Our sisters were both pushed to their deaths by men they secretly were dating, and both of them were found wearing heart necklaces. Identical heart necklaces.

It's too many coincidences. It's a pattern. A . . . modus operandi.

I have to be sure. I dig out my folder and find the CCTV images of Poppy leaving her halls of residence on the night she died. She's there with her bike, her coat open, scarf loose – and nothing but a fox necklace resting beneath it.

This isn't Poppy's necklace: it's the killer's.

'Daniel, I . . .'

He looks over at me brightly, his hair tucked behind his ear. I don't know how to tell him, so I show him. I open my hand, the heart pendant resting on my palm the way Rachel's rested on his an hour ago.

He stares at the pendant, blinking hard, then laughs, reaching for his neck.

'Oh, I must've dropped it! Thanks. It must have come loose, or . . .'

The chain is where it always is. Daniel's fingers hook around it and, slowly, he works his way down and pinches Rachel's pendant between his fingers, and peels it away from his chest. He looks down at it. Looks back at my hand. Looks to me.

'Daniel, Poppy was wearing this when the police found her, but she wasn't wearing it when she left her halls. I think – no, I *know* – the killer gave it to her that night.' I take a deep breath. 'And I think he gave that one to Rachel before she died, too.'

'What?'

'It's the same killer. A serial killer. He killed Rachel, and then two years later he killed Poppy in almost the same way. He put that necklace on both of them. It's a calling card.'

'No,' Daniel mutters. He tightens his fingers around the pendant. 'That's not right. This is *her* necklace. Rachel's.' He's getting louder now, almost shouting. 'That's why I wear it. It's hers!'

'Then why does Poppy have the exact same one? When they died in the exact same circumstances? Do you remember Rachel wearing it? Are there any other pictures of her wearing it, *not* from that night?'

'I don't know. There must be, but . . . I don't know.'

Daniel veers dangerously back into his old, manic self. He pulls at the chain, carving it into the back of his neck. He opens Facebook on his phone and scrolls through an endless stream of his sister's face, too blurred for me to see, tears springing from his eyes, blurring it for him, too.

'I can't find it,' he says. 'It's . . . it's not there.'

His face crinkles, scrunching up in sadness – then in anger. He tugs at his pendant again, but not with his usual clinging desperation. He rips it from his neck, breaking the chain, drawing blood, and throws it across the room. It hits the wall and falls, nestling in the fibres of the carpet. He digs his fingers into the duvet, hunching over, rage radiating out of him in waves.

'I've been wearing it. I've been wearing it every day for *two years*. And *he* put it on her! It wasn't even hers. Fuck!'

He balls up on the bed, covering his head, rocking, crying and screaming into the duvet. I want to scream, too. I squeeze the necklace in my hand, wishing I could crush it, melt it, mangle it beyond recognition.

When did he put this on Poppy? Was it before he pushed her? Was it a gift she was excited about? Did it make her feel special? Loved? Or was it after? Did he follow her down to that beach where she lay bleeding, dying, waiting for the waves to take her, and do it then? Did she think he'd come to rescue her? Did she think she was saved?

Daniel peels himself up and drags his nails through his hair, gulping down breaths.

'It can't be one guy,' he says. 'Poppy knew Ben, but Rachel knew Dylan. Dylan has tattoos, longer hair. And Rachel was into music, not art. They've gotta be different guys.'

I flick through the folder to Poppy's drawings, my fingers still shaking with rage. Ben smiles at Poppy in cartoon form, tall with wavy hair, wrapped up in his scarf and coat, camera around his neck.

'That trail-cam photo of Dylan in the car was taken in summer, and we can't see Ben's arms because of his winter coat. Neither picture shows his face. Dylan's hair is longer, but if that image wasn't black and white, it could easily be the same light brown as Ben's.'

'But their names are different.'

'Or they're the same. Ben Dylan. He could have been using his last name with Rachel.'

I check online, searching the combination of names – but there are too many results, and none of them are who we're looking for.

'Or both were fake. Or one of them. Maybe Dylan is his real name, and he changed it when he came to Brighton? Maybe it was a compulsion of his, to murder like this. He did it once and got away with it. He had to do it again. He couldn't resist it. He met Poppy, and he . . . he . . .'

I cover my mouth, not sure if I'm going to cry, vomit, or curse.

'Clementine . . . I'm so sorry.' Daniel claws at his knees through his jeans, avoiding my eye. 'He killed Rachel first. If the police had believed me about the murder two years ago, they could have caught him already. And he wouldn't have been around to kill Poppy, too.'

His lips shake, tears springing from his eyes again.

'I should've stopped him.'

'No. You did what you could, but it's the police who didn't listen, and it was Ben – Dylan – whatever his real name is, who did this. Don't blame yourself. *Ever*. I certainly don't.'

I try to give him a reassuring smile despite the horror we share between us. 'You have nothing to be sorry for. We'll find him. Together. Because we have the necklaces now, and because of that, our stories prove each other. It's a connection between the two. Not just murders, but serial murders that follow the same pattern. You can prove it *was* a hand pushing Rachel in front of the train, and Poppy wearing the same necklace will prove that Ben pushed her over the edge that night. The necklace proves everything. It's a link. We can show that the same killer killed twice.'

The familiar excitement of discovery fizzes in my veins, tinged with a morbid darkness.

'If we can find where he got the necklace from, maybe we can find out who he is.'

I use my phone to search Google: *silver and rose-gold heart necklaces*. Fifty-seven million results pop up. I switch to images and scroll down, looking for similar styles.

Most of them are chunky pendants, or friendship necklaces with two sides of a broken heart, or lockets. Lots have diamonds and precious stones, others are engraved. I keep scrolling, looking for the thin, contrasting metal, the elongated heart, the distinctive loops and crossed point.

It doesn't come up.

'Anything?' Daniel asks.

'No. It's not specific enough, it's showing me *all* heart necklaces. Maybe . . .'

Like I did earlier with Poppy's drawings, I open the Google Lens app. I point the camera at my palm, the pendant clear and in focus, and click the shutter. Almost immediately, a page of similar images pops up: hollow hearts, thin metal, silver and rose gold.

But they're not quite like Poppy and Rachel's. I scroll and scroll, my own heart jumping and sinking, passing sellers' pages and jewellery designers' websites – until my heart jumps and doesn't sink. I click the image and it opens in the phone's Instagram app.

It's a shot of another palm holding a necklace just like Poppy's. The hand looks like a woman's, with a wrist full of beachy jewellery made of rope and shells disappearing out of the frame, and there's sand in the background.

#newbeginnings, the caption says.

'Daniel, look.'

He shuffles closer, squinting his bloodshot eyes as I hold Poppy's necklace beside the Instagram post.

'Oh my God. You found it. You actually found it. That's it! Who is she? Can we DM her to ask where she got it? Is she the seller?'

I hit her profile.

Imogen Hawkins: trainee accountant and wannabe free spirit. RIP.

RIP? Her feed is full of beautiful beach shots: sand and waves, rocky cliffs, blue skies turning water turquoise. It's Cornwall. I lived there with my family for enough years to know. I hit the latest post: a black-and-white image of Imogen Hawkins herself, smiling on the beach in a wetsuit, her long brown hair blowing in the wind in sun-bleached waves.

> *I'm so sorry to tell you this, but Imogen passed away last week. She was twenty, with her whole life ahead of her. We'll never know for sure what happened to her out on that beach, whether she knew how dangerous the rocks were or not, but we do know that her death was unexpected and has left us all devastated. If you ever feel sad or like you can't cope, please talk to someone. There is always time to talk to someone. We'll never forget you, Imz. Love you forever – Yaz x*

'Oh my God,' Daniel mutters. 'She's dead, too. She has the necklace, and she's dead. When was this?'

'September 2017.'

Daniel's shoulders sink. 'Rachel died in the June.'

My mouth goes dry. The horror of it deepens in my gut, like missing a step in the dark.

Ben got Poppy to trust him so easily. He knew exactly what to say to her to win her over, and knew exactly how to manipulate her into keeping him a secret from us. That wasn't luck; it was skill honed through practice.

He knew exactly what to do because he'd done it many, many times before.

'It's not just them,' I say, doing the maths in my head. 'Your sister died . . . twenty-six months ago? If Imogen was killed by the same person, in the September, then that's a gap of around three or four months. He killed Poppy in February of this year, which would be around twenty months after your sister. If he approached every murder the same way and spent the same amount of time planning it, that could be a murder every three months.'

'Every three months?' Daniel asks. 'That could mean . . .'

'Six victims by the time he killed Poppy. And possibly two more since then.'

We sit in silence, staring at Poppy's art on the wall: flowers, character sketches, painted sunsets. The enormity of it is over-whelming. Seven, eight, nine other victims? Seven, eight, nine other bedrooms just like this one, beds never again to be slept in, the families in the next room torn apart over a fake suicide they blame themselves for?

'He's still out there,' I say hollowly. 'He could be hunting his next victim right now. She has no idea. She thinks she's with some-one she can trust. She doesn't know. We have to save her. We can't let anyone else die like this.'

I open my folder on my lap and start scribbling down a plan of action.

'We might not know who he is yet,' I say, 'but we've got clues. Dylan, Ben . . . Those must be fake names, and Imogen must have known him as someone else. Maybe she has the information we need to identify him. Maybe it's her friends we need to talk to, not Rachel's or Poppy's. Maybe one of them saw his face, or has a photo of them together. We can use pieces of each woman's story to validate the others. Three identical necklaces are *not* a coincidence. We can prove this now.'

I know I'm right. I believe it. Poppy, Rachel, and Imogen's deaths slot together like puzzle pieces, each building up a picture. There are other victims out there, there must be, and they'll add to this, too. Once the police start investigating, they can find the others, and from there, they can find *him*. They can stop these murders, and give the families peace. We just need to give them enough evidence to believe us.

And I know how to do that.

One necklace found on a dead woman's body is just a necklace. A second necklace found on a second woman's body shows a possible connection. A third necklace confirms it.

To prove this, and to save whoever his next victim is, we're going to need Imogen's necklace, too.

IMOGEN

17 Months Before Poppy

Sometimes the waves are too powerful to ride. They crest and break over me, knocking me off my board, and I get dragged along under the water – blind, deaf, not knowing which way is up or when I'll get to breathe again, completely at the mercy of the sea.

This is like that.

Travis and I lie together on the sand, two jellyfish beached under the Cornish sun. My bikini bottoms cling to one ankle. Our wetsuits are in tangled heaps by our boards.

I twitch my fingers against his, too exhausted to do anything else.

'Do you always carry condoms in your trunks?' I ask.

'No, but I had a feeling I might need a few today.'

'Good shout.'

A cloud drifts over the sun, easing its glare. Above me, the blue sky is framed by a curve of rock, steep cliffs hemming us into a tiny private cove, accessible only by the sea.

'I bet someone saw us.'

'Nah.' Travis stretches and moves one arm under his head, the other pointing up. 'The coastal path doesn't come out this far. This is kind of a peninsula, so the path cuts it off. Trust me, nobody can see us here.'

He speaks with the certainty of experience. 'Ah. Is this the spot you bring all your girls, then?'

'Do you really want me to answer that?' He turns to me, head resting on his thick arm, and smirks. 'Nah. Most of them don't make it this far.'

I return his smirk and stare back up at the sky.

I came to Cornwall a month ago to learn to surf, to chase waves, to stare pensively out to sea at sunset, hair perfectly tousled from the salt water, chasing a lifestyle I'd only ever seen on Instagram. I wanted a few weeks of freedom.

What's more freeing than kissing a stranger around a beach campfire? Following him to his campervan? Undressing him in the dark, scrunching fists of his long, sun-bleached hair, tasting him, smelling him, screaming out a name I'd only just learnt and would certainly never scream again?

But our paths kept crossing. We'd float in the surf, waiting for waves and philosophising about life. We'd spot each other at the same beach parties, faces lit by fire, beer bottles glinting. And every night we'd end up going home together, breathless, clawing at each other, desperate for more.

But never once anchoring it with words.

'Where are you going next?' Travis asks.

'For dinner, you mean?'

'No, which city? Which country?' He props himself up, one hand stroking over my stomach. 'A girl like you has got places to see. What's next on your list?'

Next? There is no next for me. This was it: my escape. My change of scenery. Or as my parents called it, a phase, a little summer holiday before I snap out of things and come back home to my life, like I'm supposed to.

That life is written for me already. Another year at uni working for an Accounting degree I don't want so I can join a family business I hate. A lifetime in the same old beige town with the same old beige people. Marriage with Noah – sweet, sensible, utterly boring Noah, who my parents encouraged to propose and who paws at me with unsure, fumbling hands.

I can see it already. A lifetime of perfunctory, socks-on sex with a man who is nice, who takes care of me, but who has never, ever made me scream.

How am I supposed to go back to that now when it never made me happy before?

Travis's fingertips run across my hips. I beg them to go lower, to press harder, but they hover just too high, teasing my bare skin.

'I've told you my plans,' he says. 'Get out of this country, surf on all the best beaches in the world. Be the tourist for once. That's what I want. But what about you? What do *you* want?'

Has anyone ever asked me that before? My parents didn't. And that first date with Noah, the awkward Italian meal when he got basil in his teeth and kept dropping his knife, didn't end with a question about how I felt, but rather, '*Imogen, I'm so glad you're my girlfriend now.*' And I just went along with it, thinking that's what love is. That's what life is.

But now there's a choice sprawled out beside me on the beach.

What do I want? Truly?

'I want to go everywhere,' I say. 'I want to climb Kilimanjaro and see Sydney and get a bad tattoo in Thailand and backpack across America. I want to swim with sharks and watch reindeer in the snow.' I turn to Travis, shifting my hips and trapping his hand where I want it. 'And I want *this*, all over the world.'

His fingers respond, slow and firm.

'You want passionate love affairs with handsome locals? I'm not sure they'll all be as obliging as me.'

I pull his face to mine.

'No, I want you along for the ride. I've never met anyone like you, Travis. You're just what I want.'

As I kiss him, I realise what it is I was looking for when I came down here.

I wasn't running away from my old self; I was running *towards* my true one. And my true self is confident, wild, and makes her own decisions. She takes what she wants. She owns it.

She rides the wave.

I push Travis back against the sand and straddle him, grabbing another condom from the pocket of his discarded shorts. He grabs my hips, trying to control me, to set the pace, but I pin his arms above his head and find a rhythm of my own.

This time, the power is mine.

The sun is dipping in the sky, the shadows of the cove growing cold. The water is further in than it was when we got here. It slaps against the surrounding rocks, waves coming in choppy, broken spurts.

'We'll have to be careful when we leave,' I say as Travis kisses my shoulder and zips up my wetsuit. 'Looks like it'd be easy to lose control and get dragged against those rocks. It's not exactly the best spot for a concussion.'

'No, it isn't. Someone inexperienced could easily drown here. But don't worry.' He passes me my board, then uses his fingers to cut an X across his tanned chest, smiling. 'I'll keep you safe. Cross my heart.'

CHAPTER 24

On 23 February 2019, Poppy Harris fell from the cliffs at Hope Gap and died. Further investigation without the assumption of suicide will reveal this death to have been murder.

That's the hypothesis I started with, weeks ago – one that, although correct, has become rapidly dwarfed by the last few hours of investigation. I unclip the page from the front of my folder and put a new one in its place.

Poppy Harris, Rachel Burton, and Imogen Hawkins are three young women who died in similar circumstances within a two-year period, each wearing an identical necklace. Investigation of the links and similarities between these deaths will prove the existence of a serial killer.

I unwrap the fresh packet of colour-coded dividers Daniel and I bought on the way back to the flat, and start building up the new additional sections.

After assembling what we already know about Daniel's sister, we research Imogen Hawkins: twenty years old, born in Liverpool, attended Hull University to study Accounting. News articles state that she died on a solo holiday in Cornwall two years ago, and her death was ruled as misadventure. She took her surfboard to a dangerous area and, due to her inexperience, got into difficulties and drowned after hitting her head on the rocks.

Or that's how it looked to the coroner, anyway.

We find Yaz, the friend who left the memorial post on Imogen's Instagram account, and spend over an hour debating what to say to her via direct message. In the end, we opt for a compromise between my direct approach and Daniel's cautious one.

> *Hi. I'm sorry for contacting you out of the blue like this, but are you the Yaz who was friends with Imogen Hawkins?*

We stare at the screen, waiting for a reply, but the follow-up conversation jotted down in my notebook isn't necessary. She doesn't reply. Not yet, at least. But we'll be ready when she does. We go through Imogen's photos to find any group shots of tagged friends, and note down their names as backups. Despite the importance of getting the information we need to confirm multiple murders by the same person, Daniel and I both know how easy it is to burn through possible witnesses and come across as unhinged. We have to be patient.

But patience is hard, and not a quality that comes naturally to me.

Rachel, Poppy, Imogen. It can't only be the three of them, particularly as there's a gap of almost two years between the murders of Rachel and my sister. There could be five other deaths out there incorrectly ruled as suicides – and that's assuming Rachel was the first. Who knows how long this man has been targeting women in this way?

I have to find the others.

We start with suicide deaths. We print out pages and pages of articles from local newspapers across England – *teenage girl takes own life in woods tragedy; car park death ruled as suicide* – and spread them out across the coffee table, names and smiling faces staring up at us. We cross-reference with their social media accounts, trying to find young women from the same demographics as the deaths we already know about.

'Look for interests in photography, art, music, travel, beaches,' I say, uncapping a pink highlighter. 'Poppy was from London, but she was targeted in Brighton. Maybe coastal regions are a link.'

'On it,' Daniel says, shoving his pen behind his ear and typing something into Google.

'And obviously keep an eye out for any pictures with the necklace. That'll be our best proof, if we can find it.'

The necklace is the key. It's a firm link between the victims: the calling card the killer left behind to gloat about what he'd done. Daniel and I scour the internet for it, but nothing except Imogen's Instagram post ever exactly matches the ones we keep in our pockets. It must be a custom design, but from where? If we knew that, we could trace it back to the killer.

But that's the police's task, once we give them a solid enough presentation of evidence to be taken seriously. This isn't just about Poppy any more. Next time I call 101, it'll be to report a serial killer – and I'll have the information to prove it.

Using my Reddit account, I show the necklace to as many people as possible, hoping someone will recognise it. I flood the jewellery and metalwork subs with images and posts titled *Does anyone know where this necklace came from?* but get back links to different pendants hanging from different chains. On r/AskReddit, I ask a dozen different versions of the question: *Did any of your friends/relatives ever die wearing jewellery you didn't recognise? What was it?* but get dismissive, rude answers, silence, or stories about great uncles and inscribed watches. I even try r/BereavedBySuicide – the old haunt I no longer have a place in. *Did anyone else's friend/ relative die wearing a heart necklace like this? (UK only)* I ask, along with a photo. A few users are nice enough to comment to say no, a few wanted to know why I was asking, but there was nothing of value left on any of the posts.

By Thursday morning, Yaz still hasn't responded. I message her again, and so does Daniel from his own account, but we still don't get a reply. I check my phone every few minutes, but the messages I get are not the ones I need.

> *How are things, love? Dad says you're having some time off still. Enjoy! xxxxx*

> *Hello, Clementine? It's Brenda from the helpline. Weren't you supposed to have a shift last night? I hope everything is okay!*

> *Clem, please talk to me. I'm so sorry I didn't find your sister's letters earlier. I should have checked your mail and forwarded everything months ago. I hope you're okay. x*

I send back polite replies – to Mum and Brenda, anyway. I can't talk to Jenna. I don't know what to say. It's easier to keep flicking the notifications away, unread. It's a guilt I can handle.

I'm waiting for too many things: Yaz, a chance reply from a Reddit user, a call back from Sussex Police. But they don't come.

I prod the vulnerable, anonymous users of r/BereavedBySuicide more than I should, asking further questions: *Did anyone's loved one die unexpectedly? Did you ever suspect foul play? If something feels wrong to you, that's because it might not be suicide. PM me.*

Daniel and I take this tactic offline, too. We find as many in-person bereavement support groups as we can and visit them all, flashing the necklaces around, just in case someone somewhere recognises them. But of course, nobody does, and usually we're asked to leave.

'How are we supposed to find other victims when no one will talk to us?' Daniel asks as we trudge out of another support group meeting we've been barred from. He kicks at a lamppost. 'I hate this.'

'Me too. We *know* Imogen had a necklace, so we *know* she's another victim, but we can't do anything about it until someone talks to us. I'm sick of being polite, and rational. Let's just go to Yaz and ask her about it. In person.'

'In person?'

'Yes. I did it with one of Poppy's housemates. Yaz's Facebook probably has her place of work on it, and if we go back through her social media posts we'll probably be able to find references to which days she works, or where the place is. We can approach her there, and she won't be able to ignore us.'

I check my phone as we walk, scrolling through the snatches of Yaz's life she's shared online.

'There, an art shop in Birmingham. That's not too far by train. We could go tomorrow.'

Daniel blinks at me, then laughs. 'Wow. I really didn't take you for a stalker.'

'It's not stalking! It's . . . being resourceful. If Yaz knew her well enough to have access to her Instagram account, then she *must* know something about her death. We have to try.'

'All right, then. Let's go to Birmingham.'

◆ ◆ ◆

I recognise Yaz from her Instagram photos as we look in through the window of the art shop on Friday morning: brown-skinned with a small nose ring, her dark hair pulled up into a messy bun, eyebrows as sculpted as Liam's, dressed in denim dungarees, a white T-shirt, and trainers. There's no one else inside.

'Ready?' I ask Daniel.

'Almost.' He presses a fresh nicotine patch onto his arm and rolls the sleeve of his top back down, then tucks his hair behind his ears. I frown at it.

'Wait . . . Did you get a haircut?'

'Yeah, back in Margate. Didn't you notice? I shaved, too. Thought I might be taken a bit more seriously by people if I didn't look, you know, homeless. Did it work?'

I look him up and down: his skin is brighter, despite the exhaustion of our investigation, and his clothes are clean and more grown up. His hair suits him. He looks like a normal version of himself – the person he must have been before all this. I smile.

'You look great. Let's go in.'

The shop door is already open. We head inside, passing what look like locally made candles, figurines, and paintings, and go over to Yaz. She looks up from arranging a display of printed scarves.

'Can I help you?'

'Hi. I'm Clementine, and this is Daniel. We messaged you on Instagram, but I'm not sure if you saw. We'd like to talk about your friend, Imogen Hawkins?'

Yaz's customer-service smile disappears.

'You came to my *work*?' She crosses her arms, eyeing the exit and the fastest way there.

'It's nothing bad. We're not weird or anything.'

I regret it as soon as I say it. I long for Poppy to be lurking behind me, whispering suggested phrases in my ear so I can somehow make this awkward conversation go the way I need it to.

'What's this about? Go on, then. Out with it.'

261

'All right. We're here because . . . The thing is . . . We think there's a man who—'

'We're looking for our brother,' Daniel says. He rests his arm on the counter, casually, easily – but I can see his white knuckles, his shaking legs. He continues, talking fast, regurgitating one of the cover stories we brainstormed on the train. 'I know this seems totally random, but he ran away from home a few years ago and he took some of our mum's jewellery with him, you know, to sell. And we keep an eye on all this stuff, we're always looking for him, and the other day we tried using Google Lens on an old photo of Mum's and we got this.'

He holds up his phone, showing Yaz the image of the necklace on Imogen's Instagram account.

Daniel catches my eye, silently asking for backup. I give it to him.

'That's Mum's necklace,' I say, also leaning on the counter, trying to be just as casual. 'There, in that photo. So if she had it then, it means he gave it to her. It means they knew each other. I know she died not long after this was taken, and I'm so sorry for your loss, but . . .'

'But we've been looking for him for *years*, with no trace. This is the first time we've ever got close to somewhere where he was. So we had to talk to you. We had to.'

Yaz blinks at us. 'But what does this have to do with me?'

'We just need any information you can give us,' Daniel pleads. 'Anything. This necklace was precious to Mum, so he wouldn't have given it away to just anyone. He must have cared for her, and known her well. So . . . I don't know, did she ever mention anything about him? Did she say where he might have gone afterwards?'

'I don't know anything.'

Yaz bites her lip, looking away.

'Please,' Daniel says, real desperation peeking through the act. 'We really need to find him.'

She sighs. 'Okay, all right. She *was* seeing someone in Cornwall, but I never met him or anything.'

'Did she send you any pictures?' I ask. 'Um, so we could confirm the identity?'

'No, nothing like that. Look, it's all a bit awkward, if I'm honest. She kind of went through a quarter-life crisis and ran off to learn to surf for the summer, which was great, good for her, but she had a boyfriend back home – a sweet guy, really nice – but this other guy swept her off her feet and, yeah, she was cheating on her boyfriend, so . . .'

'Are you the only person she told?'

'Yeah. And I didn't tell anyone, either.'

'Not the police or anything?'

'Nah. I told her parents she'd made a friend, you know, in case they needed to interview people down in Cornwall or whatever, but I just kind of left out the fact that she was sleeping with him.'

I mentally jot down the pattern: secret relationships, making sure nobody else knew about it.

'Did she tell you his name?' Daniel asks.

'Uh, yeah. Travis.'

Ben, Dylan, Travis. *Bastard.*

'That's him,' Daniel says, feigning a smile. 'Our brother Travis.'

'Did she tell you anything else about him? Did she say how they met, what he was like, what he looked like?'

'Um, he was helping her learn to surf, I think. Not very well, obviously.' Yaz smiles sadly, a hint of anger in it. 'Yeah, she talked about how he looked a *lot*. She was crazy about him. Said he was gorgeous.'

I pull one of Poppy's drawings out of my bag: 'Ben' with his scarf blowing in the wind, jeans turned up, boots on, brown hair wavy, eyes green, a camera around his neck.

'Like this?'

'Oh.' Yaz takes the drawing, frowning. 'Oh, no, that's not him at all.'

'What?'

'He didn't look like that. He was fit. Athletic. She said he had, like, surfer dude hair. Long, wavy, blond. And muscles. This guy is a bit . . . weedy. Hers wasn't. He was probably one of those massive guys, taller than . . .' She gestures to Daniel. 'What are you, about five-eight?'

'Five-*ten*, actually,' he says, straightening up.

'Well, taller than that, probably. And with tattoos, I think.'

'What tattoos? Where? On his arm? Just here?'

'On a lot of places, I think. On his chest, definitely. Oh, maybe a dolphin on his arm? She said something about a dolphin, and waves.'

We couldn't make out the design on 'Dylan's' arm from the trail-cam shot, but it certainly wasn't a dolphin.

'Are you sure it couldn't be him?' I ask, pointing at the drawing. 'Did she mention anything about photography? Or a camera?'

'Or music? Gigs, maybe? Vinyl?'

'Sorry, that wasn't her thing. She didn't say.'

Yaz passes the drawing back to me.

'Sorry, it must've been another Travis. Are you sure it's the same necklace? Maybe it was a different guy, or a guy your brother sold it to? I hope you find him, anyway.'

◆ ◆ ◆

I want to stay, to ask more questions until things start making sense, but Daniel tugs me out of the shop and back to the train station.

'It's no use,' he says. 'This is a dead end.'

'But, the necklace—'

'I know, it's the same one, but it isn't the same guy.' He rubs his forehead. 'I don't know how she got the necklace or how she ended up dead, but I do know that Travis sounds nothing like Ben, and nothing like the kind of person Rachel would go for. He isn't the person who killed them. He can't be.'

I don't want Daniel to be right, but I can't argue against the facts.

We're just as alone in our search as we've ever been.

CHAPTER 25

'What now?' Daniel asks as we push through the crowds at Euston Station. 'More support groups? I saw there was one over in Stratford. We could try there? Clementine?'

I pull up beside a pillar, finding a pocket of space.

'I'll do the support groups. *You* need to go back to Kent.'

'What? Why?' He grabs – instinctively – for his neck, for the comforting tug of the chain, then remembers where it is, and what it represents. 'Did I do something wrong?'

'No, not at all. But you're right about dead ends. Imogen died in an apparent suicide, the same as Poppy and Rachel, and they all had a secret boyfriend and a necklace. What if Imogen *was* murdered, but someone else did it? There could be more than one killer following the same pattern. A group of them, spread out across the country. Travis in Cornwall, Ben in Sussex, and Dylan in Kent.'

'You think they were *all* different murderers?'

'I don't know, but it would explain why Poppy never mentioned Ben having a tattoo. Maybe they're friends, or part of a sick club.'

'I . . . Damn. You're right, it *could* be that.'

'Exactly. And if it is, if Dylan is just Dylan and he never even met Poppy, there's no point you coming with me to run between support groups when you've already got all the proof you need to go to the police with. The trail-cam image proves Rachel wasn't alone on her way to the tracks that night, and the train footage backs it up. You need to go to Kent and show them. You shouldn't be wasting time here with me.'

Daniel shuffles awkwardly. 'It's not wasting time, Clem.'

'It is, and you know it. Maybe we were wrong to try to push this link between their deaths. You go to Kent, and I'll call Brighton again.'

'They don't listen to me in Kent, you know that! What's the point?'

'They'll listen to you this time.' I open my bag and pull out a plastic envelope of typed papers. 'I put everything together for you about Rachel's murder, including the stills that show she wasn't alone that night. As long as someone there looks at this, they'll have to take you seriously. And half the hard work has already been done for them in these files.'

I pass it to him.

'When did you do all this?' he asks, checking the papers.

'Last night, when you were sleeping.'

'You told me you slept, too.'

'I lied.' I smile. 'This was more important.'

He grips the envelope tightly, and stands up straight.

'All right. I'll do it. I'll talk those bastards into believing me, and then once they do, once they're taking it seriously, I'll tag you in. Even if it's different killers, the circumstances are too similar to ignore. Margate might even contact Brighton directly. Official channels and all that.'

'Exactly. Take the folder to them, prove Rachel's murder, and get the ball rolling. Go on.'

I point him towards the Underground, but he hesitates.

'Are you sure? I can stay here, with you. I don't have to go.'

'Yes, you do. You've waited long enough for evidence you can use. Go and use it.'

Daniel pulls me into a hug, his arms clamped tightly around me.

'Thank you,' he mumbles into my ear as I hug him back. 'I won't let you down.'

◆ ◆ ◆

Daniel's visit to the police in Margate is going to trigger a cascade of parallel investigations – and I need to be ready for Poppy's.

By Saturday morning, I have two envelopes prepared: one full of copies of Poppy's letters and drawings, typed-up statements, and general information supporting the murder theory, and the second with everything supporting the multiple-murder theory. Even if it isn't the same killer, the necklace indicates a pattern or modus operandi, something perhaps shared between multiple men: Ben, Dylan, and Travis. Friends? Partners in crime? Or strangers trying to outdo each other in the sickest way possible using the same parameters?

Is this a game to them?

I can't think about that. This is bigger than me, or Daniel. We need the police to take over. I pack the envelopes into my bag and head for the front door.

'Hey, hun. Where are you off to?' Liam asks from the kitchen, folding flour into a bowl of batter.

'Library,' I say quickly.

'The library? *Again?* You must've read everything in there by now.'

I twist my backpack straps, feeling the familiar guilt of lying. I still haven't told him the truth about what happened to Poppy, and why I was looking for Ben. I haven't quite worked out the best way to introduce it. '*You know that dead sister of mine? Turns out she was murdered! And so was Daniel's! Possibly by the same person! Cool, right?*

'Is Daniel with you?' Liam asks, trying to peek around my bedroom door. 'I noticed he wasn't on the sofa this morning.'

'He went back to Margate.'

'Ah. He must be single-handedly keeping Southern Rail in business, that one. Always coming and going. What did he go back for?'

It's easier to tell the truth when it's not about me.

'Do you remember me saying he lost his sister to suicide?'

'Yeah, poor guy.'

'Well, it turns out it wasn't suicide after all. She was murdered.'

'Oh my God. That's . . . that's awful. How did they find out? Do they know who did it?'

'Not yet, but once the police open their investigation, they'll find him. Daniel's taking the evidence he's gathered over there today.'

'You mean, the police don't know about it yet? *He* found out about it?'

'Yes. He found some CCTV that nobody else had access to.'

'Oh, wow. Good for him. I mean, no, not *good*, because his sister died, but you know what I mean. No wonder he always looked such a state, with all that going on. It'd wreck anyone's mental health.'

Liam sets his spoon down and tastes a fingertip of batter.

'And what about you?'

'Me? What do you mean?'

'Did you find that Ben guy you were looking for?'

'Uh, yes and no. It's complicated.' This is my moment to tell him, to get it off my chest – but I don't. Soon enough, what happened to Poppy won't be a secret any more. For now, let him enjoy his baking. 'Anyway, I should be going. See you later.'

'All right, C. Have a great day! I'll have this cake ready for you when you get back.'

He gives me a thumbs-up, but my fingers are too tightly clenched around my backpack straps to return it. I give me a brief smile and leave the flat, the music across the hall thumping as usual.

I go to the local post office, package up the envelopes together, and send them to Brighton police station. I hope they check their post more often than their messages.

My own phone pings with a notification as I exit the shop. I blink at it, shielding the screen from the sun, reading it several times.

It's a reply to one of my Reddit posts in r/BereavedBySuicide: *Did anyone else's friend/relative die wearing a necklace like this?*

> *That's weird, my daughter had the same one? Found it in her things.*

The words are linked. I click them, and a slightly blurred image opens: a rough, burly man's hand holding an identical necklace: heart-shaped, two metals, a rose-gold chain. I hit the private message button, and autocorrect makes up for my impatient fingers.

> *What happened to your daughter? When did she die? How?*

I get a message back within a minute.

> *Eliza took her own life in March 2018. She was away at university in Cardiff.*

I do the maths: she died around halfway between Rachel and Poppy. *Cardiff. Wales.* How widespread is this? How many people are involved?

What name are we looking for this time? What person?

Was your daughter seeing anyone? I type. *Did she have a boyfriend?*

> *'I don't think so. The inquest said she'd recently started taking the pill, and it caused suicidal tendencies and*

depression, but that was for her cramps. That's what her
mum told me. But I don't know.'

Another secret relationship. Another family kept in the dark.
What handbook are these men working from?
The man messages again.

Why are you asking about a necklace? Is there something
special about it? I looked at your posts. Is it linked to
suicide somehow? Is it a cult? Do girls wear them for a
reason? It's nothing like what she used to wear.

I frown.

What jewellery did she usually wear?

Skulls, spiderwebs, that kind of thing. She liked creepy
things. Always silver. That's why I remembered the neck-
lace when I saw yours. It stood out.

His next message, after a delay, is another photo link: a teenage
girl with long, dyed-black hair, dark eyeliner, steel-toed boots, and
layers of black clothes, next to a middle-aged man in a green rugby
shirt. He has his arm around her, smiling proudly, while she smirks
at him. There's a rat on her shoulder.

She was a very clever girl. She studied psychology. I guess
she was drawn to mental health because she was strug-
gling with her own. It should have been a warning sign,
really. All those skulls and black clothes and the things
she'd reblog on Tumblr. She told us the goth thing was

271

*just her style, but we should have trusted our gut. She
was never well.*

I breathe fast, anger rising in me. Anger, and realisation.

You're sure she wasn't seeing someone?

I'm sure.

But if she was, what would he look like?

After I get a response, I call Daniel, gripping the phone tight,
pacing along the street.

'Hey. I'm at the police station. Can I call you back?'

'No!'

'No? Why not?'

'I just got a message on Reddit. There's another victim. Same
necklace, university age, died about a year and a half ago. But this
one, Eliza, she was a goth. She only ever wore black.'

'A goth? That's pretty different from everyone else.'

'Yes, and I think that's the point. I think that's what he wanted.'

'He? I thought we were thinking there were multiple killers?'

'Not any more. I should have put things together sooner.'

Pacing isn't enough. I point myself in the direction of the towpath, wanting a straight line to march down.

'Each of these women were different types of people. Poppy
was an artist, Rachel was a musician, Eliza was a goth, and Imogen
was into surfing and finding herself and exploring new places.'

I keep walking. I do this at Harvard, in the library, the lab, the
apartment, turning thoughts over in my mind, searching for connections, conclusions.

'The killer murdered these women and staged their deaths as suicides so he wouldn't be caught. He wanted to get away with it. He didn't want anyone investigating a murder, so he hid it entirely. But he couldn't *know* it would work, not for sure. So maybe . . . maybe this is his backup. His failsafe. He's been killing *different* women, ones who *won't* be linked together by liking the same band or studying the same thing at uni. Their differences are part of the pattern.'

'Oh my God,' Daniel mutters. 'But how'd he find them? Why *them*? Why Rachel? Why Poppy?'

'I don't know. Actually, maybe I do. Poppy shared her art online, and Imogen was on Instagram, too. Eliza's dad mentioned something about Tumblr—'

'And Rachel had YouTube and SoundCloud for her music.'

'He found them online.' A map visualises in my head. 'He picked women at random, scattered across the UK. Not just in the south, but in Wales, too. He must have found them online and targeted them that way. And as the deaths were geographically spread out, he again limited his chances of being caught. Nobody was going to bump into someone else who this had happened to.'

'Until we did.'

'Yes. Us meeting was the one thing he couldn't control.'

I know everything I'm saying is right, but there's no joy in it. It's a breakthrough I wish I'd never had to have.

'Poppy's whole life was spread across her social media. Her likes, dislikes, her movements. It would have been easy for a stranger to see her personality and assimilate it for himself, and to create a Tinder account with a profile that she'd be sure to like.'

I hit the towpath, walking faster.

'We were looking at her drawings the wrong way. We thought she'd drawn him, the killer, but she'd only drawn who the killer was

273

for her. She drew Ben, but Ben wasn't the person in the car with your sister that night. Ben didn't teach Imogen to surf, or do whatever he did to make Eliza fall for him. He was someone different for each of them. He was just who he knew they'd want him to be.'

'Oh my God.' I can hear Daniel scraping his fingers through his hair, breathing raggedly. 'He changes how he looks, like a . . . a . . .'

'Chameleon.' I pass the family bench, digging my nails into my palm. 'He adapts to each victim by becoming exactly the kind of person they're looking for, in looks and personality. He makes them think he's their perfect match. And then once they fall for him, he kills them, and moves on to the next.'

The horror of it doesn't fit the shining, algae-green water, or the ducks lazily floating in it.

I try to imagine the person Eliza fell in love with: spiked hair? Piercings? Black nails? And Imogen: tanned muscles? Bleached hair? Woven jewellery? He could change his voice and accent with every new woman. Alter his posture or his walk. Make jokes. Make none. Change his hair colour. Grow a beard. Shave it. Wear coloured contact lenses. Tan his skin. Change it with make-up. Study his victims and their hobbies until he's word-perfect, able to take their interests and weaponise them against them.

He could become anyone he wanted to.

So how do we even know who we're looking for?

I see the UK in map-form again, pins marking the murder locations. Margate, Newquay, Brighton, Cardiff.

That Reddit user, whoever he is, is a father coping with a child's suicide, convinced that his daughter took her own life. It's a familiar story. I've lived it myself, and so has Daniel. So have my parents, and Imogen's, but . . . it's *more* familiar than that. I've spoken to someone like that before. Someone who, now I think about it,

274

claimed to wear their daughter's necklace every day as a reminder of her.

Musician, goth, surfer, artist.

Bookworm?

'I have to go,' I tell Daniel, exiting the towpath to get to the nearest Tube station. 'Show the police the envelope. Explain everything.'

'Okay. Where are you going?'

'To the helpline. I think I know who victim number five is.'

CHAPTER 26

It's midday and very much daylight in Whitechapel, but the Ripper tours still meander the streets, guides terrifying children with gory details, tourists snapping photographs of the places where women lay dead long ago.

Will Hope Gap become a place curious strangers visit because of murder podcasts and true-crime documentaries? Will Poppy be remembered for ever as a dead body on a beach rather than the talented, sensitive, stubborn, untidy, infuriating, kind, grateful, hopeful, happy person she was for almost nineteen years?

I head upstairs to the helpline as though this is just another shift, passing the logbook in reception, the white walls, the green poster with its cloying phrase: *However alone you feel, we'll always be here to talk*. I can hear murmuring from the phone room, the listeners already bringing comfort with stock responses and generic, hopeful tones.

Suicide begets suicide. It's not uncommon for someone who lost a friend or family member to suicide to feel like doing the same, and to act on it. It happened to Daniel, cutting scars into his arms and dragging him to the roof of a building. It happened to Blessing, too – the caller from a few weeks ago who told me she lost her daughter to suicide and who has worn her heart necklace every day since. That can't be a coincidence.

How many others of us are there? How many other lives has this killer ruined?

I want to ruin his.

Brenda comes out of the kitchen at the end of the corridor with a handful of mugs and biscuits and heads into the phone room, and I duck into her office. I'll have to be quick. I search around for the right folder, and eventually find it in a drawer: *Regular Callers and Call Plans.* I flick through it, searching for Blessing's name.

'Clementine?'

I snap the folder closed. Jude stands in the doorway.

'I didn't know you were coming in today. What are you doing in here?'

'I was . . . updating my handbook.'

'Oh, right.'

Neither of us move, or say anything. Jude breaks first.

'Look, about last week. I want to apologise. I overreacted about Daniel. I should have listened to what you were saying about him, and I should have trusted you. You know what you're doing. I'm sure you have your reasons – good reasons – for allowing him into your life, and it's not something you'll have done blindly. I'm sorry for doubting you. Really. I'm sorry.'

He touches his chest, right over his heart. His kind smile has returned – but right now, I don't have time to look at it. I grip the closed folder in front of me. Brenda will be back at any moment, and what happened the other night no longer matters.

'Apology accepted,' I say. 'But only if you get me a coffee.'

He laughs. 'Milk, no sugar. Coming right up.'

He leaves and I flip open the folder. Then he pops his head around the door again, smiling his gentle smile.

'I'm really glad you came back, Clementine. The phone room isn't the same without you.'

Once he's gone, properly this time, I rifle through the folder and find Blessing's details. Full name, home address, phone number. These are for our records only, to be used in emergencies and to identify incoming calls. I take a picture of her information, and type the number into my phone. I don't wait to say goodbye to anyone. I exit the office – but I can hear people coming up the stairwell. I go up it too, heading to the roof, where I'll be alone. I get out into the fresh air and press the call button, shutting the door behind me.

'Hello, can I help you?' Blessing asks in her familiar Nigerian accent. My brain goes blank for a moment; I hadn't actually thought about what I'd say. I crouch down and pull out my folder, grabbing a pen and blank page.

'Hi, Blessing. I'm from the UK Listeners helpline, and I'm terribly sorry for calling you out of the blue. This is a . . . courtesy call. A check-up. It's a new initiative we're trialling for our regular callers.'

'I see. How lovely. We've spoken before, haven't we? I recognise your voice.'

She says it like she's smiling. To anyone else, this call would be intrusive and distasteful, but Blessing is too good-natured to ever hang up. If she feels uneasy, she doesn't let it show. Perhaps she doesn't feel that way at all. Perhaps her loneliness makes even the strangest of calls worth listening to.

And now I have to reopen the wounds she's tried so hard to heal.

'So, how are you, Blessing? When we first spoke, you told me about how you've kept all your daughter's books. You also mentioned that you have a few other things of hers as keepsakes. Is that right?'

'Yes. I keep Yewande's photograph in every room, and I talk to her when I am cleaning, reading, cooking the dinner. I am a nurse, and I tell all my patients about her. I keep her present with me, always.'

'Lovely, lovely.' I clear my throat. 'And didn't you say something about wearing an item of hers? What was it, a scarf? A bracelet?'

'Her necklace. It is a pretty thing.'

'Oh? What's it like?'

'It is a heart. I do not know if it suits me, but I like to wear it all the same. She never wore jewellery, so for her to wear this, it must have been very special to her.'

'A heart? How lovely. Is it a locket? A solid pendant?'

'No, it is a . . . I do not know how to describe it. An outline? A hollow shape made of two kinds of metal. Silver and—'

'Rose gold?'

'Huh. Yes. How did you know?'

I clench my fist. I was right. Yewande is another victim, and I know the kind of hurt and pain Blessing will feel when we tell her the truth about the necklace. Her world will be shattered. Her progress lost. She'll rip the chain off her neck like Daniel did, and hate herself for ever wearing it at all.

I can't tell her the truth about it. Not now. Not yet.

Let her have another day of comfort, at least.

'I'm so sorry, Blessing, but I have to go. There's . . . another caller on the line.'

'Oh. Oh, you must answer them immediately, please. They need you more than I do.'

'Thank you.'

'No, thank you. What a nice phone call to get. Take care, my dear.'

'Goodbye.'

Yewande Arnold-Smith. I note down in my folder, putting a ring around it. I type the name into Google and, sure enough, the social media accounts come up: a Facebook profile showing her location and university course; a Twitter feed of retweeted opinions; a Goodreads account with an overflowing list of book reviews.

Yewande was an easy target. They were all easy targets. They didn't even know they were being hunted.

I cross my legs and rub my temples, the folder open in front of me.

He's been doing this for years: finding a girl, becoming everything she wants, then killing her. Why? Is it a game for him? Is he collecting them? Does he just do it because he *can*?

Where is he now? Most people have sprawling social media accounts and an online presence. I could type any random combination of first and last names into Google and find hundreds of possible victims, all with their lives laid bare for him to imitate.

Who would he go after next? What type of person? They've mostly been creative so far – the ones I know of, anyway. Is that a link? Open-minded, imaginative, kind girls? Are they more malleable? Can he twist and reshape them like the metals on the necklaces he gives them?

He must follow them, stalk them, find out *everything* about them. How else could he so perfectly present himself as someone they could fall in love with? It must be like a research project for him. Does he have a folder like mine, colour-coded, each woman broken down into hobbies, political preferences, favourite films, style, celebrity crushes? Does he brainstorm ways to make them love him? Does he get the same thrill of triumph I get when he makes a breakthrough, when he finally finds the one intrinsic piece of data that will allow him to complete his project?

What was it for Poppy? What was so special about him that he managed to get my shy, anxious sister out of the safety of her bedroom and on to the rocks of that beach?

I pick through the copies of her letters in my folder. I want to cry, and tear them up, and scream at the top of my lungs – but

I force myself to read them. Really, properly read them. Not just skimming for clues, not just looking for dates and locations for CCTV. I focus on her words, her feelings, her heart.

But as I read, I can't help but spot a pattern that's been there all along.

I've told Ben all about you!

Ben laughed so much when I told him about that time on Primrose Hill when we got soaked waiting for a sunset.

I'm not into sci-fi but Ben is, so you can be buddies when he comes to London! He says you'll have loads in common.

Ben asks about you a lot. You're going to be best friends when you finally meet!

Ben asked me if you're single today. I said you're married to science, hehe!

And, finally, in the very last letter Poppy ever wrote to me, the one Daniel and I have scrutinised for a week.

You're going to love him though, Clemmie. You have to come home this summer when he's here to visit! He says he can't wait to meet you.

I want to be wrong. I flip through the letters again, hoping the words will spontaneously rewrite themselves – but they stay the same, my sister's reprinted inky swirls unchangeable.

I flick to the portrait from Poppy's sketchbook. Ben stares up at me from behind his camera with that intense eye, and the challenge hidden within it. But now I read it differently. Not *catch me if you can,* but *see you soon.*

They talked about me. The killer asked Poppy questions, and she answered them. She knew me so well. From her, he could have learnt everything about me. All the time he was getting to know her, he could also have been getting to know me. He could have learnt everything he'd need to know to eventually inject himself into my life, and do to me exactly what he did to my sister.

Musician, goth, free spirit, painter, bookworm – and scientist?

Am I his next target?

'Clementine?'

I jump. The roof access door is thrown wide and Jude stands there, panting slightly, frustrated panic on his face. He tries to gloss over it with a casual smile.

'I was looking everywhere for you. What are you doing up here?'

He keeps smiling, but I don't smile back. I can't. Dread floods my arteries, and every heartbeat deposits more of it in my gut.

I've been back in England for six months, since the day Poppy died.

What if the killer is in my life already?

CHAPTER 27

My heartbeat hammers in my ears. The killer has been blond, dark-haired, thin, muscular, arty, athletic, green-eyed, blue-eyed. He could look like anyone; disguise himself as anything.

Why not a fellow helpline volunteer?

Jude has always been kind to me. Too kind. He draws the way Poppy does. He asks me about her. He *is* her: creative, curly-haired, always sticking a pencil behind his ear the way she used to, or making drawings for me like she did. But I've never actually seen him create one from scratch. We share the same shifts. He's here, now, when I can't even remember what day it is any more. What are the chances of that? That he'd just happen to be here now? That he'd have followed me to the roof if he was just here to answer phone calls?

He was angry when he found out I knew Daniel. He tried to get rid of him. He said he was dangerous.

Why would he think Daniel was dangerous unless he knew Daniel was a danger *to him*?

'Clementine?' Jude says again, stepping forward. He towers over me – tall like Ben, solid like Travis, tattooed like Dylan, dark-haired like the heavy metal band members Eliza idolised. 'Are you all right? What's wrong?' He glances at my phone, my folder. 'What are you doing up here?'

'Nothing. I'm . . . fine.'

I grab my things and get to my feet. I wish I could be brave and defiant, but I'm shaking. I feel sick.

I'm tall, but he's taller. His arms are strong.

It's just the two of us on this roof.

No witnesses.

His brown eyes don't feel warm and kind any more. They aren't framed by the crinkle of a smile, or glinting with understanding. There's an edge to him, a severity, like there was that night in the flat when he was warning me about Daniel.

The first time we met, after I thought Daniel jumped during our call, Jude comforted me. He tried to make me feel safe.

I don't feel safe now. I feel the chasm of the eight-storey drop behind me.

Is Jude's face the last thing Poppy saw? Did she trust those eyes like I did? Did he touch her with those hands? Push her to her death with them?

Is he the man she loved?

Has he been using her death to try to get close to me, too?

'Don't lie to me,' he says. 'Not any more. I wanted to believe you were okay, but you're not, are you? You've never been. I should have trusted my gut when you started posting about incorrect verdicts and murder and necklaces, but—'

'How do you know about that?'

I hug my folder to my chest, as though it will protect me. I step back, away from him.

He hangs his head, cursing under his breath.

'I found your Reddit account a while ago. It was an accident. I post on Suicide Watch too, and I noticed your username kept cropping up, and one night your comments were a bit more personal and I got curious and I realised it was you. I know I shouldn't have

284

kept checking what you posted, but I was worried about you. I wanted to help. Let me help you, Clementine.'

He steps forward again, hands reaching for me – hands I can't trust. Hands I don't want on me. Not now, not ever. I step back again, and hit the low wall of the roof.

'Come away from the edge, Clementine.'

I grip the wall with one hand, trying to breathe.

'We can talk about it. It doesn't have to be like this. Things will get better, I promise. This . . . theory you have, about what happened to your sister? It's not what it seems. It's depression, and denial. You're not well, Clementine. Let me help you.'

He holds his hands out to me, approaching slowly. To comfort me, or to kill me?

I dig my nails into the concrete.

He could have lunged at me the moment he saw me, but he hasn't. If he were the killer, why would he draw it out? Maybe he is here to help. Maybe he really does think I'm unwell and a danger to myself.

Or is that just what he'll tell people after I've fallen? Will he say he rushed up too late to stop it? That he reasoned with me but it didn't work? Will the impact from the fall obscure the fact that it was his hands that shoved me over the side?

I can't let that happen.

Sensing my movement, he darts forward and tries to grab me, but I dodge to the side. I swing my folder as hard as I can, aiming for his face, and catch him in the jaw. As he cries out, I duck under his arms and run for the stairs.

He calls after me, and keeps calling as I reach the bottom of the stairs and exit the building. I keep going, breathless and clammy, putting as much distance as I can between him and me.

When I glance back at the end of the street, he's standing at the exit, staring after me. Rubbing his face.

I turn away and burrow into a crowd, using them for safety as their costumed tour guide leads them down a side street.

'. . . but of course, even the most respectable gentleman walking these streets should have been viewed with suspicion. For the poor Canonical Five, the assumption that Jack the Ripper was as trustworthy as his visage implied was their biggest mistake, and not one that could ever be undone.'

We pass the doorway where Jude and I sheltered during the storm. I feel his finger brush my cheek again, his skin warm against mine. I shudder, and peel off from the group to join the main road.

I keep walking, so fast my lungs burn. The further I get from the helpline, the easier it is to breathe, to think.

Jude tried to grab me on the roof – but was that to push me, or to pull me back from the edge? Did he want to end my life, or save it? Did I hit an attacker, or attack a friend?

There's no way to know.

The killer could be Jude – but there are differences. He's been friendly to me, nothing more. I'm not seeking a relationship like Poppy was with her Tinder account. I'm not seeing anyone. I'm not in love. If Poppy's letters are indicative of a pattern, then the victims are only in danger once they fall in love. That's the moment he kills. That's when he's got what he wants from them.

But I'll never let him get that from me.

I wait on the platform for a Tube, taking deep, calm breaths.

I might not be the next victim at all. This could be paranoia, or insomnia, or self-importance. Or all three. Of course the killer would appear to take an interest in Poppy's family. He probably asked questions about Mum and Dad, too, and did the same with the other women. It doesn't mean anything that he asked about me so much. I'm not special.

But it was *me* he called from her phone that night on Hope Gap. He left that voicemail for *me*.

I shiver, even though I'm sweating. The platform is becoming crowded, new people streaming in and positioning themselves behind me. There's a helpline poster on the wall above the tracks, as there always is: *However alone you feel, we'll always be here to talk.*

He pushed Rachel. He pushed Poppy. Whether I fall for him or not, whether I know him or not, he could push me, too.

The train screeches in the tunnel, but I squeeze back through the crowd – of men, of possible killers – and up the escalators to the exit. Once out in the sunshine, I use my phone.

'Sussex Police, how can I help you?' a woman asks. She's too cheery.

'I need to speak to someone from Brighton Police. It's urgent.'

'If you submit a report to me, I can pass it on to—'

'No! I've tried that, and nobody ever gets back to me. I need to be put through to an officer, right now.'

'I'm afraid that's not how our system works any more.'

'Then what am I supposed to do? I have evidence that my sister's suicide was staged by her murderer, but nobody will speak to me!'

'Oh. Look, when did you first call? I'll see if I can check on your report for you, make sure that it got through. What's your name?'

Fist clenched, I go through the same old process of giving my details and Poppy's.

'Harris, Harris . . .' the operator says, like she's scrolling down a list. 'There we are, report submitted last week. I can confirm it was passed on to officers in the Brighton and Hove department, and it *was* looked at. In fact, someone flagged the report to say that . . . . Ah.'

'Ah?' I ask. 'What does it say? Are they looking into it? Are they going to contact me?'

'Ms Harris . . . it says here that your father has been in contact with the station to withdraw your report.'

I stop at a traffic light, a bus roaring past me.

'Excuse me?'

'That's what the note says. I'm sorry, this must be very distressing for you. I'm sure your father has your best interests at heart. Suicide is an awful thing, I'm not surprised you're struggling to cope with it.'

I can't breathe in these crowded streets, this dense air.

This is why nobody has returned my calls? Because *Dad* told them not to?

The operator on the line clears her throat. 'I can recommend some support groups, if you like? How does that—?'

I hang up, and force myself to cross the road. Why would Dad do this? Why wouldn't he want us to know the truth about Poppy?

I have to get to the café.

Mum is wiping tables when I walk in, my feet sore and blistered in my shoes. I haven't been here for days, weeks, yet everything is the same as always: rich coffee smells; cosy wooden tables and chairs; Poppy's handwriting on the menu boards and her flowery landmark paintings on the walls. The stark reminders of her at every turn.

I try not to look at them as I make my way through the tables. 'Mum?'

'Oh!' Mum jumps, clutching a cloth to her chest. 'You scared me, love. What are you doing here? I thought you were having some days off?'

'Where's Dad? I need to speak to him.'

'He's sorting out the delivery. I was about to help him, but . . .' Her smile slips. 'Sweetheart, what's the matter? I thought you'd been resting, and getting better. When did you last sleep? Have you been eating? You need to eat.'

She reaches for me, trying to fuss with my hair, my face, but I jerk away.

'I'll go and find him.'

'No. Sit down and I'll bring him to you. Have a cake. A big one. I'll be back in a minute.'

She heads for the kitchen door, but looks back before she goes through it. Her mouth is a thin, pale line.

I sink into a free seat, trying not to look at Poppy's paintings. Trying not to think about –

'Clementine? Hi!'

Alexander waves at me from his usual table in the corner, his ginger hair fiery in the sunlight and his books stacked up around him.

'I was hoping I'd bump into you. Bit last minute, I know, but I just managed to get tickets to that special screening of *Interstellar* – you know, the one with all the astrophysicists who talk through all the science after – and I was wondering if you wanted to go with me? It's next Friday. My treat.'

He smiles nervously, his cheeks pink. His glasses have slid down his freckled nose, and he pushes them back up with a finger.

I dig my nails into my knees, trying not to be sick.

Alexander has the same interests as me. He lives across the hall from me. He comes to *this* café every single day.

Did he follow me on the towpath that night to force an introduction because I'd taken too long to notice him? Was it an innocent chance meeting of two people with very specific, narrow interests, or something else?

Something contrived?

Does he even need to wear glasses? Would the freckles rub off if I touched them?

Has he swapped gushing about art for science?

The kitchen door swings open and Mum and Dad come out, but I get up and head them off at the counter, turning my back on Alexander's table. I don't want him to hear this.

'What's this about, Clem?' Dad asks. 'Your mum said—'

'Why did you tell the Brighton police not to talk to me?'

'Eh?'

'You told them not to take my calls. Why? Why did you do that?'

'I didn't. I . . .' Dad scratches his head. 'What are you on about? Calling the police? Who's been calling the police?'

'The inquest is over,' Mum says gently. 'We don't need to—'

'Poppy was murdered.'

Mum gasps. '*What?*'

'I've been trying to get the Brighton police to reopen the investigation, but they won't take my calls. They told me *you* told them to ignore my report. It sounds like you said I wasn't well, that I wasn't coping, and—'

Dad grips my shoulders. 'I never did that, sweetheart. Never. I've been worried about you, yes, we both have, but we haven't called anyone.' He exchanges a look with Mum. 'Should we call someone?'

'No! I'm fine. But Poppy was murdered.'

'Clementine,' Dad says, 'that isn't what the coroner—'

'Fred, listen to her,' Mum whispers. She clutches his sleeve, her knuckles white. 'What if she's right? What if it wasn't suicide? What if I *didn't* miss the signs?'

'I can prove it.' I pull away from Dad and dig out my folder, and flip through the sectioned and highlighted pages. 'See? See? It's all here. I found her letters, and what happened to Daniel's sister proved it. There are more victims. It's a serial killer. He—'

Dad takes the folder from me and closes it, firmly.

290

'Heather, could you check on the outside tables? I think there are some empties.'

'But, the folder . . .'

'Outside, please. I'll finish up with Clementine.'

Mum doesn't want to go, but she takes a tray and heads out anyway, looking back at us for as long as possible. Dad waits until she's out of earshot before speaking.

'I won't have you doing this to your mother. Six months she's been heartbroken, and since the inquest she's finally been getting better. She's smiling again. She's sleeping through the night. I won't let you take that away from her.'

'But, Dad, Poppy was *murdered*. I have proof. I have her letters.'

'I don't care what you think you have. Poppy took her own life, and we have to live with it. *You* have to live with that. I didn't call the police, but obviously I should have. You're not well. You need help. The police could see that, apparently, and I've pretended everything's fine for too long now. You need to see someone. A specialist. They can help you. But this . . .' He points at the folder, at its mass of research and section dividers. 'This isn't healthy. This is obsessive.'

He presses the folder back into my hands, pity in his eyes. When Sussex Police receive the package of evidence I sent them this morning, will they look at it with the same expression before tossing it into the bin?

This is what happened to Daniel.

Nobody would look at his evidence. The police didn't believe him. His mother had him sectioned. Everyone thought his story was imagined, because . . .

Because the killer made them think that?

Dad didn't call the Brighton police, but someone did. They've never returned my calls, not even the first one – and that was the morning after I found the letters. I acted as soon as I got them. They were delivered to me on the Friday, and then . . .

Wait, no. They weren't delivered to me. They were delivered to Alexander. And when I picked them up from his flat, the package was *open*.

He's watching me from his corner table. When he sees me looking, he ducks back down behind a book, pretending to read – knocking his coffee cup off the table.

Dad sighs.

'I'd better clean that up. Stay here, Clem. We'll talk about this after closing, okay?'

He rushes over with the dustpan and brush, but I don't stay. I grip my folder tight and head out on to the street, passing Mum on her way back inside – 'Clem? Where are you going now?' – and Poppy's favourite boat with the sunflowers on the towpath, and the bench where we always sat for picnics. I don't break into a run, not properly, but I move as fast as I can, glancing back, making sure I'm not being followed.

When I finally get back inside the flat, I lock the door behind me and slide the chain across, checking the peephole, just in case. Nobody. I lean against the door, eyes closed, breathing properly for the first time in hours.

Then I stagger to the kitchen and get a glass of water, glugging it down, gripping on to the counter with a chalkboard message scrawled above it: *Look on the bright side, Ms Sexy Librarian!*

The glass slips through my fingers and smashes against the floor. I whip around, checking the tiny flat, checking the seats, listening for sounds.

Liam. *Liam.*

Always friendly. Always complimenting me. Always taking an interest in me. Inviting me for drinks, wanting to spend evenings with me – why? I'm not good company, and I'm a worse friend. Nobody can be *that* nice. Not really. So why take an interest? Why pull me in for hugs? Why offer me a room here at what we both know is a ridiculously low rent?

Why *me*?

Isn't it all a bit too convenient?

There's a plate of iced cupcakes on the coffee table, a bell jar over them. Liam is always baking, filling the flat with the smell of sugar and bread and fruits and cake and pastry.

The smell of my childhood. A smell Poppy could have told him about.

I pace the empty flat. The walls are thin. Liam could have overheard everything Daniel and I spoke about. He decorated this place, and he's so often here. There could be hidden microphones, hidden cameras. I check the plant pots, just in case. I check my bedroom.

There's no lock on my door. He could be in here every time I'm out of the house, poking around. Learning things about me. Learning what I know about the killer. He's questioned me enough times about it: who was I talking to on the phone? Where have I been? What's wrong? What's *really* going on?

He could have been watching everything we did. He could have phoned Sussex Police to discredit me the night the letters arrived. He would have heard what was in them. He would have heard me planning to report it.

He might have called – but so could Alexander. *And* Jude. He was here that night, too, the night of the storm. I told Jude about the letters, didn't I? In the pub? I said I was waiting for them. I said . . .

I said I already knew Poppy had a boyfriend.

I bury my head in my hands.

I've littered my progress all through these relationships. I've left a trail of exactly how much I know without meaning to. The letters, Daniel . . .

My stomach drops.

The killer watched his victims online. He stalked them virtually, following their social media pages, learning things about them.

Does the killer have my Reddit username? I know Jude does, at least. What about the others? If the killer has that, he'll already know Daniel and I have found the necklace connection. He'll know we're looking for others. He'll know we've found Eliza.

Does he know that I know I'm next?

What will he do when he does?

The front door shakes on its hinges, a heavy fist bashing against it. I duck into my room, hiding behind the door.

'Clementine, are you there?' The banging continues. 'It's Daniel. Let me in.'

Daniel? I tiptoe over and check the peephole: his face is stretched in it, mousy brown hair dishevelled from him clawing at it, dark circles hanging under his eyes. There's nobody else in the hallway – not that I can see, anyway. I unlock the door and pull him inside, then lock it again.

'I tried,' he says, pulling a tie from his unbuttoned collar. 'I shaved, I wore a bloody tie and everything, but the police still didn't believe me. I gave them all the information and I very calmly suggested they read it ASAP, but . . .' He looks at me properly. 'Clementine? What is it? What's wrong?'

'I'm next.' Saying it out loud is worse, somehow. 'He asked Poppy all about me. That's what he does. He learns about them. He learnt about me. He did that for a reason. He's going to kill me next. He could be here already. He could be someone I know. Jude, or Alexander, or—'

'Liam?'

Daniel glances around the flat, like I did.

'He's not here,' I say, 'but he could be listening. There could be cameras, microphones. He might already know that I know.'

'Are you sure it's you, Clementine?' Daniel reaches out, so gently that his hand feels like a butterfly on my shoulder. 'Are you positive?'

'I can't be one hundred per cent certain, but I think I'm right. So, yes. I'm sure.'

Daniel nods, setting his jaw. 'Then you have to get out of here. You need to go somewhere safe. What about your parents' place?'

I shake my head. 'They wouldn't listen to me. They think I'm crazy.'

'Okay, um . . . Margate? We can hide out there, at least until the police get things going with the investigation. Maybe you can get protection. I can keep you safe until then.'

The flat is bright and colourful and comforting – but unsafe. My entire life here is unsafe.

'All right. I'll go.'

'You get your stuff from the bathroom, I'll get you some clothes.'

We separate and I gather up my toothbrush, my floss, my washbag from under the sink. Liam's products are scattered around the place – I haven't cleaned in days. I used to steal swipes of his concealer for under my eyes, hiding the shadows of insomnia from the world, but the tube sickens me now. What has he been concealing from me? What has he been hiding behind his pastel pink hair and cheerful compliments? Who is he really?

I moved in so quickly, and I kept to myself. We had our morning kitchen chats, a few shared dinners on the sofa, that night at the bar – but I never vetted him. I never got to know him. Not properly. I took him for who he appeared to be: a light-hearted extrovert; a cool, fashionable guy. But what if that's all there is? What if it's a mask I should have seen past a long time ago?

I trail out of the bathroom, leaving my washbag behind, and enter Liam's room.

Like the rest of the flat, it's a blank, white canvas covered in an explosion of colour: bright hair products across the dressing table, framed art prints, an overflowing wardrobe. I go to it, and look inside.

There are items I recognise – a spotted black-and-white jumper; ripped jeans; a peach shirt – but lots that I don't. There's a rail of scarves, some in fun prints, others in sensible ones, like tartan and plain block colours. Ben wore scarves. Ben always wore scarves. At the bottom, shoes are lined up: biker boots, polished Oxfords, sandals, high-top trainers. Different styles for different occasions – or different personas?

I check around the room, digging into drawers, sifting through magazines, looking under the bed, finding a box pushed deep underneath it. I pull it out, and take off the lid.

Wigs. Long wigs, coloured wigs, curly wigs. There are packs of contact lenses – coloured ones. Fake facial hair, and a special glue to apply it. Tattoo transfers. Fake tan. Contouring kits. Fake teeth. Dyes, prosthetic pastes, make-up of all colours.

'Daniel? You need to see this.'

Daniel joins me, and I sit in front of the box, my hands shaking. Just one thin wall separates me from Liam's treasure trove of disguises. Were those the green contact lenses Poppy fell in love with? Did that fake tan create the surfer dude chic Imogen was looking for? Was that the black wig Eliza ran her fingers through? Did a tattoo transfer of a guitar make Rachel think he was cool enough to date? And what look did Yewande fall for? The blond hair? The charmingly imperfect teeth? The pointless glasses? The –

'Uh, hey?'

Liam is in the doorway, his headphones pulled down around his neck, his sweaty gym T-shirt clinging to him. He glances at the box, and Daniel.

'Why are you going through my stuff?'

Nothing about Liam has physically changed since this morning – but he's no longer Liam.

His pink hair flops down over his face, like Ben's did in Poppy's pencil drawing. His muscles are strong, as Travis's would have been on the beaches with Imogen. Music hisses from his headphones – headphones that Dylan might have used to share music with Rachel.

I've never felt unsafe in the flat before, I've never had a reason to doubt Liam, but I doubt him now. And doubting him *hurts*.

'Why do you have these?' I ask, gripping the edge of the box. Daniel is silent beside me, and gaping. I have to be strong for both of us. 'What are they for?'

'It's hairdressing stuff?' Liam says slowly, as though I'm a child. 'You know, for my *job*?'

'No, it's not.'

He huffs out a laugh. 'Oh, so you're an expert on hairdressing now, are you?'

'You do colours, you told me. These are wigs, and fake tattoos, and contact lenses. That's not part of your job. So why do you have all this? What's it for?'

He laughs under his breath, rolling his eyes. 'Are you really questioning me about the private things in my own private room? The things you've dragged out from under my bed?'

'Yes.' I get to my feet, trying to be firm. 'Why do you have these?'

Liam crosses his arms and leans against the doorframe. It's a casual stance, but his body is tense and rigid.

'For five months I've been trying to get to know you, to be there for you. To be your *friend*. That's how you learn stuff about

297

people, you know. By talking to them. By taking an interest. Not by snooping through their stuff. Before today, have you actually ever asked me a question about myself? I can't think of one. You've been nothing but . . . indifferent. *Cold.* So why do you think it's any of your business what I keep under my bed?'

He's blocking the exit, and he knows it. Daniel and I are trapped in here. We –

'Because she deserves to know who she's living with,' Daniel says, getting up. 'And why that person would have a box of disguises hidden under his bed.'

'Disguises?'

'Yeah, disguises. Alter egos. You know, like, surfer dude? Goth? Musician? *Photographer?*'

Liam, already glaring at Daniel, shakes his head. 'What the hell are you on about?'

'We know what you've done,' Daniel says. 'Who you've hurt. Who you've *been*. Travis. Dylan. Ben.'

'Ben? Wait . . .' Liam uncrosses his arms, straightening up. 'Ben as in the photographer guy C and I have been looking for? What? You think I have something to do with that?' He looks between us, and settles on me. 'What the hell is going on here?'

'Why do you have the disguises if that's not what's going on?' I ask. 'Explain yourself. Why do you have these?'

'This is a joke, right? Yeah? It didn't land, but okay, ha-ha, let's move on now. Very funny. Let's be normal again now, though. Let's drop the spy accusations, or whatever, yeah?'

He steps towards me, but I step away, pressing myself against the window behind me.

'Seriously? You're *scared* of me now? Why? What has this guy been saying to you?'

Daniel puts himself in front of me. He's shorter than Liam, and weaker, but he tries to make himself big.

'Stay away from her. I couldn't protect Rachel from you, but I'll damn well protect Clementine.'

Liam stares incredulously at him – and then laughs. He steps further into the room, fists clenched. Daniel reaches blindly behind him for my hand, and I grip it. But Liam doesn't come for us. He grabs a bag from his wardrobe and starts shoving things inside.

'I have no idea what's going on here, but I'm out. I tried to be supportive, C, but you never wanted to talk, you never wanted to do anything actually good for you. I thought you'd be okay, but I guess not! You met this dude and suddenly you were worse than ever. You think I didn't know you weren't sleeping? That I couldn't hear you typing stuff on your laptop all night? Being obsessive? I didn't realise it was about this. I didn't realise you'd gone as insane as he is.'

Liam leaves the room, and I hear products tumble in the bathroom. He comes back, his bag slung over his shoulder.

'It's cosplay stuff, okay? My ex told me it was embarrassing and lame so I never told anyone else, but I do cosplay. That's what that stuff is. It's not a box of disguises, or whatever you seem to think. They're costumes. They're for *fun*. Get out the other boxes if you want. I'm not sure you'd call a green-and-gold caped number a *disguise*.'

Daniel's fingers dig into mine.

Liam's hurt. He has a legitimate excuse. There's a logical explanation for all of this.

But my thoughts dart around as wildly as my heartbeat.

What if this is part of his cover? What if he hid a box of cosplay items under the bed just so he could claim innocence if I ever did suspect him?

'That guy who was here,' Liam says. 'Jude? With the dark hair? I heard what he said to you when you guys carried Daniel in that night, and I agreed with him. Who is this guy? You were *fine*, C, you were healing, and then you met him and your life has messed itself up. He is dangerous. I mean, look what he's done to you. Look what he's done to us.' Liam shakes his head sadly. 'He's made you believe some mad conspiracy theory about me, what, dating your sister before she died? Having alter egos? It's nonsense, complete nonsense. He's changed you. He's messed with your head. I've never done that. I've always supported you, protected you. It's me you should trust, not him. Trust *me*.'

He reaches for me, his familiar thumb ring glinting. Exhaustion registers in my muscles and my mind, my body drained from spike after spike of adrenaline. I want this to be over. I want to be wrapped up in his gentle arms, breathing in sugar, feeling the safe, easy comfort he always gives me.

He's right. He's never given me a reason to doubt him.

But that's exactly what the killer would do, isn't it?

I recoil further behind Daniel. Liam drops his hand, hurt tugging at his face. Anger replaces it.

'Fine, be like that. Put your faith in an insane stranger instead. I tried, but I can't help you if you don't want to be helped. Stay here and go mad together for all I care. I'm done. Bye, *Clementine*.'

Liam goes and the front door slams, and relief jolts through Daniel's hand. He exhales, flopping down to sit on the bed, rubbing his face. 'Oh my God, that was close. D'you think that was something he made up, or was it true? About the cosplay?'

'I'm not sure.'

'Me neither. Maybe he's stormed off, or maybe he's running? Because we got close? Should we call the police about him?'

'I . . . I don't know.'

Liam is gone, but the feeling of unease inside me hasn't. I check the flat. He's definitely gone, but my heart is still thumping. I'm still shaking. I feel sick. I should feel safe, but I don't.

Daniel follows me to the kitchen area, and gives me a little smile.

'It's okay. You're safe now.'

But I know I'm not.

Rachel and Poppy died the same way, and the same person killed them. It's a bond Daniel and I share: both bereaved suddenly; both knowing a truth the rest of the world refuses to even consider. Nobody understands him like I do, and nobody knows my pain like he does.

But we met by chance – twice. First through the helpline, and then at my support group. Against all odds, despite the sheer number of people in the UK, we managed to find each other.

Or did he find me?

'Why did you come to my support group that night?'

'What?' Daniel frowns. 'I told you, I was staying with a friend in Croydon and that was the nearest one. It was a coincidence. I didn't go to *your* support group, I went to *a* support group. And it happened to be yours. I'm glad it was.'

He smiles again, but I can't smile back. I can't shake the feeling. It spreads inside me like a rot, making me want to gag.

We met by chance. He'd been searching for Rachel's killer for two years, but just days after meeting me, he found fresh evidence to link the case to Poppy's – by chance. He was there the night I received Poppy's letters, ones that would contain key information about the killer – by chance. And he's here now, unannounced, on the very day I realised I was being hunted – by chance.

I've seen the information and documents Daniel has sent me about Rachel's death, but I've never looked her up myself. I've never checked her family history.

Maybe she doesn't have a brother.

Or maybe she doesn't even exist.

'Clem?' Daniel asks, tilting his head. 'What's going on?'

'Show me a picture of you and Rachel together.'

'What?'

'You heard me. Show me you knew her.'

'Knew her? She's my sister! We grew up together! You know that.'

'Do I? Or do I only know what you've told me?'

Daniel's lip shakes. 'Clementine, what's going on? Do you . . . do you think I'm lying? I'd never lie to you, I—'

'Show me a picture. Now.'

'Okay, okay.' Daniel grabs his phone, and winces. 'I'm out of battery, but I'll charge it and show you.'

'Not good enough.'

'Clementine, I swear—'

'Stop saying my name!' A tear that I don't want – a sign of weakness – sneaks out of my eye, and I smack it away. 'I don't know you, not really, but you're here all the time. There are coincidences, too many coincidences. You . . . you kept touching the necklace. You wanted me to notice it, you *wanted* me to recognise it, and have this bond with you, and—'

'No! No, you've got it wrong!' Daniel is crying, too, but he doesn't bother to wipe his tears away. 'My sister is *dead*. Why would I lie about that? Why would I be the one who killed her? He kills girlfriends, not sisters!'

'How do I even know she had a brother?'

Daniel gapes at me, speechless.

'Leave.'

He finds his voice again. 'Clementine, please, no.'

'Leave.' I clench my fists and snarl at him. 'Leave!'

He backs off, hands raised to plead with me – his sleeves falling down far enough to show the healing cuts on his wrists.

'It's not me. I'm not him. Please don't make me go, Clem. *Please.*'

I stomp forward, standing my ground, forcing him to the front door.

'I don't trust you. I *can't* trust you. I can't trust anyone.'

'But you can trust *me*. You know it, Clem. She was my sister. I wouldn't hurt her. I wouldn't hurt anyone. You know that. You know *me*.'

'I don't! And that's why you have to go. Go!'

He fumbles for the door handle behind him, gulping down sobs.

'It's not me. I wouldn't. I would never do that to you. Please, I—'

'Just go!' I shove him the last of the way, my hands on his chest. His hands grip mine, just for a moment, pleading with me, begging me not to shut him out – but I pull myself free, and slam the door in his face. I drag the chain across and lean against the door, my forehead pressed to the wood.

'Please, Clementine,' Daniel begs outside. I feel him press against the door, too. 'Let me back in. *Please.*'

But I don't. I sink to the floor and cover my ears, blocking out the bangs and pleas.

I can't let him back in. I can't trust him.

For the rest of my life, I won't be able to trust any man – because any man could be *him*.

The flat is dark and the hallway is silent when I eventually unfurl and use my phone. I type five words into Google, not sure if I want to get an answer.

Rachel Burton suicide train Margate.

The results come up immediately.

Local Singer Rachel Burton Named in Railway Suicide.

Death on the Train Line: Proper Fencing Required, Says Rachel Burton's Grieving Mother.

. . . The young singer is survived by her mother, Debbie Burton, and her younger brother, Daniel.

There's a photo in the article of the three of them together: a blonde-haired mother sitting on the sofa between the girl I've seen on CCTV, Rachel, and her brother – Daniel. My Daniel. But not as I know him.

This Daniel smiles, caught mid-laugh, his hair clean and swept back, his nails unbitten, trainers still with their soles attached, an ironed T-shirt showing bare, unscarred wrists that he has no need to hide. He looks young, and happy. An ordinary person living an ordinary life.

The Burton family weeks before the tragedy, the caption says.

It's a genuine website. *Daniel* is genuine.

I claw myself up and unlock the door, but the hallway is empty.

The only person I can trust is gone.

CHAPTER 28

When Dad and I went to clear out Poppy's university bedroom after her 'suicide', everything in there was so normal. It was messy, yes, but she was always messy. There was nothing odd about it. There were in-progress canvases, half-eaten chocolate bars, a bookmarked novel. It looked, quite rightly, as though she'd left that night with every intention of coming back.

If I were to die now in an apparent suicide, nobody would have any trouble believing it.

I haven't slept in days. I can't eat. Stained coffee cups litter the tables near my haunts – the bed I can't sleep in; the sofa I don't have the energy to move from. I haven't cleaned up after myself. Grime coats the flat, and me. The person who stares back at me in the bathroom mirror is ill and haunted, hair tangled, skin pale, eyes shadowed with weeks of lost sleep.

Daniel won't answer my calls or texts. I apologise for accusing him, I beg for forgiveness, but he doesn't respond. I get messages from Jenna instead.

Clem, are you okay?

Clem! Message me back!

Your parents say they haven't heard from you for days.
What's going on? Talk to me, please.

Mum and Dad visit. I keep the door shut, but Mum presses her fingers through the letterbox and whispers to me, telling me she'll always be here if I need her. I tell her to go away.

I can't call the police. Even if 999 or the Met take me seriously enough to contact Sussex Police about Poppy, my name has already been ruined there. They'll assume I'm mentally ill, just like everyone else. If I give them Rachel's information, they'll find out about Daniel's equally invalidated claims. And Imogen and the others are no good either. Every piece of evidence we have slots together, telling a different part of the story: the blurry CCTV of Rachel being pushed on to the tracks proves murder, but only when Poppy's letters about meeting Ben on the cliff edge that night prove premeditation. Without those pieces, Imogen and Eliza's necklaces show a link between suicides, not murders.

The proof I have is a house of cards, and I don't know how to make it stand any more.

I don't know what to do. I've failed Poppy. I can't prove her murder, and because of that, I can't prove that I might be next. Asking for help would get me sent straight into psychiatric care.

I think about running. I pack my bag a few times, and unpack it again.

Where would I go? Into hiding, or back to Boston? He could follow me, and strike there. Or not strike. I'd go insane for real with the uncertainty of it, checking every face in the crowd, never feeling safe.

Or perhaps I'd go back to Boston and this would be over. I *would* be safe. But what does that mean for the next victim, and the next, and the next? It wouldn't stop with me. If I remove myself from the equation, he'll find a replacement. He'll keep doing this.

At least if it's me he's after, I can delay anyone else getting hurt.

Rationally, logically, he should have given up and moved on anyway, disappearing into another identity – but I'm a loose end, aren't I? I know too much, and I could find a way to prove it to the police. If he knows I know I'm next, perhaps he'll drop the pretence. It won't be about seduction and gaining my trust, but getting rid of me as quickly as possible. He could stab me when I go out for milk, or push me on to the Underground tracks. It could be sudden.

But I'm not sure it will be.

Daniel won't – or can't – talk to me, and he's innocent. He's Rachel's brother. I verified it on various websites, the shard of guilt inside me twisting with every new family photo or Facebook post. I should never have doubted him. I shouldn't have doubted Liam, either. The other boxes under his bed were full of superhero costumes and fantasy wigs and Victorian-style moustaches, and I found an Instagram account dating back years that documented his hobby. It can't be him either – especially as he wants nothing to do with me. He hasn't been back since he left, and I haven't reached out to apologise.

He's better off without me.

But Alexander keeps sliding magazine clippings under the door: sci-fi movie reviews, news on the latest Mars mission, new biology breakthroughs. I hear from Jude, too. He messages me on Reddit – *I'm sorry for invading your privacy, but I was worried about you* – and comes to the flat, too, knocking gently, posting something in when I don't answer: a little note, like the one he left for me at the helpline once. A cartoon version of him holding a bunch of flowers, smiling, with *I know you've been going through a lot recently, but I hope you're feeling better. I'm here if you need to talk. Jude x* written on it, and a number. I throw it in the bin, then fish it out again. It could be evidence.

If the killer is already in my life, he must be Alexander or Jude. I acted strangely around everyone that day, and Liam left, and Daniel won't speak to me. But Alexander and Jude are still trying. The notes, the visits – keeping a toe in my life, reminding me they're still there, and available, whenever I want them. Why? Why persist with this fiction when I'm no longer going to fall for it?

Unless they don't realise that I know I'm next? I acted strangely, yes, I ran from both of them – but I never accused them of anything. I never mentioned any of this to them, only to Daniel and Liam. And I haven't posted anything on Reddit since the necklaces.

If Alexander or Jude is the killer, and they've been gauging the risk via my Reddit posts, then they won't know I'm on to them. They think I've worked out the serial killer link with Daniel, and they maybe know that I've found Eliza, but that's all. They don't know the clues I found in Poppy's letters.

They're still playing the potential love interest, but the kinder and more interested in me they are, the guiltier they look. They're sticking to their original plan of trying to make me fall for them, but I'm not going to. And they don't know that. That means I'm safe, surely? Safe until they realise it won't work.

And that gives me control.

My muscles ache from inactivity as I drag myself off the sofa and to my desk, a blanket around my shoulders. I clear a space amid the litter of scrunched paper and used cups, and start two lists: *Alexander* versus *Jude*. I dig through Poppy's letters again, and pick over the pages in my folder about the other victims and the kind of men they liked; the ways in which the killer changed himself.

The way the killer targets his victims follows a pattern. Poppy was an artist, so he became a photographer. Rachel was a guitarist, so he became a drummer. Imogen wanted adventure, so he became a surfer. He presumably became a goth for Eliza, and a reader for Yewande. But it went deeper than that.

Poppy always knew what she liked, even from when she was young. Dashing Disney princes and One Direction posters turned to longing stares at floppy-haired boys in skinny jeans through the café windows. She liked brown hair. She liked green eyes. She liked a sensitive soul and a caring heart – even if she'd had no personal experience of romance at all. The Ben in her drawings is the kind of person she always wanted to fall in love with.

But I've never been like that.

I never had crushes on celebrities. I never had a favourite hairstyle or eye colour. The only 'dates' I ever went on were sprung on me after the fact, when platonic library study sessions with male students ended with them eagerly leaning in for kisses that I'd had no idea were coming. At Harvard, Jenna would whisper and point out '*cute guys*' in our lectures, but I just wanted to learn. When she introduced me to men in bars, I wanted them to go away. When she made that Tinder account for me and swiped through face after face, I didn't want to see any of them.

But when I woke up beside her in her bed that morning, sunlight casting everything with soft orange tones, her lipstick kissed away, her leg over mine, I . . . I felt it. I felt the thing Poppy had always dreamt of. And I realised that, perhaps, I'd felt it all along.

I drain the remnants from a day-old coffee cup, and rub my sore, unslept eyes.

None of this matters, because Poppy never knew what happened that night. She was already dying on that beach when we walked home together, slipping in the snow, laughing, Jenna's hand never leaving mine. It doesn't matter that Jenna is intelligent, passionate, determined, funny, kind, and carefree, because Poppy didn't know those are the traits I love. I never told her. She couldn't have known.

But she must have told the killer something, or said enough for him to formulate a persona that he thought would work. But what? Who? What did my sister *guess* would be my type?

Jude: the kind, gentle, brown-eyed man who reminds me so much of my sister, who followed me to the helpline so we'd meet, who fed me a sob story about his own attempted suicide to give us something to bond over? Or Alexander: the scientist who lives just feet away from me, who visits my parents' café every day, who seems to have studied a manual on all my hobbies and interests?

There's a scuffle of paper at the front door. I check: another magazine article slips through, unfolding on the doormat: *Cucumbers on Mars: Hydroponics of the Future.*

Jude might just be a good person, like Poppy was. He was kind to me because he knew I needed it. He wanted to help. He was giving me friendship, company.

But Alexander is a walking cliché of everything a female scientist *should* want.

I start an audio recording on my phone and shove it in my pocket, along with a small knife from the kitchen, just in case. I pull back the chair I have wedged against the door, undo the security chain, and unlock it. Then I leave the flat for the first time in . . . I don't know how many days.

It's night. I hadn't really realised, but music thuds across the hallway as it always does after dark. I have to knock loudly for a while before the door opens.

'Oh, Clementine!' Alexander jumps a little when he sees me, his curls bouncing. 'This is a surprise. I thought you might have gone away for a few days. Are you all right?'

I probably should have combed my hair before coming here, but it's too late now.

'Yes, I'm fine.'

'Oh. Good!'

He smiles. Short-sleeved shirt buttoned all the way up, glasses on, ginger hair twisted into perfectly imperfect curls.

He's a real-life version of a cartoon geek, the kind Poppy used to doodle on the backs of postcards.

'Can I come in?' I ask, not waiting for an answer before I slide past him.

'Um, yes. Of course. I was just about to get ready for bed, but . . .'

The flat is as it was last time I was here: eerily bare, undecorated, with the never-ceasing thump of music coming from the far bedroom.

'How have you been?' Alexander asks. 'I haven't seen you around lately, or your housemate.'

'He moved out. I don't know when he'll be back.'

'Oh. That's a shame.'

I walk around the flat, barefoot, pretending to be interested in the wallpaper while I look for clues. I don't know what I'm looking for. I don't really know why I'm here.

'Have you been under the weather? You look, um . . . Well, those pyjamas seem very comfy.'

'They are.' I scrape a loose tangle of hair out of my eyes. Alexander – not that that's his real name – watches me, his arms tightly crossed, bouncing from foot to foot. Shy. Unassuming.

He's trying to be like Poppy, I realise. And then I feel sick.

There is no housemate. There is no Astrophysics PhD. To catch a scientist, he became one.

What was he planning to do to me? Take me stargazing like Poppy? Lead me to a high point and then – oops! Another dead Harris sister. Was that it? Is that still it?

'Do you think the new *Star Trek* spin-off will be any good?' Alexander asks, still bobbing on his heels. 'I hope so, but you never really know what . . .'

He's talking, but I'm not listening. I watch his hands: short, neat nails like the ones pressing the camera shutter in Poppy's sketchbook drawing; fingers nervously intertwining.

I hate those hands. I *hate* them. I see through his act and see the real him: darkness in his eyes, expressionless, watching Poppy fall from the top of the cliff. Instead of helping her, he called me. He left me that answerphone message. He wanted to hurt me.

My fingers curl around the kitchen knife in my pocket.

I want to hurt him.

'. . . so I was wondering if you still might want to go?'

'Go?'

He clears his throat. 'Um, to the *Interstellar* screening? You never said, and you left the café in a hurry, so I thought I'd ask again, just in case. No pressure! But if you *do* want to go, then—'

'How did you get the tickets at such short notice?' I stare at him, hard. 'You have to book those things months in advance, but you show up at the café, last minute, with two of them?'

'I bought them months ago. Got priority booking with my mobile provider!'

'Really? And it was just a coincidence that you'd bump into me, someone who loves that film and would be totally interested in going, to give your spare ticket to?'

'Well, um, it *was* a coincidence, a great one, but I didn't buy a spare ticket. The person I bought it for dropped out.'

'Oh really? And who was that? What convenient thing happened to free up the ticket for me?'

Alexander's shoulders sag, his curls deflating somehow. I've got him, haven't I? He's about to give up and confess. He knows I'm on to him. He –

'I didn't want to have to tell you this, but . . . The ticket was for my boyfriend.' He scratches his head, staring at the floor. 'But he dumped me, and I didn't really fancy going by myself.'

My accusations die on my tongue.

'Wait, your . . . boyfriend?'

'Well, ex-boyfriend, technically.'

'You had a *boy*friend?'

'Yes.'

'You like men?'

'Yes.'

'You like girls too, though, right?'

He chokes, and shakes his head. 'I mean, I love girls! Girls are lovely! But . . . as friends. I'm, um, one hundred per cent, most definitely gay.'

'. . . Oh.'

He smiles awkwardly, cheeks and ears flushed red.

It can't be right. It *has* to be Alexander. The magazine clippings, the interest in science, the fake housemate.

Fake?

I rush to the second bedroom and burst in before Alexander can stop me. A man in a baseball cap and a headset sits at a desk, a camera pointed at him and a computer game up on his screens. He turns to me, glaring.

'Who the hell are you?' he shouts over the music. 'You ruined my kill streak!'

I back out of the room and shut the door. Alexander appears beside me.

'That's Jay, my flatmate. Sorry, he's not very friendly. Are you all right, Clementine? You look like you've seen a ghost.'

I lean back against the wall, laughing. Laughing for the first time in weeks.

It isn't him. Alexander is Alexander.

He's safe.

'You've really been gay this entire time?'

'Um, yes? That's usually how it works.' He laughs, too, and leans against the wall beside me. 'Wait, um, you didn't think I was asking you to *Interstellar* as a date, did you?'

'No, no,' I lie. 'Well, maybe. But, um, I'm not into you either, so it all works out.'

'Phew. Because I like you a lot, but not like that. I'm far more into ridiculously beautiful and out-of-my-league boys with pink hair.'

He sighs wistfully. It takes a moment for me to put it together. 'Wait, Liam? You like Liam?'

'Doesn't everyone?' He looks a little worried. 'Don't you?'

'No.' Now it's my turn to laugh. 'No, he's not really my *type*, either. Were you trying to be my friend to get closer to him?'

'No, I like you! But, um, if I managed to bump into him for five seconds while talking to you, well, that would be a bonus.' He rubs his nose. 'Sorry, I'm well aware of how pathetic that is.'

I think about how much my heart leaps when I see a new text from Jenna, and how I force myself to dismiss it without reading.

'It's not pathetic. And, just between us, he did once call you cute.'

When I'm back in the flat, I splash cold water on my face at the kitchen sink. I rub away the grime of sleeplessness and indecision and fear, feeling more like myself as half a year's accumulated negativity swirls away. Without it, my skin is raw and exposed – but ready.

I've spent the last however many days – and most of the last six months – doing exactly what the killer wanted me to: nothing. He broke me down with the phone call, the voicemail, the guilt that he knew I'd place on my own shoulders. And then when I could finally see clearly enough to blame *him*, to search for him, he ruined my name with the police. He made sure nobody would believe me. He made me too scared to try.

I was never on his radar as a victim, he just wanted me to *think* I was. To waste time. To get me acting irrationally, being paranoid, doubting good people. To ruin my own name. And it worked.

But not any more.

I need to take all my evidence to the police station and *stay there*, even if they don't believe me. I need to give them Blessing's phone number and Eliza's dad's Reddit username and Yaz's work address, and let them connect the necklaces for themselves. I can't let myself be too defeated to try. I have to believe that I can successfully present my hypothesis and get the real killer caught.

I used to always figure things out. If Poppy couldn't put a toy together, she'd bring it to me and I'd do it for her. When she was too shy to go out alone, I'd go too, holding her hand in the busy street, making sure she felt safe. That rainy Sunday afternoon on Primrose Hill, when the wind howled, she wasn't the only one hoping for a sunset.

I'd forgotten that.

I collect up my things from around the flat: letters and folder from my desk, Poppy's sketchbook from the coffee table. A pen skids out from underneath it, rolling beneath the sofa, and I stoop to retrieve it. My fingers graze something else. A book. A library book, maybe. I must have fines by now. I pull it out and smooth the cover: brown leather, spine well-worn, the kind that's often folded back over itself.

Jude's sketchbook, the one he always draws in at the helpline.

He must have dropped it here that night, after he helped get Daniel inside from the rain and threw his satchel on the floor. That seems like an age ago.

I sit and pick through the pages. It's almost entirely portraits like the ones he showed me before, imagined versions of the desperate callers we speak to during our helpline shifts. I search through and find Daniel – not the Daniel I know, but the harsh, angry one, the one Jude warned me about – and the student he said had failed his exams, and Blessing, with her headscarf and teary, smiling face.

And then after the portraits, crammed at the back, there are pages of doodles: the loose, free-thinking kind people usually do while on the phone. And at the centre of the page, there's an all too familiar heart necklace.

It's the necklace. *The* necklace. The necklace Jude couldn't possibly know about unless he'd seen it half a dozen times, on half a dozen different women's necks.

My hands shake, and something falls out of a pouch built into the back cover: a green flyer for the helpline, just like the one I received in the post after Poppy's death. There are other things in the pocket: sheets from a sketchbook with slightly different paper, torn down one side as though they've been ripped out.

Poppy's sketchbook is beside me. I open it, breathing deeply, pretending this is just a sample slide in the lab, that this is all routine – and flick to the page with her drawing of The Photographer behind his camera. The raw stubs of torn-out pages jut out of the spine. I line them up with the sheets that were tucked away in the back of Jude's sketchbook. They match.

These are the drawings the killer didn't want me to see. The ones he ripped out of Poppy's sketchbook on that clifftop.

His face, in full, smiles back at me: beard gone, hair shorter and lighter in a wash of watercolour, eyes green.

Ben. The boyfriend. The man who murdered Poppy.

It's Jude.

CHAPTER 29

When the police hunt serial killers, there's often at least one witness or survivor who goes on to describe what the attacker looked like, and from that, an artist can build a composite of features to show a representation of their face to help with identification.

My sister, dead for six months, sketched her own.

I always knew Poppy was a great artist, but I didn't realise she was this gifted. The drawing of Jude – in the guise of Ben – is immediately recognisable, even without the trappings of his dark beard, darker eyes, and long curly hair. The truth is in the shape of his nose, the shading of his cheekbone, the slant of his eyebrows. Even with an unfamiliar expression – more a smirk than a warm smile – the tiny, imperceptible details of Jude's facial structure are there.

The drawing the killer ripped out of Poppy's sketchbook is undeniably, categorically of Jude. Or should I call him Dylan? Travis? Ben?

His real name could be anything.

It's been so long since I felt this way: buoyed by the triumph of certainty. It deflates as I remember what it means, what it proves.

Jude killed my sister, and he's been carrying around these pages, this drawing, ever since. This illustration is a trophy. It must have been there, tucked away in the pocket at the back of his sketchbook, all the times we were in the phone room together. It must have been there as he showed me his drawings – probably traced somehow, or done by another artist, left just unfinished enough so he could be seen to define an eye, or shade a mouth, as though he'd created the thing from scratch. He told me stories about the people in that book. He said he'd drawn Daniel, damaged because of Rachel's death. He showed me Blessing, mourning her lost daughter, Yewande.

Both women who *he* killed.

I press my shaking hands between my knees.

What kind of narcissism does this man have, to walk around with evidence tying him to Poppy's death? To carry it in his satchel? To be so careless as to lose it?

It must have fallen out the night of the storm, when we helped Daniel up here after he cut his hand. He checked his bag in the car, didn't he? Making sure his sketchbook wasn't damaged by the rain. Making sure his trophy was intact. But his bag was open, he threw it down by the sofa, the sketchbook slipped out and got kicked underneath . . .

But surely he wouldn't have just left it? He'd always keep an eye on it, he's meticulous about these things, he covers his tracks so well, he's careful, he's—

Emotional.

That was the night he realised Daniel and I were in contact. He knew I almost had Poppy's letters, and he must have suggested that Uber home as a way to get inside. But Daniel was there. He wanted to drive a wedge between us, to stop us putting things together and realising the link between us, but he couldn't. I defended Daniel. I asked Jude to leave. He was angry. Distracted. By the time he realised he'd lost it, it would have been too late: we weren't on speaking terms, and I didn't go back to the helpline until I needed

Blessing's contact details. Even then, we argued on the roof. I hit him with my folder. I ran from him.

Why hasn't he tried to get it back? He must know this is where he lost it. He's been messaging me on Reddit, slipping notes through the door, knocking, but he never asked me to look for the sketchbook.

Because he doesn't want to draw attention to it. If I'd found it right away, he would have been arrested immediately. But he hasn't been, because I didn't. If he asks me for it, I might look through it. But if he could get inside this flat, he could search without me knowing. He could make sure I don't see his trophy. His plan would still be on.

I gather up the notes he's been pushing through the letterbox: caring messages with cutesy little cartoons on them. He's been trying to get in here for days, but gently. Patiently. Trying to earn back my trust.

He *doesn't* know what I know. He thinks I still don't know I'm being hunted. He's a step behind.

More than a step. Because now I have the one extra piece of evidence I need to prove that Poppy was murdered.

Thanks for the gift, *Jude.*

It's hard to sleep when my brain is buzzing in my skull, but exhaustion wins out – for a few hours, anyway. I leave the flat early the next morning, skin scrubbed clean in the shower, in a fresh shirt, with all my evidence organised neatly in my backpack. But I don't go to the police station. I get a train to Margate.

There's someone who needs to see this before the police do.

Daniel never told me his address, but I go to the road mentioned in one of the local news articles about Rachel's death and wander the street until I find it: a small semi-detached house with one paving slab missing by the front door, four sets of handprints pressed into the long-dried cement.

Careful not to tread on them, I approach and ring the doorbell.

There's movement through the pane of dimpled glass in the door, and eventually a woman opens it, her wavy, grey-rooted blonde hair pulled back with a scrunchie, her leggings and baggy jumper faded. Post litters the floor.

'Hello. Deborah Burton?'

'Debbie.' Her voice is tired. Everything about her is tired. 'What's this about?'

'I'm sorry for turning up out of the blue like this, but I'm looking for your son, Daniel. Do you know where he is?'

'Why?' Debbie clutches the edge of the door, as though she's about to shut it on me. 'What do you want?'

'I'd like to talk to him. I said something I shouldn't have the last time we spoke, and he deserves an apology.'

Debbie blinks at me, closing the door another inch.

'We're friends,' I add. 'Or we were. I hope we can be again, but maybe he—'

'You're a friend of Danny's?'

'Yes. We met in London.'

'London! Is that where he was? He never tells me.' She pulls the door wide, stepping back in fluffy slippers, an abrupt smile on her face. 'Come in, come in! Any friend of Danny's is always welcome. I'll make some tea. Do you take sugar? I have some biscuits somewhere. Do you like Hobnobs?'

She doesn't wait for a response. She leaves the door open and pads away, slippers shuffling, chatting away cheerily about this and that. I step over the cemented handprints and follow her.

The house has a dark, stagnant quality about it: a few too many curtains shut when they should be open; thick films of dust on picture frames.

Rachel grins in glasses by a Christmas tree with what must be her first guitar, gap-toothed, while a smaller, similarly mousy-haired boy screams in the background, his fire engine discarded on the floor, torn paper in his fists. Sunburnt and sticky, the siblings sit together under a parasol at a plastic table by a pool, Daniel waving, Rachel sneaking a handful of chips from his plate. In matching uniforms with a dappled grey background, Rachel smiles with confidence in fashionable glasses – older, head tilted – while Daniel twists his fingers together on his lap, nails bitten, stretched thin from a sudden growth spurt, skin marked with deep, angry clusters of acne that he tries to hide behind his hair.

'Poor boy,' Debbie says, passing me a cup of tea. 'They bullied him so much at that school, he used to come home in tears. I had to send him to another one in the end, after the difficulties.'

'Difficulties?'

'You know how it is. A decade of verbal abuse, every single day, but *he's* the one who got expelled for fighting back once. Children can be so cruel. At least he had his sister.'

They are alike. Similar face shape, identical noses, same not-quite-blond, not-quite-brown hair. I imagine them bickering, like Daniel told me: Rachel stealing his chips, Daniel pushing her in the pool. Fights that end in laughter and a truce.

'I'm sorry for your loss,' I say. 'She seemed like a lovely person.'

'She was. Just like her dad.' Debbie sips her tea, both hands twisted around her mug.

She's still wearing her wedding ring, despite Daniel's father dying years ago. There are pictures of him, too; the kitchen wall a collage of memories of the people she's lost.

'She and her dad used to have such games together. I'd hear them screaming with laughter up there. I still hear them, sometimes. It was his idea to get her the guitar, you know. Before he died in that accident. He never got to see her learn to play it. She wrote songs for him. I can't remember them now. I do, sometimes. A little tune comes to me now and then. Maybe it's Rachel, playing it through the floorboards.'

Debbie hums a disparate, eerie tune.

'I have home videos of them somewhere. Would you like to see?'

'Actually, I need to talk to Daniel.' I put my tea by the kitchen sink. It's weak and stone cold; she must have forgotten to put the kettle on. 'Do you know where he is?'

Debbie sips her tea again, still clutching it as though it brings her warmth.

'Oh, yes. He's upstairs.' She points upwards to the still, silent first floor. 'Shall I show you?'

'I think I can find it myself.'

'All right.' She smiles again, and shuffles back into the dark, dusty living room. 'I'll find that video for you. Rachel sings at a talent show. It's quite spectacular. It really is such a shame she can't sing any more. At least I have my tapes.'

She hums to herself again, picking through a cabinet as though browsing for entertainment.

Upstairs is just as gloomy. A double room with an unmade bed is visible at the top of the steps, boxes of pills and prescriptions stacked up beside it. There's a bathroom next to it and then, at the front of the house, two doors with matching wooden signs: *Rachel* and *Daniel*.

I knock on the latter.

'Leave me alone,' a muffled voice replies.

I knock again.

'I said leave me alone, Mum!'

I inch the door open.

The room is dark and musty. Light creeps in through the gap in the curtains, picking out a desk, a computer, a crumpled mass of bedsheets with a tangle of matted hair sticking out. The hair disappears, Daniel curling up and burrowing under the duvet, hiding from the light.

'Go away!'

'Daniel? It's me.'

The bedsheets twitch, then go oddly still.

'Clementine?'

'Yes.'

'Are you . . . are you really here?'

'Yes.'

Daniel turns over and peels back the duvet, his eyes glinting from the shadows as he checks for himself. I wave. He clutches the sheets to his chest.

'What are you doing here?'

'I came to apologise. I'm sorry for not trusting you. All you've ever done is support me, but I wouldn't even listen to you. It was wrong, and I'm sorry.'

He hugs the sheets tighter.

'You thought I was the killer.'

'I know, but I was wrong.'

'I begged you to let me back in. I pleaded with you.' He sniffles, taking difficult breaths. 'But you wouldn't listen. You looked at me like . . . like you didn't trust me.'

'I know. But I checked and found all the proof about your sister online, just like you said, but you'd already gone. I called you, I tried to get in touch, but you didn't respond. So I came here.'

'You called me?'

'Yes, that first night, and every day since. You didn't answer, and I was worried you'd maybe . . . done something.'

'Oh.' He wipes his face on the sheet and sits up. 'I didn't get a message. I thought . . .'

He reaches for his phone on the windowsill, knocking the curtain back further as he grabs it. The screen is smashed, as though he hurled it there. He holds it in his hand, chewing on his lips.

'I thought you hated me. I thought . . . I'd never see you again.'

His room looks like the flat. Mess surrounds him, empty bottles on the bedside table and tissues scattered on the floor. An ashtray overflows, stale smoke and sweat clinging to the air. His greasy hair is in knotted clumps, his T-shirt dirty, his beard overgrown again, lips cracked, wrists thin – new red scratches on the skin. He wraps the sheets around them, hiding them, using them to press the tears off his cheeks.

I spent days in the flat, hiding, too scared and sad and wrecked to get out.

And Daniel did the same.

'I'm here now,' I say, sitting next to him on the bed and unzipping my bag. 'And I need to show you something.'

He shuffles over, rubbing his eyes. 'Poppy's sketchbook? Wait, are those . . .' I line up the stumps with the torn sketchbook pages I've put in plastic wallets. The full portraits of Jude as Ben stare back at us through the polythene. 'Where did you get those? Is that—?'

'Jude. I found them in Jude's sketchbook. These are the pages the killer ripped out that night.'

Daniel blinks. 'How did you get Jude's stuff? You went back and stole it from the helpline? Why would you—?'

'I didn't. He dropped it at the flat that night. I found it. This ties him to Poppy. He must have kept these as a trophy. But as soon as we take it to the police, they've got him. There must be fingerprints all over this. It's *his* sketchbook, and the pages from *her* sketchbook are covered in drawings of him. It's definitive proof.'

'And you found it.' Daniel smiles at me, and grabs my hand. 'You found the person who took our sisters from us.'

'And we're both going to get him arrested. They'll need both our stories if we're going to prove he's a serial killer. Let's go to London and do this together.'

A train horn echoes somewhere nearby, the carriages rattling on the tracks. Daniel and his mother have to listen to that every day: a constant, timetabled reminder of the death of their loved one. Daniel winces. It still hurts him, even after all this time.

'Okay,' he says. 'I'll come.'

I wait in his room while he showers, stripping the bed for washing and throwing the windows wide to air it out. Aside from the mess and accumulated clutter of two difficult years, it's the bedroom of a normal, happy young adult. There's a gaming computer, shelves of discs, a boxset of *Battlestar Galactica*, a set of weights, two skateboards, books, and a pinboard with a map of the world on it, printed images of places he wants to visit one day stuck to it.

When Daniel gets back, he looks different. The grime is washed away, his hair is combed back off his face, and his beard is gone again. In fresh clothes and with the hope we now both share, he looks neater, healthier. He looks ready.

And so am I.

CHAPTER 30

We don't get back to London until early evening, so Daniel and I decide to wait until tomorrow to go to the police. We go for a walk instead, stretching our legs in Regent's Park. It's light still, the sun casting long shadows on the grass, but the chilly air brings the promise of autumn. It's September now. Leaves are beginning to crisp and curl, and in a few weeks, they'll fall in orange heaps across the Harvard campus. They'll do that here, too, lining the streets, collecting in clumps, ready and waiting for Poppy to kick through them in her chunky boots as she always did. She loved autumn: the earlier sunsets, the frosted cobwebs, the colours.

'Aren't we going up there?' Daniel asks, as I cut off Primrose Hill and lead him back towards the flat.

'We should get back. It'll be dark soon.'

I've already seen the powdery orange glow coming from the horizon, and the pink-kissed clouds above it. I don't want to be up there during a sunset that Poppy can't see.

'Whoa, this place looks worse than my room,' Daniel jokes when we get to the flat. He goes around it, picking up the things on the doormat, the empty cups from my room, the rubbish, but his flurry of cleaning is a pretence. I can see him checking behind doors, making sure the flat is completely empty. I'm grateful for it. He checks the fridge.

'Yikes. I'm gonna nip to the shop and get some fresh milk. Need anything?'

'Some coffee would be good.'

It's the most normal thing we've ever said to each other, as though we're housemates in a dull sitcom and there is nothing remotely unusual about us.

He grins. 'Be right back.'

I tidy up to keep myself from pacing until Daniel comes back with coffee, milk, two nicotine patches slapped to his arm, and a big bottle of vodka.

'Thought we could take the edge off a bit before tomorrow. What do you think?'

I smile at him. 'I think I'll get the glasses.'

We sit on the sofa together, and Daniel fills two of Liam's shot glasses. He clinks his against mine.

'To catching this bastard, once and for all.'

The alcohol tastes foul, but I swallow it anyway. We have the evidence we need now, and by tomorrow we will have proved it. That's worth celebrating.

'How long do you think Jude was working on you for?' Daniel asks. 'Straight after Poppy? Or was there a gap?'

'I'm not sure. I only noticed him a few weeks ago – it was that night when you called, and I thought you'd fallen. He comforted me. He seemed so nice . . .'

In hindsight, his kindness seems sickly and cloying, and his soft touches slimy. Daniel refills our glasses, and pushes mine into my hand. I down it, focusing on the taste instead of my emotions.

'It makes me sick to think of it now. I spent time with him. I talked to him about Poppy, about trying to cope with the loss – and he was the one who killed her. This whole time.'

Another refill; another shot.

'I know,' Daniel says. 'I keep thinking about that time I met him. He sat right there and wanted to talk to me, like he was a mate, like he actually cared. He must've known who I am. He knew who he killed, and who she was to me. He must've loved that. He must've been laughing at me.'

'And me. For months, I didn't even know Poppy had been murdered, let alone by him. He must have watched me every shift, trying to find the right time to introduce himself. And he picked when I was at my lowest.'

I pour the drinks this time.

'He followed you to the helpline. He saw a way to get to you, and—'

'Not necessarily.' I pick through my folder and find the UK Listeners flyer that was in Jude's sketchbook, now preserved behind plastic like the rest of Jude's things. 'I got the idea to volunteer there because I got one of these through the door at my parents' place, after Poppy's funeral. I assumed it was a national recruitment drive or something, but now I think *he* posted it. He wanted me to volunteer. He lured me there. He knew which narrative he wanted to try on me.'

'This isn't just some guy,' Daniel mutters. 'He planned everything out. He knew *just* how to get to you. And it nearly worked.'

Daniel refills our glasses again, but I don't drink mine.

'What do you mean?'

'Well, you know . . .' Daniel shrugs, not meeting my eye. 'You liked him. I could tell.'

'Well, yes. He was always kind to me.'

'I've been thinking about that night, when I was waiting outside in the rain. Like, if I hadn't been there, he'd have come up here with you, and then it would've been too late. You'd already have been involved. He could've got you that night, or in the morning after Liam left. And then I never would have known about the necklaces. I'd still be wearing mine. And Jude would be on to someone else.'

Daniel sips his drink, wincing on it.

'Oh, I mean, I liked him – but not like *that*.'

I can't help but laugh at Daniel's expression.

'What? But, like, he became the person *you* want. He's tall, dark, handsome, you know? That's not your thing? I thought it was.' I shake my head, and Daniel laughs, too. 'Oh. That's weird. How'd he get it so wrong?'

I fiddle with my glass. 'I don't know if he got anything wrong, exactly. I could tell he was nice-looking, but . . . he wasn't what *I* was looking for.'

'Yeah, but, how? Why?'

'Because . . .' I've never said it out loud. I never even allowed myself to think it, really. 'Because there was already someone else.'

Jenna.

The night Poppy died was the first night we ever spent together. Jenna whispered her love into my ear, she kissed promises into my lips, she told me she'd always felt this way about me – but I couldn't say it back. I was too unsure, too awkward. I didn't know what to say, or how.

But in the glow of the morning, before she woke up, I knew what I felt. I knew that I used to stare at her across the lecture hall, that I used to pretend not to know where lab samples were so I'd have an excuse to talk to her, that seeing her in the kitchen first thing in the morning was the best part of the day, and saying good-night in the evening was the worst. I knew what I wanted to say.

But then Dad called. Poppy was dead. And that perfect night became something to regret.

I pushed Jenna away. I could barely face opening her messages, let alone replying to them. I let it drag on, becoming the new normal. I got used to the daily pain of a caring text I didn't deserve to receive; the sting of shame every time I didn't respond.

I shouldn't have treated her that way. I tried not to think about her. I convinced myself she felt sorry for me, that the texts were out of pity – or that she was ashamed of me, as ashamed as I was of myself. I hated myself so much that I wanted her to hate me, too.

But I don't want that any more.

I can't change the fact that I ignored the killer's call that night and didn't raise the alarm, or that my inaction let Poppy's murder go undiscovered for six months. Those regrets will live with me. But this one doesn't have to.

If there's a normal future out there for me, it begins with talking to Jenna.

'Why did you come to Margate today?' Daniel asks softly.

'You deserved to know about Jude. Rachel was his victim, too.'

'But you didn't have to go all that way.'

'I was worried about you,' I admit. 'I hadn't heard from you, and I thought . . . I thought the worst. I went to make sure you were okay, and to bring you back with me. I wanted you here for this. Actually, no.'

I take his hand, smiling.

'I *needed* you here for this. We're in this together, remember?'

Daniel smiles, too – the kind of smile from the old family photos at his house in Margate.

He grips my hand back, and uses his other one to gently tuck a piece of hair behind my ear.

And then he kisses me.

I'm paralysed for a moment, with his thumb caressing my ear, his lips soft against mine. But I reach for his shoulder and gently push us apart. His eyes open again.

'Oh, Daniel, I'm so sorry, but . . .'

I don't finish the sentence. The happiness falls from his face and he regresses back to the Daniel I first met: hurt, damaged, lost.

'You don't . . . You don't feel the same?' His hand feels clammy, holding mine too tight. 'At all?'

'I think you're lovely, I do, and I care about you, but—'

'But not like *that*?'

I shake my head. 'Not like that.'

He drops my hand and buries his own between his knees, staring down at them.

'So, when you said there was someone else . . .'

'I meant someone in Boston. From before. Her name's Jenna.'

'Wait . . .' Daniel looks up, his hurt giving way to confusion. '*Jenna?* A girl?'

'Yes.' I take a deep breath. 'I was with her the night Poppy died. That's why I missed the call. I told myself it was a mistake, but . . . it wasn't. It meant something. It still does.'

'Oh. Wow,' Daniel says blankly. 'I had no idea.'

'That's because I didn't tell you. I've never told anyone. I'm not good with this sort of thing.'

I smile, but Daniel can't see. He's covered his face with his hands.

'Daniel, I'm so sorry. I didn't mean to give you the wrong impression. I should have said something. Are you all right?' He doesn't answer. 'Daniel?'

'Yeah.' He rubs his face and resurfaces, laughing. 'Sorry, yeah, I'm fine. Fine! Just *slightly* mortified about making a pass at a lesbian.'

'I really am sorry.'

'God, no, don't apologise! It's my own fault for being an idiot and misinterpreting things. I should have known you wouldn't feel the same. I was stupid to think otherwise.' He claws his hair off his face, chuckling. 'Sorry for making things weird. Can we maybe agree to be friends and, like, never talk about this again? Ever?'

'Deal.'

'Phew. Now I need a drink.' He grabs the vodka bottle and heads into the kitchen, checking the fridge. 'Ooh, I could do us a smoothie cocktail? Sound good?'

'Um, sure,' I say, glad for a distraction. 'Do you need help?'

'Nah, I've got it.'

He smiles, but his teeth are gritted in embarrassment as he turns away from me and starts checking the cupboards. I leave him to it, and sort through our evidence to take to the police tomorrow. The ripped stubs in Poppy's sketchbook and the torn pages I found tucked into Jude's are what will seal it: two jigsaw pieces that slot together to prove Jude was Ben. I've been careful not to touch them again. The police will find Jude's fingerprints and it'll prove he was there. It's the piece of evidence that validates everything.

What was he thinking, carrying it around in his sketchbook?

Daniel comes back with two frothy pink drinks, and hands me one. It even has one of Liam's cocktail umbrellas in it.

'To friendship,' Daniel says, raising his. 'And to forgetting all awkward advances made on gay friends under the influence of shots.'

'And to justice.'

'Yeah. That too.'

We both take a sip, and gag: Daniel manages to swallow his, but I spit mine back out.

'No, you can't reject my cocktail, too,' Daniel says, laughing. 'I'll never live that down. Come on, let's do this together. Three, two . . . one!'

I force down the drink, which is a horrid mixture of fruit and . . . sour chalk? He must have dug some of Liam's more daring spirits out of the cupboard. I get to the end of it and slam the empty glass on the table, wiping my mouth.

'Disgusting,' Daniel says, shuddering.

'Somehow even worse by the end. Why was it chalky?'

'Dusty glass, maybe? Sorry about that.'

We slump back on the sofa, feeling the soft fuzziness of alcohol in the bloodstream. We chat more, going over our plan for tomorrow, discussing the best way to present our evidence. Despite the kiss, I feel comfortable here, with Daniel. But maybe he doesn't feel the same.

'Are you sure you're okay?' I ask. 'About earlier. I'm sorry I never said anything about Jenna. If I led you on, I'm really—'

He holds up his hand.

'It's fine. Seriously, I'm fine. Nothing has changed.'

'Do you mean that, though?'

'Of course I mean it. We're friends – partners – and nothing is ever, *ever* going to change that.'

He smiles, points his index fingers, and slots them into an X shape over his chest.

'Cross my heart.'

RACHEL

20 Months Before Poppy

Never leave computers unattended: that's always been our family motto. A logged-in laptop means a hideous desktop wallpaper you'll never scrub from your memory, or an embarrassing Facebook update you'll never live down. One time I got hold of Dan's phone and renamed his crush as *Mum*, and he actually messaged her to ask for more spot cream from the shops. Classic.

He's out when I get home, but his dark room has the blue-tinged glow of an illuminated computer screen.

I might have travelled to the other side of the world and back, but some things never change.

What shall I put as his background? Manky feet? A dead fish? That photo of him from when he was thirteen and he had broccoli stuck in his brace, zoomed right in?

I nudge his screensaver away and go to click the browser search bar – but Reddit is open, and there's a list of posts filling the page.

Girls are only good for one thing

Even my mom's a slut

Women are spoilt little bitches and even the fat ones think they're better than me

Feminism is the worst thing that ever happened in the history of the universe

I hope that bitch who laughed at me at the bar last night DIES

Um, what the hell? Why is his homepage full of misogyny from forums about r/MensRights and r/TheBlackPill? It's like an incel highlights reel – the creepy little virgins who hate women for not sleeping with them.

This can't be right. Is this a friend's account? A fake trolling account? It must be a joke.

I check his account. He's been on the site since he was thirteen, and he's posted a long list of things himself. It's in reverse order. I scroll to the bottom and work my way up.

It starts with innocent posts about Marvel movies in safer parts of the website, but then things change.

How do you know if you're unlovable?

Girls won't even look at me.

I'd rather be dead than be this ugly forever.

He writes about being hideous – other users commiserating with him, saying they are, too – and unloved, being bullied at school, mocked by his older sister. *It isn't your fault*, another user says to him in a comment, *it's girls. They think they're better than you,* but they're not. This is feminism. Even the repulsive ones think they're too good for us.

Did I mock him? I teased, maybe, but it was a joke. It's what we did. We traded insults, but it didn't mean anything. He knows that, doesn't he?

Doesn't he?

New school, but the girls are still bitches.

Rejected again. Thinking of starting a rumour about her. Ideas??

Skinny guy here. Is hitting the gym worth it? Other ways to bulk up?

Are there stretches or something to make yourself taller?

Got called cute today. What do you think? y/n

Got some of those shoes with hidden lifts. Can pass for almost 6ft if I style my hair right.

The lifts work! Got a phone number! Girls really do only care about height.

That feeling when you realise you got given a fake number . . .

Any good (men's) foundation recs?? Need to hide this acne

Best ways to talk to girls?

How do you start conversations?

Tried to kiss a girl and she slapped me. Yay, physical contact!!

Nearly got laid tonight, but her friend said she was too drunk and took her home. Wasted all my booze!

Is my Tinder broken? No matches

Me = no matches, hot guy model whose pics I stole = loads

Hot girls are so shallow

Why do girls think they're so much better than me???

I'm sick of being ignored by bang average bitches.

Kinda starting to hate girls, lol.

I hate our society. Girls have all the power but they should have NONE

I'm done with this

Wish there was a way to make girls feel as shit as they make me feel.

Ever wanted to punch a girl right in her smug—

'What are you doing in my room?'

Dan switches the light on, glaring at me. I pretend he didn't startle the crap out of me, and glare back.

'What's all this bollocks? You're an incel now?'

'You read my stuff?' He flinches angrily.

'I was going to give you a truly horrific screensaver, but I accidentally found something much worse. It's a joke, right? A troll account?'

He shrugs, and crosses his arms. 'Whatever.'

'Dan, come on, you don't actually believe this stuff, do you? That . . . that women are sluts? That they're shallow and deserve to be punched?'

'You said it, not me.'

He smirks, jutting his chin out – showing off the jaw of stubble he always wanted. He used to be a skinny kid who'd spend hours in front of the mirror, chugging protein powder, begging for facial hair, covering spots with concealer three shades too dark, trying out chat-up lines, flexing muscles that wouldn't grow. He'd come home from school wet from being pushed in the pond, his phone dead, or with gum in his hair, or with a growing black eye. My friends used to laugh at his braces, at the way he followed them around the house during sleepovers, staring creepily from beneath an oily forehead, voice breaking when he tried to talk to them. He didn't go to parties. He never had a girlfriend. He used to kiss his poster of Megan Fox every night before bed.

Grown up in an adult's body, he's like an angry child with a loaded gun.

'This *better* be a joke. Mum didn't raise you to be like this, Dan.'

'Mum didn't raise us at all, did she? She's a depressive loser, always knocking herself out with pills and falling asleep in front of the TV. It's pathetic. If she'd been around more, she'd have raised *you* right.'

'Me? You're the one in a Reddit cult!'

'Yeah, but you're part of this whole cult of women, aren't you? Bet you only shag hot guys, right? Bet you look down your nose at everyone. Bet you think you deserve the best, even though you're plain and you've got no tits.'

I let it wash off me, like the thousands of insults we traded as kids.

'You're sounding dangerously like a full-on misogynist right now.'

'It's not misogyny if it's true. Girls are stuck-up bitches. All of them. They gave me hell when I was younger, and why? Because I wasn't Chris Hemsworth? Because I wasn't six foot? Because I had bad skin? They think they deserve hot guys, but they don't. They don't deserve anything.'

I rub my temples. 'Dan, what the hell? This isn't you. You were a nice kid, you don't have to be—'

'A nice kid? You never called me nice. You bullied me, Rachel. You humiliated me in front of your friends, and you drove away anyone who might have been mine. You made my life hell. *You* did that. That's why I had to move to boarding school. That's why I'm like this, okay? Because of you. Because of girls like you.'

'Don't blame me for your behaviour. I'm sorry if I hurt you when we were kids, I am, but that doesn't mean you get to take it out on other girls. That's crazy. How can you be okay with that? Your posts make it sound like you want to *hurt* women. That's not healthy. It's not normal.'

'Screw normal. You know what normal *used* to be? Women weren't picky and they'd be loyal, but then feminism happened and suddenly women want only the best – they want models with huge bank accounts, and they think they're *entitled* to men like that, even if they're fat and ugly and have nothing to offer, just because they're *women*. It makes me sick. Attractiveness is a scale, and the top eighty per cent of women only want to date the top twenty per cent of men. That means average and less-than-average girls want more, they think they're better than us. How is that fair? Women like that hurt me my entire life because I'm not in that top twenty per cent. But who decides what's hot? They do. They write the fucking rules, and they wrote them to exclude me. It's bullshit.'

He's shaking when he finishes his rant. That's what it is: regurgitated lines he's probably seen hundreds of times before on Reddit, shoved together into some kind of extremist mantra. He believes this stuff. He probably practises it in front of a mirror.

I get up from his computer desk, wishing I could tower over him like I used to when we were younger.

'Dad would be ashamed of you.'

He scoffs. 'He'd be proud of me for speaking up. Every man in the world would be proud of me.'

'Not all men are insecure misogynists with tiny dicks.'

'Like you'd even feel a big dick if you found one. You're probably stretched out from riding the cock carousel all over Europe.'

'Ugh, spoken like a true virgin. That's not how the female anatomy works.'

'I'm not a virgin!'

'Really? Because those posts sounded a lot like the ravings of a guy who's angry he's never had sex before. You're a virgin because nobody wants to go anywhere near you.'

'Shut up.'

'No, *virgin.*'

'Shut up, *slut!*'

We stand apart, both baring our teeth, fists clenched, as though we're kids again and the bickering and hairpulling and arm scratching has gone too far. But there's no Dad to storm over and separate us, and no Mum to distract us with ice lollies and a truce.

We aren't children any more.

I used to win all our fights, but I can't beat him simply by being older any more. Not physically, anyway. But there are other ways.

'You're not ugly,' I say. 'You never were. You were just a kid, like anyone else at that school. So what if you had spots? So did I. So did everyone! People didn't dislike you because you were ugly, or because you were short. They disliked you because you were *weird*. You stalked girls, you said weird things, you never washed your hair, you bit your nails, you skulked around glaring at people. You weren't nice enough to be liked. You still aren't, even though you look fine. You say everything is the fault of these girls for not fancying you, but can you blame them? The problem was never your outer shell, it was who you are inside. They could see how rotten and repulsive you are. That shone through like a lighthouse. It still does. The problem is you. *You.*'

I prod his chest. He's snarling at me, and I know I shouldn't say it, I *definitely* shouldn't say it, but screw it, I'm going to.

'The only way you'd ever get laid is if you pretended to be someone else entirely, because no girl, anywhere, would actually want to have sex with *you.*'

He rushes at me and shoves me in the chest, hard enough to knock me off balance, to make me fall – and my head cracks against something hard, and everything goes black.

Dad was a big man. We used to play the firefighter game when I was little, where he'd throw me over his shoulder and run up and down the stairs, going back to my bedroom again and again to rescue my guitar, my dolls, my teddy bears from the imaginary blaze.

He heaves me over his shoulder now, but we don't stop for toys. My head hurts. I try to tell him, but he doesn't hear. Mum's in the living room, stretched out on the sofa. I wave, but she doesn't see. She's sleeping. Then she's gone. I try to reach for her, to drag my way back, but my head hurts too much and now we're outside, the fire gone, fresh air in my lungs, our hands pressed into the cement by the front door: Mum, Dad, Daniel, and me.

Something drops on to the cement. Something red. I think it came from me. I try to touch my head, but I can't get my arms to move. They dangle limply like empty sleeves.

I hear the car unlock. I'm hurt, aren't I? Dad is taking me to the hospital, like when I got the cast on my leg and he told me I was a very brave girl. But it's my head that's hurt now. It hurts so much.

Dad swears again. He *never* swears. I'm in the car, but there's no seatbelt. It's dark. There's fabric above my head, and I'm cold, and the door closes above me, and I roll around when the engine starts and the car swerves around corners.

Dad drives for seconds or hours, I'm not sure which, but when we stop, he looks different. He's wearing glasses just like mine, and a top with stripes that's just like mine, too.

'Is this the hospital?'

He doesn't answer me. I'm not sure I said it out loud. He pulls off the top and the glasses and shoves them on to me, and wipes at my face. He checks around and pulls me out of the car for another round of the firefighter game.

'I missed you, Dad,' I say – or don't say, maybe. I think it, at least, as my arms swing limply again and my head lolls. Even with my glasses on, things are blurry. There's a building, and trees. A metal fence. A gap in the fence.

Dad sets me on my feet, holding me upright from behind. I sag in his arms, unable to stand. There are noises: a rumble, getting louder; a horn. The bushes in front of me dance. Light reflects on metal tracks behind them.

Dad moves me right up to the bush, and the noise gets louder. Metal clacks. Electricity thrashes. The horn blares. Dad shoves me forward past the bush, and light blinds me as I fall.

I don't remember this part of the game.

CHAPTER 31

It's a coincidence. It must be. Crossing the heart like that is probably a move so common that loads of people do it. It's not strange. There's nothing special about it. It means nothing that Poppy wrote about seeing it, again and again, from the man who went on to murder her.

The man who is supposed to now be hunting me.

'Everything okay?' Daniel asks.

'Um, yeah, I just . . . I need some water.'

'I'll get you some.'

He gets up, smiling. There's nothing sinister about him. Nothing has changed. He's the same Daniel I've always known: scruffy and fragile, like a flower battered by a storm.

I smile back.

No. I've wrongly accused him once, and I can't betray him by accusing him again. I *trust* him. The news articles confirmed who he is, who Rachel was to him. He's a victim, like me. He isn't a killer. He couldn't possibly be.

Jude is the killer. I have his sketchbook. Inside it are the sketches of his own face that he ripped from Poppy's sketchbook, and the recruitment flyer he sent to me to lure me to the helpline.

The helpline where I first met Daniel.

Doubt seeps in, like water flooding a sinking ship.

That night forms again in my mind: handing out the mugs with Brenda; Jude smiling; other listeners answering ringing phones only to put them down again.

'*Another snap call*,' Brenda said. '*There have been lots of those lately.*'

Calling and hanging up. Why? Because the callers were too scared to talk, or because they only wanted to talk to a specific person?

Because the killer wanted to talk to *me*?

That was just days before the inquest. The killer would have known that, wouldn't he? He'd keep tabs on me. He'd know when I might be particularly vulnerable. And then after the inquest, when I was at the support group, there he was: Daniel. He followed me out when I left early. He made sure we connected. He cried, breaking down, showing me the worst parts of himself.

Bonding himself to me through our shared trauma.

No. This is the drink talking, the fuzziness in my head. I've always felt safe with him. I *am* safe with him. I'm safer than I have been in six months.

But that's exactly how the killer would want me to feel, isn't it?

'There you go.'

Daniel passes me a water glass and sits back down next to me. He's still smiling. I try my best to return it. I try to drink, too, but my throat is too tight. I put the glass back down.

Our 'evidence' against Jude is across the table. I flip through the drawings of him in the guise of Ben, the ones on the pages that came from Poppy's sketchbook. He has lighter hair, a scarf, a smile, no beard – but it's definitely Jude's face. I move them aside and look at Poppy's drawing of The Photographer behind his camera.

Is it the same style? Aren't the lines straighter in the pictures of Jude? More precise? Like a tracing of a photograph? Isn't The

Photographer more wispy somehow? Isn't his eye ever so slightly, almost imperceptibly different?

Jude's sketchbook. I flip the pages with my nail, looking at the portraits of callers I've seen before. The angry, devastated divorced man; the student who felt nothing. And Blessing.

Her soft, round face is cheerful and loving, despite her tears. Her hair is swept up in a silk scarf in a beautiful print, and her daughter's necklace hangs around her neck, like she told me it did.

But it's the wrong necklace.

The one she described to me was identical to Poppy's. Her daughter Yewande *is* one of the victims, and Jude supposedly is her killer – but he's drawn a solid, heart-shaped locket. Why would he draw a locket if he knew it was a different style? To throw me off the scent? To make sure I didn't recognise it?

But if so, why sketch the real necklace at the back of the book, where I might still see it? Why carry around these pages from Poppy's sketchbook in his bag when they clearly show his face? Why take that risk? Why be so careless as to leave this incriminating evidence behind and not try harder to retrieve it?

But I already know the answer to these questions. I've known it since Daniel made that cross on his chest.

Jude isn't the killer.

Daniel is.

That's why he kissed me. That's why he made his move.

Our plan was to go to the police tomorrow, but we never will.

It was always his plan to kill me tonight.

'I'm . . . I'm going to the shop,' I say, getting up. I stagger, grabbing the back of the sofa for support. Too much alcohol. Why did I drink with him? Stupid. *Stupid.*

'What for?'

'Milk.'

'I got that earlier.'

'Um, toothpaste. Ran out of toothpaste. Be back in a few minutes.'

'No, you've got loads. I saw it. Sit back down, Clem.'

He's still smiling, still being friendly. I swallow the rising vomit in my throat.

He tried to frame Jude. He wanted me to find Jude's sketchbook under the sofa and match the loose sheets to the ones missing from Poppy's. He must have torn out the blank pages from her sketchbook on the cliff edge that night and kept them for when he needed them. He must have found pictures of Jude online and traced them onto the page. He left them there for me to find.

Because he killed my sister, and many other women.

And I'm next.

If I can just get outside or to Alexander's flat, I'll be okay. As long as he doesn't know I know, I'll be okay.

'I need some fresh air. Be right back.'

I head for the front door – and end up on the floor. My legs feel like lead suddenly, and my head spins. I claw myself back up, hanging on to the wall – and fall again.

The world is spinning. This isn't right. This shouldn't be happening. It was just vodka, and we only had a few. It doesn't make sense.

I can't move, I can't get to the door, but I have my phone. I get it from my pocket, my fingers feeling like jelly, and get it on the carpet in front of me. *Calls. Favourites. Jenna.*

Daniel crouches down in front of me, blocking the way to the door, and firmly presses on the End Call button. He takes the phone, tutting.

'You know, for a scientist, I thought you'd be smarter than this.'

Now he looks different. The smile is still there – but this time it is sinister, and smirking. His whole face has changed. He's holding it differently, somehow. He's no longer the man I knew. He never was. He was always this.

'Help!' I shout. 'Help me!'

Daniel chuckles.

'Nobody can hear you. There's that music across the hall, remember? It's just you and me tonight, and nobody's going to interrupt us. Not after you drove Liam away.'

I know he's right, but I don't want him to be. I try to get up again, shouting, screaming – but I can't get the words out loud enough. Everything is slurred, as though my tongue won't follow directions. I manage to sit up against the wall, and shuffle back along it. But not far, and not fast. Daniel moves closer and reaches for my shoulder, and I can't stop him.

'What was . . .' I focus on my facial muscles, forcing the words out. '. . . in that drink?'

'Hey, you figured it out!' He grimaces. 'You won't like it, I'm afraid. You remember those packets of sleeping pills and antidepressants you've had hidden away in a drawer for months? The ones I found while snooping around your room every time you were in the shower? Well, I made you a little cocktail, as promised.'

He disappears into the kitchen and comes back out, showing me several empty blister packs and boxes.

'I mean, I'm not a scientist or anything, but I'm pretty sure that's a lethal dose. Eliza died from less. You know that slut let me fuck her the first night we met? It was too easy.'

No. *No.* Not like this. I force my hand up to my mouth and shove my fingers down my throat, trying to bring everything up – but I haven't even moved. I'm still slumped against the wall, arms weak, brain slow and sluggish, weighed down by pills on top of pills, crushed and liquidised, absorbing easily into my bloodstream.

And there's nothing I can do to stop it.

'You should be grateful, you know. There are worse ways to die. You're gonna slip away and it'll be all peaceful. Not like it was for Poppy.' He leans in close, still smirking. 'She screamed.'

My body responds this time.

Even though my arm blurs in front of me, I feel my nails connect with his face. He pulls back, jagged scratches running down his cheek, deep enough to bleed. My arm thuds back to the floor, but he raises his, swinging it at my face.

'You bitch!'

But he stops. He sighs, recomposing himself.

'I guess I deserved that.'

'Why?' I manage to say, loud enough for him to hear. 'Why did you hurt her? She . . . she loved you.'

'She didn't love *me*, she loved Ben! None of them loved me. They wouldn't have given a damn about me if they knew me. They wanted Mr Perfect and nothing less, so that's what I gave them. I became just who they wanted, and they were so arrogant and conceited that they never even found it suspicious that I liked all the same things as them, that I doted on them, that I was crazy about them. They could've had hundreds, thousands of nice, average guys, but they didn't want them. They only wanted the best. They thought they *deserved* the best. So I became the best, and showed them just how wrong they were to overlook the others.'

His words sound echoey and disordered, some rushed and some delayed, reaching my ears at different times. Drowsiness pulls at my eyelids, but I fight it off. I sort through the fragments of speech, decoding it, finding the meaning.

'Poppy . . . wasn't like that. She was . . . kind.'

'They're never kind. None of them are. Not even you.'

He moves in close again, blood congealing on his cheek.

'I thought you were different, but you're not. You're as bad as the rest of them.'

348

My body is dulled, and slow, but my heart pounds in my chest. I feel it all over, in every vein. Panic.

I have to fight this. I have to do *something*.

'You won't get away with it,' I slur. 'They'll catch you.'

'Who, me? Daniel Burton? But I wasn't even *there* that night.' He laughs smugly, and pulls something from his pocket. 'Fake beard from when I went to the shops earlier. Reversible jacket, too. Daniel left, but a random guy in a beard came back to the flats. Pretty solid alibi, that. Not that anyone's gonna be looking for a murderer. This will clearly be a suicide.'

'But . . . people know. The police, my parents.'

'Well, they didn't believe you the first time, did they?' He says it like I'm a child. 'The Brighton police think you're clinically insane, driven mad by the grief of your sister's suicide. So do your parents, and Liam, probably. Everyone. You've been acting irrationally for weeks, just like I hoped you would. An overdose, alone in your flat after pushing away everyone who loves you? Sounds like suicide to me.'

'There's proof. There's—'

'What, like this?' He goes to the coffee table and comes back with wads of evidence, chucking it on the floor. He pulls out one of Poppy's letters – the last one, the one about meeting Ben at Hope Gap, the original – and burns it with his lighter.

I cry out again, helplessly, as Poppy's looping, excited writing disappears to nothing, the page curling and falling away until all that's left is an embossed flower at the top, and two words: '*Hey, Clemmie!*'

Her last words, gone.

I can't see properly. I blink harder, and feel wetness on my cheeks.

Daniel is using my phone.

'You really need a better passcode than pi,' he says. 'Copies of the letters, deleted! Posts about the necklaces, deleted! Your Reddit posts, deleted!'

It's gone. All the research, the proof, and it's gone. And there'll be nobody left to investigate my murder.

I blink and Liam's chalkboard is here, Daniel carefully, carefully writing two words: *I'm sorry.* But in my handwriting.

'I used to forge permission slips and stuff when I was at school. Good, right? No arguing with that suicide note.'

I blink again, and the chalkboard's back in the kitchen.

'They'll find . . . necklace link,' I say, trying to taunt him, to slow him down somehow, but my words come out weak and pathetic.

He scoffs. 'What necklace link? Did you really think I'd be stupid enough to connect every murder back to my sister's? I had them made after, for the others. Rachel never had a heart necklace. I just pretended she did, because I thought you'd recognise it. You were supposed to see it and feel the connection between us, just the two of us, but it took you so long to even notice it, and then when you did, you went ahead and found out about Imogen and the others – well, *some* of the others – and ruined it. I knew I should have deleted that Instagram post. I wasn't as careful back then. I've learnt a lot since, though.'

'But . . . you wore it. Rachel's necklace.'

'Silly Clementine. That wasn't her necklace. It's always been yours.'

His hands are around my neck, and something cold settles against my skin. I glance down, and see the pointed, overlapping tips of a silver and rose-gold heart on my chest.

'I was just keeping it warm for you.'

He shoves his hand into my pocket and rips out Poppy's necklace – the one he gave her before he killed her. He tosses it in the air and catches it, playing with it.

'Guess I'll take this one back. That way, everyone will think poor little Clementine was so sad she decided to put on her sister's necklace and join her. Good story, right? Even you'd believe that.'

I can't keep my eyes open – or maybe I don't want to. He squats down in front me, bragging about faking the trail-cam image he showed me, editing in the necklace, making 'Dylan' the same build as Jude to help frame him. There was no Dylan. There was never a Dylan. He murdered his own sister and got a taste for it.

'And I thought, if I got away with it once, why not twice? Why not more? There are so many you don't know about – that you'll *never* know about. And after I'm done with you, I'll keep going.'

Daniel keeps talking, but I don't know what he's saying. His words meld together, echoing, booming, whispering, fading in and out. I fade in and out. My head lolls, my limbs hanging limply, darkness pressing on my eyelids. I like the dark. It's soft and swaddling, like a warm blanket. I'm tired. So tired.

But I don't want to sleep. Not yet.

I force my eyes back open, blinking until things come into focus. It's too bright at first. Too white. There are sounds I don't understand: running water; a coarse brushing.

My body stretches out ahead of me, oddly shaped, clothed in underwear and a vest. Rippling. Distorted. Water churning, loudly, by my feet.

I'm in the bath, propped up a little against the side, and the rising water is up to my chest.

'They're gonna love this at the inquest,' Daniel says. '*Suicide due to the psychological impact of losing her sister in similar circumstances. Easy.*'

He hums to himself, the scratching sound continuing. My heavy eyes follow it. My arm is raised out of the water and Daniel holds it, scrubbing at my nails with a brush. I try to pull away, but even with the help of gravity, I don't have the strength.

He's scrubbing away the DNA evidence from when I scratched him.

My thoughts are so slowed, so dulled, that the fresh panic kicks in late. The water is rising, and I can't move. I can't sit up or climb out. I can't escape.

I'm going to drown, just like Poppy did.

I claw with my toes, trying to grasp the chain for the plug stopper, but Daniel spots me. He rips the chain free and drops it into the water, where I can't reach it.

I try to breathe through the panic, the drowsiness, the pain in my gut. I have to live long enough to do something. There must be a way out. There's always an answer. I've never not found an answer.

Evidence destroyed, Daniel slides my arm back into the water, careful not to cause any bruises. I realise why he didn't hit me earlier when I scratched him, and why he incapacitated me with pills instead of forcing me into the bath with his hands.

It has to look like a suicide, and defensive injuries will undermine that. It will raise questions. Cast doubt.

He's killed enough times to know how to get away with it.

The water is at my chin, and rising fast. Daniel clasps his hands on the edge of the bath and leans on them, his head tilted, smiling sadly.

'I really thought you were different, Clementine. Those other girls, they were so shallow and arrogant and up themselves, but you never were. You hid your looks behind glasses because you didn't care, it didn't matter to you, and I loved that. Even before I met you, I loved that. With the others, I had to play an act. I had to pretend to be the person they wanted. And I've been so many people over the years. More than you know. More than you can imagine. Nice guys, bad boys. Photographers.'

Like a glitching image, he switches between fragments of personas: hair suavely swept back or boyishly forward; shoulders slouched or rigid; his face kind or confident or devious. He leans in close, pressing the shutter on an imaginary camera. His eye bores into mine: the one from Poppy's drawing. How didn't I see it before? How didn't I notice?

Maybe I didn't want to.

'I thought I didn't have to do all that with you,' he says. 'I believed in you. I *respected* you. I thought you were above looks and the stupid games and the compliments and all the other hoops I had to jump through for the others, but you're not, are you? You're worse than them. I gave you a soulmate, someone who knows your pain and your loneliness. I gave you a broken person, someone who trusted you with his feelings, with his scars.' He taps his wrist. '*Real* scars, cut just for you. He was your comfort, your confidant, the person who believed you when nobody else did. He was the only person on this whole planet who understood how you felt, and the only one who cared about you enough to help. He was all that, he loved you – and you still didn't want him. You didn't want *me.*'

He reaches down and caresses my cheek, fingers flexing as though resisting the urge to scratch.

'This is what you deserve, you ugly bitch. All you've done is prove I was always right about females.'

Daniel's face ripples as though I'm already underwater, distorting into shards of the person I used to care for. But that person never existed. Daniel helped me investigate a murder *he* committed. He held me as I mourned the sister *he* took from me.

And why? Because he couldn't handle rejection? My sister and the others died because of one man's fragile ego?

I tilt my head, forcing my mouth free of the water, even though it means slipping a little further down the bath.

'You're pathetic.' My words come out as a slurred mess, but it's enough to turn Daniel's smugness to a clenched snarl. 'You're a failure.'

Daniel chews on his anger, gripping the edge of the bath with white knuckles.

'You think this is failure? I have all the power. I'm in control. You can't reject me if you're dead.'

'I already rejected you,' I force out, my brain struggling to string the words together. 'I said no.'

'The next girl won't. Know where I'm gonna go? Boston. Find Jenna. Make her say yes.'

'You can't. She likes *girls*.'

'No, she just thinks she does.' He scoffs. 'She was probably just using you until a hot enough guy came along. That's what lesbians do. You're just killing time, being sluts with each other while you wait for something better, for some ridiculously perfect guy that you *think* you deserve. Well, I can be that perfect guy. I put too much faith in you, but I'll go back to basics with Jenna. Work out, go for the geek chic thing. I'll get her. And I'll kill her, too.'

'No—'

Water floods my mouth, making me choke. I can't speak.

'And when I've fucked her and killed her, just like I did to Poppy, who's gonna be the real failure, huh? Who's gonna feel like a piece of shit? Not me.'

Daniel's hand clamps on to the top of my head, applying force – pushing me down. The water covers my mouth, and splashes against my nose as I try to gasp through it.

'This could've been different. If you'd just loved me . . . But you didn't, and now you have to end up like the rest. Goodbye, *Clemmie*. Say hi to your sister for me.'

And he pushes me under the water.

He doesn't hold me down, because there's no need. I can't move, I can't save myself. He stares for a moment, blurred through the water, then disappears.

I'm alone, under the water.

And I'm going to die.

Someone will find me in this dirty flat, with weeks of unhinged behaviour behind me, and make their assumptions. My evidence has been destroyed. There's no DNA under my nails; no defensive injuries. Soon I'll be a body on a slab, like Poppy was. Just like all the other victims were. Blank canvases with *suicide* painted over us by a murderer. Our voices taken away.

I can't let that happen.

I put every bit of energy and focus I have into moving my arms. I reach for the necklace around my throat and pull it, hard, as hard as I can – and the chain breaks. I grip the pendant between my fingers and flop my other arm on to my stomach. I dig the sharp metal point of the necklace into my skin and press down, as far as it will go, and tear it through my soft, soaked flesh.

M

I keep going, letter after letter, carving a message into my arm for the coroner to find.

Darkness bleeds into my vision, the rippling ceiling becoming a grey blur through the water, sound echoing oddly as my last breath comes back out, bubbling up, leaving me forever. My lungs burn and contract as I make the last cut, gasping for oxygen that isn't there, water flooding inside, panic pounding within every useless, paralysed cell.

The pendant slips from my fingers. My hands float.

MUrDer stands out on my arm, a red mist of blood seeping into the water. My eyes close.

I hope it's enough.

I don't believe in an afterlife, but I think of Poppy as I die. I open my eyes and I'm in the surf at Hope Gap, sand beneath me, waves lapping coolly over my legs. Poppy stands above me, looking down, smiling. She smells like she used to: coconut hair products, smudges of paint. She leans down and offers me her hand, a sunset burning in the sky above us, the light casting a pink glow on her hair.

'*No, C! What happened?*

She pulls me out of the water with both hands, stronger than she should be, and cradles me on the sand.

'*Stay with me, C. Stay with me until help gets here.*'

The sunset fades, and I wrap my arms around her.

I will stay.

CHAPTER 32

Darkness, and then light. Stars. They come and go, twinkling and then fading to black, but I fight to see them: glowing planets; misty white galaxies. Then they're gone again. The darkness is safe and warm and easy, but I don't want it. I want the sights. I want to see.

Between long, slow blinks, the stars decode themselves: tiny bulbs blinking on machines; light from a corridor leaking in through a partly open door. It catches on the folds of bedsheets, the plastic tubes attached to a hand.

My hand.

It comes back in a rush: the bath; the rising water; my head being forced beneath the surface. I can't get out. I can't scream for help. I can't breathe.

'Clem? It's okay, Clem. You're safe. You're in the hospital. Don't try to get up.'

But I have to get up. Daniel smirks through the water, distorted. Not the person I knew. A killer. He killed Poppy. He burnt her letters. He got away.

'I have to go.' My throat feels like broken glass. 'I need to—'

'Rest. You need to rest.'

But I can't rest. Not now. I try to kick the sheets away, but I'm weak.

More blurred fragments of memory come to me: the bitter drink; Daniel leaving a message on the chalkboard in my handwriting. A suicide note.

'It wasn't me.' The words hurt. They come out as hoarse whispers, not the shouts I want. 'I didn't do this.'

'I know.'

'It was Daniel. He killed Poppy. Tried to kill me. Killed others. I have to stop him.'

'Clem, it's all right.'

'It isn't!' I struggle, trying to get out of bed. 'I have to find him. He burnt Poppy's letters. He got away. I need to find him!'

'You don't. Clem, listen to me. *Listen*. He's already been arrested. He's in custody. Everything's fine. You're fine.' Fingers sweep loose hair off my face and tuck it behind my ear. 'Trust me, okay?'

Fingers settle gently on my arm and I open my eyes, turning to the person beside me.

Her chair is pulled close, but she's out of it now, perching on the edge of the bed. A dimmed lamp glows behind her, bringing out the warmth in her dark hair, her darker eyes. Her red lips.

'Jenna?'

'Hey,' she says, smiling.

'What are you doing here?'

'Checking up on you. In case you forgot, you weren't replying to my texts.' Her hand is where she left it, lingering against my neck. She clears her throat and pulls it back. 'I should get your parents. They told me to wake them when you woke up.'

I follow her gaze. Mum and Dad are on the seats in the corridor, hands close together as though they fell asleep holding them.

'What happened?' I ask, as the shock of seeing Jenna fades and the questions come. 'I . . . I thought I died. How am I here?'

'Liam found you. He went to your apartment to check on you. Got there just in time.'

'He came back to the flat?' I rub my head. 'But, why? Why then?'

'Uh, because I asked him to. You probably don't remember, but I got a call from you that night. It only lasted a second, but it was pretty out of character and you didn't answer when I called back. So I messaged Liam, and—'

'Wait, wait. How did you message Liam? You don't know him.'

She smiles. 'I do, actually. We've been in contact for a few weeks. He found me online because he was worried about you. He wanted to know if you were okay. But, uh, I didn't really know either, so we weren't much help to each other. But after you called, I messaged him. He was in a bar around the corner and went straight over to check on you.'

'Oh.' A familiar guilt needles at me. 'I was awful to him. I . . . I thought I couldn't trust him. I can't believe he still cared enough to check on me after that.'

'Hey, come on, now. What's a little murder accusation among friends, eh?'

Liam stands in the doorway with two coffees, leaning casually against the frame. He grins and rushes over, resting the cups on the table and jumping to sit on the other edge of the bed. I wince.

'Oh, crap, sorry. Now we're even, I guess.'

'We're not,' I say. 'Liam, I'm so sorry. I should never have treated you like that, or gone through your room, or made you feel like you couldn't even stay in your own flat. I'm sorry I didn't listen to you about . . . about Daniel. But thank you for being there for me anyway.'

'Any time, hun.' He takes my hand and squeezes it, smiling. Even though my eyes are suddenly blurry, I know it's an infectious smile. 'You've not been yourself these past few months, and I totally get why. It's fine. But I'm looking forward to meeting the real C sometime soon.'

I sniff, wiping at my eyes.

'What happened after you came back? You said they found Daniel?'

'He was arrested today.' Jenna checks the clock on the wall: it's almost 3 a.m. 'Well, yesterday. He was trying to board a boat to France. Now he's in jail.'

'But how did anyone know to do that? I had all this evidence about what he did, about Poppy and how everything was staged and there were other victims, but he destroyed my evidence. I saw him do it. He . . .' I look down at the tube taped to my hand, avoiding both their gazes. 'He burnt the last letter she ever wrote me.'

'Oh, Clem. I'm so sorry,' Jenna says. Liam squeezes my hand again.

'I didn't even realise it was him until that night. He tricked me. He pretended we were in it together, he acted like he was helping me, but he wasn't. He's the one who killed her. All that time, he knew he'd killed her. But I didn't. I fell for it. I'm so stupid.'

'You're not.' Jenna rubs my shoulder, shuffling closer to me on the bed. 'You outsmarted him without even trying. They caught him because of you.'

'What do you mean?'

'Okay, are you ready for this?' Jenna flicks her hair off her shoulders, and starts counting on her fingers. 'One – you scratched that son of a bitch's face. Liam passed him on the stairs as he was leaving. Pretty suspicious, right?'

'Super-suspicious,' Liam says.

'Two – you left us a message.' She taps my arm. It's bandaged. 'Suspicious guy leaving the scene of a suicide with a scratched face while the person upstairs put it in writing that it was murder? It's not a great plan. And three – you sent two folders of evidence and theories to Brighton police station a week ago. Once your dad realised what Daniel had tried to do to you, he got in touch with them. He said you'd mentioned them not listening to you before, and he wouldn't get off the phone with them until they looked into it. The folders were just sitting on someone's desk. Apparently Daniel had pretended to be your dad and warned them not to talk to you. Your dad put them straight.'

'He's been great, C. He made sure people knew what really happened. You still need to fill in some blanks for the police, but they believe you. You proved it.'

I rub my bandaged arm, feeling the sting from the letters carved beneath: *murder.*

'I tried to tell Dad before, but he didn't listen.'

'Yeah, he told us.' Jenna shifts, crossing her legs. She glances into the hallway, making sure my parents are still sleeping. 'He's sorry, Clem. He knows he messed up. He—'

'Blamed me. For Poppy. For missing her call that night.'

'That's not it.'

'It is. I know it wasn't even Poppy who called me, but I didn't answer and my parents blamed me for what happened to her.' I sigh. 'They're right. Maybe I could have done something if I'd answered. I could have called someone, the coastguard, the police, and—'

'No.' Jenna forces herself into my field of view. I've been doing my best to avoid looking at her. 'That's not it, at all. Look, this isn't for me to say, it's between you and them, but . . . They thought they lost a daughter to suicide, and they were hurting. They thought they'd let her down somehow by missing the signs. Nobody should blame themselves for that, suicide is nobody's fault, but they did. And I think if your parents were hard on you, it was because it was easier than being hard on themselves. But they always loved you, Clem. That never changed. They're on your side.'

I sigh and pull my knees up to my chest, staring at the wall.

'Maybe, but they'll still always blame me for not answering that call. If I had, she might still be here.'

Jenna and Liam glance at each other.

'Oh, Clem. Is that what you've been punishing yourself with all this time? That you could have saved her?'

Liam leans forward and puts his hands on my knees. I feel Jenna's palm rest on my shoulder.

'C, there was nothing you could have done differently that would have changed what happened to Poppy, and your parents know that.'

'You need to find a way to believe it, too.'

I close my eyes. I don't want to picture the beach, but I have to. I see it again, as I did during the inquest: the dummy falling, hitting the cliff, falling again. The injuries were unsurvivable. Even if it was the sea that drowned her, she couldn't have survived.

She was dead before I missed that call.

Jenna passes me a tissue and I dab it at my eyes.

For the last six months, Poppy has been my everything. I've studied her life, immersed myself in her past, read every letter she wrote to me as though she were speaking to me now. She's been alive for me, in a way. I've carried the ghost of her with me into the present, and all the time I've been hunting her killer, it's been justified. It was for a reason.

But she doesn't belong here any more. One day soon, I'm going to have to let her fade back into the past. I'll have to let her go.

I did everything I could for her. I defended her happiness, uncovered her murder, helped catch her killer who took her life.

Maybe the last thing I can do for her is to promise to live mine.

'Right, we're gonna need more coffee,' Liam says, jumping off the bed and heading for the door. I wince again. 'Sorry. I'll get doughnuts, too. Lots of doughnuts.'

'Liam, wait.'

He spins on the spot, his hand on the door.

'Just in case I forget. You know our neighbour with the curly ginger hair? Alexander?'

'Yeah?'

'You should ask him out for a drink sometime.'

Liam looks shocked for a second, then laughs, nodding to himself. 'Hmm, Alexander. Will do.' He flashes me a thumbs-up, and pulls the door shut behind him.

The room is awkwardly quiet without him. Jenna and I were alone here before, but this feels different. She's filled me in on the important things that happened while I wasn't around. And now it's my turn to do the same for her.

'Clem, I—'

'No, let me go first. Please.' I sit up, scraping my hair behind my ears. No more hiding. 'Jenna, I'm sorry. For all of it. That morning when I got my dad's phone call, I didn't know how to react, so I just . . . didn't. I shut down, and I shut you out.'

'You don't need to apologise. You were in shock and grief because a terrible thing happened to you. I understand.'

'No, I don't want you to just forgive me like that. I was in the wrong. Grief isn't an excuse to hurt someone you . . . care about. You were so kind to me, you were there for me every single day, you sent me Poppy's letters . . . And I couldn't even reply to a text. You didn't deserve that, however much pain I was in. However much I wanted to push you away.'

She sighs, facing away from me on the edge of the bed. 'It's my fault you felt that way in the first place.'

'What do you mean?'

363

'I should never have dragged you to the bar that night. I shouldn't have forced you to do things you didn't want to do. I was so ashamed of myself. I made you feel like you couldn't trust me. I ruined our friendship.'

'No, I did that.'

'*No*, Clem. I'm so sorry for what I did. Of course you didn't want to talk to me for so long – I was the reason you didn't answer that call. You must have hated me so much.'

'Never.'

I kneel up and hug her. She gasps slightly, taken off-guard.

'Jenna, I hated myself, not you. I isolated myself because it's what I thought I deserved. To be alone, to be unloved. I thought I didn't deserve to be happy. And . . . and I was always happy with you. Always. Especially that night.'

She turns in my arms, her hands sliding gently across my back. I look into her brown eyes, the ones I was scared would always remind me of Poppy. But in them, there is only her.

'Clementine, come back to Boston, and be happy with me. You deserve it.'

I burrow against her and she clings to me in return. We hold each other, swaying, our heartbeats syncing. I close my eyes, feeling her silky hair between my fingers, pulling her to me, breathing in the smell I've missed.

Harvard: coffee, textbooks and, of course, Jenna.

A life I can go back to.

◆　◆　◆

We let my parents sleep for another hour or so before Jenna unwinds herself from me to wake them up.

There is so much to say to them. Do they know how Daniel implanted himself into Poppy's life – wooing her, kissing her, making her fall in love with a lie? Would they want to know that? Losing Poppy is a trauma we all share equally, but what happened after is mine. Poppy's killer held me when I cried about her; coaxed out vulnerabilities I have never shown to anyone else. He was a friend.

Losing that friend – realising he never really existed – is a different kind of grief altogether.

Mum and Dad rush in, and I know there will be explanations and apologies in the future. But not yet. We hold each other on the bed, Mum stroking my hair, Dad sobbing into my shoulder, feeling the raw vein of grief that runs through all of us.

We're a triangle again, like we used to be before Poppy was born. But she isn't gone.

She's at the centre, and she always will be.

EPILOGUE

'It's the first holiday without her. Mom. She used to get all the gifts together and we'd buy a tree from this place off the highway and she'd get a new ornament for it every year from the places we'd go on vacation, and . . . now there's nothing. My dad can't face it. I can't either. The boxes are still in the basement. We didn't talk about it, we just ignored it. Like, Christmas was cancelled by default. And I just . . . I keep thinking that this is life now, right? Every holiday is ruined, 'cause she's not there. We'll never have the family meals, or exchange gifts we don't actually like, or plan vacations, celebrate birthdays, she'll never come to graduation or meet any grandkids . . . And it's like, do I even want kids? Am I gonna be around to have them? Can I last years of this, without her? Is it worth it? Really? When everything's worse?'

The caller sucks in air through his teeth, and I shift in my seat. The phone room is large, the listeners spread out, tinsel wrapped around ponytails and foil streamers strung across the ceiling. Lights blink intermittently on a fibreglass tree.

I lift my pen off the notebook Jude sent me – pausing my swirling doodles of stars and spaceships.

'I know it hurts,' I say, 'but the first year will always be the hardest. The first birthday, and yes, the first Christmas. They're milestones that our loved ones are missing. But I've heard it gets easier as time goes on. We adjust.'

'I don't know if I wanna adjust.'

'I know.' I take a deep breath, swapping the phone to my other ear. 'I lost someone recently, too.'

'Is that why you're here? Talking people out of suicide on Christmas?'

'Yes, it is. My sister died a little less than a year ago. It was sudden.'

'So was Mom. Car accident.'

'It's difficult when you can't prepare for it. When you couldn't say goodbye.'

'I did, at the hospital. I don't know if she heard, but I said it.'

'I'm glad you could say it.'

I think for a moment. The caller is young, male. There's every chance he is holding a handgun.

'I spoke to a caller once,' I say, 'who told me she keeps her daughter's memory alive by keeping her present. She reads the books her daughter used to write in, and talks to her about them.' I bite my lip. 'She's not trying to forget what happened or the pain it caused, but rather to channel it into something else.'

'Be glad my mom's dead? That's your advice?'

'No, not at all. Losing someone you love is awful. Indescribably. But just because it's awful today, doesn't mean it'll be as awful tomorrow. Maybe there are ways to cope. You can pack away Christmas if you like, you can ignore it because it's too painful, or you can face it. You can share stories with your dad about your mum's roast potatoes, or make a new tradition of you buying a new ornament every year. You can make her a part of things even when she isn't there. You can celebrate her.'

'Isn't that worse, though? Doesn't it make you sadder?'

'Maybe, at first. But life goes on for those of us who are left behind, and we can choose how we live it.'

'But I don't want to live it.'

'Maybe not today, and maybe not tomorrow. But if you end your life now, you'll never know if there were better days to come. And isn't it worth hanging on to see if there are any?'

The man – a boy, really – exhales. Then he goes silent for a while.

'Hello? Are you still there? Are you okay?'

'Yeah,' he says, clearing his throat. 'Sorry. I was just trying to figure out where the hell I'm gonna get a new ornament on Christmas.'

At the end of my shift, I wave to the other volunteers and head out on to the streets of Boston, the air crisp, sunlight peeking through the clouds as the day draws to a close.

I always thought I'd invite Poppy to visit someday. I could have shown her around, pointed out the three ginger housecats who always sleep on the same basement windowsill on our block, or taken her to the café by the river for what Jenna calls the city's best hot chocolates. It never happened, but I still like to think about it. Maybe I'll always have those daydreams, even when I'm old: my younger sister, frozen at age eighteen, skipping around a world that outlived her.

It's so strange to hear people talk about her like they knew her. Once the news outlets found out about a new British serial killer – one killing the most marketable of victims: pretty young women – my sister's murder went from something nobody would believe to something everybody wanted to talk about. Who were these dead girls? Why did they captivate the killer? What were they wearing?

The bloggers and podcasters are more delicate than the press, at least. No direct interaction, no doorstep questions. They picked her social media clean, just as I did all those months ago, but all they can do is lace that information together. They don't know the real Poppy, just like I'll never know the real Imogen, Yewande, Sasha, Eliza, or Rachel.

The police haven't found the others yet. There have been no new victims discovered since Sasha Baxter, an Animation student from Leicester. She died eight months before Poppy did.

I know there are more out there. I can feel it. The police checked every database and log for heart necklaces found on young women after apparent suicides, but Sasha's was the only one that came up. But what if something was mislabelled or lost? Would a necklace stay on after a fall or a collision with a train? What if a victim was discovered before she died – could her jewellery have been removed in a hospital and swept up by loved ones who didn't look at it? Could it have been stolen from her body?

Daniel targeted vulnerable women, people away from home or isolated somehow. It's so easy for things to slip through the cracks. For people to slip through. What if his other victims were so isolated and alone that their bodies haven't even been found yet?

Daniel won't talk. He sits smugly in every police interview, arms crossed, smirking as he says, '*No comment.*'

I made the mistake of searching for his name online, once. He writes to people, apparently. Won't admit the murders, but has a manifesto about women that they published for him – about what we do and don't deserve. Men online are championing him now, setting up websites and subreddits in his honour faster than they can be banned. There was even a thread where they posted images of his victims and asked users to rank them: *Who would YOU bang and kill first?*

I don't look at those forums any more. I check in with the police every so often, but there's rarely anything new they can tell me. I keep the search going for other victims, raising awareness in whatever way I can: sharing images of the necklace; contacting the families of possible victims. It's intrusive, I know. Sometimes I feel like the journalists I despise, marching into people's lives and disturbing their healing, getting their hopes up. The desire for closure is so strong that some families come to me themselves, utterly convinced their loved one must have been a victim – even if they died after Daniel was arrested. For so many of us, even the worst answer is better than not knowing.

I cross the bridge towards home, turning up the collar of my coat, the ends of my hair fluttering in the breeze. I like the bob Liam cut for me before I left London. It was time for a change.

In a lot of ways, life is how it used to be: Harvard; research; returning each night to our apartment with the door that always, always sticks. The things I loved so much from before. But my life is no longer just that. It's that, plus grief. Plus trauma. It's as though I've picked up a new hobby that takes precedence over all my old ones, one I keep going back to even though I keep hitting the same wall, again and again. I squeeze it in whenever I can, staying up late, getting up early, devoting my lunch hours to it.

I have to find those other women. Daniel won't name them, he won't even confirm them, but if I find them, they get their truth back. The world can know their stories; their families can get closure. They can escape the lie Daniel put them in, just like Poppy did.

I have to do that for them. I *will* do that for them.

But today, it's Christmas. Mum and Dad are waiting at the apartment for me, drinking eggnog and watching old movies with Jenna, working towards new family traditions now that our old ones are gone. That's good. That's healthy.

I'm working on healthy.

I pause halfway across the bridge. The sky to the west is on fire. Reds and oranges shimmer on the surface of the Charles and press through the gaps between buildings, crosscut by the spindly branches of leafless trees. Above, the night sky stretches over, pushing the colours together like a concertina, the thin, wispy clouds bathed in a peachy pink.

I feel for the pendant Jenna got for me: a real poppy preserved in glass. I wrap my fingers around it.

I never cared much about sunsets, but Poppy did.

Now, I watch them for her.

ACKNOWLEDGEMENTS

In January 2019, delirious with a cold as the snow fell on the foxes in my garden, I watched *Conversations with a Killer: The Ted Bundy Tapes* on Netflix and had an idea for a novel.

Thank you to my agent, Hannah Schofield, for championing that idea and guiding it from a garbled, badly explained pitch to a polished novel. You knew this book would be *the book*, but it only got there because of your patience and unwavering support. I'm so grateful and lucky to have you on my side.

Thank you to Luigi Bonomi and the whole team at LBA for shortlisting me in the 2017 *Daily Mail* First Crime Novel Competition. Your belief in my writing was a lifeline at a time when I was drowning, and although it took me almost two years to pull myself to shore, you gave me something to aim for.

Thank you to Leodora Darlington for reading this book and loving it as much as I hoped an editor someday would. It was always my dream to be published, and you and the team at Thomas & Mercer made that a reality for me. I will be forever grateful.

Thank you to Writers United – to Helen, Carol, Sue, Jo, Laura, Gareth, Paul, Susan, Joan, Caroline, Bean, Anya, Libby, Suzanne, and all the others who have come and gone since our accidental inception all those years ago. Thank you for the critiques, the company, the cheerleading, and the wine-fuelled giggles in Pizza

Expresses across the country. We may be more friends than a writing group these days, but I love and support every one of you. So many of you are already published, and I truly believe the rest of you will be, too. Onwards and upwards, as we always say.

Thank you to the Pitch Wars class of 2015. I may have spent most of the years lurking and living vicariously through your successes, but I'm truly grateful for being a part of such a diverse and knowledgeable community, and for the help you've offered whenever I've asked. Kat, thank you for being a great friend and a fantastic CP, and thank you to Rebecca for the early support you gave to this book when it was barely a few chapters long. Jamie, thank you for being you.

Thank you to the Reddit communities who scooped me up when I was at my lowest, and the friends I made in the worst of times: Ashley, Mike, Marissa. Look at us now. And Craig, thank you for the long walks and the long talks during that time, even when there was nothing left to say.

And finally, thank you to my family. To my parents for their generous support while I pursued this unlikely dream; to my brother Robbie for our ever-comforting *Star Trek* discussions; to Hannah for her flawless rapping during our kitchen discos; and to my sister Alice, for so often being the Clementine to my Poppy. Oscar and Nancy, you're far too young for this book, but I hope you read it someday and can be proud of what your Auntie Lucy made. I know I am.

ABOUT THE AUTHOR

Lucy Goacher was born and raised in Worthing, and can often be found braving the windy weather on the seafront. She has an English degree and a Master's in Creative and Critical Writing from the University of Sussex, and was a finalist in the 2017 *Daily Mail* First Novel Competition. *The Edge* is her first novel.

Her time is split between writing, pampering her cat, and photographing the urban foxes who visit her garden every night for dinner – much to her cat's annoyance.

You can follow Lucy (and her foxes) on Twitter and Instagram: @goachwriter.